KATIE COTUGNO

HOW *to* LOVE

BALZER + BRAY
An Imprint of HarperCollins P

Balzer + Bray is an imprint of HarperCollins Publishers.

How to Love
 For information address HarperCollins Children's Books, a division of HarperCollins Publishers, 195 Broadway, New York, NY 10007.
www.epicreads.com

Produced by Alloy Entertainment
1700 Broadway, New York, NY 10019
www.alloyentertainment.com

Library of Congress Cataloging-in-Publication Data
Cotugno, Katie.
How to love : a novel / Katie Cotugno.—First edition.
pages cm
Summary: A tumultuous love affair between Reena and Sawyer ends when Sawyer abruptly abandons their Florida town, causing Reena to bear their child alone and struggle with mistrust when Sawyer returns three years later.
ISBN 978-0-06-221636-6 (pbk.)
ISBN 978-0-06-239021-9 (Can. ed.)
[1. Teenage pregnancy—Juvenile fiction. 2. Teenage mothers—Juvenile fiction. 3. Drug abuse—Juvenile fiction. 4. Teenage pregnancy—Fiction. 5. Teenage mothers—Fiction. 6. Drug abuse—Fiction. 7. Love—Fiction.] I. Title.
PZ7.C8297 Ho 2013 2012276016
[Fic]—dc23 CIP
AC

Typography by Liz Dresner
15 16 17 18 19 PC/RRDH 10 9 8 7 6 5 4 3 2 1

First paperback edition, 2015

For Jackie, who read everything first

1

After

I've been looking for Sawyer for half a lifetime when I find him standing in front of the Slurpee machine at the 7-Eleven on Federal Highway, gazing through the window at the frozen, neon-bright churning like he's expecting the mysteries of the universe to be revealed to him from inside.

Come to think of it, maybe he is.

I stop. I stare. I need gum and a soda and a box of animal crackers for Hannah, but already I know I'm going to be walking out of this place empty-handed. I'm due at my stupid accounting class in fifteen minutes. Water from the storm outside drips from my all-purpose braid and onto the dingy linoleum; a tiny puddle forms around my feet.

"Hey, Reena." Just like that, just like always, I'm caught.

He's fitting a lid onto his plastic cup, careful, but nobody has ever sneaked up on Sawyer LeGrande in his entire life, and when he turns to face me it's like he's not even a little bit surprised. His hair is buzzed nearly clean off.

"Hey, Sawyer," I say slowly, a sound like waves and roaring in my head. I slip my index finger through my key ring and squeeze, the cold metal biting into the flesh of my palm as it occurs to me how unfair it is that after all this time God knows where, he shows up tan and luminescent to find me looking like half-drowned trailer trash. I have no makeup on. My jeans have big holes in both knees. I'm at least ten pounds fatter than I was the last time we saw each other, but before I have time to be properly humiliated he's bypassed the corn chips and beef jerky and is hugging me tight. Like it's something we do a lot.

He smells the same, is the first thing I notice, like bar soap and things that grow in the ground. I blink. "I didn't know," I begin, not entirely sure which particular ignorance I'm about to confess: all of them, maybe, eighteen years' worth of universal truths everybody was smart enough to figure out except for me.

"I just got back yesterday," he says. "I haven't been to the restaurant yet." He grins one of those slow smiles of his, crooked, the kind I've been trying to write out of my system since seventh grade. "I think maybe I'm surprising a lot of people."

"You think?" I snap, before I can stop it.

Sawyer stops smiling. "I . . . yeah," he says. "I think."

"Right." I can't come up with anything better than that. I can't can't come up with anything at all, which is how it always was with Sawyer, though you'd like to imagine I'd have outgrown at least some of it by now. Back when we used to work the same shifts at Antonia's I'd be forever dropping plates and forgetting which orders went where, mixing up checks. One night when I was fifteen and he was behind the bar, a woman at one of my tables ordered a Sex on the Beach and it took me so long to work up enough guts to say the words to him that she complained to my father about the slow service and I had to clean the kitchen after we closed.

"My mom told me . . ." he says now—trailing off, trying again. "About . . ."

I imagine letting him dangle there indefinitely, a hanged man, but in the end I'm the one who breaks first. "Hannah," I supply, wondering what else his mother told him. I can't stop staring at his face. "Her name is Hannah."

"Yeah. I mean." Sawyer looks uncomfortable, like he's waiting for something else to happen. For me to just come out and say it, maybe—*Welcome back, how was your trip, we made a baby*—but I keep my jaw clamped firmly shut. *Let him wonder for once*, I think meanly. *Let him sweat it out for a change.* The Slurpee's bright green, like a space alien. My braid's left a wet spot on my shirt. Sawyer shifts his weight awkwardly. "She said."

We stand there. We breathe. I can hear the hum and clatter of the market all around us, everything chilly and refrigerator-bright. There's a huge, garish poster of pretzel dogs over his left shoulder. I have pictured this going differently.

"Well," I say after a minute, aiming for casual and missing by roughly the distance between here and the other side of the world. "It's good to run into you. I should probably get what I came for, or like—" I stop, peel a stray hair off my forehead, glance up at the buzzing fluorescent lights. "Sawyer, I really gotta go."

His jaw twitches, infinitesimal, the kind of thing you'd never notice if you hadn't spent your entire adolescence doing things like looking at his jaw. "Reena . . ."

"Oh, buddy, please don't." I don't want to make it easy on him. I shouldn't have to. Not when he's the one who disappeared, took off without even saying *Good-bye, see you later, I love you*. Not when he's the one who just *left*. "Look, whatever you're going to tell me, don't worry about it. It all turned out fine, right?"

"No, it didn't." He gazes at me and I am remembering so clearly how he looked when he was eight, when he was eleven, when he was seventeen. Sawyer and I were only together for a few months before he left, but he was my golden boy for so long before that, he would have taken the guts of me with him even if we'd never been a couple at all.

I shrug and look around at the ice cream, at the displays of chewing tobacco and chips. I shake my head. "Sure it did."

"Come on, Reena." Sawyer rocks back on his heels like I've shoved him. "Don't blow me off here."

"Don't blow *you* off?" It comes out a lot louder than I mean it to, and I hate myself for letting him know that I still think about him, that I carry him around inside my skin. "Everybody thought you were dead in an alley someplace, Sawyer. *I* thought you were dead in an alley someplace. So maybe I'm not the best person to talk to about feeling like you're getting blown off."

It sounds nasty and composed, and for one second my mighty magician Sawyer looks so helpless, so completely sorry, that it almost breaks my heart all over again. "Don't do that," I order quietly. "It's not fair."

"I'm not," he says, shaking his head, recovering. "I'm not."

I roll my eyes. "Sawyer, just—"

"You look really good, Reena."

Just like that he's back to taming lions; this whole thing is so surreal I almost smile. "Shut up," I tell him, trying to mean it.

"What? You *do*." As if he's got some sixth sense for nearly breaking me, Sawyer grins. "Am I going to see you around?"

"Are you going to *be* around?"

"Yeah." Sawyer nods. "I think so."

"Well." I shrug like somebody whose hands aren't shaking, whose throat hasn't closed like a fist. I only just finally got used to him being gone. "I live here."

"I want to meet that baby of yours."

"I mean, she lives here, too." I'm aware that there are other people in this aisle, normal convenience-store shoppers whose worlds haven't taken a sharp and unexpected curve this fine morning. One of them nudges me out of the way to get to the Cheetos. Outside it's still pouring like crazy, like maybe the end of the world is at hand. I breathe out as steadily as I can manage. "Bye, Sawyer."

"See you, Reena," he tells me, and if I didn't know better I'd think it was a promise.

2

Before

"Gin," Allie said triumphantly, dropping her last card onto my quilted bedspread and raising her sharp chin in victory. "You're finished."

"Ugh. Seriously?" I flopped back onto the pillows, dropped my feet into her lap. We'd spent most of the afternoon mired in a ridiculously complicated version of rummy governed by a rigid and intricate roster of house rules we'd never been able to explain to anyone else—which didn't actually matter, seeing as how the only people we ever played with were each other. "I quit."

"It's not quitting if you already lost," she said, reaching over to my dresser and scrolling through the music on my laptop. The sunny pop she liked best chorused from the tinny speakers. "At that point it's just . . . conceding."

I laughed and kicked at her a bit, just gently. "Jerk."

"You are."

"Your mom is."

We hung out in silence for a little while, comfortable and familiar. Allie picked idly at a fray in the hem of my jeans. On the wall was a poster of the Bridge of Sighs in Venice, another of Paris at dusk—both speckled with little grease spots in the corners from the tacky stuff I'd used to position and reposition them until they were just exactly right. It was the spring of our freshman year, almost summer; the world felt endless and impossibly small.

"Hey, girls?" My stepmother, Soledad, appeared in the doorway, dark hair knotted neatly on top of her head. "Roger and Lyd'll be here any minute," she said to me. "Can you come down and set the table for me? Allie, honey," she continued, not bothering to wait for my reply—I'd say yes, obviously. I always said yes. "Do you want to stay for dinner?"

Allie frowned, glancing at the alarm clock on my nightstand. "I should probably get home," she said, sighing. She'd gotten busted for shoplifting *again* a couple of weeks before, a pair of plastic sunglasses and a silky scarf from the Gap this time, and her parents were keeping her on a pretty tight leash. "Thanks, though."

"Okay." Soledad smiled and tapped the doorjamb twice

before she turned around, the delicate metal of her wedding ring clicking against the paint. "Make sure you set an extra place, Serena, will you?" she called over her shoulder. "Sawyer's coming tonight, too, I think."

Right away Allie and I looked at each other, eyes going wide. "I can stay," she announced immediately, bolting upright like a prairie dog. "I'll call my . . . uh. Yeah. I can definitely stay."

I laughed so hard I almost fell right off the bed, thinking even as I tried to pull it together that I was going to need to put on some makeup. "You are so *obvious*," I said, heaving myself up and onto the carpet, heading for the hallway as casually as somebody whose heart wasn't jackhammering inside her chest. "Come on, nerd. You can fold the napkins."

Lydia LeGrande blew into the kitchen like a tropical storm twenty minutes later, all confidence and chunky necklaces, dropping a cursory kiss on my cheek. "How you doing, Reena?" she asked, not waiting for me to answer before setting a tray of fancy cheese on the counter and peeling the plastic wrap away. Roger followed with a bottle of wine, navigating his considerable bulk with surprising deftness, and put a hand at my upper back to say hello. "Hiya, chickie," he said.

The LeGrandes were my father and Soledad's closest friends, partners both in the restaurant where we all worked and for vacations down to the Keys, outdoor concerts at

Holiday Park. Their games of Outburst were loud and legendary. Lydia had gone to college with my mom. She and Roger had introduced my mother and father to begin with, and when my mother died of complications from multiple sclerosis when I was four and my father was too busy raging at God to think about things like lunches and clean socks, Lydia was the one who hired Soledad to move in with us, not realizing at the time that she'd found him a second wife just like she'd found him a first. A little over a decade later and they still came for dinner often—but *not*, for the most part, with their son.

Tonight, though, luck was in my corner or the moons of some far-off planet were aligned, because sure enough, Sawyer skulked in behind them, jeans and a T-shirt and his dark, wavy hair. Around his neck was the tiny half-moon pendant he always wore, tarnished and thin. "You," my father said to him by way of greeting, ambling in from the yard where he'd been lighting up the grill. Allie and I were still setting the table; she was clutching a handful of forks. "I have a record I want you to listen to. An actual record. Herbie Hancock. Come with me."

"My son's in a mood," Roger muttered, warning, but Sawyer just kissed Soledad hello and nodded at my father, following him out into the living room where the big stereo was. Sawyer was his godson, had grown up drifting through the crowded hallways of our house; my father had taught him to play the piano more than a decade before.

"Hey, Reena," he said distractedly, nodding at me as he passed by—close enough that I could smell him, soapy and faintly warm. I'd seen him at work a few days earlier. He hadn't come for dinner in nearly a year.

I swallowed, heart tapping at my rib cage like pebbles at a windowpane. "Hey."

Sawyer was two years ahead of us at school, a junior, although he seemed way older—closer to my brother Cade's age than mine. He'd always been that way, for as long as I could remember, like he'd already lived a thousand different lives. He tended bar at the restaurant and showed up to class when he felt like it and ignored me, for the most part: not in a malicious way, but in the way that you ignore a message on the side of a building you see every day. I was part of the scenery, blending in, so familiar as to be completely invisible to the naked eye.

Allie, though. Allie was hard to ignore.

"Hey, Sawyer," she called out now, curly hair bouncing with the shake of her pretty head. She'd changed her clothes, borrowed one of my tank tops—simple black with skinny straps, nothing fancy. Her shoulders were covered with freckles from the sun. "Long time no see."

Sawyer stopped and looked at her with some interest. Roger had followed Soledad onto the patio by this point; my father had disappeared into the living room. Lydia was making herself at home in the kitchen as usual, rummaging through the silverware drawer for knives to go with her cheeses. Allie just smiled.

I was watching carefully. They knew each other, sure, from any number of family parties, birthdays, and graduations. They passed each other in the hallways at school. They weren't friends, though, not by any stretch of the imagination, which was why I was so surprised when he grinned back, slow and easy. "No kidding," he told her, tipping his chin in her direction. "Long time no see."

3

After

"*Sawyer LeGrande* is home?"

I'm livid when I stomp into the house a full two hours ahead of schedule, back from the 7-Eleven and banging my way into the kitchen with all the grace and equanimity of a hand grenade. I've been driving in panicky circles through the still-biblical downpour like if I don't keep moving something bad is going to happen, like chance favors those in motion and the odds are already stacked. Outside, the palm trees bend in supplication. My car stalled at three different lights.

"What?" Soledad snaps to attention. She's been chopping carrots at the counter and the knife clatters into the basin; she swears softly in Spanish before jerking her thumb to her mouth. Hannah, who's sitting in her high chair macerating

a gritty-skinned tomato from my father's garden, begins to shriek. She's small and dark-haired and fierce, my girl; when she really puts her mind to it, her howl can seem to come from a creature ten times her size. "*Mama*," she wails, that last long *a* like the universe has totally wronged her. I tuck her against the curve of my body and begin to pace like some nervous feline, a lioness or lynx.

"It's okay," I lie, whispering nonsense until she quiets, watery pulp slipping through her chubby fists. "That was scary. I know. It's okay." I look back at my stepmother, who's still sucking the blood from her finger and staring at me in disbelief. "Sawyer LeGrande," I repeat, like maybe there's possibly some other Sawyer she thinks I'm talking about. "Hanging out by the Slurpees."

Soledad takes a moment to process that information, then: "What flavor?"

I blink at her. "What *flavor*?"

"That's what I'm asking."

"What the hell kind of question is that?"

"Watch it," she reminds me, and I look guiltily at Hannah. Already my kid is toddling and full of jabber, gobbling the universe with a terrific kind of greed, and I know it's only a matter of time before she gets to preschool and starts asking her teacher why today's snack is so shitty.

"Sorry," I mutter, planting a kiss against her warm, downy head as she smashes a little bit of tomato into my face. "Your mom is a trash mouth."

"Did you skip your class?" Soledad asks, and I'm about to tell her exactly where community college falls on my list of priorities in this particular moment when my brother lets himself in through the back door, my father close behind him. There was a managers' meeting at the restaurant this afternoon, I remember all of a sudden.

"Ladies." Cade glances at me briefly, heads directly for the fridge. He was a fullback on our high school's football team, once upon a time, and he still eats like he's bulking up for a game. "Saw Aaron at the gym this morning."

I ignore him—and the reference to my boyfriend—as if I haven't even heard. "Did you know Sawyer is home?" I ask instead. I don't mean to sound as crazy as I do, so close to hysterical; I take a deep breath, bounce Hannah on my hip, and try to contain the overflow. "Did you?"

"No," Cade says immediately, but suddenly he won't look at me and the back of my neck is prickling. He frowns at the contents of the refrigerator, like there's something really interesting going on in there. "Did you drink all the OJ?" he asks.

"Kincade, I am going to ask you again—"

"What?" He sounds pissed at me now, irritated. "I didn't *know*, exactly—"

"Cade!"

"Reena." My father steps between us like we're seven and twelve instead of eighteen and twenty-three, like maybe I'm about to pull some bratty little-sister move involving a shin-kick or a punch to the back of the head. Like maybe I'm not standing here holding a child of my own. "Enough," he says, and I turn on him. My father and Sawyer's have been friends since they were children; they've owned the restaurant for more than a decade, are godfathers to each other's sons. There is no way in the breathing world that if Sawyer LeGrande so much as crossed the state line into Florida, my father didn't hear about it.

"What about you?" I demand, trying to keep my voice steady. His hair is going gray at the temples. Hannah squirms unhappily in my arms. "You must have known."

My father nods. "Yes," he says, and looks at me evenly. One thing he never does is lie.

"And you didn't *tell* me?"

He doesn't reply for a minute, like he's thinking. Dark spots from the rainstorm are flecked across his shirt. "No," he says, when he's ready. "I didn't."

None of this is new information, but still it hits like something with physical force, a pillowcase full of nickels or God sending a flood for forty days. "Why *not*?" I ask, and it comes out a lot sadder than I mean it to.

"Reena—"

"Soledad, *please*."

"I didn't tell you he was here," my father says slowly, and he is the very theology of calm, "because I was hoping he wasn't going to stay."

Well.

All three of them are looking at me, waiting. Soledad's got a hand pressed to her heart. Cade is still standing at the refrigerator, all bulk and muscle, watchful.

"OJ's in the door," I tell him finally, and take Hannah upstairs for her nap.

4

Before

"We're getting too old for this," Allie declared suddenly. We were wasting the morning on the swing set at the far corner of her parents' huge, immaculate backyard: just the two of us, just like usual, her corn-yellow hair brushing the grass as she leaned back as far as she could.

"We *are* too old for it," I said. I was lying upside down on the plastic slide, knees bent, hands groping without luck for a dandelion or some crabgrass to pick at. Allie's dad was fanatical about the lawn. We were fifteen that summer, not quite driving, perpetually bumming rides off a couple of Allie's older friends. "That's the point. Shut up and swing."

"Fine," she said, laughing. "Maybe I will." Then, on

second thought, righting herself with a dizzy shake of her head: "Want to go get coffee?"

I frowned. In a minute it was going to be too hot to keep lying like this, but the reason Allie wanted to go get coffee was because her friend Lauren Werner worked at Bump and Grind and gave out free iced mochas, and I hated Lauren Werner's guts. "Do *you* want coffee?"

Allie considered that one for a moment, eyes narrowing behind her enormous tortoiseshell sunglasses. "No," she said eventually, heaving a put-upon sigh. "I just want to *go* someplace."

I was about to suggest an early movie, or maybe coffee at the bookstore instead, but just then her mom appeared at the sliding door to the kitchen, her hair the same perfect blond as Allie's but bobbed short and sensible. "Girls?" she called, leaning against the doorjamb, one bare foot coming up to scratch her opposite knee. "I made muffins, if you're hungry!"

"Don't fall for it," Allie said immediately. "They're full of flax."

"Don't tell her that!" her mom yelled back. Mrs. Ballard had ears like a bat. "They are not. Just try one, Reena."

"Okay," I agreed, after a moment. I was agreeable in general, and anyway I had to pee. I flipped myself backward off the slide and wandered toward the house across the deep, lucid green of the grass, the heat like a wall of syrup even this early in the day. "I'm coming."

"Get cards, too!" Allie called, any and all plans for leaving the yard suddenly forgotten. We were playing only old-person card games that summer: bridge and pinochle, euchre and hearts. It was this thing Allie had us doing, the latest in a long sequence of summers with themes like *French Braid Pigtails* and *The Katharine Hepburn Movie Canon*. "And paper and pen!"

"Anything else"—I shot her a look over my shoulder—"Your Majesty?"

Allie grinned her biggest and goofiest, flinging one rubber flip-flop off her foot in my general direction. "Pleeease?"

"We'll see."

I peed and got the cards from her bedroom and opened the makeup case on her dresser, digging around for the Risky Business lip gloss I knew she'd gotten at the mall earlier that week. I pulled out some eye shadow and a couple of tampons but didn't see it, and was about to give up when my fingers curled around a tarnished, silver half-moon on a thin rope that I recognized—immediately, without even thinking about it, the way you recognize your own face in the mirror—as Sawyer LeGrande's.

I blinked. I swallowed. I stood there for I don't know how long, central air humming quietly in the background and my bare feet sinking into the pale gray wall-to-wall carpet, fresh with vacuum marks from the Ballards' cleaning lady, Valencia. Finally I went outside—right past Mrs.

Ballard, who was holding a paper plate with two flaxseed blueberry muffins, the thought of which, suddenly, made me feel a little sick.

Allie looked up as I approached. She was hanging from the rings at this point, flipping herself over and over like we'd done when we were small, tan legs kicking. "Where's the poison muffins?" she asked. Then, seeing my face: "What?"

I held the necklace out in front of me like it was radioactive, pendant swinging. "Did you steal this?" I demanded, and even to my own ears I sounded shrill.

Allie let go of the jungle gym. Her whole expression changed in a way I'd never seen before, almost accusatory, a security grate going down. "Were you going through my stuff?" she asked.

"Was I *what*?" I was startled. We went through each other's stuff all the time, Allie and me, no problem. She could have recited the contents of my desk drawers off the top of her head. "I was looking for the Risky Business."

Allie blinked. "Oh," she said, and just like that she looked normal again. She dug the tube out of the back pocket of her shorts. "Here."

"Thanks." I put it on, still staring. The silver moon bounced off my knuckles, and when I handed her the lip gloss back, she took that, too, out of sight like a sleight of hand. "So?" I prodded. "Did you steal it?"

"Did I steal it?" she repeated. "What do you think? I'm some kind of freaky klepto?"

"Oh, like you've never stolen anything before."

Allie cocked her head to the side like, *fair point.* "I stole that lip gloss, actually," she admitted.

"*What?*" I said. "At the mall? I thought you paid for it."

"I just told you I did." She shrugged. "It was when you were smelling the perfumes."

Oh, for God's sake. I sat down hard right in the middle of the lawn, flopping backward and looking at the clear, unforgiving sky. The air felt like a wet blanket. "You gotta knock that off."

"I know," she said, and lay down beside me. Neither of us said anything for a minute. I could hear her stomach growling and the faint sound of wasps nearby.

"Al," I said eventually, trying to keep my voice even, not wanting to sound as slightly hysterical as I felt. She'd been my best friend since we were four. "Where did you get that necklace?"

Allie sighed like a white flag waving, like I was just going to torture the truth out of her anyway and it was easier to tell me the truth. "I didn't steal it," she said.

I felt all the breath whoosh out of me, dizzy even though I was already lying down. "I didn't think so," I told her, and as it came out of my mouth I realized it was true. "He gave it to you?"

Allie nodded. She rolled over onto her side, propped herself up on one sharp elbow to look me in the face. "I was going to tell you," she said finally. "I didn't know how."

I pushed the heels of my hands into my eyes, colors exploding like fireworks, like something detonating inside my head. "Sawyer LeGrande gave you that necklace," I repeated, and I almost cracked up laughing, that's how ridiculous it sounded out loud. "Since when are you hanging out with *Sawyer LeGrande*?"

There was that edge in my voice again, that crazy shrillness, but Allie just shrugged. "Few weeks?"

"A few *weeks*?"

"Three?"

"Three?" I sat up fast, and now I really was dizzy. In the yard it was very, very hot. "And we're only just talking about it *now*?"

"Oh, come on, Reena," she said, getting up herself, red-cheeked and with a hint of a challenge in her voice. "Like you're the easiest person in the world to tell stuff to. Especially this."

"That's not true," I said. "That's not true, and it's not fair to—"

"I'm sorry," she said immediately, recalibrating. "You're right. I'm sorry. I should have mentioned it to you."

"Should have *mentioned* it to me?"

"Okay, can you stop repeating everything I say?"

"I'm not re—" I caught myself just in time. "Al, this isn't some random person, this is Sawyer Le—"

"What do you want to know?"

What did I want to *know*? I stared at her, openmouthed

and stupid. I had no idea what questions to ask. I felt, absurdly and with some panic, that I might be about to burst into tears.

"Come on," she said softly, and after a moment nudged at me with her knee. She hated having people mad at her, Allie; had almost no tolerance for it at all. "Don't look at me like that. Not you."

"I'm not looking at you like anything," I told her. "I'm just . . . looking at you."

"Your face is doing a funny thing."

"It is not!" I laughed, a weird little bark that didn't sound anything like my normal laugh, even to me. "This is just what I look like."

"It is *not* what you look like," she corrected. "Stop. We're just hanging out. He's friends with Lauren. I saw him one day at Bump and Grind and he asked if I wanted to, you know—"

"If you wanted to *what*, exactly?"

"If I wanted to hang out! It's not a big deal." Suddenly Allie looked at me a little more closely, like a thought was just occurring to her. The tips of her ears were red from the sun. "You're not, like, really upset, are you?" she asked me. "I mean, I know we always joke about how hot he is and stuff, but you don't actually, like . . . I mean, if you really care—"

"I *don't*," I protested immediately, like if I could deliver the lie with enough emphasis, it would somehow make it even a little bit true. In the back of my head I knew Allie was right: I was famous for keeping my emotions to myself. If she didn't realize how much—how *hugely*—I felt whatever it was I felt for Sawyer, then chances are it was my fault for never letting on.

It was too late to tell her now, though, sitting there in the yard like I had on a hundred other summer mornings—not if Sawyer had already chosen her. Not if they'd already chosen each other. The only thing to do now was to protect myself with the lie.

"It's fine," I continued, shrugging nonchalantly. "You guys should do whatever makes you happy." I probably would have kept going—offered to help them pick out a china pattern for their wedding, maybe—but thank God there was Mrs. Ballard back at the screen door, voice like a Klaxon across the empty yard.

"Girls!" She sounded annoyed this time, impatient. I wondered how much she'd heard. "Do you want these or not?"

"We don't want 'em, Ma!" Allie yelled, and then turned back to me expectantly. But I was already getting to my feet, brushing my shorts off, and arranging my face into a mask of easy, artificial calm.

"I want them," I said, even though I didn't really. I crossed the grass, the sun beating down on my dark curtain of hair. "I'm coming," I called, leaving Allie behind.

5

After

I wander downstairs once Hannah is in bed for the night, thinking I might do some school reading at the picnic table in the yard. It's humid and swampy out, the air thick with mosquitoes, but frankly it's not worse than any other night and I feel too big for these walls anyway.

I spend a lot of time out here in the evenings, tethered to the house with one ear out for the baby, feet up on a lounge chair and the odd lizard scurrying up the trunk of the orange tree. The damp air curls the pages of my books. I'll do schoolwork or click around on Facebook, talk with Soledad if she's feeling chatty. I used to try to write out here sometimes, before I finally gave up and stopped tormenting myself—the blank screen like a sweeping accusation from the person I used to be back in high school, everything I said I was going to do and didn't.

Tonight my father's beaten me out here, though, already hard at work in the garden he's kept since Cade and I were babies, pulling the aphids off his tomato plants. He's listening to Sarah Vaughan through the kitchen window. Soil is caked into the creases of his palms.

I almost turn around, just cut my losses and go—I'm still angry with him from earlier, absolutely, but that's not the whole story, not by a long shot. I knew from the second I saw him that Sawyer turning up here was going to unearth all kinds of nastiness for my father, and just standing near him I'm hit with that familiar sear of frustration and shame. For a second I'm sixteen again, pregnant and hopeless, every careful plan for my future scattered like hayseed in a dry wind.

Still: That was before.

"How's it going?" I venture, crossing the patio to be near him. The slate is warm under my feet.

My father glances up at me, then back at his tall, spindly plants. His doctor says gardening's good for his heart, although that's not why he does it. "All right, I suppose." He sighs, rubs at a prickly green leaf with the pad of his thumb. "Worried about rot." I watch as he moves on to the zucchini, the bright yellow summer squash. He'll finish with Soledad's rosebushes, just like always, pruning them back before they climb clear up the side of the house and take over like something out of a fairy tale.

We had an aboveground pool back here, once upon a time, but my father had it pulled out when we were kids, citing upkeep costs and childhood drowning statistics. "Besides," he said at the time, "Roger and Lydia are happy to have you over there. You can use their pool whenever you want."

It's true Cade and I spent hours over there when we were little, jumping off the diving board and turning somersaults in the clear blue water. I try to imagine it now, showing up with Hannah and our bathing suits. *We're just here to have a swim.* It might be worth it just to see the look on Lydia's face.

"What?" he asks, going to work on the bell peppers. The pruners click neatly in his hand.

I snap to attention. "Hmm?"

"You're smirking."

"Oh." I hadn't even realized he was looking. Something tells me he wouldn't be as amused by the mental image as I am. "I don't mean to."

I told my father I was pregnant and he didn't speak to me for eleven weeks. I only blame him a little: His own parents died when he was seven, and he was, quite literally, raised by the nuns in Saint Tammany Parish in Louisiana. He fully intended to become a priest until he met my mother; he confesses every Friday and keeps a Saint Christopher medal tucked inside his shirt. In his heart he's a musician but his soul is that of the most serious of altar boys, and the fact that he didn't send me away to some convent until I had the baby is probably a testament to the mercy of the God that we've always prayed to in my house.

It got better once Hannah was born—better, I suspect, once I wasn't so visibly, aggressively huge—and in the last year or so we've reached an uneasy kind of truce. Still, the anger he reserves for Sawyer is damn near bottomless, and it doesn't surprise me that I'm going to catch the overflow now that my proverbial boyfriend is back.

Penance. Right.

"I was going to read out here for a while," I say finally, for lack of anything better. I'm still clutching my textbook in one arm.

My father frowns. "It's dark for that, Reena."

Go away is what he means. I don't know why I feel compelled to try. "It's dark for aphid-picking, too," I point out.

He sighs again, like I'm being difficult on purpose, like I'm deliberately missing the point. "Well," he says after a moment, and when he finally turns to face me, it's so quiet I can hear the neighbors' sprinkler hissing endlessly next door. "I suppose you're right."

6

Before

"I suck," was the first thing Allie said when I picked up the receiver, her number appearing on the caller ID for the first time in almost a week. I was sitting on my bed reading the travel magazines Soledad had picked up for me at the bookstore, imagining myself wandering the markets of Provence or sitting on the beach in a cove in Kauai. "I totally owe you a phone call."

"You don't suck," I told her, although the truth is she sucked a little. It was the end of the summer. Sophomore year started in a few days. August had seeped away in a kind of weird, lonely fugue state: I'd played an awful lot of solitaire. I'd spent a lot of time alone. "You're busy. I get it."

"No, I do," she argued. "I'm the worst. I miss you

desperately. Come over. My parents have some law-firm benefit thing tonight. Come on," she said, when I hesitated. "It'll remind you how much you love me."

I thought for one mean second about turning her down, claiming other plans and spending another night watching *Law & Order* reruns with Soledad, but in the end that was too bleak to contemplate, and besides: I missed her desperately, too.

"Yeah," I said, after a minute. I got to the end of *Travel + Leisure*, flung its glossy pages onto the floor. "Of course."

I biked the familiar streets that led to Allie's parents' development, everything green and rain-forest-damp. My tires skidded slickly against the blacktop. I leaned my bike against the side of the garage and scratched idly at a mosquito bite on the jut of my collarbone as I waited for Allie to open the door.

Lauren Werner opened it instead.

"Serena!" she said in a voice like a Fruit Roll-Up, tart and vaguely sticky, nothing organic there at all. "I didn't know you were coming."

I stared at her for a minute, her slinky top and honey-brown hair. "Yeah," I said eventually. I was wearing stretched-out jeans rolled up into capri pants, a white Hanes undershirt that might have belonged to my brother at some point, and a pair of Birkenstock clogs. "Ditto."

"Allie's around here somewhere," she told me, leading

the way into the front hall like this was a place I'd never been before, like I'd need to be pointed in the direction of the bathroom and told where to hang up my imaginary coat. I followed dumbly. In the living room were half a dozen kids I recognized from the hallways at school, maybe a grade or two ahead of us—a girl from my chem class, a guy who worked the counter at Bump and Grind. I could see a couple more people hanging out in the kitchen: not a big party, definitely, but still, being there felt like being in a dream where you're someplace you recognize but it looks weirdly different, everything just a degree or two off from true north. "I always forget you guys are friends."

"Uh, yup," I said vaguely, doing my best to ignore her garden-variety bitchiness and still trying to get my bearings. The AC wasn't working, and the air in the hallway was tepid and aquarium-damp. "We're friends."

Just then Allie appeared, flushed and grinning, throwing her skinny arms around my neck. "Hi!" she said, and in that second she looked so happy to see me that I forgot myself and smiled back. That was the thing about Allie, one of the reasons I loved her so much: When she made you the object of all her terrifying, kinetic energy, it was like standing in a puddle of sun. "You're here!"

"I'm here," I said, letting her spin me around on the tile in a swooping little dance. "You know," I said, once she'd dipped me and, deciding that was enough dancing for now, begun to yank me gently down the hall, "maybe you could have mentioned on the phone that half of school was going to be at your house so that I could have, you know, bathed."

"What are you talking about?" she asked, frowning. "You look adorable."

"I look twelve."

"You look arty and cool."

"Okay." I snorted. "I do not look *arty* or *cool*—"

"Hey, Reena."

I startled, looked around, and tried not to gasp too audibly: There was Sawyer standing behind me, in jeans and a T-shirt, leather cord looped around his wrist. A plastic cup dangled by its lip from his hand.

"Hey," I said.

I saw Sawyer pretty often, actually, hanging around at the restaurant or sitting in front of us at church on Sunday, at my house taking lessons from my dad. However much I thought about him—and I thought about him a *lot*—I was reasonably adept at keeping it together when he was around, careful not to tip my hand and thereby make my entire life completely unbearable.

I had never seen him in Allie's kitchen before. I had never seen him slide a casual arm around her shoulders, one hand sifting through her wispy hair. Seeing it now felt slow and painful, like a muscle tearing. I had no earthly clue where I should look.

In the end it didn't matter, because already he was leading her away without even trying; he just stepped back and she followed, like a magnet or a high-frequency sound. "Get a drink and come down to the basement," she called to me, distracted. "We're gonna play flip cup in a minute."

And then she was gone.

I stood there for a second. I tried to look very, very calm. Finally I slipped past the two girls at the counter, out the sliding door, and across the covered patio, avoiding the bright patch thrown by the floodlight affixed to the back of the house. I made straight for the swing set, wet from this afternoon's rainstorm, the air still so humid it felt like breathing spiderwebs.

I sat.

I wasn't shy, exactly. That's never what it was. I just didn't know how to *do* this, is all, the clang and chatter of high school. And more than that, I didn't particularly want to learn. My whole life Cade had teased me for my total inability to handle more than one or two friends at a time; ten minutes in Allie's crowded kitchen left me feeling like some wild animal dropped into a completely foreign habitat, a tiger in the tundra or a penguin in the woods. I wasn't unpopular, exactly. I was just . . . unequipped.

It was one thing when I had Allie around to help fight my wars, I thought as I sat there. She could do all the talking when I was feeling tongue-tied, vocalize feelings on behalf of both of us: *Reena and I thought that movie was stupid. Reena and I would love to go.* Lately, though, not only did it feel like she didn't have the time or patience to parse my silences, but on top of that she'd taken the person I wanted most in the entire world.

It was my own fault, I thought again, swinging slowly back and forth without much of a long-term plan. I didn't know how to open up to people. I didn't know how to be the kind of person who did. I couldn't figure out how Allie—

"What are you doing?"

Sawyer sidled across the damp, hissing grass, hands in his pockets. I hadn't seen him coming. He'd edged around the floodlight, too.

"Um." I groped around for plausible deniability and, finding none, had to settle for the truth. "Hiding."

Sawyer raised his eyebrows, paused against the slide. He was barefoot and casual-looking, like someone who just lived in his body sort of carelessly, all muscle and bone. "From anything in particular?"

Everyone, as a matter of fact, but it didn't feel like the kind of thing I could say to Sawyer LeGrande. "That," I began instead, stalling, "is a very good question."

"Well." Sawyer sat down on the swing next to me and rocked back and forth a little, long legs planted, just normal, like we did this all the time. "You suck at hiding, because I found you in, like, one second."

"Were you *looking*?" I blurted, and then, before he could answer: "I wasn't so much doing it as a game."

Sawyer considered that. "No," he said eventually. "I guess not." He swung for another minute, quiet. We'd never been alone like this before. "This isn't really your scene, huh?" he asked.

"What's that?" I asked, just this side of defensive. I felt my spine straighten up, a reflex: He'd hit a little close to the artery. My fingertips curled tightly around the edge of the swing. "People having a good time?"

Sawyer laughed like he thought I was clever, like I might have a secret to share. "That's not what I mean. Bunch of slacker types screwing around. I don't know. Lauren Werner."

That got my attention, as if he hadn't had it already. I squinted a bit, trying to gauge the expression on his face. It was frustratingly dark out here; fine for brooding, sure, but for all the world I wanted to pull him into the light and just . . . *look*. "I thought you and Lauren Werner were friends."

Sawyer shrugged. "We are, I guess. But she's . . . I mean . . ." He stopped. It looked like he was thinking about it, like he hadn't totally decided how much he wanted to reveal. "You know."

"I really, *really* do," I told him, and the way I said it cracked him up again. I grinned. I tried to remember the last time I'd made him laugh—a long time ago, definitely, back when we were still little kids running around with my brother, playing tag in the grove behind his house. It used to take them forever to catch me back then. I'd freeze and go quiet among the trees.

We sat there for another minute, swinging. I could hear the frogs calling out above my head. Inside Allie's house something crashed to the floor, followed by a spray of laughter. I winced.

"You ever wish you were still, like, eight years old?" Sawyer asked suddenly.

I blinked at him, startled: It felt like he could open up my head and see inside. I took a beat to recover, slid my feet out of my clogs and rubbed them cautiously through the cool, damp grass. "Nah." It felt weirdly dangerous to look at him, like staring at the surface of the sun. "I only ever wish I was old enough to leave."

Sawyer didn't answer for what felt like an eternity. Finally I glanced up and found him looking back. Something weird and new and personal charged between us in the darkness, a gaze too long to be an accident. Another moment passed before he grinned. "For what it's worth," he said, and here he bumped the hard knob of my bare ankle with his own, gentle, "I think you look arty."

"I don't—" I started, but then there was Allie crossing the lawn, a dark swath through the pool of light Sawyer and I had both avoided so carefully, like a stage actress finding her mark.

"There you are!" she called brightly—so pretty even in jeans and a tank top, curves and curly hair. Of course he would have chosen her. "My two favorites."

"Here we are," Sawyer agreed, eyes on me for a single

beat longer before turning his attention to Allie. "Reena was hiding."

"That's 'cause she's mad at me," Allie said, subtle as a border collie, reaching for the chain link and giving my swing a little shake. She smelled like malt lemonade and her mother's perfume.

Sawyer cocked his head to the side. "I don't know about that," he told her, getting to his feet. "I'll see you inside." He glanced at me one more time, quick. "Later, Reena."

"What were you guys talking about?" she asked when Sawyer was gone, taking his place on the swing set and winding around in a circle so the chain twisted up, then letting herself go in a dizzy rush. "You and the boy king."

"Nothing," I told her, shrugging. I slid my shoes back onto my feet a little urgently, as if I might possibly need to run someplace in the immediate future. "He just wanted to know what I was doing out here."

Allie looked at me sideways, face screwing up a bit, like she didn't quite trust me to tell her the truth. "What *were* you doing out here?" she asked.

"Seriously?" I gaped, a hot little flare of annoyance inside my chest. "I mean—*seriously*?"

Allie blinked, her gray eyes wide and innocent—her *I don't know how that stuff got in my purse* expression, normally reserved for her parents and shopping mall security guards. I didn't like her turning that look on me. "What?"

"You totally blindsided me with those people in there!" I

couldn't get a foothold with her lately. It felt like I was hanging on by my nails. "I came over to watch TV and eat pizza or something, not play flip cup with a bunch of strangers."

"They're not *strangers*," she corrected sharply. Heat lightning flickered in the distance, there and gone again. "They're all from school. And I knew you wouldn't come if I told you Lauren was going to be here, so—"

"Yeah," I interrupted. She wasn't listening to me. "I know. That's my point."

"Well, where does that leave me?" Allie asked, huffing a little. "*They're* my friends, too, Reena. I like them. They're not, like, bad, shady people. They're nice."

"I never said they weren't nice," I argued. "I never even said they're the reason you totally dropped off the face of the earth this whole summer, which—"

"I told you I'm sorry!" Her voice rose a little, almost whining. "If you could quit making it so hard for me to include you—"

"Maybe I don't want to be included in this stuff, Al! I hate this stuff! I just want to do normal stuff, like always—"

"Card games and *Bringing Up Baby*?" Allie frowned. The air was swampy out here, oppressive. I wanted to hop on my bike and speed away. "Is that what you want to do, really? Is that still fun to you? Come on, Reena," she prodded when I didn't answer. "People like you. They all just think *you* don't like *them*."

"I mean," I said. "I *don't* like them, generally."

"You don't even know them!" she exploded, then, nastily: "You like *Sawyer*."

And *that*—God. That stung.

"Okay." I stood up then, wiped my clammy palms on the rain-wet backside of my jeans, because nope, *nope*, we were not going to have that conversation, not now—not when I was already feeling weird and lonely and homesick, embarrassed by everything I wanted and didn't have. I glanced up at the row of palm trees at the property line, trying to keep it together. Suddenly even the backyard felt sinister, familiar places gone threatening and strange in the dark. "You want to win this fight, Al, you can win this fight, that's cool. I'll see you."

"You're right," she said immediately, getting up and following me across the lawn. "I'm sorry. I'm not trying to be bitchy."

"Oh, really?" I stopped and stared at her, hands on my hips. I wanted to hit rewind on this night and on this summer, for this bizarre alternate universe to bend over on itself again and for everything to go back to the way it was supposed to be. *Ever wish you were eight years old?*

"No!" she exclaimed. "I'm trying to have a conversation with you. Jesus! I miss you! I want to talk to you about stuff."

"Really," I repeated coldly, and Allie rolled her eyes. "Like what, exactly?"

"I don't know." She shrugged, almost helpless, skinny hands fluttering in front of her like dragonflies. "You know what I mean. He's . . . I don't know. He's not what we thought he was."

"He's a vampire?" I deadpanned.

That made her mad. "Okay," Allie said angrily. "*You* want to win this fight, Reena? You can win it. You can ice me out. But I'm just trying to be honest with you. I know you think I'm this horrible person, and I know you think I did this horrible thing, like I *stole* him from you or something—"

"I never said that—"

"But I did you a favor. If you can't handle coming to my house and playing flip cup with Lauren Werner, you definitely couldn't handle having sex with Sawyer LeGrande."

I reeled for a second. I stood there. I thought, very clearly, of the word *devastated*.

"Look, Reena." As soon as it was out there Allie knew she'd crossed some boundary, some line of demarcation so clearly marked that once she'd breached it our lives would always be divided into when we were little kids and when we weren't, neatly bisected into the then and the now. I looked at her for one more moment, and then I turned around. Thunder rumbled over my head, loud and ominous, a storm about to break.

"*Reena*," Allie called behind me, more forcefully this time, but by then I was already gone.

7

After

One thing about living in South Florida is that everywhere you go is violently air-conditioned, the tabernacle included. It's sixty-five degrees inside Our Lady of the Miraculous Medal when we walk into church on Sunday, has been since God invented HVAC. Forever and ever, amen.

We're church families, the LeGrandes and us: christenings and confirmations, spaghetti dinners and Sunday school. My father and Soledad were married in this building. In middle school I used to stop in to light candles for my mom. Even at my most miserable and lonely and pregnant I sat right behind Sawyer's parents every weekend in the seventh pew on the right, and though I think that at this point his family and mine love and hate each other with equal intensity, the Profession of Faith is just one more thing we've always done together, world without end.

Today I've barely gotten Hannah's sausage-link arms into the sweater Soledad finished just this week when Sawyer sidles in flanked by Roger and Lydia, his hands shoved deep into his dark jeans and sunglasses hanging from the *V* of his button-down. Everyone, even Sawyer, wears a collared shirt to church.

"Hey, everybody," he whispers, as they slide into the row in front of us. My father ignores him. My brother only glares. His wife, Stefanie, is gaping a little in a way that makes me want to smack her across her round, curious face: *Yes, Stef, he's good-looking. Yes, Stef, he's back.*

Jesus Christ, everybody. Pull it together.

Soledad is apparently the only member of my family with a modicum of grace, not that this comes as any kind of revelation. "Hi, Sawyer," she says to him, voice tempered as always by traces of a childhood spent in Cuba. Beside him, his mother is glowing, radiating light, and why shouldn't she be? Just like the story promised, her prodigal returned. "It's good to see you."

He kisses Soledad's cheek before he turns to look at Hannah, and for nearly a full minute they stare at each other, silent. There is a moment when I do not breathe. Sawyer has always been full of nervous habits, perpetually tapping his fingers or rubbing hard at a muscle at his neck—it's part of what makes girls fall in love with him—but now he goes still as winter, like the blood has dried up in his veins.

Lydia clears her throat. Hannah fidgets. Sawyer looks at me like I've broken his beating heart.

"Nice work," is all he says, and I laugh.

Back when we were together I used to spend my Sunday mornings in church poking Sawyer in the back, waiting until no one was looking and quietly snapping the elastic on the boxers peeking out the rear of his pants. He'd reach behind and grab my hand, the two of us thumb wrestling until Soledad or Lydia noticed and elbowed one or both of us in the side. "Pay attention," they'd hiss, and then turn back to the priest and pretty much leave us to our own devices.

We were sweethearts. It's a thing that happened. It's over now. It's fine.

Halfway through the psalm and Hannah's wriggles turn to whimpers; her body is thermal and heavy in my arms. She's crabby, is all. She didn't sleep well last night—neither of us slept very well last night, if you want to know the truth—but in this second it feels like she's on to me, all terrifying toddler intuition. In this second it feels like she knows.

I scoop her up and head for the aisle, because in another second we're both going to lose it, right in the middle of a reading from Paul's letter to the Corinthians: *Behold, I tell you a mystery.* We burst through the doors at the back, straight into a blinding shock of light.

"I never liked Paul much anyway," I tell Hannah once we're hidden away in the courtyard outside the church, a flagstone patio peopled by half a dozen life-size statues of angels and saints, like some kind of weird religious cocktail party hosted by the apostle Bartholomew. I set Hannah on her feet and let her walk. Summer in Broward County is brutal and haunted, all palm trees and the green tangle of sea grapes wound around the grotto on the lawn. Hannah grabs at a cluster of Spanish moss with her pudgy starfish hands. "Oh, boy," I say. "Whatcha got over there, chick?"

"Oh, boy," she repeats, and I grin. Hannah's a hugely beautiful kid, dark-haired and sloe-eyed, even taking into account the fact that I grew her inside my body and therefore might possibly be a little prejudiced. Strangers stop and say she's beautiful all the time. "Oh, *boy*!"

I sit down on a wooden bench to watch her. A taciturn Virgin Mary holds court on top of a dried-up fountain at the edge of the patio, a missing chunk of plaster where her veil should meet her dress. I think of my own mom, whom I hardly remember—just a waterfall of dark hair and the faint smell of lavender—and wonder if she'd have any secrets to share. I run my thumb over the jagged edge of stone, waiting. Soledad prays to Mary for virtually everything and swears that Mary answers every time, but if either this mother or mine have any advice to dispense, at the moment they are holding their tongues.

"Fat lot of help you are," I tell them, and jump up to catch my kid before she falls.

8

Before

I had no friends in tenth grade.

Okay, that's dramatic. I had friends. I didn't eat lunch alone on a toilet seat or anything. Mostly, I just didn't eat lunch. I went to the library. I hung out on the bleachers and read. When I did go to the cafeteria, I sat with Shelby, the new hostess at the restaurant. Shelby was a junior; she'd just moved from Tucson with her mom and her twin brother, Aaron, although he'd only needed about two days in the pestilent swamp of South Florida to decide there was absolutely no way he could ever live here. He'd fled to New Hampshire to live with their dad before school had even started. Shelby had hair like a flaming neon carrot and a mouth like a merchant marine; she wore tiny silver hoops all up the side of her left ear and was dating the captain of the girls' soccer team. I'd automatically assumed she thought I was too boring to breathe air until the day she plopped her tray right next to mine and demanded to know what was up with the food in this godforsaken place like maybe we'd been friends all our lives.

"It sucks," I told her, blinking in grateful surprise. "That's . . . basically what's up."

Shelby grinned, handed me half the Kit Kat she was unwrapping. "Looks that way."

She was giving me a ride to work one afternoon, nineties girl rock blaring from the speakers in her decrepit Volvo wagon as she pulled out of the parking lot, when she snorted and gestured out the windshield with her chin. "Is that the bartender?" she asked, squinting a little. "From the restaurant?"

I followed her gaze to the side of the building, half hidden by a row of dry, browning shrubs: In the shadow cast by the overhang above the side door of the gym, Allie and Sawyer were pressed against the concrete, his palm sliding steadily up her skirt.

"Yeah," I said slowly. For a second it felt hard to breathe, like there was something unfamiliar taking up space in my chest beside my heart and lungs. "Yeah, that's him."

"People gettin' at it in broad daylight," Shelby said

brightly, pulling out into traffic. "That's how you know the terrorists haven't won." Then she looked at me, her pale eyebrows knitting together. "What?" she asked. "Shit, sorry. Are you one of those people who's really sensitive about terrorist jokes?"

That made me laugh. "I'm not particularly sensitive about anything," I lied, glancing out the window for another half a second before tilting my head up to stare at the fat, heavy clouds.

The year ground on in that way—Halloween, Thanksgiving. I finally got my learner's permit. I spent a whole lot of time with my journal. Soledad watched me carefully, cataloging the narrowing parameters of my teenage life like an anthropologist conducting a field study: *school, work, home. Rinse, repeat.* I didn't tell her about Allie and Sawyer—never told her about Allie and *me*—but that didn't stop her from knowing. "Do you want to talk about this?" she asked me once, Saturday night and three episodes into a *Bridezillas* marathon on cable.

I shrugged like I didn't have the slightest idea what she meant. "Talk about what?" I wondered blandly.

Soledad rolled her eyes.

I called Allie once, for the record. She didn't pick up, and I didn't leave a message.

Also for the record: She didn't call me back.

The answer, I always thought, was to get out of town.

I'd always liked to read about foreign places—I'd been getting *National Geographic* since I was ten—but that winter I was absolutely insatiable, camped out on my bed surrounded by travel books from the library, their cellophane jackets sticky with dust. I plotted. I made lists. I stayed up all night clicking through blog after blog, stories and pictures of women who spent years in Morocco and Tanzania and the South of France—then mapped my own itinerary, tracing my route with a silver Sharpie like some kind of imaginary Silk Road.

I wanted so, so badly to leave.

"Where you going tonight?" my father asked me one evening, hovering in the doorway of my bedroom, tonic and lime in his hand. He'd been playing the piano downstairs, and somewhere in my head I'd dimly registered the quiet, the way you notice the dishwasher kicking off.

"Chicago," I told him cheerfully, looking up from the pictures of Oak Park on my laptop. He'd had a heart attack a couple of years before, my father, collapsing in the parking lot outside my eighth-grade graduation; I tried to be cheerful with him whenever I could. "Or possibly Copenhagen."

"Chicago's a pretty good music town," he told me, nodding like he was thinking about it, like it was a place I might actually be headed. "You might want to lay over in the kitchen first, though. Soledad's making pesto."

I smiled and closed my computer, rolled myself off the bed. "Be right there."

One morning that spring I got a note in homeroom saying I needed to go to Guidance by the end of the day, which left me feeling startled and uneasy. I'd never been called to the office before. I wondered if I was in trouble for something I didn't know I'd done, or if some well-meaning Samaritan had expressed concern about my ability to cope with the tyranny of high school in general. "We've noticed you're socially inept," I pictured the counselor saying, her jowly face tilted to the side to show how well she was listening. "You stare out the window constantly. You're obsessive, and you spend too much time in your own brain."

"No kidding," I imagined replying, hitching my backpack up on one shoulder and heading down the hall toward English. "Tell me something I don't know."

I spent all morning with a hard little knot of anxiety lodged someplace in my middle, then knocked tentatively on the door of the office at the beginning of my lunch period. The air smelled like coffee and dust. I was expecting to meet with Mrs. Ortum, the older, slightly daffy-looking counselor who'd run all our ninth-grade seminars and whose husband, apparently, had made a hundred million dollars in tech stocks, but in her place was a dark-haired young woman I'd never seen before, a little plaque printed with MS. BOWEN on the desk.

"Hi, Serena," she said, smiling warmly. "Come on in." I had no idea how she knew who I was, but she was pretty and smart-looking in a way that immediately made me want to please her. I found myself smiling back.

"You're not in trouble," she said, as soon as I was seated. The sleeves of her starchy white button-down were rolled halfway up her arms. "Everybody I've had in here so far keeps thinking they're in trouble." She picked up a file folder, tapped it against her desk for a moment. Reading upside down, I could see that it contained my transcripts. "I'm new here, so I'm just kind of going through my lists and trying to get to know everyone I can."

She asked me how my classes were going and if I had an after-school job, taking notes on a yellow legal pad as I answered as vaguely as possible. A bright turquoise costume ring glittered on the middle finger of her left hand. There was a carafe of water on the desk beside her, the fancy kind we used at the restaurant, with round slices of lemon floating inside. It seemed weirdly glamorous for school. Most of the faculty carried plastic travel mugs with bank logos on them.

"Have you given much thought yet to college?" she asked finally, sitting back in her uncomfortable-looking chair and gazing at me shrewdly. She'd put the pen and paper back down on the desk.

"A little," I told her, which was a lie. In fact, I thought about college constantly, of where I might go and the people I might meet there. There was, at this very moment, a course catalog from Northwestern on my desk at home so well-thumbed it was basically falling apart, the writing program bookmarked with a neon yellow Post-it. I could have recited their arts and sciences requirements from memory. "But I'm only a sophomore, so I figured I had some time."

"Well," Ms. Bowen said, "that's actually what I wanted to talk to you about. I've been looking at your records, Serena, and they're really impressive. A 4.0 GPA every semester you've been here, straight honors track since last year. I'd like to see you participating in an extracurricular or two, but the fact is that if you stay on this track, keep taking those APs and doing well on them, you could be eligible for graduation a full year early." She leaned forward a bit, almost conspiratorial. She looked excited for me. "Is that something you might be interested in working toward?"

It took me a minute to absorb that information. *A full year early. Eligible for graduation.* I stared at her for a moment, blinking; in the outer office I could hear the sounds of the copier jamming, an assistant's frustrated *dang.*

Ms. Bowen took my hesitation as reluctance; she cocked her glossy head to the side, the same sympathetic pose I'd imagined earlier. "Of course, you certainly don't have to," she amended. "I know plenty of students who wouldn't want to miss out on being a senior, and everything that goes with it. I just wanted to let you know that you had the opt—"

"I'd love to," I interrupted quickly. I thought of airplanes and huge, drafty lecture halls, locks on cages springing free. "What do you need me to do?"

What Ms. Bowen needed me to do was pretty simple, at least for the time being: keep doing well in my classes, make a list of the schools I wanted to apply to, and get myself an SAT study book. "We'll find you some volunteer work for the summer," she promised, eyes shining like maybe she was just as excited about the prospect of pulling this off as I was. "Beef up your transcripts a bit."

In May, two of the waitresses quit, so on top of the extra studying I worked like a demon, three nights a week and then doubles every weekend. I lived in black pants and a starchy white shirt. My father and Roger bought Antonia's when I was a little girl and I'd been waiting tables just about that long, knew the menu and the regulars all by heart. The truth is, I'd always liked being there: the place all tin ceiling and subway tiles, white linen tablecloths like a hundred communion dresses. There was always a band set up by the bar.

The guys playing tonight were some of my favorites, a quasi-ridiculous oldies ensemble who covered a lot of Sam Cooke, and I sang along under my breath while I zipped a couple of credit cards through the computer beside the bar. Sometime during the second verse I realized I wasn't alone:

Sawyer was leaning against the hatch and watching me, a wry, secret smile on his face.

I snapped my jaw shut, blushing and surprised: Sawyer wasn't even *working* tonight. He hadn't been on the schedule. I hadn't done anything nice to my hair. He was wearing jeans and a T-shirt, street clothes. He was giving off the heat from outside. "Don't tease," I ordered, bouncing back after a minute, trying like hell not to let on that my feelings for him hadn't let up even a little, though he'd been dating Allie for more than seven months. "It's not nice."

Sawyer shrugged and just kept standing, like he had no place in the world to be other than here. "I'm not teasing," he told me, and in truth, he didn't actually seem to be. "'Bring It On Home to Me'? That's a good song."

"That's a *great* song," I corrected, and he grinned.

"You sound like your dad."

"Nah. He likes Otis Redding." I tore a receipt out of the printer, smiled back. "What are you doing here?"

Sawyer tilted his head. "Looking for you."

"Right." I snorted, slipping the cards back into the billfolds. "Your mom was floating around earlier." Lydia wasn't super involved in the day-to-day running of the restaurant, though her fingerprints were everywhere if you knew where to look: the formal antique portraits affixed to the doors of the restrooms, the Edison bulbs hanging above the bar. Lydia was an artist herself, a photographer, but her family had made a fortune with a chain of successful steak houses up and down the Eastern Seaboard, and she probably had a better head for the food business than either Roger or my dad. She'd turn up from time to time, watchful, an expression on her face like she was working out secret sums in her mind. The busboys were all terrified of her; Shelby called her Dragon Lady behind her back. I tried to stay out of her way.

The one person Lydia never seemed to turn her cool, eagle-eyed artist's scrutiny on was Sawyer. He was her only son, her Best Beloved: He'd had surgery when he was a baby to repair a literal hole in his heart, a fact Allie and I had always thought was enormously, unbearably romantic, and as long as I'd known Lydia she'd been ferociously protective of him. "She probably makes you have a blood test before you're allowed to be his girlfriend," Allie'd hypothesized at my house late one night, both of us dissolving into giggles—not that it seemed to have stopped her, in the end.

I was about to head back toward the floor when Sawyer reached out and grabbed me by the wrist. "Reena." There was something urgent and unexpected about the way he said it, like he'd almost told me a secret and then changed his mind. "Why don't I ever see you around anymore?"

I blinked at him, disbelieving. He was still holding on to my arm. "Maybe I'm better at hiding than you thought."

Sawyer took just long enough to answer that I was sure he had no idea what I was talking about: It had been a long time since that night in Allie's yard, after all, and he'd probably forgotten it immediately. I was about to backpedal when he smiled. "Maybe," he said, letting go but not moving away at all. "But I'm serious."

"Yeah, well." I felt my eyebrows arc. "Me, too."

"What are you doing tonight?" he asked.

I cocked my head, glanced around. The band had segued into "It's All Right." I could see my father talking to a couple of regulars at the other end of the bar. "Working?" I said.

Sawyer rolled his eyes at me. "Thank you, princess. I mean after that."

"Going home?"

"Come hang out."

"With you?" I blurted, and Sawyer smirked, lazy as the Cheshire cat disappearing from the tree.

"Yeah, Reena. With me."

In all the years I had known him—and I'd known him, more or less, since I was born—Sawyer had never once asked me to go anywhere. It took me a second to recover. Still, I shook my head like an instinct, like something I knew in my gut. I thought of the party at Allie's, Lauren Werner and the crowds of people I didn't know how to navigate. "Listen, Sawyer. Allie and I don't really . . ." I trailed off, tried again, wondered what she'd told him. "I mean, we're not so much . . . hanging out."

Sawyer frowned, and there was that expression again,

like he'd come here to tell me something specific. "I didn't mean with Allie," he said.

Oh.

"Oh," I said. I looked at him for a moment, then back over at my father with his coffee and his grin. "Sawyer—"

"Come on, Reena," he said, already slightly impatient. I got the feeling this was all the convincing he was going to try to do. "It's just me."

I thought of Allie and of valuables gone missing: of lip gloss slipped in pockets and crushes filched right out from under your nose. No matter how I tried to justify it, this was a capital crime of friendship. It was treason, even if she'd done it first.

"Yeah," I said. Behind me the music was ending, one final chord and the crash of a snare. "Yeah, I can hang out."

9

After

After church I take Hannah back to the house for lunch and strap her into the high chair, slicing some fruit to keep her busy while I toast some wheat bread. "Hey, lady, can you say *banana*?" I ask her, and Hannah repeats it back obediently. "Good girl," I tell her happily, holding my hand up for a high five. Dumb as it sounds, I didn't totally realize when I was pregnant that Hannah would have an actual personality separate from mine, but sure enough it comes out more and more every day: She likes ice cream and avocados and dancing to Beyoncé in the back of the car, her small body moving with surprising enthusiasm inside the confines of her safety seat. She's talking more and more now, baby jabber and snatches of conversation repeated back to me. It's kind of the coolest thing ever.

Soledad comes in and drops her purse on the counter, swipes a chunk of banana off the cutting board. I snort. "That's for Hannah."

"Sorry. Starving." She smooths an affectionate hand over the top of Hannah's head. "So, Lydia talked to me when we were leaving," she tells me, not bothering to work her way up to it at all. "She wants to take Hannah to the library one day this week to get her a card."

"What? Why?" I spread a little bit of peanut butter on the toast and cut it into tiny triangles, then put it on the tray of the high chair. "There you go, baby girl." I glance at Soledad, wrinkle my nose. "What does she need a card for? She's fourteen months old. *I* take out books for her."

"I know that. But I guess Lyd wants to spend some time with her."

My spine straightens. "Really."

Sol stares back. "Really."

"How special."

Growing up, I spent more time with Lydia than with any of my aunts or cousins, which is why it doesn't totally make sense that I've never gotten over being afraid of her. When I was ten and eleven she and Soledad and I used to go out to expensive lunches and get pedicures, reading gossip magazines and picking out our favorite dresses on each page. She's got a successful photography business and trolls flea markets looking for cool antique rugs for her hallways; she bought me an incredible rose-quartz necklace when I turned thirteen. She's never turned the full force of her dragon-lady tendencies on me, not exactly, but still I've always found her totally terrifying, the way I'd be scared of a she-wolf or a teacher I couldn't impress. I can't get over the notion that there's something huge and important about me that she finds totally lacking.

On top of which, until this morning she's showed about as much interest in Hannah as one might show for memorizing the finer details of the Terms and Conditions agreement on iTunes. So it's possible I'm not feeling a whole lot of Catholic charity toward one Lydia LeGrande at this particular juncture.

"I think we're busy that day," I announce grandly, and my stepmother rolls her eyes.

"I didn't tell you a day."

"Well, Hannah and I have a very busy social calendar."

Soledad smirks, just the tiniest bit. "Reena."

"Sawyer's been back for a *day* and suddenly she's angling for a Grandmother of the Year Award? Seriously?" I scowl, pouring milk into Hannah's sippy cup. "When was the last time you even saw her *hold* this kid? *Never* is the answer, in case you were wondering. *Never*."

"Never," Hannah echoes cheerfully, tossing some peanut butter toast onto the floor.

Soledad raises her eyebrows. "Reena," she says again, more quietly this time. "Calm down."

"You calm down." God, that makes me mad. "No. I say no. And why was she talking to you, anyway? If she wants to talk to me she can talk to me. I'm right here. I've *been* right here, if you remember, for the last *two years*."

Soledad nods slowly. I can't tell if she's disapproving or maybe a little impressed. "Yes, sweetheart," she says after a moment, and presses a kiss to my temple before she goes. "I remember."

My cell rings just as Hannah goes down for her nap, and I dig it out from the bottom of my bag, where it vibrates beneath a bottle of ibuprofen and a board book of *The Very Hungry Caterpillar*. It's Aaron. I smile. "Hey, mister," I say, wedging the phone between my ear and my shoulder as I dash down the stairs. I wave good-bye to Soledad and hurry out the back door. "What's up?"

"Corner of Las Olas and Third Ave," he tells me, a delighted grin evident in his voice. "Suck on *that*."

"What? No way." There's this drag queen who looks like Celine Dion that hangs out around town, and if Aaron can prove he's seen her, I have to buy dinner, that's the game. Aaron buys dinner more often than not. "Did you get a picture?"

"What do you think, it's my first rodeo?" He laughs. "Of course I got a picture. Steaks on you, Chicken Little. You still around tonight?"

I hesitate. Aaron is Shelby's twin brother, the one who

moved to New Hampshire before I could ever meet him in high school. Now he's a boat mechanic at a marina on the Intracoastal and probably the best thing to ever happen to me, dating-wise. Still, this day's not even half over and all I want is to sit, very quietly, in a room all by myself. "How's tomorrow?" I ask, hedging.

"Tomorrow works," he says good-naturedly. "Take a drive downtown in the meantime, see if you can't catch her yourself. We'll go Dutch."

"How generous," I tease—they're my rules, after all. "Listen, I'm working brunch, so I've gotta go, but—"

"Yeah, yeah. No worries," he says, and then, hesitating: "You okay, though? You sound . . . I don't know. Something."

The thing about Aaron is that I could probably tell him, no problem. He's a reasonable human, more easygoing than I've ever hoped to be in all my time on this earth. Odds are he wouldn't be weird about Sawyer turning up out of nowhere. Odds are he'd be totally cool.

Still, though. Still.

"Tired," I answer, which technically isn't lying. "I'll see you tomorrow night."

"Where the hell have you been?" is the first thing Shelby says when I get into work ten minutes later, before *Hi* or *How are you?* or anything else remotely civil. She's home for the summer from college in Massachusetts, where she's learning to be a doctor and also to talk like the characters in *Good Will Hunting*. Shelby flew back to Broward in the middle of her freshman year to help me deliver Hannah, memorizing all the bones in the human body between my contractions and charming the nurses into helping her with her homework. She was eighteen years old, and she was my labor coach. Not everybody has a friend like that.

"I had to put the baby down," I tell her, glancing around the empty restaurant. We don't start seating until noon on Sundays, and it's only a quarter of.

Shelby makes a face. "Uh-huh." She looks at me pointedly as the phone on the podium rings, like she knows exactly what—exactly *who*—I'm searching for, and doesn't know why I'm wasting her time trying to be slick about it. "Good morning. Antonia's," she says, all syrup, but she's staring at me like my hair is on fire as she scribbles in the reservation book, and I stand there and wait for what's next.

"First of all," she tells me once she hangs up, sex-kitten purr gone and replaced by her hybrid half-accent—Shelby's lived all over the country, and you can hear it in her voice. "Super-Sperm Sawyer is in the kitchen with Finch at this very moment. So probably you should start there."

"*Shh*," I hiss, eyes darting toward the back of the house. I open my mouth to explain, although in the end all I can come up with is "He was at church, too."

"Yeah," Shelby says all attitude. "I bet."

I stare at her. "What does that even *mean*?"

Shelby shrugs. "I don't know. I don't like his hair. It

makes him look like a cancer patient." Shelby has never been one to reserve judgment. "Why didn't you *call* me?"

"I didn't know it was going to hit local news outlets so fast," I say, sinking into an empty chair. I've had a headache for the last twenty-four hours and think longingly of the ibuprofen in my purse, though at this particular moment even finding a glass of water feels like an Olympic endeavor.

"Oh, don't even joke." She stops, looks at me. "Did you tell my brother?"

I roll my eyes. "There's nothing to tell."

"Bull*shit.* Reena," she begins, voice going soft and urgent. If she's nice to me I'm going to burst into tears. I start to shake my head but here he comes though the swinging doors from the kitchen, and even after all this time the room seems to orbit around him, like he's got a perpetual spotlight on him everywhere he goes. I think, suddenly: *Risen from the dead.*

"Ladies," Sawyer says gallantly. He's got another Slurpee in his hand, enormous, pink and bright through the clear plastic cup.

"Ladies?" Shelby snarls. Shelby has never been afraid of Sawyer. Shelby has never been afraid of much of anything, so far as I can tell. "Seriously? Two years later and the best you can do is *ladies*?"

"I was going for casual," he tells her, wrinkling his nose and smiling, half bashful. His mouth is faintly red with the dye. "Did I overplay? I overplayed."

"A little bit." Shelby rolls her eyes. "I'm going to need a drink."

"Really?" Cade looks up from across the dining room and frowns, but doesn't actually make any move to stop her. Cade's always been a little gobsmacked by Shelby. "We're not even open yet."

"Bloody Marys!" she says cheerily, heading for the bar. "I'll make you one, too, Kincade." She flips up the partition, nudges my brother out of her way. "What about you, Sawyer? Can I offer you a strong alcoholic beverage to help take the edge off being yourself?"

Sawyer and I snort at the same time; he looks over at me, smirking, and holds up his Slurpee like a toast in my direction. "I'm good," he says, eyes on my face.

"Really." Shelby's eyebrows hitch as she reaches for the tomato juice. "What are you, off the sauce?"

"As it were."

"A bartender who doesn't drink anymore? How romantic."

"Yeah, well." Sawyer nods and slides onto a barstool. "I'm a romantic kind of guy."

Oh, *come on*. Cade looks like he's about to projectile vomit all over the restaurant and, frankly, I don't blame him. I'm feeling a little queasy myself. I get up and head back to the office to punch my time card, then set about completing as many menial tasks as I can find: folding napkins and stacking glassware, refilling ketchup bottles, which grosses me out to no end. I keep my hands busy. I work. We're slammed for brunch every Sunday, the wait skyrocketing to an hour or more, and once Shelby opens the doors it's bread and smiles until midafternoon. When I finally have a minute to glance over at the bar, Sawyer's disappeared into the teeming crush of bodies, like maybe he was never there at all.

10

Before

"Who with?" was the first thing my father wanted to know when I told him I was going out for a bit after work—a fair enough question, seeing as how I'd spent the last eight months hanging out with no one so much as the pizza delivery guy from Papa Gino's. He'd been chatting with the drummer in the band and he smelled like coffee and cologne, familiar; it was a smell I thought I'd miss when I left home.

"Allie," I blurted, not knowing I was going to lie until I did it. "With Allie."

I don't know why I didn't tell him. There was no reason to think he'd say I couldn't go: Sawyer was his godson, after all, heir to his musical talent in practice if not by blood.

Still, he'd have wanted to know the *where*s and *why*s and the *what are you doing*s, and a thousand other things I could only begin to guess. For now it just seemed neater not to say.

"Allie," he said slowly, slipping one bearlike arm around my shoulders. "There's a name I haven't heard in a while."

"Um," I said. "Yeah."

My father shrugged, nodding at one of the waiters to comp a round of drinks. He trusted me. He'd never had a reason not to. "Have a good time," he said, lips against my forehead in a distracted good-bye kiss. "Home by curfew."

"Yeah," I said again. "Of course."

I found Sawyer in the back hallway, leaning against the door to the office and scrolling through his phone, vaguely bored. "Did you just lie to your dad about me?" he asked, smirking a little.

"Yes," I said.

The smirk bloomed into a grin. "Well, okay then," he told me, perversely delighted. "Long as I know where I stand. You ready?"

"Sure," I said, hoping against hope that he couldn't tell what a big deal this was for me—that just the thought of being alone with him had my stomach doing the kind of gymnastic tumble that would have made Béla Károlyi proud.

Sawyer held the back door open and I followed him across the parking lot to his ancient Jeep. He didn't talk. I had no idea where we were going, and at this point it felt a little late to ask: I opened my mouth, hesitated, shut it again. Sawyer didn't seem bothered at all.

I glanced around the Jeep as surreptitiously as I could manage, beginning a list in my head as he hit the gas. *Floor of Sawyer LeGrande's car, a complete inventory: empty Snapple bottle, peach iced tea, check.* Duke Ellington Live at Newport 1956, *check. Dashboard: sunglasses, check. Tree-shaped air freshener still in the package, check. Mix CD with Allie Ballard's handwriting on the label, check.*

I closed my eyes for a second. Allie used to make me mixes all the time, songs for my birthday and Christmas and springtime and Tuesdays. My favorite was called "The Bad Behavior Mix": sixty minutes of ridiculous hip-hop capped with Phil Collins's "A Groovy Kind of Love," presented to me on the occasion of our first high school dance. We ended up back at my house by nine thirty that night, making brownies with Soledad and shouting along with Kanye, doubled over in hysterical giggles.

I didn't mean to sigh, never even heard myself do it, but I must have, because Sawyer glanced over at me as he turned onto A1A, sharp features lit reddish by the neon lights on the dash. "Long day?" he asked.

"Yeah," I said, letting him think that it was the monotony of service work getting me down and not the absolute hopelessness of being in this Jeep with him, his eyes glittering a hundred thousand adjectives beyond green. "Kind of."

Sawyer nodded. "You want ice cream?"

I blinked. "Ice cream?" I repeated. I don't know what I'd been expecting, but it . . . wasn't that.

"Yeah, princess, ice cream." Sawyer laughed as he pulled into a parking spot, not bothering to wait for my answer. "What did you think I was gonna offer you, like, some glue to sniff?"

"No!" I said, although to be honest, he was probably closer to the truth than not. I unbuckled my seat belt and climbed out of the car. "No."

"You think I'm so sketchy." He bumped my shoulder with his as we crossed the parking lot, so lightly I thought it was probably an accident. "Like, way tougher than I actually am."

I shook my head and looked away. "I really don't," I promised.

"Okay," he said, in a voice like he thought I was full of shit but didn't particularly mind. "Whatever you say."

We ordered at the counter and I dug in my purse for my wallet, pulling out a set of house keys and my *Lonely Planet* to get to the bottom of the bag. Sawyer pushed my hand away. "I got it," he told me, handing over a wrinkled ten to the cashier. He nodded at my book. "Planning a trip?"

"Yeah," I said. "I mean, no." It suddenly felt enormously stupid, this game I played with myself, like hopscotch or Barbie. "It's for my admissions essay."

"To college?" Sawyer raised his eyebrows, licked the dripping bottom of my cone before handing it over. It was an old-fashioned shop, wood paneling and knickknacks on the walls, an antique cash register that sprung open with a loud ring. I smelled sugar and cold air. "Already?"

I nodded. "Northwestern," I told him. "I'm graduating a year early, so I'm going to apply in the fall."

Sawyer tilted his head to one side. "That's ambitious."

"I'm ambitious."

"I know," he said, taking his own ice cream and herding me back toward the door, holding it open with one foot as I scooted through. "So that's what your essay's about, then?" he asked as we crossed the lot toward the car, navigating a teeming crowd of noisy, restless kids about our age, shouts and laughter. "Traveling?"

"Yeah, kind of." I shook my head, embarrassed. "It's stupid."

"I doubt that." We were back at his Jeep by this point. Sawyer climbed up on the hood to eat his cone, angled his head at the empty space beside him until I got the message and pulled my sneakers up onto the bumper along with him. "Tell me."

"Ugh, fine." I rolled my eyes a little, blushing in the dark. "The program I'm applying to is for creative nonfiction, you know? Travel writing." The words sounded wooden and unfamiliar; this wasn't something I'd told a lot of people besides Allie. "So I'm writing the essay like a travel guide, basically—go here, do this, avoid this gross hotel—only instead of it being about a particular place, it's actually about, like—my life." I shrugged again, embarrassed. "Or like, the life I want to have."

"That's not stupid." Sawyer was grinning. "That's cool. I want to read it when you're done."

I snorted. "Yeah, right."

"I'm serious," Sawyer said, considering. His white T-shirt seemed to glow in the light from the storefronts. "Early graduation, huh?" he asked after a moment. "You're that desperate to get out of here?"

"No," I explained, "it's not that. I mean, of course I'll miss my family and everybody. I love my family, I just . . ." I shrugged. I didn't know how you could explain something like loneliness to someone like Sawyer—the feeling that I had to find something to wrap my hands around, and that whatever it was, it wasn't here. "There's not a whole lot for me here, you know?"

Sawyer smiled a bit, unreadable. "So I better hang out with you while I can, is that what you're saying?"

Which—what? What was going *on* here? I had no earthly idea what he was after. "Pretty much," was all I said.

We sat in silence for a little while, watching the cars go by on the highway. I ate my ice cream. I waited. "You're quiet," he said eventually.

I considered that for a moment. "Well," I said, "so are you."

"Reena." We were close enough that our arms were touching, warm and the slightest bit sticky with heat. "Why are you here?"

I looked at him sideways. My heart was a foot on a kick drum inside my chest. "You tell me."

Sawyer shook his head. "I'm serious."

"Are you?"

"Yeah," he said. "I really am."

"Sawyer." I hesitated, blushing. I was ninety percent sure I was completely misunderstanding whatever was happening here. "Look. Allie's my friend. Or *was* my friend, at least, and—"

"Don't you get tired?" he interrupted.

I stopped. "Of what?"

Sawyer shrugged. "Being who everybody thinks you are."

"What? No." I shook my head, stalling, and glanced out across the highway at the strip malls and the palm trees. I smelled wet pavement and car exhaust. "Who else would I possibly be?"

Sawyer seemed to know I was faking; he looked at me for a second in a way that made me almost nervous, like he could see the tissue underneath my skin. Fighting the creeping feeling that I was in way, *way* over my head, I did what any rational human being would do when confronted with a question she didn't want to answer, by a person she'd had a miserable crush on for two presidential terms:

I nudged my cone right up into his face.

"I'm sorry," I said immediately, giggling a little hysterically. "Jesus Christ. I'm sorry. I can't believe I just did that."

Sawyer stared at me for a second, ice cream smudged over his mouth and his nose. "I . . . kind of can't believe you did, either," he said, but he was laughing. When he put his free hand on the back of my skull and kissed me, I tasted chocolate and rainbow sprinkles. I didn't even close my eyes.

He pulled back a little bit. "Is it okay that I just did that?" he asked, after a second or two.

I nodded dumbly.

"Did you like it as much as I did?"

I nodded again.

"Are you ever going to talk to me again in your whole life?"

I nodded. "I mean," I said, recovering slightly, thoughts skittering like moths at the panicky edges of my brain. "Yes."

Sawyer grinned. "Okay," he said. He tossed the rest of his ice cream into a nearby trash can and cupped both of his hands around my face. "Good."

He was still kissing me when his cell phone rang inside his jeans a minute later, and I made to pull away but his grip tightened, a gentle fist in my hair. "Ignore it. Ignore it," he muttered, and I did for a minute, but then mine started ringing, too.

"Sawyer," I said, reaching for my purse even as the rest of me was still otherwise engaged. "Sawyer, it's my house. I have to pick it up. Hello?" I said, while—oh God, oh *hell*, we were in the middle of a parking lot and my *dad* was on the phone—Sawyer moved his mouth down to my neck. "Hi. What's up?"

"Reena," my father said, and there was a sound in his voice I'd never heard before, panic and anger. "Oh, thank God. Where in the hell are you?"

I jumped off the hood of that Jeep so fast that I just about took Sawyer's head off, squeezing my eyes shut as I tried to figure out what to say: I'd lied to my father for the first time in my *entire life* and I was caught. How was that even possible?

I was still trying to come up with an answer when he pushed on: "Are you with Allie?" he demanded.

I curled my free hand into a fist, felt my nails dig into my palm. Sawyer was watching me carefully. I fumbled around for something plausible, finally had to settle for the truth. "No," I admitted. "No, I'm not."

"Thank God," he said again, then, to whomever was in the room with him, Soledad or Cade: "She's okay. I've got her."

"What?" I said sharply. Suddenly I was very, very afraid. "What's going on?"

"Reena," he said, and I knew I'd never forget this as long as I lived, the neon lights of the ice cream place in the near distance, the curious expression on Sawyer LeGrande's pretty face, and the tiny shards of glass embedded in the asphalt, like something fragile and bright had only just exploded there. "I have to tell you something bad."

11

After

I don't see Sawyer for the rest of my Sunday brunch shift, although he might as well be breathing down my neck the whole time the way everybody's talking about him—like he's some visiting movie star and not a degenerate who up and abandoned everybody who ever gave half a damn. The regulars are delighted to see him. The waitresses can't get over his hair. He's been traveling this whole time, Finch tells me in the kitchen, rambling around the country like a tumbleweed or Jack Kerouac, with no particular destination in mind.

"*Traveling,*" I repeat slowly, the colossal unfairness of it hitting me with a force so physical I actually grab the edge of the prep table until I steady out. I feel like my insides have been excavated, like I'm some screwed-up ghost version of myself. "How nice for him."

By five fifteen, all I want to do is go home and curl into a ball under the covers, but right after I punch my card I turn around and he's there in the doorway of the office, rubbing at the stubble on his cheek.

"Jesus Christ," I say, louder than I mean to. "You scared the shit out of me."

"Sorry," Sawyer says, in a voice like he's actually not. He slouches casually against the jamb. For the first time since he turned up, I let myself stare at him for longer than a second, more than a quick, hungry glance out of the corner of my eye: He's broader than he was when he left here. The hair on his arms is bleached pale from the sun. Sawyer is patient; he stands there and he lets me look.

"What?" I snap, when I'm finished.

His lips twitch. "Nothing," he says.

I pick up my purse and dig through it for my car keys, pushing *The Very Hungry Caterpillar* out of the way for the second time today. "Have you been here all afternoon?" I ask, eyes on the jumbled contents of my bag so I don't have to look at him.

"No." As soon as he says it I look up at him anyway. Sawyer shakes his head. "I looked at the schedule."

"Why?"

"To catch you when you were leaving."

"Well," I say as nastily as I can manage, finally putting

my hands on my keys, "mission accomplished. Here I go."

Sawyer doesn't move from the doorway. "Looked pretty busy today," he says. "Have to get used to it again, I guess."

My eyes narrow. "Why's that?" I demand. We have another bartender now, a fiftyish guy named Joe who's always sending me home with lollipops for Hannah, even though she's too young to eat them. "You're not *picking up shifts*, are you?"

"Are you going to kill me if I say yes?"

"Possibly," I tell him, and he smiles like I'm trying to be funny. I'm not trying to be funny. I think I might burst into tears. "Can you stop?" I ask, voice brittle. For a while Hannah was doing this thing when she got upset where she clamped her hands over her ears and screamed. "I mean it. I'm not—just—*stop*."

Sawyer quits smiling, makes a move to come toward me. I hold out my hands to keep him away.

"Reena," he starts.

"Seriously," I tell him. "You can't just come here after all this time and try to joke around with me and act like nothing happened. That's not— Stuff *happened*, Sawyer. You can't just be *back*."

Sawyer shrugs once, just barely. He looks so much older than he did. "I am back, though," he tells me softly. "You gotta . . . I am."

The hideous thing is this: I want to forgive him. Even after everything, I do. A baby before my seventeenth birthday and a future as lonely as the surface of the moon and still just the sight of him feels like a homecoming, like a song I used to know but somehow forgot.

And God in his golden heaven, how completely messed up is *that*?

"Stay away from me," I mutter, and shove past him out of the room.

"How was work?" Soledad wants to know when I get back to the house a while later. She's sitting cross-legged on the sofa, wearing her reading glasses and working intently on the crossword in the paper. Soledad learned English when she was twenty-two and still she does the *New York Times* crossword puzzle in pen, and that's only one of the reasons why I love her.

"Sucked, thanks. Hey, pretty lady," I say, scooping Hannah up from where she's playing on the floor and planting noisy raspberries on her tummy until she's giggling like gangbusters, squirming happily in my arms. "How was your day, huh? You have fun today?"

"She was a dream," Soledad reports, same thing she says every time she watches Hannah. They spend a lot of time together, and I like the idea of her as a second mom to Hannah, just like she was to me. Soledad lived with our family for nearly a decade before my father asked her to marry him, another piece of this family clicking quietly into place. *It is not good for man to be alone.*

"Where is he?" I ask her now, toeing off my sneakers and hefting Hannah onto my hip. My dad has been avoiding me since our run-in at the tomato plants, studiously absent whenever I'm around. The baby chatters happily into my ear.

"In the yard again. Reena . . ." Soledad looks sorry. Sometimes her voice reminds me of water over a fire, the steam rushing up like that. "You might want to give him some time."

"Oh." I nod. I'm not entirely sure what she's worried about, his temper or his heart. Both, most likely: When I used the computer this morning I saw her recent Google search for the effects of stress on cardiac conditions. "Okay. You know, I was thinking of taking the baby for a ride."

"We're supposed to meet Roger and Lyd in a little bit anyway," Soledad tells me. "Gonna check out that new place on Las Olas." She looks like she wants to say something else, and for a moment I almost ask her how it's possible that my father can eat a friendly dinner with Sawyer's parents, size up the culinary competition, but can't find it in his heart to look at me. In the end, though, both of us let it lie. "Have a good time," is all she says.

"We will. Come on, you," I tell the baby, and bring her upstairs for a change before we go. "We're road trippin'."

Hannah had wicked colic when she was an infant; she didn't sleep for more than a couple of hours at a time until she was nearly six months old. Changing her feeding schedule didn't work. Laying her down on the dryer didn't work. Backrubs didn't work, and neither did long soaks in the baby tub. Soledad helped as much as she could, but in the end it was Hannah and me sitting on the floor and crying, two men trapped in a mine. I honestly had no idea what to do.

She did like driving, though, and if I wasn't too exhausted to get behind the wheel of a car, it usually wasn't too long before she'd pass out in the backseat—head lolled back, tiny fist shoved in her mouth. Still, for the first hour or so the slightest stop would wake her, so I took to driving for miles on the interstate, where there was no threat of red lights or pedestrians to slow us down. Once, I ran out of gas in Miami and had to call Cade to come get us. Another night I made it all the way to Vero before I realized it was probably time to head home.

Eventually, Hannah's bellyaches subsided and our moonlight excursions up and down 95 became less and less frequent. I haven't driven this stretch of highway in months. But tonight, as the baby drifts off to dreamland to the dependable droning of public-radio jazz, the scene out the windows is as familiar as home.

12

Before

Sawyer didn't say a word as he sped away from the ice cream shop and toward the hospital, went quiet as nighttime and just as still. A gorge had opened up inside my chest. The CD in the stereo was still spinning, old Louis Armstrong Sawyer must have gotten from my dad, and I reached forward and clicked it off. "It's bad, right?" I asked.

Sawyer shrugged once, eyes on the asphalt in front of him. "I don't know."

"It must be bad, right? If she's already in surgery and my dad wouldn't—" I broke off, the words swallowed up by guilt and confusion and this huge, endless fear. I dug my fingernails into the passenger seat, willing the car to go faster. "It must be bad."

"I said I don't *know*, Reena," he told me, and I was quiet after that.

We parked in the cavernous garage at the hospital and got lost on the way to the ER, the two of us wandering the corridors like some panicky, overgrown Hansel and Gretel. "This way," Sawyer said finally, and I followed him dumbly down a freezing, fluorescent hallway, then through a set of doors and into chaos.

There was a crowd in the waiting room, small but restless: Allie's parents and Sawyer's, Lydia with her wild hair secured in a complicated knot. Lauren Werner was there, crying noisily. And there were my father and Soledad, watchful and waiting, somehow already gutted like carcasses or husks. Soledad looked heartbroken. My father looked old.

They got to their feet as I ran across the wide expanse of linoleum, and I saw my father's eyes narrow in confusion: On the phone we had never actually established where I was or who I was with, and now here was Sawyer close behind me, throwing off fear and heat.

Allie's boyfriend, I thought, for the hundredth time in the last fifteen minutes. *I was with Allie's boyfriend.*

He didn't have time to ask, though, because Allie's mom had spotted me and was rushing forward, grabbing me so tightly it was painful. I felt my ribs scrape together inside my chest. "She's dead," Mrs. Ballard wailed. It was a sound I'd never heard before and, if it pleases God, a sound I would like never to hear again. "Reena, baby. Our girl is gone."

I thought, very clearly: *This isn't happening.*

I thought, very clearly: *This is our fault.*

I stood there with Allie's mom for a while, let her sob into the limp fabric of my shirt. I didn't cry. I didn't do much of anything, to be honest; I felt frozen, bizarrely quiet, like something had been hermetically sealed inside me. I heard the whine of an ambulance in the distance, the whoosh of a door whispering shut. Finally Mr. Ballard pried her gently out of my arms.

"We didn't make up yet," I told him.

"Reena." That was Soledad, coming closer, but I stepped away, out of her reach.

"I'm serious," I said, and my voice was louder this time. I was having a hard time getting what was going on. "We weren't—we were . . ."

I trailed off as Soledad wrapped her arms around me, stood there loose-limbed and bewildered while she whispered Spanish prayers into my ear. "I'm not *kidding*," I told her, voice cracking. I felt my ribs start to collapse. I looked up one last time before I stopped remembering anything, just in time to see the sharp, jagged pleat of Sawyer's backbone as I watched him slip out the sliding doors.

13

After

Aaron and I have a date planned for Friday night, so I meet him down at the marina at the end of his shift. I stroll along the wide, weathered dock and find him chatting with Lorraine, a big-haired retiree from New Jersey whose taste in clothing definitely skews toward the noisy: At the moment, she's wearing cheetah-print leggings. She and her husband, Hank, have been docking their boat, the *Hanky Panky*, at the marina for fifteen years, but every time I see her she makes a big show of telling me how Aaron's her favorite mechanic.

"Ree-na," she calls cheerfully when she sees me, waving her straw hat in greeting. Lorraine treats everybody like a long-lost friend. "I was at your place the other night! The short ribs were di-vine. I told Hank he was going to have to roll me home."

We chat for a bit about the restaurant, how crowded the Intracoastal's been. Eventually Hank turns up, ruddy and heavyset, and they send us "young people" on our way. Aaron slides his hand into the back pocket of my jeans as we head for the car. "I've got a pair of pants just like hers," he tells me quietly, and I throw my head back and laugh.

Aaron is appalled that I've lived fifteen minutes from the ocean my entire life and have somehow never eaten a lobster roll, so he takes me to this divey place on a pier in Lauderdale, picnic benches and beer in plastic cups. Souvenir shops glow white and neon along the beachfront. Tourists wander by in various stages of sunburned undress.

"This is a Maine thing, though!" I protest, pulling a handful of napkins from the dispenser on the table. "Aren't lobster rolls a Maine thing?"

Aaron shrugs. "Maine, schmaine," he says, then laughs. "I mean, yes. These are probably Yankee lobsters, which means they hauled their slow crustacean selves all the way down here so that you could have this experience, so *probably* you should quit complaining."

"I'm not complaining," I tell him, and smile. There's a pile of onion rings on a plate between us. The last of the sunset catches the gold in his hair. "Actually, I'm happy as a clam."

Aaron groans. "Was that a seafood pun?" he asks, and I cackle dorkily. "Really? *Really?*"

After Aaron finished high school in New Hampshire, he worked on fishing boats in Gloucester, Massachusetts, for a couple of years before he moved to Florida at the beginning of the summer. He picked up Shelby from work every night for two weeks before I realized he wasn't doing it to make Shelby's life easier.

"You realize I'm not fun," I told him, the first time he asked me out. "I have a kid. I'm not fun. Even before I had a kid, I wasn't fun."

"You're totally boring," he agreed, nodding seriously. We were standing on the sidewalk outside Antonia's after eleven, the smell of heat and car exhaust and the ocean somewhere underneath. "Definitely." Then he laughed, and it felt like something warm and liquid cracking open inside my chest. "How's this weekend?" he asked, and that was that.

Tonight we finish our sandwiches and wander down the beach for a while in the dark. The sand is gritty and familiar beneath my feet. I chat to him for a while about the classes I'm taking, lit and art history and accounting at the community college in Broward, a last-ditch attempt to keep my brain from turning to soup inside my head.

"We still on for Saturday?" he asks, when we're back at my car. We kiss up against the side of it for a while, the faint zing of peppermint gum behind his teeth, but Cade and Stefanie have the baby, and I promised I'd pick her up by ten.

"Absolutely," I say with a grin, though in truth I totally forgot until right now. There's a barbecue at his mom's house, a family thing with Shelby and everybody that he told me about last week. At some point I'm going to have to make a salad. "Pick us up around one?"

"Will do." Aaron kisses me good-bye and knocks twice on the roof before I go, *Get home safe*. The lights look like a carnival in the rearview.

Hannah fights me on her nap the next morning, and we're already running a little behind by the time I get her changed and make it down to the kitchen to finish packing the diaper bag. I bump the swinging door open with one hip and find Sawyer standing there, dressed in his work clothes, looking at the baby pictures on the fridge. I freeze. "Wha—?"

"I didn't know you were here," he says immediately, trying to head me off at the pass before I can lay into him. "My dad just needed to drop some paperwork off for your dad. Your car wasn't— I didn't know you were here."

"It was making a noise," I say. I stop in the doorway and watch him for a second, remembering: I used to find him like this all the time when we were together, just hanging out in my house as if he lived here, or wanted to. I swallow, hold the baby a little tighter. "Cade took it in this morning."

Sawyer nods. "You said stay away from you."

"I did." I bounce Hannah on my hip and rummage around in the fridge for the lidded cups of juice I put there last night, her pudgy hands rooting through my hair. It feels claustrophobic in here, like the walls are closing in. Our kitchen is small and outdated, a dark, awkward afterthought of a space. "I was being dramatic."

Sawyer shrugs. "You're allowed."

"I wasn't asking for permission." The baby moves from my hair to my earring, yanking a little, and I do my best to disentangle her without dropping an armful of Tupperware. "Hannah, baby," I mutter, nudging her away as gently as I can. "Love of my earthly life."

Sawyer takes a tentative step closer. "Need a hand?"

"Nope." I don't even think about it, it just comes right out, like the mean thing to say is always on the tip of my tongue. Then I sigh. "You want to hold her?" I ask.

He looks genuinely surprised, which makes me feel kind of shitty. "Yeah," he says, right away. "Yeah, if that's okay."

So I take a deep breath and hand over my baby girl—watching the placement of his hands, her head, even though she's way too old for me to have to worry about that, and anyway he's absurdly careful, like he's holding a bomb. He looks totally, nakedly terrified. I almost laugh.

Hannah whimpers for a moment like she's going to start to fuss, and he dances around a little to stave off her cries. "Hey there, Hannah," he says, once she relaxes. "Hey, pretty girl."

Hannah smiles like the fog burning off in the morning. I glance sharply away. This close together they look so, *so* alike, olive skin and their sharp, intelligent faces. It makes my heart swoop sort of unpleasantly, a pinball machine on *tilt*. "Hi!" she says cheerfully.

Sawyer stares a moment. "She talks?" he asks, clearly surprised.

"I mean, she's a human person," I say snottily, then: "Sorry." I give him some room, fingertips curling around the back of a kitchen chair. "That was—sorry."

"It's okay." Sawyer shrugs, looks for a minute at the apple curve of Hannah's cheek. "You get that I didn't know, right?" he says quietly.

I flinch and clear my throat, glancing carefully away. "Know what?" I ask, all ignorance, as vanilla-bland as humanly possible.

"Please don't." Sawyer's green eyes darken; there's a set to his moody jaw. "Look," he says. "You get to hate me. That's . . . whatever. That's okay. But don't jerk me around about this, Reena. If she's not mine—"

"Are you *kidding* me?" I gape at him, because seriously, the *balls*. "Of course she is!" In some kind of bizarre reflexive counter-illustration of my point, I snatch the baby out of his arms. Hannah startles. "Jesus Christ, Sawyer—"

"Well, then just say that!" Sawyer shakes his head. "Reena, I didn't call anybody. Nobody knew how to find me. You know that. I didn't know you were—if I'd have *known*, then—"

"Then what, exactly?" I snap. "You'd have stepped up? Or you'd have offered to pay for me to—"

"Don't," he interrupts, looking not at me but at the baby. "Come on. That sucks. That's shitty."

"Am I *wrong*?"

"Yes!" he explodes, and then hesitates, rubbing hard at the back of his neck. "I don't know."

"Yeah," I tell him. I shove a container of Goldfish and some grapes into the baby bag, packing up one-handed. "That's what I thought."

Sawyer shakes his head again, frustrated, like I'm being deliberately obtuse. "I have no idea what I would have done, Reena. You know what I was like. I was screwed up. That's why I left to begin with." He sighs loudly, scrubs a hand over his bristly head. "But I'm here now."

I hitch Hannah up on my hip. "Evidently."

"I'm not going anywhere," Sawyer tells me, ignoring the acidic coat of sarcasm on my words. He moves deftly out of my way as I bounce around the kitchen, like he can anticipate where I'm going to go next. "I want to be here. I want to do whatever I can do to be a part of this."

I open my mouth to say something snotty, then close it again. Suddenly I am so, so tired. I am tired like I've had two years of no sleep at all. "Okay," I tell him. "Fine."

Sawyer's eyes widen, like he was expecting me to tell him to go screw off. I guess I can't exactly blame him. "Okay?"

I shrug. "That's what I said."

We stand there for a minute, a cautious détente. I wait. The baby rests her heavy head on my shoulder like she's bored of us, settling in.

"What about the park?" Sawyer asks, after a measure or two.

I blink at him. "The park?"

"Public place," Sawyer explains, picking Hannah's baby sunglasses up off the counter and handing them to me. "Middle of the day."

I roll my eyes, but I take the glasses. "Oh, stop it," I say.

"Made you smile."

"Congratulations," I tell him, snorting a bit. I perch the sunglasses on top of Hannah's head, careful. She only likes to wear them about half the time.

Sawyer is grinning. "How's tomorrow?"

I sigh. "Tomorrow is fine."

"Reena, sweetheart—" Soledad pokes her head through the swinging door into the kitchen and stops cold when she sees us. Her dark eyebrows twitch.

"Ma'am," Sawyer says. If he was wearing a hat he would tip it, I'm sure.

"Hi, Sawyer." To me, pointedly: "Aaron is here."

"Yup." I heft the baby bag onto my shoulder, brush Hannah's dark cap of baby hair out of her face. "I'll be out in a sec."

"So," Sawyer says, once she's gone, and of course now he's going to push his luck. "Aaron."

I roll my eyes. "I have a boyfriend, Sawyer, Jesus. I know that's difficult to believe, but—"

"It's not difficult."

"Well." I don't know what to say to that, exactly. My heart is tapping away against my ribs. "Okay. I'll see you."

"Absolutely," he says, but he follows me out of the kitchen like a shadow and I know he knows exactly what he's doing. Aaron is standing in the living room, half watching the TV Soledad left on, shorts and flip-flops and an easy, unhurried grin.

"Hi," I say.

"Hi," says Aaron.

"Hi," says Sawyer.

We stand there, the three of us. We look at one another. Soledad's got an expression on her face like she thinks I've lost my mind. "Aaron," she says, when it's clear I have no intention of making any kind of introduction. "This is Sawyer. Sawyer, Aaron."

"Good to meet you," says Aaron.

"Likewise," says Sawyer.

"Well!" I say brightly. In a second I'm going to burst out laughing, but only to avoid some other, less desirable reaction. "We've gotta go."

Sawyer nods slowly. He gazes at Aaron and then at me. "I'll see you tomorrow," he says, the faintest hint of a smirk at the edges of his mouth.

Smug bastard. "Yup," I say. "Bye." I kiss Soledad and

grab Aaron by the wrist, screen door smacking soundly shut behind us. I pretty much run to the car.

"So," Aaron says, when we're buckled. "That was him."

I have never, in all the time we've known each other, said a single word to Aaron about Sawyer. "Yeah," I tell him after a moment. "That was him."

Aaron turns the key in the ignition. "I thought he'd be taller," is all he says.

14

Before

I got stung by a wasp the morning of Allie's funeral service. It was three wet, humid days after she wrapped her cute little car around a tree three blocks outside her parents' development, thus leaving this world for the next in a spectacular act of theatrical *stupidity* so distinctly Allie that in some crazy, perverse way it made me miss her even more than I already did.

She'd been drunk, was the news that spread through school the week it happened, her blood alcohol level a tenth of a point over the legal limit for an adult in the state of Florida, never mind that Allie was sixteen years old. Grief counselors set up shop in the office. We sat through a mandatory assembly about the dangers of drunk driving;

kids pinned purple ribbons to the straps of their backpacks. Apparently Lauren Werner got questioned by the cops.

It was Wednesday, and raining. I kept waiting to cry.

A flaming red welt the size of a walnut on the back of my knee seemed as good a reason as any to give up on this particular day, and I camped out in bed from the time we got home from church until Soledad knocked on my door just before the dinner rush. "Enough, girlfriend," she said, hitting the switch and filling the room with tepid yellow light. "You gotta get up."

"I'm sleeping," I muttered into the pillow, even though I wasn't. I'd spent the afternoon hidden under the quilt and wide awake, tracing the wobbly line of a crack in the plaster ceiling and waiting for her footsteps on the stairs. My knee itched and smarted. I'd scratched until it bled.

"Cade says you're on the schedule for tonight."

"Cade's a filthy liar."

I heard my father pause in the doorway, the slow cadence of his heavy tread. The AC swished and muttered, asthmatic. "Leave her be, Sol. I can call somebody to fill in."

"Leo—" she began, ready to fight him. I think I was freaking her out.

"Don't worry about it," I said, throwing off the quilt. "I'll get up."

"Are you sure?" My father was unconvinced. I wondered if he was thinking about my mother, about funeral flowers and headstones and lives cut short too soon. I wondered what would have happened if I asked him. We hardly ever talked about my mom.

"Sure," I lied instead, heaving my heavy self up off the mattress. "I'll meet you at the car in ten minutes."

"He's worried about you," Soledad said when he was gone, opening my closet and reaching for my black work pants. Her long, dark hair hung loosely down her back.

I swung my feet over the side of the bed and shrugged. "You're not?"

"I'm waiting for you to *talk* to me, Reena. But if you don't want to do that—"

"I have to get dressed," I interrupted, "if you want me to go to work."

"Watch your tone, please." Soledad tossed the pants in my direction, plus a white blouse that had, frankly, seen better days. She'd asked me three times what had happened the night of the accident, where I'd been and why I'd lied and what I was doing with Sawyer to begin with. She thought I was holding out on purpose, a surly teenager thing, or that maybe I'd been at the party myself and knew something I wasn't saying. I couldn't tell her that the truth was a million times worse. "But fine, have it your way. You might want to put a little blush on before you go."

I frowned. "Thanks a lot."

"It's after five, sweetheart. I'm trying to move things along. Put something on that leg, too, or you'll be at it all night."

The restaurant was packed, the soupy heat of summer in Florida overcoming the industrial air-conditioning, sweat pooling in the creases of my elbows. Sawyer was missing from behind the overflowing bar. "Hiya, chickie," his dad greeted me instead, pulling pint glasses from the dishwasher and arranging them in towering stacks beside the taps. Roger was tall and solid, quick smile and a temper to match. He flipped up the hatch and came toward me, slung a familiar arm around my shoulders. "You hangin' in?"

I nodded, extricated myself as politely as I could manage. I really didn't feel like being touched. "I'm okay," I told him, the lie like a getaway car. All I wanted was for nobody to talk to me for the foreseeable future, to curl myself up into the smallest of balls and disappear.

The night melted by. I delivered order after order of Finch's cornmeal-fried catfish and smiled blandly at dozens of customers, losing myself in the hum and clatter of forks on plates and the steady one-two step of the band set up by the bar. I'd almost managed to wipe every stray thought from my head when I rounded a corner, slammed into one of the cocktail waitresses, and sent a full tray crashing to the tile floor.

It was only a couple of dishes, broken china the busboys could take care of in under a minute, but it was enough to completely undo me. I hurried through the breezeway toward the patio, ducking around a barback and squeezing past the line for the ladies' room. My heart was a trembling snare inside my chest. *Why did you think you could do this?* I wondered desperately, edging around one of the prep cooks idling on his break. *It's not working.*

"What's not working?" That was Cade, materializing behind me in all his football-star, Abercrombie glory and catching my arm. I hadn't even realized I'd spoken aloud and was burning under his close big-brother scrutiny. I really, really didn't want to talk.

"Too hot in here," I muttered, brushing past him. "Patio open?"

"It's raining," he warned even as he stepped back. I think he was afraid of me, too.

"It's always raining. I'll be fine."

I left him behind and pushed through the double glass doors. The sprawling back patio was sanctuary-silent, deserted owing to the rain, which, I realized now as I stood beneath it, wasn't really rain at all but the kind of sneaky mist you can't even feel until the moment you notice you're somehow soaking wet. Milkweed wound through the wrought-iron fence; white lights twinkled in the palm trees. A few deep breaths and my frantic heart had almost slowed before I realized I wasn't alone.

"Oh!" I yelped when I saw him, sitting with his head bent and his elbows on his knees on the giant glider at the far end of the yard. It was reflex, just the one skittish syllable. I stopped so fast I almost tripped.

Sawyer glanced up with the barest flicker of interest, stared like he didn't know who I was. I'd seen him that morning at the funeral and the blankness of his expression had intrigued me, made me wonder if there was anything beating and alive beneath it. Even close up, there was no way to tell.

"Sorry," I said, almost over my shoulder as I turned to run away from this place forever, or probably just for tonight. We hadn't talked since the scene at the hospital. I couldn't imagine what we'd possibly begin to say. "I didn't . . . nobody told me you were out here. Sorry."

"No," Sawyer said, not entirely friendly. "You're all right. Stay."

I stopped and looked at him. He was still wearing his clothes from that morning, gray tie hanging loose from his neck, funeral shoes shining like onyx. In church he'd kept his eyes fixed straight ahead. "I don't think— I should really—"

"I mean it." He glanced at me sideways. "Don't look so scared, Serena. I'm not going to hurt you."

God, that wasn't what I was afraid of, not by a long shot: What *scared* me was that I was a person capable of still feeling the things I felt for him after everything that had happened. What scared me was that my best friend was gone. Sawyer was the one person in the world who could maybe understand that, the one person who knew what we'd done, and for a second I almost told him everything: why Allie and I had stopped being friends to begin with, how I'd wanted him for so long I didn't even remember what it was like not to. In the end I chickened out instead. "I'm not," I lied, shaking my head like even the idea was ridiculous.

Sawyer snorted, a low animal noise. He slid over and made room. "Prove it," he said.

"I . . . Fine." Annoyed and bewildered and unprepared, I crossed the expanse of patio between us and perched carefully on the edge of the glider. He smelled faintly of soap and sweat and the air was warmer near him, like his body gave off more heat than normal. "Here I am."

"Here you are." He was holding a half-empty green bottle and he ran his thumb once around the rim, offered it to me without looking me in the face. "You working?"

"Yeah." I took it from him, wrapping my hands around the cool glass and hoping he wouldn't notice if I didn't actually drink any of it. "Well, sort of." There was a feeling in my chest like a moth against a windowpane, the desperate scrape of wings. "I just broke a bunch of plates."

Sawyer raised his eyebrows. "On purpose?" he asked.

"No."

"No," he repeated, looking at me finally, smiling a small, languid smile I'd seen a hundred times before in the decade and a half I'd lived on his periphery. "I guess not."

Sawyer sighed. I waited. We sat quiet as death and just as still and listened to the wasps as they sang their elegies high in the leaves above our heads.

15

After

Aaron and Shelby's mom lives in a kitschy little bungalow out in Poinsettia Heights, cool tile floors and spiny green succulents exploding like alien life-forms all over the raised deck that surrounds the pool. Hannah's in heaven, drifting through the cool blue water in her yellow plastic baby raft, no shortage of middle-aged women in neon-flowered bathing suits to coo over her and her star-shaped kiddie sunglasses.

Eventually her small fingers go pruney, and we climb carefully up onto the deck, water from my hair running in cold rivulets down my back. Hannah's body feels cool and slippery, like a seal's. I wrap her in a hooded towel that looks like a bug-eyed frog and take her inside to get changed, stopping in the kitchen on our way back to pull some snacks out of the bag I packed this morning. Shelby's rooting around in the fridge for a lime to go with her beer. "Was wondering where you got to," she says, holding out the bottle. She's wearing cargo shorts and flip-flops, wet hair knotted at the nape of her neck. "You want?"

I glance over the line of baby cacti on the windowsill, taking in the big, inclusive tribe in the yard. "I'm not going to drink underage in front of your entire family."

"Oh, like anybody cares. You're already here with your illegitimate child and they all love you. Speaking of: What about you, baby girl?" she says to Hannah. "Mai tai? Margarita?" She glances at me, frowns. "What?" she asks. "I'm kidding. I'm not actually going to make your kid a margarita. She's a baby. That would be bad form."

"Huh?" I blink at her, distracted, still gazing out at the crowd on the deck. "No, no. I'm sorry. I wasn't even really listening."

"Well, *thanks*," she says faux-snottily. Then, bumping my shoulder with hers: "Hey. How you doing over there?"

I shrug, trying for a bright smile and probably missing. "I'm fine," I promise. "Not really sleeping so well."

"Yeah." Shelby breaks off as two of her teenage cousins amble through the kitchen, bony elbows and legs like gazelles. "Look," she says, when we're alone again. "You can talk to me. I know it's weird now because you date my goony brother and you're hanging out with all my fat aunts and whatnot, but you talked to me before that and, you know. It doesn't mean you can't tell me stuff. You can tell me stuff."

I hand the baby her Goldfish, stalling, but it's useless to do that with Shelby. She waits me out every time. "Sawyer was at my house today," I confess finally, eating a couple of crackers myself for good measure. "We had, you know, *the talk*."

"The *I know we're really Catholic but this is where babies come from* talk?" Shelby laughs, blue eyes going wide. "No offense, Reena, but you probably should have had that one like, two years ago, you know what I'm saying?"

"Oh, you're very funny." I make a face. "The *we made a baby and here she is* talk, smartass."

"Ooh," she says, leaning back against the counter with her beer bottle, clicking the glass mouth lightly against her front teeth. "*That* talk. How'd it go?"

"Fine," I say again. "I don't know. Nothing the rest of the universe didn't know already, right? We're going to hang out tomorrow, all three of us."

"As a family?" she blurts, and I physically startle at the sound of it. Is that what we are, the three of us? That can't possibly be what we are.

"Um, yeah," I say after a moment. "I guess so."

"Well." Shelby's quiet, and I know from experience that she's working the logic of it out in her mind like some kind of medical puzzle: muscle and tendon, cartilage and bone.

"That's a good thing, isn't it? I mean, for better or for worse, Sawyer is your—"

"Don't say it," I plead, knowing what's coming. Shelby loves this particular phrase.

"—baby daddy. There's bound to be some big feelings there, or whatever, but that doesn't mean he shouldn't be in your kid's life. Right, Hannah?" she asks, taking the orange cracker the baby proffers, kissing her crumby hand. "You want your hot but degenerate father to take you to Disney World and stuff, don't you?"

I laugh, I can't help it. "Can you cut it out?" I beg.

"I'm teasing. I'm sorry, I'm not being helpful." She slips her free arm around my waist as we head back out into the sunshine and noise. "Just, you know, don't forget all the shitty stuff he did. And remember that you're happy now."

"Yeah," I tell her, still distracted, glancing at the crowd around the table. Shelby's uncles are arguing politics good-naturedly; her cousins are playing a noisy game of Marco Polo. I think again of families, hers and mine and Sawyer's, of what exactly they look like and what exactly they do.

Shelby's looking at me hard. "You *are* happy now, aren't you?" she asks.

At the grill, Aaron is burning a hot dog because that's how I like to eat them, a cloud of smoke like a dark corona around his face. "Yeah," I repeat, more certainly this time. "Yeah, of course."

16

Before

Sawyer pretty much disappeared the summer after Allie died, lying so low as to go practically subterranean, skulking around bars on the seedier side of Broward and getting into loud, rowdy fights. In June he got arrested on a drunk and disorderly charge. In July he wound up with a broken hand. In August he finally mentioned to his parents that, by the way, he had no intention whatsoever of shipping off to college like he was supposed to, which, while not exactly a revelation to anybody following along at home, had Roger and Lydia practically apoplectic and turned the restaurant into a backdrop for all kinds of huge LeGrande family drama.

"His dad flipped the hell out," Cade told me on the ride home one night, the rain a steady patter on the windshield, the wipers a rhythmic swoosh. It's a myth that boys don't like to gossip: Cade in particular couldn't keep a secret to save his life. "Said he had to move out of the house if he didn't go to school. They dropped a lot of money on his tuition deposit."

"That's what I figured." The LeGrandes were richer than us, I knew, but not rich enough that things like college deposits didn't matter. Still, I suspected Lydia would probably be more upset than anyone else: Sawyer was, after all, the one living soul she never had a critical word for. Even if she'd never admit it to anyone, I could only imagine how much his apparent commitment to complete and total self-immolation got under her skin.

It got under mine, too, obviously, but it wasn't like I was going to say that out loud.

The college thing sort of made sense to me, though. Even before everything happened, I remember thinking how odd it was that he was headed to FSU, *Go Seminoles,* just like every other senior in the state—how *pedestrian*, as if somebody like Sawyer should be headed for pastures way greener than keg parties or freshman seminars on the history of Western civilization. He should have been haunting cafés in New York or playing open mics in California, slouching around looking beautiful and waiting to get discovered.

Or, you know, traveling the world with some girl who was into that kind of thing.

Whatever.

"So," I said, affecting a carefully honed poker face and glancing at Cade out of the corner of my eye. "Where's he going to live?"

Cade shrugged. "With some friends in Dania, I think. There's a bunch of them living in some split-level off the highway. Roger was all pissed off about that, too, because apparently you can, like, smell the meth cooking all up and down the street."

"Sounds very attractive." I slipped my shoes off, put my bare feet up on the dash. "Did he say why he's not going?"

"I dunno. He's pretty screwed up, I guess." Here my brother hesitated, glancing at me sort of nervously. We didn't talk very much about Allie in my house. It felt like everyone was a little bit afraid of what I might do if they brought her up—go off like an improvised explosive, maybe, glass and shrapnel everywhere you looked. Three months in the ground and it was almost like she'd never existed in the first place, like maybe she'd only ever been my imaginary friend. "Because of everything that happened."

"Right." I swallowed the sudden thickness in my throat. "Well," I said brightly, "State is filled with screwups. He'd have fit right in."

One thing Sawyer definitely *wasn't* doing was showing up for his shifts at the restaurant, which is why I was so surprised when I came in to work the dinner shift one Friday in September and found him mixing a mojito at the bar. "Hey," he said, grabbing a rag and wiping a spill from the glossy surface, barely looking up. "Your dad said to come find him when you got in."

"Do you still *work* here?" I blurted, my backpack slipping from my shoulder. I was used to not seeing him by this point, used to the notion that we were never going to talk about anything: that I was going to spend the next twelve months in a sinkhole of guilt and confusion and sadness, and then I was going to leave. For a second I thought of that night in the parking lot, the taste of chocolate ice cream and the feeling of his fingers on my neck.

You kissed me, I thought as I looked at him. *You kissed me and then Allie died.* For a second it felt like she was sitting at the bar in front of me, sharp chin cradled in one skinny hand—both of us watching Sawyer just like we used to, back when watching Sawyer never felt like something that hurt.

Now he tilted his head, lips barely quirking. "It's nice to see you, too," he told me, snapping me back to the present. Just like that, Allie was gone.

"That's not what I meant." I blushed. "It's just . . . you know. Been a while."

"I guess so." He rattled the shaker a couple of times, poured its contents over ice and added a couple of mint leaves for garnish. Sawyer had been tending the bar at Antonia's practically since puberty; he could have mixed drinks in his sleep. "You miss me?"

"No," I said immediately. I glanced around, skittish—it was early yet, three or four people nursing drinks at the bar. *The Best of Ella Fitzgerald* pumped in through the speakers, afternoon music. "I don't know."

I picked up my bag again, ready to go find my father, but Sawyer wasn't finished. "I saw you the other day," he told me. "In your car, by the flea market."

I blinked. "What were you doing at the flea market?"

"I wasn't *at* the flea ma— I had band practice," he said, as if perusing antiques and collectibles was any more ridiculous than the rest of the James Dean/James Franco crap he'd been doing. "Our drummer lives over near there."

"How do you play piano with a broken hand?" I asked him, and Sawyer grinned wryly.

"It's not broken anymore, princess." He nodded for me to sit down on an empty stool and, once I did, slid some pretzels down in my direction. I glanced at the clock above the bar—I had a couple of minutes before I needed to punch in.

"Is that what you've been doing instead of coming to work?" I asked, cautious. "Playing with your band?"

"You mean as opposed to pursuing higher education?"

I shrugged. "As opposed to . . . whatever."

"I guess," Sawyer said. "I don't know. We play at the Prime Meridian sometimes." He raised his eyebrows like a dare. "You should come."

The Prime Meridian was a seedy little club off the highway in Dania, Bud Light and bouncers who didn't bother to card. People got stabbed at the Prime Meridian. "Why don't you ever play here?" I asked, without comment.

Sawyer snorted like that was hilarious. "My father would love that, I'm sure."

"Why?" I shot back. "Do you suck that bad?"

"Hey, now." He laughed again. "We're freaking awesome, Serena."

"Well," I said, fidgeting. "I'm sure you are."

A guy at the end of the bar ordered a scotch and soda; Sawyer stood up and reached for a bottle on the top shelf, shirt riding up his rib cage to reveal a small tattoo winding above the waistband of his jeans, a curling green infinity that I recognized from my calc book. "Did that hurt?" I asked as he scooped ice into a rocks glass.

"Did what hurt?"

I gestured vaguely. "On your back."

"Oh. Nah." Sawyer handed the guy his drink and leaned over the bar like he was going to tell me a secret. I smelled polished wood and limes. "I'm really manly."

"Right," I said, leaning in a little bit myself without meaning to. "Obviously."

He tapped the bar twice, like a rhythm, and straightened up. "What about you, princess?" he asked me, in a voice like maybe he was kidding and maybe he wasn't. "You got tattoos nobody knows about?"

I was opening my mouth to answer when my father came through the swinging doors at the far end of the restaurant. He stopped when he caught us at the bar. "Reena," he said sharply—and I think he was more surprised than anything else, but still we'd never talked about what I'd been doing with Sawyer that night at the hospital, and one look at his face said he didn't like what he saw. "You know I don't want you sitting up there when we have customers. Come on."

"Sorry," I said, scrambling down from the barstool. My skin felt tight and hot. I didn't look at Sawyer as I headed back to the office, two minutes late to punch in.

17

After

"It's not a date," I promise Soledad the next morning, when she asks for the particulars of my playground trip with Sawyer and Hannah. She's sitting at the table drinking her favorite chai latte from an old Northwestern mug she ordered a million years ago, her tawny skin smooth and makeup-free. I really, really hate that mug. "He just wants to spend a little time with Hannah, so I said he could." I tickle Hannah's feet in her high chair, and she giggles. "Kiss, please," I demand, then wait for her to plant one on me before I turn back to Sol. "I actually think it's very adult behavior on my part."

Soledad eyes me over her latte like she thinks perhaps

the lady doth protest too much. "I hear you and Hannah have a very busy social calendar," is all she says.

"Oh, you're hilarious." I scowl.

Now it's three thirty and 89 degrees out, and Sawyer and I are pushing Hannah in the baby swings on the playground outside the elementary school, asphalt warm and sticky under our feet. My car is still at the mechanic's and Sawyer picked me up at the house, just like he used to; Count Basie was on the stereo and I had to concentrate hard on looking out the window, on not breaking to smithereens right there in the front seat. I don't remember why I agreed to this. It didn't even seem like a good idea at the time.

"So what made you change your mind?" he wants to know now. He's dressed in jeans and a T-shirt, baseball cap pulled down low over his forehead, and I'm shocked to realize that he looks not like a rock star or a runaway boyfriend, but like a dad. He's got another Slurpee and he brought me one, too, Coke-flavored and freezing, sweating pleasantly in my hand.

I raise my eyebrows, make him work. "About?"

"I don't know," he says, taking over as I step away from the swing set. We've been trading back-and-forth for nearly half an hour, steady like a metronome. Hannah could swing for days, chubby baby legs kicking happily; she figured out clapping a few months ago, and every once in a while she smacks her hands together with some kind of secret baby glee. "This. Me."

I shake my head. "I haven't changed my mind about you."

Sawyer snorts. "Ouch."

"Sawyer—" I break off, huffing a little. "I'm trying, you know?"

"I know," he says.

We push in silence, patient. The sun glares. My lungs ache like they're full of dust, dry and barren. "What was the best place you visited?" I ask finally, not so much because I want to know—it's almost safer not to, I think—but because I can't imagine what else to ask him and the quiet shreds my nerves. There's a map of the United States stenciled in bright paint on the blacktop. I wonder if small things like that will ever stop making me sad about everything I missed out on. "What was your favorite?"

Sawyer glances at me once, like he's surprised, and then thinks a moment. "Nashville," he decides eventually. "You would really like Nashville."

I hum a little, noncommittal. "Would I."

"Yeah, Reena," he tells me. "I think you would."

"Out," Hannah says, quite clearly, and Sawyer grins.

"Out?" he repeats.

"Out!"

"Okay, then. Out it is." He lifts her from the swing and sets her on the ground; she toddles happily toward the sandbox, quick and unsteady. "My mom says it's been good for her," he tells me. "Hannah, I mean, having all her grandparents around, and you, and—" He smiles, a little shyly. "She says she's really smart."

Well, that gets my attention. "Your mom said that?" I ask, disbelieving—Hannah's smart all right, but if it has anything to do with the keen interest shown by her grandparents, then I'm the Cardinal of Rome. "Seriously?"

"Uh, yeah." Sawyer looks suddenly uncomfortable, like he thinks he's possibly misstepped—it's not an expression I remember from back when we were together, him so sure of himself all the time. "Why, is that not . . . ?"

It boggles me a little, though not as much as you'd think. Lydia's probably pulling out every stop she can think of to get Sawyer to stick around this time, and if that means convincing him that everybody gets along great around these parts, that we're all some kind of modern, blended family—well, then, so be it. Still, for some reason I don't have it in me to give her away, not explicitly: It feels like a lot of work for nothing, on top of which it's not entirely out of the realm of possibility that there's some small part of me hoping it will work and he'll stay.

I shrug. "No, she's definitely something," I say, not bothering to qualify which *she* I might be referring to or what that something might possibly be. I nod at Hannah, who's calling my name from the edge of the sandbox. "Here I come, babycakes!"

Sawyer looks at me like he's not totally buying what I'm selling; he doesn't push me on it, though, like maybe we've got some tacit agreement to play nice with each other on this hot, sunny afternoon. "So, hey," he says instead, as we follow Hannah on a scenic tour of the playground, sun bleaching white on the back of her neck. She squats down to grab a handful of sand and almost loses her balance, and I reach out a steadying hand. "Are you still writing?"

I laugh before I can stop it, a low angry cackle like the Wicked Witch of the West. I try not to feel bitter. It doesn't always work. "No," I tell him. "No, not really."

Sawyer frowns. "That's too bad."

"It's fine," I say, hoping he'll drop it, but:

"Why'd you stop?"

"Because." I shrug and dig some sunscreen out of my bag for the baby. It's possible this isn't even the real answer, but at the moment it's the best I can do. "You can't be a travel writer if you've never gone anywhere."

Sawyer takes some time to absorb that. With the hat, it's kind of hard to see his face. "Fair enough," he says after a minute, and he doesn't ask me any questions after that. Instead he looks at the swing set, at the baseball diamond, at Hannah. He squats down in the sand and digs in.

We get home and my father is fixing himself a snack in the kitchen, leftover chicken and rice from the other night, skinless and low-fat like Soledad always makes for him. The radio croons, the public jazz station out of Miami that he likes. "Hi," I say, putting Hannah in her chair and pushing her sweat-dampened hair off her face. I collect a few stray Cheerios from this morning, toss them into the sink.

My father nods at me, impassive. His cholesterol and blood pressure medications are lined up along the counter. In the last year or so he's put on weight.

"We were at the park," I tell him.

"So I heard." He nods again.

"With Sawyer," I continue.

"So I heard." Mother of God, he nods a third time.

Oh, come off *it*, I almost snap. Instead I take a deep breath, steadying. "All right," I say, surrendering. With the possible exception of Soledad, we're none of us emoters in my family. Still, my father can out-silence anybody, even me. "Can we just . . . address the fact that this is happening?"

"What's that?"

That makes me mad. "You know what," I say, an edge in my voice I can't totally file down. "Him being here. Any of it."

My father sighs. "Reena, I don't really see that there's anything to talk about. You know how I feel. You make your own choices. Do what you want." This morning's paper sits on the table, and he opens it to the international news. "There's food," he says, without looking up.

"Okay," I say finally, and open the refrigerator. "Just . . . okay."

Not so long ago, in my art class we read about the Renaissance and how for a long time afterward it was almost impossible for Italian artists to make anything. All that history there already, they figured. What was the point?

18

Before

"I think you're sticky," my father was telling my brother as I came out of the kitchen one windy Saturday night at the restaurant, Homecoming weekend of my third and, with any luck, final year of high school. There was a dance I could have gone to. I picked up an extra shift instead. It was after midnight and Antonia's was empty, my work shoes squeaking on the hardwood floor.

"Well, what is it? It's like, a— What's the word? It starts with a P." That was Cade, leaning against the bar in his discount-warehouse suit—he'd gotten promoted that fall, was managing days and some weekends. He and his fiancée, Stef, were saving up to buy a house.

"It's a plasma," Sawyer said. He was unloading glasses

from the dishwasher behind the bar, and he smiled at me as I approached. "Here, ask Reena. Reena will know."

"What will I know?" I set my plate full of pancakes on the bar and hopped up on a stool. My hair was falling out of its braid, I could feel it.

"Okay," said Cade, around a mouthful of bar pretzels. "Reena. If I throw a bucket of blood on you"—he paused dramatically—"are you wet?"

I blinked. "What?"

"Are you wet," my father repeated, like this was somehow a logical question. He was festive and silly tonight—he got like that sometimes, around the boys. It made him seem younger than he was.

I set my fork down. "First of all, that's disgusting. Second of all"—I turned to Sawyer—"why is that something I would know?"

"'Cause you're smart," he replied reasonably. "And smart people know stuff."

"Oh, well, in that case." I rolled my eyes, dorkily pleased. I'd taken the SATs again that morning, as a matter of fact, trying to pull my math score up even more—the next in a logical sequence of steps, I thought, toward getting the hell out of town. "Anyway, I think he's right. I think you're more sticky than you are wet."

"Ha. Good girl," my father said, vindicated. He kissed the top of my head. "I'm going to get out of here before Soledad calls the police. You want to come with me, or have Cade drive you after he closes?"

"Um." I hesitated, looking in every conceivable direction except for the one I wanted to be looking in. I should have gone home, actually—I'd joined the school paper at Ms. Bowen's behest and was writing an Around Town column about street festivals and new stores on Federal Highway. I had 250 words on a sculpture park near the beach due first thing Monday morning. "I can stick around for a while."

Sawyer noticed my plate once my father had gone and Cade, flush with his new managerial responsibilities, went back to the office to run the night's totals. "Aw, not fair," he said, his face a sad, silly caricature. "Finch made you pancakes?"

I nodded happily, digging into the fluffy stack sitting on my plate. "Finch loves me."

"And really, who can blame him?" Sawyer hooked a pair of wineglasses onto the rack above his head. Then he reached across the bar, took my fork out of my hand, and helped himself to a big bite.

"Oh, come on!" I cried, playing at irritated. "Get your own."

"Yours are better," he said, mouth full.

I huffed a little, delighted and trying not to look it. "You know, not all of us want your germs."

"Reena," he replied mildly, handing back the fork. "You already got my germs."

I froze for just one second, and then I started to laugh. It was the closest we'd come to talking about it—the only indication he'd given me that he even remembered it had happened—and hearing him say it loosened some knot I hadn't even realized was pressing on the muscles in my chest. I giggled like a maniac for a minute, absurdly relieved, crazy hyena giggles, like I hadn't laughed in a year. "Shut up," I managed, once I finally got my breath.

"There you go, Reena." Sawyer grinned, revealing two perfectly straight rows of white teeth. "You're so serious all the time, I swear. I crack you and it makes my damn night."

"Yeah, well." I took a breath, calmed down a bit. "I do what I can."

"Mm-hmm." Sawyer wandered over to the piano and made himself comfortable on the bench. Though my father put a down payment on Antonia's all those years ago in part so he'd always have a place to play his music, it only took a couple of months for him to realize that the care and keeping of a restaurant required more time and effort than he had anticipated. Now he sat at the baby grand only once or twice a month, a special occasion. The rest of the time, he booked bands.

"Any requests, ma'am?" Sawyer asked, clever hands already splayed over the keys. He started with a few quick scales, flew through the opening of a Dave Matthews song that was one of Cade's favorites, then launched into some West Coast–style jazz I knew my father must have taught him. Dave Brubeck, I recognized after a moment. Car-commercial music.

Is there anything you're not good at? I wanted to ask him, but I just smiled, reached behind me, and pulled the rubber band out of my hair. "Play whatever you want. I'll just listen."

"I wish everybody was that easy. Come sit."

I slid off the barstool and onto the piano bench. Somewhere in the back of my head I thought of the old pictures I'd seen of my parents sitting at the upright in my grandmother's house, the dark gaze of my mother, Antonia herself, fixed on my father's young face as he played.

"You should wear your hair down more," Sawyer said, glancing at me, hands moving fast through a piece I didn't know. Our thighs were touching. "It looks nice like that."

I laughed, but Sawyer just shook his head. "I'm serious," he said, still playing. His voice went low and quiet. "I noticed you, you know that? Even before last spring I did."

Before last spring you were dating my dead best friend, I thought and didn't say. Instead I hedged. "That so?"

"Yeah." Sawyer shrugged. "You're just . . . different."

"Different," I repeated. I thought of Lauren Werner, of the fact that at this very moment, everybody else in my grade was at Homecoming except for me. I got tired of being different, is the truth of it. It wore on me. "What, from Allie?"

That was the wrong thing to say. Sawyer kept his fingers on the keys, didn't miss a chord, but his whole body tensed. I thought of the strings inside the piano. "Sorry," I said, backpedaling. I hadn't even meant to bring her up, not overtly—she was just on my mind so much, still, like the six months since the car crash hadn't done anything to dull how much I missed her. You'd think losing her almost a full year before she actually died would have cushioned the blow, somehow; instead I just felt it more and more. "I shouldn't have— I just meant—"

"It's fine," Sawyer said shortly, but for the first time all night I didn't like the sound of his voice. I wondered how much he thought about her. I wondered if he thought about her at all.

"Okay, but . . ."

"I said it's okay, Reena."

We sat in awkward, testy silence for a moment until Cade emerged from the kitchen. "Taking requests?" he asked, then noticed our stony faces and looked, sort of accusingly, at Sawyer. "What's wrong?"

"Nothing," I said too loudly, keeping my expression as neutral as humanly possible and feeling certain that I'd just pulled this apart, whatever it even was, faster than I'd known it could be destroyed. "Everything's great."

19

After

I've got a midterm to take in the Modern American Novel, a class I was sort of excited about when it turned up in the Broward College course catalog last semester, which just goes to show how delusional I really am. For some reason I was picturing lively, sophisticated conversations about the great writers of the last few generations; instead the lecture is delivered by a fleshy middle-aged professor who's not so much boring as blatantly bored, who eyes us with vague pity through an owly pair of glasses and periodically administers multiple-choice quizzes I'm fairly certain he's printing off the Internet. "You are my penance for a misspent life," he announced on the first day of class, before assigning *The Things They Carried* and two books by John Updike and pretty much washing his hands of us entirely. I like to imagine that one of these days I'll be able to walk into a class at Broward without thinking of Ms. Bowen and how disappointed she'd be, but to be honest it hasn't happened yet.

This morning I park my car and head down the chilly hallway toward the classroom, past the bulletin board with flyers for intramural flag football games and two-for-one happy hour at a bar near campus. Par for the course, I don't have a hell of a lot in common with my classmates, although I feel like at this point that's absolutely more my fault than theirs. I've been to coffee a couple of times with some girls from my accounting class, but for the most part my time at BC has not been the social bonanza Shelby hoped it might be. Basically it feels a lot like high school, only without gym.

I sit down at one of the long tables and tick the appropriate boxes with my number 2 pencil, then hand in my test at the front of the room where good old Professor Orrin is reading the *Atlantic* on his phone. He nods at me distractedly before returning his attention to the screen. I hurry down the stairs into the parking lot, cross the shimmering blacktop to where my car sits waiting. There's more than fiction on my mind today.

Allie's old house has been empty for ages: Her parents moved to Tampa not long after the accident, and the new owners foreclosed inside a year. It just sits there in the swooping curve of the cul-de-sac now, gap-toothed and vaguely haunted-looking, waiting for whatever's coming next.

Allie's buried at Forest Lawn, but I've never been much for cemeteries, and anyway, whoever's beneath that headstone—*beloved angel, darling girl*—that's not the Allie I knew. And maybe the girl I fought with all those nights ago in the unforgiving glare of the patio light wasn't the Allie I knew, either, but sometimes I can still find her here in her old backyard. I come by to look every now and again, if it's summer or I'm lonely or afraid.

This afternoon, though—half a week since our date at the playground, who knows how long since my father looked me in the eye—I'm not the only one hanging around the Ballards' old development. Sawyer's rusty Jeep is parked in the driveway, unmistakable. I shake my head, disbelieving, as if there's some invisible string that kept us tethered the entire time he was away and that's tightening now, a slip-knot hooked around my wrist.

"You're trespassing, you know," I call, wandering across the scruffy expanse of dry, brown grass, Allie's dad's beloved lawn gone wild and weedy. It occurs to me, not for the first time, that things change whether you're around to notice them or not.

"I know," he says. "What are you doing here?"

"What am *I* doing here?" I sit down on the swing next to him just like we sat all those nights ago outside the party, rubber burning the backs of my thighs. "What are *you* doing here?"

Sawyer shrugs. "I was in the neighborhood. I don't

know. I feel like I never really . . ." He trails off, going quiet, one sneaker toeing the ground. "I think about her sometimes, you know?"

"Yeah," I tell him, which is an understatement. "I do."

"I thought about her a lot while I was gone." He raises his head to look at me, like a challenge. "Thought about you, too."

I ignore that last part, shaking my head a little as I gaze across the yard at the empty patio, the darkened windows filmed with grime. I grew up in this yard—Allie and I slept out here every summer, the two of us in a pup tent with a Coleman camping lantern and a radio, listening to the Top 40 countdown. In second grade I tumbled off these monkey bars and fractured both my wrists. "She'd be in college," I tell him. "If she hadn't . . . if she'd lived. We both would be, maybe."

Sawyer nods slowly. "Maybe," he agrees, eyes narrowing the slightest bit, like he's trying to figure out how much of it I blame him for. I don't know if it's more or less than he thinks.

"She was gonna go to Barnard," I continue. It feels a little bit like finding my voice to say it after all this time. "And I was going to come to New York after college, and we were going to get some fancy apartment by Central Park and dress up for regular life. She always said that, when we were younger—that we'd dress up for regular life." I gaze down at my shorts and T-shirt, a loose-fitting Red Sox ringer Shelby brought back from school for me. "As you can see, I've really taken that sentiment to heart."

Sawyer smiles. "For what it's worth," he says, dark eyebrows arcing, "I think you look arty."

He bumps at my ankle, careful. After a moment I bump at his in return.

20

Before

"So," Sawyer said out of nowhere, "did you ever finish your essay?"

"What?" I blinked at him. I was sitting at a back table, wrapping silverware into little white-cloth-napkin burritos, one leg tucked under me. It was almost Thanksgiving of junior year. Sawyer and I had edged around each other for weeks since the night on the piano bench, careful; I tracked his distant orbit from the corner of my eye. The restaurant rustled, steady, a current ferrying us through. "My essay?"

"The travel guide thing," he elaborated. A gray undershirt peeked out from beneath the collar of his button-down. "For Northwestern."

"Yeah, no, I know what you're talking about." I finished with the roll-ups, stacked the last of them into a wicker basket on the tabletop. "I just didn't think you remembered that."

"Well," he said, shrugging, "I do."

Imagine that. "It's almost done," I told him. In fact, I was halfway through my third draft of the stupid thing, sure there was something important I was leaving out. Ms. Bowen had looked at it, and so had my English teacher. Noelle, the snippy blond editor of the school paper, had read a copy and pronounced it *satisfactory*, which out of her mouth was actually a huge compliment—up to her standards, maybe. But not to mine. "Just fixing a few more things."

"That's cool. I still wanna see it." He hesitated a minute, just standing there with his hands shoved in his pockets, watching me. "You got a break right now?" he asked. "I'm supposed to pick up some CDs from Animal."

I felt my eyebrows rise. "Animal?"

"He's my drummer."

"Like in *Muppet Babies*?"

"Yeah, like in *Muppet Babies*." Sawyer grinned. "Come on, come with me. We'll stop and grab you a soda or something. Whatever the kids are drinking these days."

"Absinthe, mostly," I said, hesitating, not wanting to let on just how much I'd been hoping for an invitation like this one these past few weeks. Finally, taking a breath: "Sure, okay." I stood up, untied my apron. "Just let me tell my dad I'm going."

I poked my head into the cluttered office my father shared with Roger, papers stacked on the desktop and photos of both our families on the walls. "Can I take my break?" I asked. "It's, like, super slow."

He looked at me over the top of his computer monitor, reading glasses perched on the bridge of his nose. "Sure. Where you going?"

"Thanks," I said, then, quickly: "I'm going to run some errands with Sawyer."

"With Sawyer?" His eyebrows shot up so fast, I thought they might be in danger of springing off his head entirely.

"Yes."

"All right," he said, hesitating, a look on his face like maybe he wished there was a valid reason for him to say no. "Be careful."

"Will do."

"Did you lie this time?" Sawyer asked when I returned. He was holding my shoulder bag in one hand and his car keys in the other, leaning against the bar.

"No," I told him, sort of surprised that he remembered. "I told the truth."

This time of day there wasn't a ton of traffic near the restaurant, just crappy antiques shops and cracked pavement. The engine hummed behind my knees. Sawyer flicked the button on the stereo, and the CD in the player clicked to life: Miles Davis, I recognized after a moment. *Bitches Brew.*

"I really like the stuff he did right before this," I said, nodding at the radio as Sawyer glanced over his shoulder and merged. "*Kind of Blue* and all that. I mean, I know everybody really likes this album, it's good, but if you ever see pictures of him from around this time they're just so awful and sad. He's dressed like Tina Turner all the time."

Sawyer laughed. "Listen to you. I didn't know you were into this stuff."

I shrugged. "I wouldn't say I'm into it, exactly. But you don't live in my house for sixteen years without picking some of it up."

"I guess not," he said. "Anyway, my iPod's floating around here someplace. Put on whatever you want."

I nodded and looked around until I found it, settled on some old Solomon Burke. "Good?" I asked after a moment, as the horns started up.

"This works." Sawyer was grinning. He tapped his fingers on the underside of the steering wheel as he drove. "Your dad introduced me to all this stuff, you know that? When he used to give me lessons."

"I remember." I used to sit in the kitchen and listen. "He was really bummed when Cade and I turned out to be tone-deaf." I smiled. "Just one more in a long line of parental disappointments, I guess."

"I don't know about *that*." He shook his head. "You guys are, like, the perfect children. Everybody knows how proud he is of you."

I pulled one leg up onto the seat as we turned a corner, rested my chin on my knee. "Well, *your* dad is—"

Sawyer cut me off. "What if we don't talk about my dad?"

"He's proud of you," I protested.

"He's a dick." Sawyer hit the brakes like punctuation, no arguments, and it occurred to me that for all our years and years of proximity, maybe I didn't actually know what it was like to be a LeGrande.

"This is it," he said a moment later, unbuckling his seat belt and scrubbing a hand through his wavy hair. We were sitting in front of a little gray bungalow in dire need of a guest spot on a home improvement show: The porch sagged, one of the front windows was cracked, and the lawn was all but dead. Soledad would have had an aneurysm just looking at it, and I was pretty sure Lydia LeGrande wouldn't have been particularly impressed, either. "You wanna just wait here?"

"Oh," I said. I wondered briefly which one of us embarrassed him, Animal or me, or if maybe I'd just pushed him too far again. "Yeah, sure."

"The house is pretty grody," Sawyer said by way of explanation, shaking his head. "It's a bunch of guys that live here, so . . . I don't know, I don't want to, like, appall you or anything."

"No, it's fine. I'll be here."

I leaned my head back to listen to the music and, to my credit, managed to wait until about thirty seconds after he had disappeared inside the house—the front door was unlocked, and he strolled right in—before conducting a more thorough investigation of the contents of the Jeep. I twisted around to have a look at the backseat: A faded blue sweatshirt and an old issue of *Rolling Stone* were crumpled together on the floor, but other than that, he'd cleaned up. Allie's mix CD was gone. A couple of bar tabs sat beneath some coins in the well between the two front seats, and—oh God, that's what you get for being so nosy—there were two condoms tucked in the compartment where you're supposed to keep your toll money. I could feel myself blushing, even though there was no one else in the Jeep. Jesus. Shelby would get a kick out of that one, I knew.

"Hey," Sawyer said, and I jumped as he opened the door. "Ready to go?"

"Sure. Where are the CDs?"

"CDs?" He looked at me blankly.

"Yeah," I said. "You said you were getting—"

"Oh, right, right." Sawyer nodded. "He didn't have them."

"Oh." He was lying, clearly. I thought of bar fights and shady characters, wondered what kind of run I'd just taken part in.

"He's sort of a space case," he continued as we pulled out onto the main road. "Animal, I mean. His real name is Peter. But you can't be in a rock-and-roll band with a name like Peter."

"Sure you can," I countered. "What about Pete Townshend?"

"Okay, well—"

"Pete Seeger."

"Yeah, but—"

"Peter, Paul and Mary."

"Peter, Paul and Mary were not a rock-and-roll band!"

"But they sang about drugs." I was enjoying myself. "So if your argument is that people named Peter are too uptight for drug-type singing, then Peter of Peter, Paul and Mary clearly illustrates otherwise."

"You know, I think I liked you better when you didn't talk." Sawyer was laughing. "You want a milkshake or something? Baskin-Robbins is on the way back."

"Nah. Just a soda is fine."

"Your call," he said, switching lanes and executing a particularly skilled parallel park outside a Chinese grocery on A1A. I hopped out onto the sidewalk, the sun warm and reassuring on my skin.

"Oh!" I said happily, once we were inside. Sunrise Grocery was just a glorified convenience store, but there was always some kind of unusual produce stacked on the stand near the door—I'd written a column about it for the paper, actually, and something called an Ugli fruit. "They have pomegranates."

"Pomegranates?" Sawyer tossed a pack of gum on the counter and began rooting around in his back pocket for his wallet. "You want one?"

I paused, retrieved a bottle of Coke from the refrigerated case near the door. "Yes, actually."

Sawyer laughed. "So get one. Get me one, too, actually. I've never had one before."

"You've never had a pomegranate?" I asked, setting the pair of softball-size fruits on the counter.

"Nope."

"And you've lived here your whole life?"

"Longer than you, even."

"That makes me feel sad for you."

"Cue the violins," he agreed. He dropped his change into the "leave a penny" basket and handed me the plastic bag. "Here," he said. "Peace offering."

I raised my eyebrows. "Are we fighting?"

"I don't know," he said, holding the door open. We crossed the sidewalk to the Jeep and climbed inside. "You tell me."

I thought about it for a second, about the night in the restaurant and how he'd totally shut down on me as soon as I said Allie's name. "No," I said after a minute. I reached into the grocery bag and fumbled around until I produced one fat pomegranate. "I think we're good." Then, taking a deep breath and cracking it open with my thumbnails: "Do you miss her?"

Sawyer hadn't been expecting that from me, that was for sure. I hadn't been expecting it, either—normally I was the one who didn't want to talk about painful stuff—but it felt like one of us had to say it. I looked up and watched six different expressions play over Sawyer's face: surprise, sorrow, something I thought looked a lot like guilt. Finally he settled on mild irritation. "Of course I do," he said, in a voice like on second thought maybe we were fighting after all. "Seriously, what kind of question is that?"

I shrugged, defensive. "Well, I know—"

"We were in a fight when it happened," Sawyer interrupted roughly. "So." He shrugged once, all shoulders like he hadn't wanted to admit that and was annoyed I'd gotten it out of him. He didn't look at me as he put the car in drive. "Take from that what you will."

I blinked. "Fighting about what?" I blurted before I could stop myself. For all the mental energy I'd spent on the idea of Sawyer and Allie together, I'd never pictured them arguing. I thought of the night he'd kissed me, the sense I'd gotten like there was something he'd wanted to say and hadn't. "I mean, not that it's any of my business, I just—"

"Whatever." Sawyer shook his head, decisive. "It's not important. Talking about it doesn't change anything." A beat later, though, as if maybe he'd reconsidered: "Do *you* miss her?"

"I—" I broke off, tried to think how to explain it. This was my best friend since preschool we were talking about: the girl whose snack and math homework I'd shared since before I had memorized my own phone number, who'd buried her cold, annoying little feet underneath me during a thousand different movie nights and showed me how to use a tampon. She'd grown up in my kitchen, she was my shadow self—or, more likely, I was hers—and now she was gone forever. I wondered again how much Allie had told him about why she and I had stopped being friends.

"Yeah," I said to him finally. "Yeah, I miss her a lot."

Sawyer nodded, visibly uncomfortable. *Talking about it doesn't change anything*, he'd said; normally I would have agreed wholeheartedly, but there was something about Allie that was different. It seemed to me she was sitting in the car with us, flesh and blood and her feet up on the back-seat, complaining about the radio. I wondered how it was possible that Sawyer didn't feel that way, too.

I was working up the guts to push him a little bit further when he pulled over suddenly, the Jeep grinding to an abrupt stop on the side of the road. We were still four or five blocks away from the restaurant.

"What are you doing?" I asked, a little shrill.

He laughed and shrugged and just like that we were normal again, like he didn't like the trajectory of the conver-sation and had decided to bend it to his will. "I'm going to eat my damn pomegranate."

"You're out of your mind," I said, but I dug into the bag again and handed it over. I felt Allie slip out through the back door, leaving Sawyer and me alone in the car again, just the two of us.

"Possibly," he agreed. "How do I eat this?"

"Just bust it open and eat the seeds."

I watched carefully as he did it, was relieved when he smiled a moment later. "Tastes like fruit punch." He ate thoughtfully for a moment, then: "So how come you don't have a boyfriend?"

I almost choked. *"What?"*

"You heard me."

"Who says I don't have a boyfriend?"

He raised his eyebrows. There was a day's worth of stubble on his chin and pomegranate juice on his bottom lip. "Do you?"

"No," I admitted. I picked a bit at the skin of the pomegranate, digging at it with my nail. "But give me a little credit, at least. Theoretically, I could have one."

"Theoretically, you could," he agreed. "But why don't you?"

"Because I'm cold and unfriendly."

Sawyer laughed, slung one arm behind the headrest of the passenger seat. Out the window, cars whizzed by, dozens of strangers going about their business, totally oblivious to whatever it was that might be happening inside Sawyer's Jeep. "No, you're not."

"Oh, I am," I said. "Ask anybody. An ice queen, even."

"No, you're not." He was serious now. "You just hold yourself back, is all. It's kind of . . . intriguing."

"Right," I managed, shaking my head.

"Why can't you take a compliment?"

"Why do you ask so many questions?" I fired back.

"Why do I make you blush so much?"

"You don't!" I put my hand to my cheek. Sure enough, it was burning hot beneath my palm. "Crap," I said, embarrassed. Still, I shifted my body toward him in the passenger seat, pulled one knee up to rest my chin on. I wanted to see where this conversation was going.

"Ice queens don't blush," Sawyer said matter-of-factly, like he was pleased with himself. "Ergo: You're not an ice queen."

I rolled my eyes. "How scientific."

Sawyer shrugged. "It's just logic. So who do you like?"

"Who do I like?" I laughed, knowing he enjoyed making me uncomfortable. Enjoying it myself. "What are we, in sixth grade?"

"Humor me."

"I don't like anybody."

"Nobody?"

"Nope. Ice queen."

"Stop saying that. I don't believe you. Everybody likes somebody."

"Okay," I said, hoping the deep breath I took wasn't audible. "Well, then, who do *you* like?"

"No fair," he said. "I asked you first."

I shook my head. "I am not having this conversation with you."

"You're blushing again," he said cheerily, extracting a few more seeds from the pale rind of the pomegranate. Out the window, the sun shimmered white. He put one sticky hand on my cheek and tilted my face forward, confident, and when he kissed me it was sugar-sweet and magenta, like something I'd lived near all my life but never tried.

"Ice queen," he muttered when it was over, like he'd set out to prove his point and been successful. "I don't buy it, Reena. Not for a second."

21

After

Literally every pair of jeans I own has holes in it and Soledad's got plans of her own, so I strap Hannah into her car seat and take her for what, I hope, will be the world's shortest and most efficient trip to the Galleria on East Sunrise Boulevard. The mall smells like chlorine and Cinnabon. A perky high-school salesgirl carries my stuff into the dressing room, her shorts so tiny that the pockets stick out the hem against her tan, skinny legs. "She's so cute," she tells me, smiling at Hannah, who's passed out asleep in her stroller with one spitty fist crammed into her mouth. "Are you babysitting?"

"Nope," I tell her quickly. I get this question a lot and it used to fluster the crap out of me—I'd stutter my way through explanations to bank tellers and baristas, both of us wishing to God they hadn't asked. Eventually I found it was better to be clear and direct. "She's all mine."

The salesgirl's eyes widen, just for a second. She's probably only a year or so younger than me. "Oh," she says brightly, averting her eyes as she hangs the jeans on the hook inside the brightly lit cubicle. "That's great."

I've barely gotten the door locked and my pants unzipped before Hannah wakes up, flushed and cranky. "Hey, baby girl," I say with a smile, trying to head her off at the pass. "We'll be out of here in two seconds, okay?"

No dice. Hannah whimpers as I try to shimmy in and out of the first pair of pants; by the time it becomes clear to me that everything I've picked out is at least a size too small she's smack in the middle of a truly spectacular tantrum, screaming like she's being tortured as I lift her out of the stroller, do what I can to calm her down.

"Everything okay in there?" the salesgirl calls shrilly.

"Yup," I call back, trying to sound like I know what I'm doing. I *do* know what I'm doing, really; I try to remember that as I press my lips to Hannah's forehead. "We're fine."

We're not, though: Hannah needs a change, and she won't stop crying. There's not going to be any shopping today. I get my own holey jeans on as fast as humanly possible, Hannah all hiccups and hollers and the occasional furious "Nooo!" As I hightail it out of the store I'm painfully aware that I look like something out of one of those MTV reality shows people watch to feel better about their own lives.

"Oh, too bad," the salesgirl calls behind me. "None of them worked?"

All I want is to head home and give up for the day, but I told Aaron we'd come by after the mall for pizza and a movie, some thriller I agreed to against my better judgment. "Relax," he tells me halfway through, laughing as I almost jump off the couch for the third time in twenty minutes. I hate scary movies, is the truth.

"You relax. Bitch is *toast*," I reply, reaching for the popcorn on the coffee table and nodding at the girl detective on-screen. Hannah's asleep in Aaron's bedroom. Maxie, the bulldog, is snoozing on the floor.

"Nah." Aaron pulls me closer, one bear-paw hand playing idly in my hair. He smells like saltwater and soap, clean. "She's too cute. The cute ones never die."

"In what universe?" I ask, laughing. I'm about to lean into his shoulder when my phone starts making noise in the depths of my purse: the Rolling Stones, I realize after a second, "Sympathy for the Devil." My heart does a funny thing inside my chest. Junior year of high school Shelby changed the ringtone on my cell so that it played "Sympathy for the Devil" when Sawyer called. When I hear it now, I just sort of . . . freeze.

Aaron starts laughing, and then looks at my face and frowns. "Who's that?" he asks as I dig the phone out of my bag.

"Nobody," I say, recovering, hitting the red IGNORE button. "It's just . . . a joke."

"Is it Sawyer?" He doesn't sound particularly happy about the idea. The light from the TV flickers blue across his face.

"Yeah," I confess—no reason to lie, right? Nothing going on. "But I don't need to talk to him, so."

"So," Aaron fires back, unconvinced. "What's he calling for, then?"

That surprises me a little—it's the first suspicion I've seen out of him, really, and it must show on my face, because he backpedals. "Look," he says. "I'm not trying to be a dick. I just—"

"No, I know," I say. "It's fine. I have no idea what he wants, honestly. But I don't particularly care, either. I'm hanging out with you right now, you know?"

"Okay," Aaron says eventually, and we hang out for a while, twenty lazy minutes on the sofa once the movie is over. He was right, for what it's worth: The plucky policewoman lived to fight crime another day.

"Can I ask you a question?" he says once I start to extricate myself—it's getting late, and I glance around for my flip-flops. "What would happen if you stayed?"

"I can't," I say automatically, a reflex, though for a

moment I wonder how it would feel to say yes. "I mean, the baby is here, and—"

"I mean." He looks disappointed for a second, gets a look on his face like *no kidding*: The first time I brought Hannah to Aaron's, he bought covers for all the electrical outlets. "I wasn't going to send her home in a cab."

"I know." Here's the thing: I really, really like him. You don't need a map to navigate the level terrain of Aaron's heart. Still, staying over feels like a big deal for some reason, a step I don't know if I'm a hundred percent ready to take with him: I think of my phone ringing earlier, "Sympathy for the Devil." Try to stop thinking about it.

At last I smile, scratch through the sandy hair at the nape of Aaron's neck. "Another time," I promise, and head into the bedroom to get my girl.

Sawyer calls again when I'm on the way home, Mick Jagger twanging out from the depths of my shoulder bag. I fish for the phone and glance over my shoulder at Hannah in her baby seat, but she's dead to the world. My car smells like Cheerios and hand sanitizer. "We don't want any," I tell him, instead of hello.

"You haven't even heard what I'm selling." Sawyer's laughing; I can hear it in his voice.

I frown at the road in front of me, all grim neon strip malls and fast-food restaurants. I am so, so tired of driving this route. "I don't need to."

"Sure you do."

"Knives?" I ask, merging onto the highway. "Vinyl siding? Flood insurance?"

"Better," he tells me, full of promises. "Let me cook you dinner."

Oh God. *"What?"*

"Dinner," he repeats more slowly, like maybe the problem was in his enunciation. "Tonight."

"It's nine thirty."

"It's European."

"At your *house*?"

"Well, that's where my kitchen is," he says logically.

I roll my eyes. The highway is pretty empty at this hour, the darkened silhouettes of palm trees studding the median and the red glow of scattered taillights up ahead. The windshield fogs up a bit from the humidity, and I swipe at it with the flat of my palm. "Where are your parents?"

"At the restaurant."

There's no way. "I already ate."

"Eat again," he suggests, undeterred.

"I don't think so."

He's quiet for a minute like he's regrouping, changing tactics. "Where are you?" is what he tries next.

I check on Hannah in the mirror one more time. "In the car."

"Where *were* you?"

I sigh. "At Aaron's."

"Ah." Sawyer sounds satisfied. "*That's* why you didn't pick up."

"Maybe I didn't pick up because I didn't want to talk to you."

"That's not what it was," he says confidently. "You just picked up now, didn't you?"

God, he is so *annoying*. And, I guess, right. "We were watching a movie."

"What movie?"

"Who are you, my father?" I dig around in the console for some gum, shove a piece between my teeth and bite down hard. "A scary one, I don't know."

"You hate scary movies."

"Maybe I like them now."

"Come over."

"Sawyer." I should hang up, really. I don't know why I'm still on the phone. "No."

"Why not? Come on, Reena," he says. "I want to see you."

"You saw me the other day."

"I want to see you again."

That's a bad idea, is what that is. That is a truly terrible idea. "I have to go," I manage finally. There is no reason in the world for me to want to say yes as much as I do. I'm passing by the airport at this point: the planes low-flying and larger-than-life, all of that coming and going and me just exactly where I've always been. "I'm driving, remember? It's not safe."

For a second Sawyer doesn't answer. I'm expecting him to come back with some new and creative sales pitch, but in the end all he says is, "No." He sighs a bit like I've defeated him, and all at once I'm surprised by how it doesn't feel like a victory at all. "No, I guess it's not."

At home I get the baby into her crib without event and wander around the house for a while, restless. I drink some water standing next to the sink. I go up to my bedroom and stare at Sawyer's number in my phone's contact list—dial six numbers, then hedge and hang up (my whole life a holding pattern, some variation on *wait and see*). I pace.

Finally I come downstairs.

Soledad and my father are sitting in the living room, watching *Law & Order* on the couch. "Can you guys do me a favor?" I say, hovering on the bottom stair like a ghost and willing myself not to sound so timid.

They both look up expectantly. It's not often that I ask. "What do you need, sweetheart?" Soledad answers, and the endearment makes me feel about one inch tall.

"Can you keep an ear out for Hannah?" I ask her. "I've got something I need to do."

22

Before

I was sitting on a desk in the newspaper office, half listening to an eager sophomore pitch an exposé on cafeteria cleanliness, when I felt my phone vibrate inside my back pocket. I ignored it at first—Noelle, our editor, was hugely uptight about texting during meetings—but it buzzed again a minute later, insistent. I fished it out as discreetly as I could.

Look up, the text message said.

I did, and gasped out loud: Sawyer was standing in the hallway at the windowed door to the classroom, arms crossed and looking faintly amused. He tipped his head in greeting when he caught my eye and I grinned hugely, heart tipping sideways a bit. *What are you doing here?* I mouthed.

"Uh, Reena." I snapped to attention. I wasn't the only one who'd noticed Sawyer: Noelle shot me a look that could have taken the bark right off a coconut palm. "Do we have your attention here, or not so much?"

"I'm sorry," I told her, blushing. Everybody was watching now. Sawyer looked like he was about to crack up. I grabbed my backpack off the chair beside me, made for the door. "I just remembered someplace I really have to be."

"So," Sawyer said when I got out into the hallway, pushing me up against a locker and kissing me hello like it had been a lot longer than a couple of days since we'd seen each other. "That was very slick, what you did in there."

"Shut up," I said, laughing. I shoved him gently in the shoulders, let him carry my backpack down the hallway like something out of a teen movie. We'd been hanging out more and more lately, going for long drives along the water and hitting up Sonic for Cherry Limeades, making out until my mouth went smudgy and red. "How'd you even get in here, anyway?"

"I have ways." Sawyer shrugged. "Actually, some freshman girl let me in."

I snorted, rolled my eyes. "Of course she did."

"Of course," Sawyer echoed. "So how are things in the world of print journalism?" he asked next, opening up the door for me and stepping out into the early-winter dusk. "On the eve of extinction as always?"

"I mean, I don't know," I said, smiling. "I might have

been able to answer that a little better if you hadn't just yanked me out of my meeting before it was over."

Sawyer pulled a face. "I didn't *yank* you anyplace," he countered, grabbing my wrist and doing just that, pulling me into him so he could get an arm around my shoulders.

"Right." I laughed and leaned closer, the waffle of his thermal shirt warm against my cheek. "No, it's good. Noelle's starting to give me some feature stuff besides the column, which is cool. I'm covering the winter musical, I'll have you know."

Sawyer raised his eyebrows. "Fancy."

I pouted up at him. "It is!"

"I know," he said, and kissed me again. "That's awesome, Reena." Then, as he flipped the key in the driver's side door of the Jeep: "So what are you doing tonight, anything? Do you have plans?"

Well, sort of, if homework counted. "Was thinking I'd jet down to Havana for the weekend, actually," I told him, figuring sarcasm was the safest way to go here. Sawyer was definitely acting pretty boyfriend-esque lately, picking me up from school on the days I didn't ride with Shelby and leaving pomegranates on my front porch. Still, whatever was going on between us was still achingly gray and amorphous: He hadn't made any declarations, and I certainly wasn't going to be the one to make them first. Instead, I waited. I kept watch. "Check out the nightlife."

"Oh, I see." Sawyer slid his hand behind my headrest, backed the Jeep out of his spot. "Well, if you think you could maybe blow off El Presidente just for tonight, we're playing at the Prime Meridian later. You should come and see us, meet everybody."

Everybody.

On the nights we spent goofing around in the restaurant or hanging out on his parents' front porch, it was easy to forget that Sawyer lived an entire life into which I had no point of entry—that he hung out with friends I'd never met, played music I'd never heard. I didn't like to think about where he was when he didn't pick up his cell phone, weekends I spent with Shelby or by myself doing mundane, high-school-life-type things. It made me feel nervous. It made me feel weird.

"Yeah." I smiled and willed down the slimy greenish mass of anxiety I already felt forming in the pit of my stomach. "You know, it's sort of a bitch to get to Cuba, anyway, so."

"I mean, customs alone." Sawyer grinned, pulled up in front of my house, and tugged at some hair that had fallen out of my ponytail. "I'll pick you up at nine."

The Prime Meridian wasn't nice. Sandwiched between a pet store and a sketchy Chinese restaurant in a strip mall off the highway, it was long and narrow and boasted a tiny stage in back, a raised platform a foot or so off the ground.

The bar was strung with multicolored Christmas lights and tended by a scowly guy who was, in all seriousness, probably seven feet tall. It smelled like beer and cigarettes, too many people in too small a space.

I'd been here with Allie once, back at the beginning of high school, both of us wearing far too much makeup and dressed in our tightest jeans. We'd taken one look inside and fled for the fluorescent safety of last call at Panera Bread, but I figured she'd probably returned at some point, more likely than not with the same boy who was currently steering me through the crowd, one hand on my lower back. The idea made me feel sick-sad, the same way I did whenever I thought about Allie and Sawyer.

"I have to go set up," Sawyer said over the noisy chatter of the crowd, once he'd settled me at the far end of the bar. "Are you going to be okay by yourself? Mike said he'd keep you out of trouble."

Mike, the giant bartender, nodded gruffly in my general direction and I nodded a little, sweating: It was stifling hot at the Prime Meridian. "Yeah, I'll be fine. No worries."

"Good." He found my hand and squeezed once, fleeting. "Make sure you cheer real loud."

Sawyer left me and headed for the stage, where a couple of guys were already assembling a drum kit, connecting an amp. I watched them for a while, until the drummer—Animal himself, presumably—caught me and nudged Sawyer. He said something, but I couldn't make out what.

I tried to get comfortable on the stool, to not stare at anybody, to look like I belonged here. I wished for a notebook. I wished for a pen. Probably a girl writing in a bar was weird, but not as weird as a girl who was just sitting around all by herself and sweating, with nowhere to comfortably look. I wished I'd asked Shelby to come.

"You want something?" Mike wanted to know, leaning over the bar so I could hear him.

I nodded. "Just a Coke. With a lot of ice."

He raised his eyebrows at me. "That all?"

"That's all."

"Good girl."

I just shrugged. That's me, I wanted to tell him. Serena Montero, good girl at large. I should have had business cards printed up.

I chewed ice cubes as the bar filled, as another guy climbed onstage and began tuning a guitar. People kept making their way through the door, and I glanced around warily as a group of three or four girls positioned themselves almost directly in front of me. There was definitely a target market in the Prime Meridian that night, a whole lot of American Apparel up in there. "Um," I said, as Mike passed by. "Can I ask you a question?"

"You just did." He looked impatient; he was busy.

"Do they play here a lot?"

"Every few weeks or so."

"Is it always like this? The . . . crowd, I mean?"

"What, the lady brigade?" Mike smirked, glanced around. "Pretty much." He looked at me for another moment. "You need something else?"

Yes. *How the hell did I not know this was a popular band?* I wanted to yell, but the lead singer, who wore a green T-shirt with MY OTHER RIDE IS YOUR MOM emblazoned across the front, approached the mic. "We're the Platonic Ideal," he announced, as the drums started up behind him. "How are you guys doing?"

I looked back at Mike and just shook my head. "No," I said slowly, which was useless—I couldn't even hear my own voice. "I think I'm good for now."

The members of the Platonic Ideal were all variations on a theme, shaggy-haired boys with bad attitudes and Converse sneakers, but it worked for them—didn't hurt that their melodies were gorgeous, the harmonies right on. The kid on the keyboard had braces, I noted with a smile, and the guitarist, who was wearing aviator sunglasses even though it was muddy dark, and whom I vaguely remembered Sawyer referring to as Iceman, had a lot more John Mayer in him than he probably wanted to admit.

Sawyer, though, my Sawyer LeGrande, was very obviously their token looker—dark jeans slouched low on his narrow hips and a belt buckle the size of a saucer. He wore a plain white T-shirt, the kind you buy at Walmart in packs of three for six dollars, but of course he looked like a million bucks, all angles and muscles and fierce concentration. I plucked another ice cube from my glass.

He knew how to play the girls, too, in particular a coven of about four or five who were standing right next to the stage, singing along to every song and positively wiggling. *Wiggling.* Jesus. Sawyer played the bass and didn't say much, just grinned occasionally, tapped one sneaker-clad foot on the stage, and sang his songs. He had a pretty voice, all yearning tenor, velvety and sad.

I shifted in my seat, out of sorts and aching; I couldn't get over the sneaking suspicion that I was sitting exactly where I didn't want to sit. I'd gotten this far and still all I could manage to do was watch him from across the room and wish there was a way to capture him, to write him down—the girl in the yard at the party, hiding outside the pool of light.

He talked to those girls between songs, the Wiggles, laughing like he knew them, crouched down at the edge of the stage. "Sawyer, take off your shirt," called one of them from farther back, loud enough for everyone to hear, and probably she was half kidding, but still I almost choked to death.

"You first," he shot back.

Finally I got up to pee, snaking my way through the crowd and trying to get manhandled as little as possible. When I was finished I pushed out the front door, ignoring the tight knot of people standing around a pickup in the parking lot, glass bottles sweating in their hands. I stared into the pet store window for a while, at the puppies and kitties sleeping in their tiny crates. I pulled out my phone to call Shelby.

"Domino's," she answered cheerfully.

"This place is full of skanks."

"Of course it is." She sounded amused. I could hear the TV in the background, the grisly crime shows she liked. "It's nasty."

"None of them are old enough to be here, though. I mean, I'm not old enough to be here, either, but at least my skirt's not up my ass in the middle of January."

"True," Shelby agreed. "True, you do wait until the summer months to wear your skirt up your ass."

"Shut up." I laughed in spite of myself. "I'm serious. Did you know this was, like, a band that people actually come to see?"

"How would I have known that?" she asked. "You're the one who's going to write her doctoral dissertation on the life and times of Sawyer LeGrande."

"I think I need to leave."

"'Cause of the skanks?"

"I feel like a groupie, Shelby." I kicked at some loose concrete, a little kid having a tantrum. "I like him so stupidly much."

"I know you do." Shelby blew a raspberry on the other end of the phone. Her patience for Sawyer was limited,

I knew. For a moment I let myself think about Allie, the way we could spend an entire ninth-grade afternoon deconstructing his new haircut or the way he pronounced the letter *L.* It was just one more thing I missed about her, like her weird bony ankles and how much she loved corny knock-knock jokes, the shorthand and secret language of a friendship that went back a decade or more. "You want me to come pick you up?"

I sighed, pulled it together. "No, I'll be okay. I'm a big girl."

"You are indeed. Call me if you change your mind."

"Thanks." I hung up, tapped the pads of my fingers once against the pet store window, and dragged myself back inside. I'd lost my seat, so I got another Coke from Mike and contented myself with watching the rest of the show smushed against the wall, one arm crossed over my chest like a shield. They'd just announced their last song when I felt a hand on my shoulder, heard a singsong kind of lilt in my ear.

"Se-ree-na. What are you doing here?"

I turned around, flinching at the touch, and there was Lauren Werner. Of course. She was wearing designer jeans and a tank top made to look like it was weathered, a delicate amethyst pendant on a skinny chain around her neck. Already I wanted to die. Or, better yet, for her to die.

"Hey. I, um . . ." *Pull it together, Reena, Jesus.* I felt caught out, like she'd found me doing something illicit. "Came with Sawyer, actually."

That surprised her. Her eyes narrowed, cunning and feline. "Really? Are you guys, like . . . ," she said, an accusation. "Dating?"

"What? No, no," I said quickly. "We're just— Our dads own a business together, so . . ."

So.

"No kidding." Lauren looked me over. I could smell her perfume, faint and expensive. "He never mentioned that. You have that bewildered, first-time Sawyer LeGrande look, sort of. But I guess you've known each other since you were just little grommets?"

I squinted. "Something like that."

"That's cute!" she said. "He's great, isn't he?" I started to reply, but she just kept right on talking. "And I guess you, you know, had Allie in common and everything."

Oh, *wow*. I was about half a second away from running for the door again, calling Shelby, hitchhiking if I had to, but Sawyer appeared behind me just then, slipped a hand into my back pocket by way of hello. I turned around; he was warm and damp with sweat. "Hey, Laur," he said. "You taking good care of this one?"

"Oh, the best," I answered for her.

"We're old friends," she put in.

They chatted a little about some party they'd been to a couple of weekends ago, some people I'd never heard of, before she disappeared back into the crowd, smiling her good-bye in a way that looked, frankly, like a threat. Sawyer didn't notice.

"So what'd you think?" he asked me, once she was gone.

I took a deep breath, put my game face on. "Freaking awesome, clearly."

He grinned, and then frowned. "What's wrong?"

"Nothing," I said, blinking. "Just a little tired."

"You want me to take you home?"

I shook my head. "No. Stay if you want. I can call Shelby to pick me up."

"No, don't do that," he said. "Don't go. Give me a few minutes and we'll get out of here."

"Sawyer—"

"It's totally fine," he promised.

It was more than a few minutes. It was three more Cokes and two trips to the sketchy bathroom and meeting about thirty exceedingly good-looking and mostly female friends of Sawyer's, several of whom actually said, "Oh, she's so cute!" as if I wasn't there and also was four years old. It was after midnight by the time we made it out the door.

I settled carefully into the passenger side of the Jeep, pressed against the door, as far away from him as that night on the patio at the restaurant months and months ago. He must have been thinking the same thing, because he rolled his eyes at me.

"Oh, stop," he said, reaching over and picking up my hand. His calluses scraped my palm as he pulled me across the seat, until I was almost sitting in his lap. "I'm sorry we stayed so long. I didn't realize how late it was."

I shook my head. "No, it's not that."

Sawyer smiled. "You had a shitty time, Reena. You can say it."

"I wouldn't call it shitty," I said.

"Then what *would* you call it?" He was picking at the seam on my jeans, fingers moving absently up and down my thigh.

I shrugged helplessly. "I really did like your band."

"Good, but that's not what I asked."

"Sawyer . . ." I sighed. "I'm not your type."

He raised his eyebrows. "What's my type?"

Allie. Lauren. The Wiggles. "Not me."

"What does that even mean?"

"I'm not good at this stuff. I don't like . . ." Bars. Girls telling you to get naked. Feeling like a fan. ". . . big groups of people. I'm not, like, super social. I'm not your type."

"Who cares? I hate my type. I want you." He twisted the end of my ponytail between two of his fingers. "Why are you upset?"

"I don't know." I shrugged. *I want you*, he'd said. "I hate Lauren." To start with.

His face cracked open into a grin. "No shit."

"How long have you guys been friends?" I asked, as he put the Jeep in drive and pulled out of the lot.

"Since freshman year?" he said, checking behind him. "I don't know. She dated Iceman for a while."

"Did you ever . . . ?" I trailed off, regretting even before the words had gotten out.

But he was smiling. "Did we ever *what*, Reena?"

I looked down, away. "Forget it."

"Would that bother you?"

"Maybe."

"No."

"Good."

He glanced at the clock on the dash. We were headed for the highway at this point. If Sawyer made a left we'd end up at my house, and his parents'; a right would take us south, toward the street where Sawyer lived now. He stopped the Jeep at a red light. "Do you need to call your dad?" he asked.

I shook my head. Our parents had spent the evening together, at a retirement dinner for one of the restaurant's longtime regulars. I pictured them in the banquet room, weirdly comforted by the idea of them all in one place. I hadn't been lying when I told Sawyer I'd miss them when I left home. "I didn't know how long it would go, the show, so I told him I'd probably just stay at Shelby's."

Sawyer nodded, didn't say anything for a long time. The stereo hummed. "Do you want to come over for a little while?" he asked me, and there was a moment before I answered in which I didn't breathe at all. My face felt warm. The light turned green.

"Reena?" he asked again.

"Yeah." I nodded. "I can come over."

23

After

It's after ten thirty but the humidity is still bearing down by the time I get to Sawyer's parents' house, and the weight of the air feels physical, something I'd like to throw off. It rained a couple of hours ago—it rains every single day, world without end—and the grass is slick under my feet.

I ring twice and worry he won't even be there—or worse, that his parents will be—but when he finally opens the door, the house behind him is quiet save for the low hum of a radio somewhere. A pair of dark-rimmed glasses is perched on his nose. "When did you go blind?" I ask.

"Always have been." Sawyer shrugs like he's not even surprised to see me. "Couldn't admit it."

"Oh." I nod once, curtly. "Do you still want to make me dinner?"

That makes him smile. "Yeah," he says, and steps back to let me through. "Yeah, absolutely. Come in."

I follow him through the living room, past the multitude of black-and-white family portraits on the dining room walls—Lydia's work is all up and down the hallways. When I was a little girl she used to let me take pictures with her heavy 35mm, showed me how to develop them in the dark-room she'd set up in the downstairs bathroom. I remember feeling so nervous to screw up around her even then that my hands would shake as I tried to hold the camera, a whole roll full of blurry, focusless shots.

I know the LeGrandes' house almost as well as I know my own: I've sat through a dozen Super Bowls on the leather couch in the den here, eaten king cake on the sun-porch every Fat Tuesday for years and years. I know where they keep the spoons and recycling and extra toilet paper, all the secrets and all the smells.

"You like risotto?" Sawyer asks.

"Um." That is . . . not what I expected when he said *dinner*. I blink. "Sure."

Sawyer flicks on the light in the kitchen and the room goes clinically bright, all pale-green tile and gleaming stainless-steel appliances. "So," he says, lifting a pot off the hanging rack above the island, "how's Aaron?"

I snort a little. "Can you stop saying his name like that?"

"How am I saying it?"

"I don't know." The snort turns into a laugh, a little hysterical. I feel like every organ in my body has lodged itself somewhere in the back of my throat. "However you're saying it."

"I'm not saying it any way." Sawyer shrugs. "*Aaron*'s from the Bible."

I hop up on the counter. "Aaron works on boats."

Sawyer nods slowly, like he's absorbing that information, like there's an old-fashioned card catalog in his head and he just filed Aaron into the drawer for shit he's frankly not crazy about but suspects he needs to live with for the time being. "Is he good with the baby?"

"I wouldn't be with him if he wasn't," I say snottily, then: "Can we please not talk about Aaron?"

Sawyer grins like, *As you wish*. "What do you want to talk about?"

"I don't know," I say. "Whatever normal people talk about. Baseball."

"You want to talk about baseball?"

"No." I raise my hands and drop them again, useless. "I don't actually even know anything about baseball."

"Me either." He's cutting up an onion now, quick and expert like Finch taught us all when we were kids. "Is this weird?" he asks once it's in the pot, glancing at me out of the corner of his eye. "You have a look on your face like you think this is really, really weird."

"Well," I say, shrugging, picking at my ragged cuticles. "It's a little weird."

"Yeah," he echoes. Then, after a beat: "She kept everything the same. Like, my bedroom and stuff."

"Who?" I ask. "Your mother?" In truth I'm not really listening, instead watching him toast the rice, pour in a ladleful of stock. Clearly he's comfortable doing it—clearly he's done it before—but still it's somehow unnatural, like a tree beginning to speak.

"Uh-huh. What?" he asks when he catches me staring. "This is how you make risotto."

"I know how to make risotto," I tell him. My heels kick softly at the cabinets. "I'm just surprised you do."

"I know how to do lots of things I didn't used to know how to do," he answers, and we're definitely not talking about dinner anymore. The air crackles: too many electrons, like you could reach out and grab them and feel them buzz inside your hand. I look away.

"Anyway," I say, too loudly. "Your mom. Your bedroom. I guess she just . . . I don't know. I guess she knew you'd be back."

"I guess so."

"She missed you."

"Did she?" he asks. He stirs the rice one more time before he abandons the stove, and, oh God. He stops when he's standing right between my knees.

"Yeah," I tell him slowly, glancing down. His hands have

landed on my thighs. "I think she kind of did." When I look up at him we're face-to-face like commuters on a packed train at rush hour, and I really need half a second to . . . "Just," I say, "hold on."

"Reena—" he begins, but I cut him off.

"Stop." I shake my head. "Just don't . . . I just need to—" and I'm going to say *think a minute* but instead there is the sudden press of lips and faces, tongues in each other's mouths like every stunted *love you* is hidden in the wet darkness there. I could act surprised, but this is why I came here, isn't it? This is what I've wanted since the morning he turned up. I get my arms around his neck, hard and clutching. After a moment, I hear him say my name.

24

Before

It didn't take long to get from the Prime Meridian to the crumbling stucco house where Sawyer was living with a bunch of his buddies. He clicked the radio off as he coasted up the driveway, took me by the hand and led me up the stairs of a small deck, through the unlocked back door. The kitchen was illuminated by a coiled fluorescent bulb affixed to the ceiling that cast a greenish tinge over the speckled linoleum, the ancient appliances: pretty much what I'd expected, save for—I noted with a little smile—a plastic bowl of pomegranates on the table.

"So who exactly lives here?" I asked finally. He hadn't spoken since inviting me over, but as he shrugged out of his hoodie he answered easily, like there hadn't even been a pause.

"Well, me and Iceman, plus Animal's brother Lou, and Lou's friend Charlie, all the time. But usually there are some other people staying over." Sawyer paused, moved toward the fridge. "I think everybody's probably gone for the night, though. You hungry?"

I shook my head.

"Me neither," he agreed and kissed me, pressing me back against the fridge and tracing the line of my jaw. It felt like my entire body was liquefying. Goosebumps popped up on my arms, and I couldn't get over the notion that the floor wasn't quite even. The blood, I thought vaguely, was having a hard time getting to the places it needed to be.

"You cold?" he asked, when my frigid hands grazed the back of his neck, the tag at the collar of his T-shirt.

"No."

"Okay." Then, in my ear, though there was no one around to hear him even if he yelled: "Do you want to get out of this kitchen?"

"Um." Just for one second, I let go of him to brace one arm behind me, against the handle on the refrigerator door. I felt like the cats I'd sometimes see stopped cold in the middle of the road late at night as I drove home from Shelby's. Like I'd gotten to the top of the high dive and suddenly remembered that I didn't know how to swim.

It wasn't the God thing. I was a habitual Catholic, not a devout one; my religion was incidental to whatever was going on here. I was just—afraid. Not in a bad way, necessarily, but the way I'd been brought up to fear hurricanes: something powerful coming, better board up the glass.

"It's okay, sweetheart," he said, gently prying my hand off the door, linking our fingers together. Just—of course he would know. "We can stay right here."

"No." I shook my head, stubborn. "Let's go."

Sawyer looked at me closely, one hand cupping the side of my face. "Are you sure?"

"I'm sure."

"Reena—"

"Sawyer. You've done it before, right?"

"Yeah, Reena." He smiled in that half-bashful way he had sometimes, glancing down. "I've done it before."

"Well, then," I said. "Show me how."

He nodded, bit his bottom lip. "Okay."

Sawyer's bedroom smelled lemony, Pledge layered on top of pot. He didn't bother with a light—in fact, I wasn't even sure if there was one—but I could see in the glow of the fixture in the hallway that his room was neat and orderly and sparse. I glanced around: a freestanding bookshelf, an expensive-looking stereo sitting on the floor, a mattress with no box spring. The closet was a little bit open, and inside was an enormous pile of junk—sneakers, books, other teenage-boy refuse I couldn't see clearly in the half-light. I smiled. Cade was famous for that at home, dumping all his crap into his closet or shoving it under his bed on the occasions when

Soledad forbade him to come downstairs until his room was clean—holidays, mostly, or when we were having company.

Pledge. Company. I cocked my head to the side. "Can I ask you a question?"

"Hmm? Shoot." He reached down and flicked the power button on the stereo, fiddled with the radio dial; we could get the USF station, sometimes, and Sawyer had told me once that they did a good blues show late at night.

"Did you clean for me?"

"What? No." He straightened up a little too quickly, ran a hand through his hair a little too fast. "No. Why?"

"You did. You cleaned for me."

"Reena . . ." He looked embarrassed. "I don't want you to think I was, like, planning on bringing you back here."

I perched on the edge of the bed, smirked at him. "You weren't?"

"Well . . ." He shook his head. "I don't know, Reena. I'm not going to pretend I didn't think about it. And this place is a dump."

"It's not a dump," I lied.

"It's a dump. And if you were going to come here, I wanted it to at least be a dump where there's not shit everywhere."

"Who *are* you?" I asked, laughing. I felt drunk, almost. I was glad to be sitting down.

"You know who I am," he said, and I was about to reply, but Sawyer LeGrande was gently, so gently, pushing me backward into his bed, and that was the end of that. "Reena," he muttered. "You need to tell me if you want to stop, okay?"

"Yeah," I said, and smiled. "I really don't."

He kissed me for a long time, on top of the sheets and then underneath them. My shirt hit the bedroom floor with a sigh. There was a small but unmistakable scar on his chest, from the surgery he'd had when he was little; he was salty like the ocean and I was fascinated by the way he was put together, the dips between his fingers and the muscles in his back. I reached for the button on his Levi's, and Sawyer took a deep, shaky breath. "We're gonna go slow, okay?" he told me. "We're gonna go so slow."

I wanted to stay awake when it was over. I wanted to look carefully, to remember every single detail so I could write it all down later and not lose it, not ever, but I felt sleepy and sluggish, like I was trying to swim through syrup. "Can you stay here?" he mumbled, and I don't remember replying, but when I woke up the dawn was dripping gray outside, and I was all alone.

I reached down to the chilly hardwood to retrieve my T-shirt, tried to think and not to panic. I hadn't heard him leave. His roommates would be back by now, wouldn't they? What the hell was I going to do, just wander downstairs and say hi? I felt freaked out and weirdly disoriented, totally and completely out of my league.

I got dressed as quickly as possible, crossed the room to nudge my feet into my flip-flops where they'd landed in the corner near the window. I braced my hand on the sill to keep my balance, was looking down when something shiny caught my eye: Tucked in a pair of Sawyer's hipster sneakers was a crumpled plastic baggie, the cellophane catching the light. Inside that was half a dozen little white pills.

Holy *shit.*

They could be aspirin, I told myself as I bent down to fish them out, knowing even as the explanation occurred to me that I was being totally ridiculous. There was no way this wasn't bad news. They were probably painkillers, I thought with a grim kind of realization, but clearly Sawyer wasn't about to pop 'em for an end-of-the-day headache.

I was wondering if there was a way for me to slip out of the house without anyone noticing when I heard somebody in the hallway; I shoved the baggie back where I'd found it, wedged my flip-flops successfully onto my feet. Sawyer nudged the door open, a fat pomegranate in each hand. "Hey, lady," he said easily, grinning at me like his was a world where good things happened often, and like—just possibly—I was one. "How'd you sleep?"

"Um." I exhaled, grateful he hadn't caught me snooping. In spite of everything, I felt myself smile at the sight of him, sleep-rumpled and happy. He'd pulled a pair of jeans on, last night's shirt. "Hey," I said. "Good."

He handed me one of the pomegranates, sat down cross-legged on the bed. "You okay?"

"Uh-huh." I nodded. "I just woke up, and . . ." I stopped. It sounded silly now, the idea that I thought he'd disappeared on me.

"What'd you think, I left?" He kissed the side of my forehead. "Man, you think I am such a weasel." He cracked open his pomegranate, swearing softly as the juice dripped onto his sheets. He dug at the seeds for a minute and then held up a hunk of the rind. He looked curious. "What happens if I eat the hard part?" he wanted to know.

I looked at him, still smiling, the warm flush of his full attention; even the pills seemed less sinister all of a sudden, that sharp slice of panic already fading away. Maybe I was wrong, I thought. Maybe I really didn't know what I'd seen. "A pomegranate grows in your stomach," I told him.

"Really?"

"If you're lucky."

Sawyer grinned and sank down on the mattress beside me. "Oh, I'm real lucky," he said.

It was close to lunchtime when Sawyer drove me home. I crept in through the back door, hoping to sneak straight upstairs, but my father was in the kitchen drinking coffee. "How was Shelby's?" he asked me quietly, one thumb ringing around the edge of his mug.

"Good," I said.

"Good," he repeated. Then, as I made for the staircase: "Reena."

Uh-oh. I turned around, eyes widening. I felt like he could see right through my skin. "Yup?"

"Sit down."

"I was just going to—"

"Serena." His voice rose suddenly, and I thought of Moses on Mount Sinai, the voice of God and the burning bush. "I don't know if you were or were not with Shelby last night, but I do know that this needs to stop right now."

I blinked, tried ignorance. My cheeks were very warm. "What does?"

His eyes narrowed. "Please don't insult me."

"I'm not," I said. I was holding on to the edge of the countertop, clutching at it with my fingertips. "I don't mean to."

"Please don't think I'm so ignorant that I don't know what's going on with you and Sawyer, all right?" He looked so uncomfortable that I almost felt sorry for him. "I might not know what, exactly—and I get the feeling, quite frankly, that I don't *want* to know exactly what—but I am telling you now that you need to put a stop to it before you do something you'll regret."

I glanced instinctively out the window, but of course there was nothing to see there: I'd had Sawyer drop me halfway down the block.

My father saw me looking, rubbed a hand across the side

of his face. "Reena," he said, more softly this time. "I love you. But you are on very thin ice here. And I don't think you understand what you're dealing with."

I squinted at him. "Meaning . . ."

"Meaning, Sawyer has a lot of problems."

Bald denial was my first instinct. "Oh, Daddy, he does not."

"There are things you don't know about him, Serena. There are things you don't know about the world. And maybe that's my fault, maybe I've kept you from—"

"Can you stop?" I asked sharply. It was the closest to the edge I ever got with him, but I just— I did not want to be having this conversation. I didn't need anyone else telling me all the things I didn't know. "It's not like that. He's not just some random—" I broke off, tried to think how to explain it to him. "You *know* Sawyer."

My father looked at me like he'd never seen me before in his life, like he honestly had no idea what to do with me at all. "Yes, Reena," he said finally. "I do."

We stared at each other, like a standoff. For a moment I wished for my mom—someone to take my side in all of this. Eventually I shrugged and raised my chin. "Can I go?"

I was expecting an argument, but my father just sort of sagged. "Go ahead," he told me finally, and as I pushed through the door into the living room I was almost sure I heard him sigh.

25

After

I bite at Sawyer's bottom lip in his parents' kitchen; I run my hands up over the fuzz where his hair used to be. "There you are," he says after a minute, two palms on either side of my face like he wants to make sure I'm not planning to go anywhere. He's smiling hard and bright against my mouth.

"Hi." Kissing him feels familiar but also new, a song they haven't played on the radio in a really long time. "Risotto needs a stir."

"Who cares?" He's got his teeth at the place where my neck meets my shoulder and is lifting me up off the counter the tiniest bit. "God, Reena," he murmurs, nosing close to my ear. "I missed you so freaking much."

"Shh," I hush him, concentrating. He tastes like salt and

summer, the same. "No, you didn't."

Right away Sawyer gets that look on his face like I've slapped him, and he sets me down on the counter with a thud that sings up through my spine.

"Ow! What the hell, Sawyer?" I reach behind me to rub my tailbone. "That hurt."

"Sorry." His face softens for a moment. "But I don't know how much I appreciate you constantly acting like you don't believe a single word that comes out of my mouth."

I bark out a brittle little laugh, incredulous. "I *don't* believe a single word that comes out of your mouth."

"Why?"

"Because you're a liar!"

"Well, then why are you here?" he explodes.

I glare at him, embarrassed. This was a mistake. I knew it was a mistake coming in, and I did it anyway. *Slow learner*, I think, hating myself and Sawyer equally. *Stupid girl.*

"Look, Reena," Sawyer says quietly. He gets a little closer again, careful, warm breath at the spot behind my ear. "Sooner or later, I think we're going to do this."

I jerk away like he's radioactive. "The hell we are."

"We are," he says, like it's that simple. I want to jump down off the counter, but he's standing in my way. "And don't talk like you don't want to, either, because if you didn't, you wouldn't be showing up at my house at eleven o'clock at night so I could make you a second dinner you don't even want to eat." He looks so sure of himself I could kill him. "But I'm not going to let it happen until you forgive me."

"Well, then, I guess we won't be doing it for a hundred thousand years."

Sawyer snorts. "I guess not."

"Oh, suddenly you're into delayed gratification?" I'm striking out in every direction, indiscriminate. I want to hurt him as fast and as badly as I can. On the stove the rice is boiling over, an angry hiss.

"You're pissed," he says, eyes narrowing. I can tell that blow landed, but it doesn't feel as satisfying as it should. "So I'm going to let that one slide."

"How charitable of you."

Sawyer shrugs. "If I just wanted sex, I could get sex. Trust me, I've done it. But I want you."

I seriously almost slap him. "God, you are such an *ass*."

"It's a sickness."

"Yeah, we should throw you a fund-raiser."

He grins. "You're getting feisty in your old age."

"Well." I want to mark up this perfect kitchen, pull the pans off the rack and draw on the walls like the baby with a Sharpie. "Getting knocked up and walked out on will do that to a person."

"I didn't know you were pregnant!"

"I don't care!"

Sawyer sighs noisily. "So what are you going to do, storm out on me again? Because—"

"Yes, actually," I fire back. This time I do hop down onto the tile, shove him roughly out of my way. "That's exactly what I'm going to do." I grab my shoulder bag off the table, brush past him. The smell of burning rice sticks to my T-shirt clear across town.

I get home and head upstairs to check on the baby, anger and exhaustion and that infinite embarrassment still rattling around like loose coins inside my head. The house is cool and silent, the hallway dark save for the glow of Hannah's nightlight spilling dimly out the half-open door; I get in there and find her wide-awake and waiting, calm as the surface of a cool, placid lake. "Hi, Mama," she says cheerfully, grinning like possibly she stayed up just to talk to me and is pleased with herself for being so clever. Her eyes are fathoms and fathoms deep.

"Hi, baby." I drop my purse on the floor and cross the carpet, suddenly a hundred percent sure I'm about to cry. I'm just stupidly relieved to see her, is all, this twenty-pound miracle I thought for sure would make me a prisoner, hands and feet bound zip-tie secure. It does feel like that some days, to be honest, but right now I'm bone-grindingly glad.

I swallow the tears, smile back. "Hi, Hannah," I say again, lifting her out of the crib and cuddling her against me, rubbing her warm downy head against my cheek. She's getting heavy lately, more toddler than baby. It makes me feel weirdly nostalgic and bittersweet. "Whatcha still doing up, huh?"

Hannah doesn't answer—she's got words but not so much conversation yet—and instead she just snuggles into my body, surprisingly strong arms coming up around my neck. "Mama," she murmurs again.

"I am your mama," I tell her, sinking down into the rocking chair and smoothing patterns with my palm across her tiny baby back. "I'm the only one you've got, poor thing."

26

Before

God help me, he didn't call.

Like . . . ever.

The first couple of days after I slept over weren't so bad. He was probably just busy, I reasoned, as I made a big show of not looking at my cell phone—of trying not to be that girl. I had homework to finish. I had articles to write. On Monday I worked a party at the restaurant, tucking the extra tips into my pocket at the end of the evening, telling myself it was seed money for whatever awesome adventures were waiting for me after graduation.

It was fine, I promised myself in the ladies' room mirror. I was fine.

Two days turned into three, though, and then five—and

soon a week had passed. I wanted to crawl out of my skin. I skulked around near the Flea, where his band practiced. I called my own cell on the landline, on the off chance I'd somehow randomly stopped getting service in my house.

"Well," I muttered out loud, when it rang just right as rain—thinking of my father, thinking of Allie, thinking of all the things I actually didn't know. *Well.*

I didn't cry. I planned instead. I dug out all my travel books and bought an armful of new ones, retracing my old routes and making notes: Macedonia and Mykonos, Joshua Tree and Big Sky. I priced tours of the Pyramids on Kayak and Expedia. I took virtual tours of hotels in Prague.

That worked okay, on occasion.

Other nights, not so much.

Tired of watching me pace the upstairs hallway like a zoo animal, Soledad sent me out on whatever errands she could think of: milk, Tylenol, bank deposits. I turned up the AC and drove. That didn't always help, either, though: One night right around Valentine's Day, I finally cracked and headed south down 95 toward Sawyer's, my father's plastic-covered dry cleaning hanging in the backseat. The windows were dark, driveway empty. I cruised by again to make sure.

"So, okay," Shelby said, when I confessed over French fries in the cafeteria the following afternoon, head in my hands over my sad little cup of yogurt. She'd broken up with her soccer-star girlfriend over Christmas, had spent more or less the entire break sacked out on my bed watching all six seasons of *Lost* on DVD and muttering monosyllabic answers every time I asked if she was okay. It occurred to me that relationships basically sucked no matter where you fell on the Kinsey scale. "That was a low moment."

I cleaned out my closet. I interviewed the couple playing Sandy and Danny in the winter musical for the paper. I dropped by Ms. Bowen's office—again—to make sure Northwestern had gotten all my application materials.

"We're all set, Reena," she promised, smooth forehead creasing a little as she looked across the desk in my direction. She was wearing her dark hair pulled up into a topknot. Her short nails were painted a deep purplish red. "Nothing to do now but relax and wait."

"I know," I said, and even as I tried to tamp it down I could feel the edge creeping into my voice. *Relax and wait* was the story of my life lately; it was hard to take it from her on top of everyone else. "I just—" I shifted my backpack to my other shoulder, fidgeting. All of a sudden I felt weirdly close to tears. "It's really important that I get in, is all."

"Reena." Now she really did look concerned, all her guidance counselor instincts coming online at once. "Are you okay?"

God, for a second I almost told her everything: Sawyer and Allie and how lonely I felt lately, how badly I needed to get out of this place. The way she was looking at me, her face open and intelligent—something about her made me think she'd listen. Something about her made me think she'd be able to help. Still, spilling my guts to my *guidance counselor* of all people? That was pathetic. That was *absurd*.

"Yeah," I told her, smiling as hard and as brightly as I could manage. I probably looked deranged. "I'm great."

I got A's on all my midterms. I went into Lauderdale to go shopping with Shelby. I started working my way through Sylvia Plath's *Collected Poems*, but that made Soledad really nervous, so I switched to Jane Austen so she could sleep without worrying I was going to put my head in the oven or something.

Which I wasn't.

Probably.

I felt so incredibly, unforgivably *stupid*, was the worst part—the lamest kind of stereotype, the dumbest kind of fool. I remembered that night outside the party at Allie's house, the pitying look on her sharp, familiar face: *You definitely couldn't handle having sex with Sawyer LeGrande*. I'd had sex with Sawyer, all right—I'd given him something I couldn't get back—and now he was done, game over, thanks for playing. It was gross. It was *predictable*.

It hurt like nothing else in my life.

Weeks passed. Life hummed on. At night I sighed and mapped out my future, staring at the moon outside my window and wondering where on earth I might go.

27

After

There's a farmers' market on Las Olas where I like to take the baby on weekends, buying heavy bagfuls of cheap yellow lemons and watching the spry retirees. I get Hannah a chocolate chip cookie from the organic bake sale and she lounges happily in the stroller while I shop: rosemary for Soledad, avocados for my father. I buy eleven kumquats, because I like the way they look.

Aaron's been coming with us lately—he's a sucker for this Nutella bread that's basically just cake, chocolate, and hazelnut with an orange-sugar glaze—and this morning he meets us by the fountain just like always, trendy sneakers and the sturdy expanse of his body, one hand in my back pocket as we walk. Aaron is the only person in my life who makes me feel legitimately small.

He's quiet today, though, sort of broody. His forehead is furrowed underneath his cap. "What's up?" I ask finally, reaching for a sip of his limeade, nudging his solid shoulder with mine. He smells clean and citrusy, like the soap in the bathroom at his place; there's a tiny cleft in his chin where my thumb fits almost exactly. "You're being weird."

Aaron shrugs, noncommittal. I'm expecting a *no, I'm not* or a *don't worry about it,* the kind of *guess what's in my head* I'm used to when it comes to the men in my life, but instead he sits down on a bench near the soaps and beeswax candles and scrubs a hand through his sandy hair. "Can I ask you a question without you freaking out?" he starts.

Right away my whole body goes cautious, perking up like a ferret—but how could he possibly know? "Yeah, definitely," I reply. I think of Cade and me as kids, playing dumb like that. I pull the stroller closer, so I can see the baby's face. "Of course."

"Did you go to Sawyer's after you left my place the other night?"

Um.

"Did you *follow* me?" is the first thing I come up with, from zero to completely wigged in 2.5 seconds. The sun is beating down on my neck. There are, like, six different emotions happening here right now, no question—guilt and this weird indignation, anger at Sawyer and myself. Most of all I'm scared I've blown this. Aaron looks at me like I'm insane.

"No," he says immediately. "Jesus. I saw Lorraine at work, and she mentioned she saw you over there. I don't know. I'm just asking—"

"*Lorraine* followed me?"

"Reena, nobody was following you!" Aaron looks a little annoyed. "Calm down for a second. She lives over there. Near the LeGrandes, I guess. She knows them, so she mentioned it to me."

I—oh. "That's it?" I ask.

Aaron frowns. "Is there something else?"

"No," I say quickly. "No, definitely not." He doesn't know. I'm being crazy. "I'm being crazy," I tell him, staring hard at the pavement between my feet. "I'm sorry." I rub at the base of my ponytail for a second, trying to figure out how to play this. I know I can be secretive. It's not a quality I particularly like in myself, but there's no way I can tell him the whole truth. What happened with Sawyer was a stupid mistake, some bizarre one-time muscle-memory thing. It's never going to happen again. "I'm sorry. Yes, I saw Sawyer the other night."

"You did?" Aaron says—and God, his *face*, I feel terrible, I feel like the worst person in the world. He looks pissed, yeah, but more than that he looks *hurt*. "Seriously?"

"He's Hannah's dad, Aaron." I'm being deliberately deceptive, as if somehow that's all Sawyer is—somebody I knew a long time ago, a footnote in my life as it stands. It's not fair of me, I know that, but just—the last thing I want to do is mess things up with Aaron. "Of course I'm going to see him now that he's back. He wants to be in the baby's life, and we just need to . . . figure out how that's going to look, I guess."

I reach for his hand, run my thumb over the calluses on the pads of his fingers—there's a scar in the meat of his palm, long and thin, from a piece of jagged metal on a schooner he helped restore back in New Hampshire. Sometimes I wonder what would have happened if Aaron had stayed in Broward for high school—if I'd have noticed him then, his wry smile and the flecks of amber in his dark brown eyes, or if I'd have been too dumb and distracted to see.

He shrugs now, a hint of sulky mulishness I've never seen from him before. "No, I know," he says finally. He looks at Hannah for a minute, takes the damp, half-chewed cookie she holds out to him with no hesitation at all. "Look, Reena," he tells me. "I grew up with a lot of bullshit in my life, okay? I don't operate like that anymore. I like you a lot. I want you to *know* that I like you a lot. But if you're not at a place in your life where this can go somewhere . . ." Aaron shakes his head. "I guess I'd just rather have that out there now."

I feel myself blushing, this warm pleased flush that starts in my chest and radiates outward, my whole body heating up in a way that has nothing to do with the humidity index. I get my hands on either side of his face and plant a kiss against his mouth. "I like *you* a lot," I tell him, fingertips scritching though the hair at the base of his skull. "This is just . . . I don't know, an unexpected development, or something. But there's nothing going on between me and Sawyer, okay?" I swallow the guilt and uncertainty, smile as he reaches up to tuck a bit of hair behind my ear. "I would tell you if there was."

After a moment Aaron half smiles back at me, reluctant. A brass band sets up at the end of the street. Eventually he holds out his hand and we head back through the market: crowds and orange citrus, the sunshine state.

At the beginning of the summer, Shelby and I had a standing date for yoga after my art class on Thursday mornings, but then for three weeks in a row one or both of us were so late that we couldn't get in, so now we have a standing date for breakfast at the Greek diner across from the yoga place for which we are always, mysteriously, right on time.

She's there before me today, sitting at our usual table with two iced coffees in front of her, and she nudges the darker one toward me as I sit down. "Watch out," she says quietly, red hair falling like a theater curtain over her face. "Marjorie's in a mood."

"Good to know." Marjorie is the extremely tall, extremely skinny waitress who works this shift at Mount

Olympus. Half the time she's thrilled to see us and half the time she hates our guts, and there is virtually no rhyme or rhythm or way of predicting at all. It adds a real element of surprise to a Western omelet. I nod briskly, reach for a menu. "I'll choose fast."

"I think you better." Shelby dumps some more cream into her coffee, takes an experimental sip and wrinkles her freckled nose. "So what'd you learn in school today, honey?" she asks, once I've ordered—very politely—a couple of eggs over easy. "You have any homework for me to sign?"

I grin. "Got some spelling words you could quiz me on, if you want." Shelby's the one who got me to sign up at Broward to begin with, right after Hannah was born. She was worried, and probably rightly, that I'd never see anybody my own age again if I wasn't required to show up someplace where they took attendance. "Dork."

We drink coffee and try, with negligible success, to get Marjorie to smile when she brings us our food. We make plans to take the baby to the beach. Shelby's dating a girl named Cara up in Boston now, a political communications major with huge hipster glasses about whom I am desperately curious and who, Shelby tells me, might be coming down at the end of the summer. "You'll like each other," she promises, although secretly I can't imagine Shelby's sad teen-mom friend from home is particularly high on this chick's list of must-meets. Still, Shelby seems so *happy*; I sort of can't wait to lay eyes on the reason why.

"So," she says as I'm finishing my toast, and just from the barely perceptible change in her tone, already I've got the sinking feeling I know where this is going. "You and Sawyer."

"Me and Sawyer what?" I say, and it comes out a little more defensive than I mean. I take a deep breath, file the ragged edges down. "Did Aaron say something to you?"

"Did my brother talk to me about his girl problems?" Shelby snorts. "No." She reaches over and snags the last few abandoned home fries off my plate. "He also kind of doesn't have to, though." She shrugs, like *What can you do*. "Twin thing."

I nod, chew slowly. "Right."

"Right." Shelby takes a long sip of her coffee, then sits back in the booth and eyes me across the cracked Formica. She can do this; I know from experience. She can wait me out.

"What?" I demand finally, literally throwing up my hands. My fork clatters on the table. Marjorie shoots me a filthy look. "There's nothing happening with Sawyer. Believe me. Sawyer is a disaster. Me and Sawyer *together* is a disaster."

"And yet?" Shelby prompts, then repeats it three more times: "And yet, and yet, and yet." She grins, like she's trying to take the sting out. "That's from a poem, right? I feel like that's from a poem."

I snort. "Probably," I tell her mildly, doing my best to rein it in. I feel like the worst kind of turncoat. Because what happened with Sawyer—one-time thing or not—is bigger than just messing around on Aaron. It's a hundred times more complicated than that: Shelby and her family have only ever taken care of me. *My* family has only ever taken care of me, really, and here I am lying to everyone like it's junior year of high school all over again. I hate it. I'm not doing it. No way.

Shelby only shrugs. "Look," she tells me. "I'm not going to sit here and tell you I don't have any kind of emotional stake here. I love you; I love my stupid brother. Of course I want you guys both to be happy. And of course I want you both to be happy together, if you can."

"Shelby—" I start, and she holds up a hand to stop me.

"But if you *can't*—and I've seen this movie before, I know how stuff goes with you and Sawyer—then as long as you're not shitty about it, I just want to tell you that I'm going to really try and not be shitty about it, either." She shrugs again, like she's tired of this conversation. "He likes you, though. Aaron does. I can tell."

"I like him," I tell her immediately: a reflex, like looking up at the sound of my name. "I like him a ton."

"Well," she says. "Good." Shelby frowns, peers across the diner for Marjorie. "I think I should have ordered extra bacon," she tells me, and we don't talk about it again after that.

28

Before

One damp afternoon at the end of February, I swung by the restaurant during my free period, hurrying—I wasn't working, but I'd left my calc book in the office the night before and wanted to see if I could grab it before I had to get back to school for a newspaper meeting.

"Goddamnit," was the first thing I heard. The restaurant was deserted—the lull between lunch and dinner—and Roger's voice was booming from the office. "Where in the hell have you been?"

"Look, it's not gonna happen again." That was Sawyer. Sawyer was here. I froze. Where had he been? He'd been gone? I hadn't seen him in weeks, since the night I'd stayed over, but I figured he'd been avoiding me.

"You bet your ass it won't. We're not doing this. I'm not going to have police officers calling my house. I'm not having you disappearing for weeks at a time. If you want to live in that squalor and throw away your education and ruin your life, that's your business, but I won't have any part of it."

Police? What the hell had he *done*? I thought of the not-aspirin in his sneaker the night I'd slept over. I thought of his broken hand from last year. I stood there like I'd been hit by lightning, fingertips scrabbling the edge of a tablecloth, feeling absolutely one hundred percent rooted to the floor.

"Get out of my sight, Sawyer. I don't even want to look at you."

I could hear my heart beating, fast and skittish. I crept a little closer to hear. "For God's sake, Dad—" Sawyer started, but Roger cut him off, closed for business.

"I mean it. And don't you dare swear at me."

"Fine." I heard Sawyer get up, and I made for the front door as fast as humanly possible. I tried to keep it as quiet as I could, but the strap of my bag caught on the back of a chair and I had to pause to untangle it. My hands shook as I worked it free.

"Oh," Sawyer said, when he rounded the corner and saw me. He looked *pissed*. "Hey."

"I didn't hear anything," I replied immediately, then backtracked. "I mean. Hi. I, um, left my book."

"In the office," he told me with the vaguest hint of a

smile—blink and gone. He hadn't shaved. "On the desk. I figured that was yours."

"Yeah. Well." I started to move past him, but he caught me by the wrist.

"Where're you going?"

"To get my book," I said, glancing fast, down at our hands, up at his face, back down again. It came out bitchier than I meant.

"Aha." He squeezed once, let go of my arm. "Sounds like a plan."

"Yeah. So. I'm going to go and . . . do that."

Sawyer nodded. "Okay."

I made my way into the office, mumbled a greeting at Roger, grabbed the damn textbook, and fled back outside. Sawyer's Jeep was parked at the curb, and he was leaning against the driver's side, arms and ankles crossed. "Need a ride?" he asked.

I swallowed. "No."

"Want one anyway?"

"Sawyer . . ." The wind was blowing. A car sped by. "I have a meeting."

He shrugged. "Skip it."

"No."

"Why not?"

Are you kidding me? I almost asked. *Because I'm trying to get you out of my system. Because I don't always like the way I act when I'm with you. Because we had sex, and you fell off the face of the earth.*

"Why did the cops call your house?" I asked instead.

Sawyer grinned. "I thought you didn't hear anything."

"I lied."

"Fair enough. Take a ride with me and I'll tell you."

"That's how girls get killed."

"How's that?"

"They get in the car with sketchy guys."

Sawyer just cocked an eyebrow. "A walk, then."

I should have said no. I should have gone to my stupid meeting. I should have done basically anything else besides what I actually wound up doing, but that had never stopped me before when it came to Sawyer, and even as I thought about the abject hell these last few weeks had been, I nodded instead. "A quick one," I said after a minute. "Around the block."

Sawyer nodded once, considering. "Around the block," he said.

We set off in the direction of Grove Street underneath the bright February sky—past a jewelry store, the dry cleaners. This felt a little ridiculous. For a while, neither one of us talked. "So here I am," I told him finally. "Walking. What did the police want?"

Sawyer shrugged. "I got in a little trouble at a bar. Drank too much."

I rolled my eyes before I could stop it. "Do you think that makes you more interesting or something?"

"Hmm?" That got his attention. "What's that?"

"The whole brooding, king-of-pain thing you do." I felt punch-drunk. He was gone already; I had nothing to lose. "I mean, I know girls fall for it. I fell for it. But do you think it makes you more interesting? Because, you know?" I shrugged. "It doesn't."

"No." Sawyer smirked a little, impossible to read. "I guess it doesn't."

"Can I ask you something else?"

"Go ahead," he allowed. "Hit me."

"Why did you waste your time with me?" I was comforted by the rhythm of my boots on the sidewalk, for some reason found courage there. "I mean, those girls . . . the ones at your concert, or the ones who come into the restaurant. I feel like they probably would have . . . I feel like it probably would have taken at least a little less effort with them. Less of a preamble."

Sawyer stopped walking. "I don't want them. I told you that."

"Right. You hate your type."

"Reena, I'm sorry I didn't—"

"It doesn't matter," I said, cutting him off, lying. "I mean, I wasn't really expecting anything from you anyway."

"Ouch." Sawyer exhaled, ran his tongue over his teeth. "You should talk to my dad."

"See? That's what I'm talking about. Poor you. When really you're just full of garbage, and I don't know why I let you get to me like that when I'm going to leave in a few months anyway, and probably never come back in a million years unless it's Christmas and I need someone to buy me a coat. Or something."

"I know you're getting out of here, Reena." Sawyer sighed. "You don't need to play the smart card with me, okay? I know how smart you are. Look," he said, grabbing my wrist again, pulling me around a corner with enough force that my backpack thudded off the side of the building. My heart was banging away behind my ribs. "I got a little skittish, okay? I do that sometimes. Get a little freaked. But I don't want to do that with you. I don't want to get scared."

I huffed a bit. "Stop it."

"I'm serious," he said softly. He had both wrists, and then he slid his grip down so he was holding my hands. "And I know you have no reason to believe me. *I* probably wouldn't believe me. I'd probably think I was full of shit. But I *like* you."

I shook my head, stubborn. "Right."

"I do. I like your brain." Sawyer grinned. "And I like the rest of you, too, if you don't mind me saying so."

Somewhere in my head, a little pilot in a little airplane was doing his best to prevent a fiery crash, shouting *mayday* with no one to hear. "Cut it out," I managed, but by this point I wasn't fooling either one of us. "I'm not kidding."

"Me neither."

"You wouldn't have ever said another word to me if I hadn't been—"

"You're wrong," he interrupted. "It would have taken me a little time, probably. But I would have gotten there."

"I sincerely doubt it."

"I'll have to prove otherwise."

I shifted my weight from boot to boot, uncertain. A silent war was raging in my chest. "I'm serious about the college thing," I told him finally, as if it was some kind of compromise—an escape hatch, a contingency plan, a way to protect my heart. "I'm gonna hear from schools soon. I'm not long for this world."

"Duly noted." Sawyer smiled. "But I want to be with you."

"Do you always get what you want?" I started, but I only got halfway through that particular inquiry because Sawyer was leaning in and kissing me up against the side of the building, warm hands on either side of my face. And in the heat thrown from his body, somehow my questions evaporated into the humid Florida air.

29

After

Aaron takes me out for Mexican a few nights later (I spotted the Celine Dion drag queen in CVS with an *Us Weekly* and a family pack of peanut M&Ms, which makes it his turn to buy). We order margaritas and fish tacos at a table near the band. The restaurant is just around the corner from his place, and we head back there afterward, his steady fingers threaded through mine.

I keep up my end of the conversation like a star, frankly, so chatty I'm borderline manic, but underneath I'm feeling edgy and out of sorts—restless and almost panicky, like I'm pressing at the inside of my skin trying to get out. It's just garden-variety anxiety, probably, but I hardly hear a word he says all night.

The truth: I can't stop thinking about Sawyer.

"Okay," Aaron protests finally, pulling back a bit. We're on the couch in his living room, one of his big hands cupped at the base of my neck. I feel tense from the tips of my ears all the way down to my ankles. "Now *you're* the one who's being weird."

I'm surprised he's noticed, actually, that he's tuned-in enough to be able to tell. I'm not used to that kind of attention. I don't know if I like it or not. "Who, me?" I ask, bluffing, eyes wide and innocent. "I'm fine."

He doesn't believe me—I can tell that he doesn't believe me—but he lets me kiss him for another minute before he tries again. "Reena," he says, rubbing his palm up and down my arm. "Come on. You can talk to me."

I *could* tell him, I think, and I *almost* tell him, but instead I just sort of charge ahead. "What if I stayed tonight?" I ask. "I could go pick up the baby and then come back here, and—" I break off. "You know. Stay."

Aaron looks surprised, like he wasn't expecting that from me. "Sure," he says slowly, a pleased smile spreading over his face. "I'd love that, if that's what you want to do."

"I . . . yeah," I say, voice pitched a little high and desperate even to my own ears. "Yes."

His grin falters a bit, just around the edges. "Are you sure?"

"Aaron—" I open my mouth to reassure him, to say, *Of course, I want to*, but when my answer comes, it's from somewhere inside me that I didn't even know existed, some small, hidden place that wouldn't show up on a map. "I think we should take a break."

Um.

"What?" For a second he looks totally and completely baffled, like I'm speaking a language he's never heard before, and I guess I can't really blame him—fifteen seconds ago I was asking to stay the night. "I don't—" He blinks at me, like he thinks I'm being crazy. "Why?"

"I just—" As soon as it's out of my mouth I know it's true, that whatever I'm trying to do here isn't working. That I've been trying to force a key inside a lock that doesn't fit. "I think I need a break, you know? With everything that's been going on with my family, and school—"

"What? What's going on with *school*?" That's a bullshit explanation, and Aaron knows it. He's still staring at me like he's been blindsided, anger just starting to creep in. "Is this about Sawyer?"

"It's not," I say immediately, still pacing. "I promise it's not."

"Really?" His voice rises, just a shred. "I guess I just don't really get where it's coming from if it's not coming from Sawyer."

"It's coming from me!" I burst out. It's the nearest I've ever come to boiling over with him: I keep my feelings clutched close. "I'm restless, or something, I don't know."

"So let's go somewhere!" he suggests. "Let's go to the Keys or something. We can take Hannah, sit on the beach for a couple of days."

You're not understanding me, I want to tell him. It's so much bigger than that. But how *could* he understand, really? I've never bothered to explain.

The worst part is that I can see myself being happy with Aaron. I can see myself settling down here in a little house with the baby, safe near his family and mine. I'd finish my degree at a state school. I'd wait tables at the restaurant while Hannah grows up. I can see it all laid out for me, as neat and small and pleasant as a weekend in the Keys, and it makes me want to scream like nothing else I have ever experienced. I can't live like this forever. I *can't*.

"That's not the solution," I manage, voice shaking a little—God, already I'm thinking there's an outside chance I'm the stupidest woman ever born. "Look, Aaron, you deserve somebody who's going to be a hundred percent—"

"Don't do that," he interrupts quietly, and that's how I know I've made him angry. "Don't make it about what I deserve. If you don't want to be with me, then fine, but at the very least just tell me the truth."

And because he deserves that much at the very least, I just . . . nod. "I'm sorry," I tell him, shrugging helplessly. I feel like the eye of a hurricane, panicky and calm. "But I think I need to go."

Aaron looks at me for a minute like I've wrecked him, like I'm not the person he thought I was at all. "Yeah," he says finally, shrugging back—the slightest lift of his shoulders, hurt and unconvinced. "I guess you do."

30

Before

"Look at him," Shelby said, crossing a party of five off her list as she stood at the podium on Thursday night—spring break of junior year, the beach teeming, the whole restaurant packed. She gestured toward the bar, looking disgusted. "He thinks he's Don Juan fricking DeMarco. You know, if I was all over the clientele like that, you can bet your ass I'd hear about it. Or, God forbid, if you were."

"What?" I glanced behind me, a basket of bread in one hand and a pitcher of water in the other, and tried to appear as uninterested as humanly possible. I knew Shelby wasn't exactly a giant fan of whatever I had going on with Sawyer. "You call it hanging out, I call it masochism," she was fond of saying, wrinkling her freckly nose. "Potato, po-tah-to."

And maybe it *was* masochism: Sure enough, at this particular moment Sawyer was leaning over the bar, engaged in animated, definitely flirty conversation with two girls I half recognized from school.

"Hm," was all I said before delivering the bread basket, doing my best to ignore the thick, sour shot of jealousy, the dropping sensation in my chest. We weren't even technically *dating*, I didn't think. Two weeks after the scene on the sidewalk, and I still didn't know what we were.

Whatever. It was fine. Sawyer liked girls. Right now he liked these girls.

Except, I realized as I passed Shelby on my way back to the kitchen, they were both holding half-empty wineglasses. "Oh, what an ass," I muttered.

"Nolan, party of four?" Shelby called. She turned to me, perched primly on her stool. "Do it. Cowboy up."

I made my way over to the bar, glared until I caught his attention. "Talk to you for a sec?"

He grinned at me, pulled the rag off his shoulder and dropped it below the counter. "Hey, beautiful."

"Don't call me that," I snapped, as he followed me into the back hallway, near the office.

Sawyer frowned. "Why not?"

"Because it's not nice." I scowled and glanced at the girls, one of whom had SEXY spelled out in rhinestones across her shirt. I hated that. It was like having to explain a joke. "Do you ever think? I mean . . ." I paused, struggled to find words. "Do you ever *think*?"

"I don't—" Sawyer put his hand on my arm. "What are you talking about?"

I wriggled out of his grasp. "Did you serve them?"

"Did I serve who?"

"Those girls." I nodded in their direction. "Helga and Olga, or whatever the hell their names are." I swallowed. "Did you serve them?"

"Yeah," he said, no hesitation at all. He looked confused. "Why?"

"They're in my gym class, Sawyer. They're in high school."

"Oh." He glanced at them, then back at me. "Whoops."

"Whoops?" I sounded shrewish, I knew, but at this point I didn't care. "Really, *whoops*? That's a good way for my dad to lose his liquor license."

"Reena, relax. Nobody's gonna lose their license. I didn't think to check, but—"

"All I'm saying is that maybe if you'd spent a little less time—" I broke off. A little less time *what*, exactly? Looking at hot girls was what, but I couldn't say that out loud.

Sawyer blinked at me. "Wow," he said, after a moment. "Okay. You're pissed."

"Yeah, I am."

"It's sort of cute." Two indentations that just missed being dimples appeared at the corners of his mouth.

"Stop saying stuff like that to me." I scowled. "You know, not every girl in the whole world is impressed by you."

He nodded seriously. "About three-quarters."

My God, he was such a bastard sometimes. I could have screamed.

Shelby swooped in just then, cool fingers curling around my wrist. "Quite the crowd you got over there, chief," she said, nodding at the bar.

He nodded. "I'm on it," he said, looking at me. "Reena—"

"Forget it," I said, shaking my head. "Forget it."

I stomped off, plastered a smile on my face, went back to my tables, and steamed my way through the dinner rush. A couple of hours later I was standing in the back hallway, looking out the window at the patio and drinking a cup of coffee, when I heard him come up behind me. "Slacker," he called me, by way of hello.

"I'm on my break."

"I know. I'm kidding. Listen, Reena, about before—"

"Don't," I interrupted. Already I felt stupid, felt jealous, felt young. "I don't want to talk about it."

"I dropped the ball, okay? I'm sorry. But nobody got hurt."

"Sure. You're right." I started to brush past him, but he grabbed my arm. I pulled away. "Don't."

"Why?" He looked genuinely confused. He looked like Christopher Robin. "Reena, I don't know what your problem is with me tonight, but—"

Just then Sawyer's words were cut off by the loud, shrill whoop of the fire alarm: I saw his face crease, his eyes widen. "Holy shit," he said softly, and when I turned to look behind me, I saw the smoke leaking from the kitchen door.

"Oh my God."

"Shit. Move," he said, flipping the handle on the back door and pushing me through. I could hear people yelling inside.

"Sawyer, my dad—"

"Reena!" He grabbed at my arm and steered me onto the patio. My coffee cup smashed on the pavement. "Go."

It was a grease fire, I learned later, small and fast and stinking. Nobody was hurt, but the damage in the kitchen was enough to close us down for the rest of the weekend. Dark, damp-looking stains crept up the walls like crooked fingers; the whole dining room reeked of oil and smoke.

My father put a hand on my shoulder as I sat alone in a booth a couple of hours later. He'd already sent Shelby and the rest of the waitstaff home. "I have a couple of things to finish up here," he said. He looked exhausted; earlier I'd seen him munching Tums and I let myself worry, for one quick minute, about the stress on his heart. The idea that we could have lost the restaurant made me feel panicky and protective of the place and my father both. I thought of leaving for college in a few months and felt a pang of missing him, even though he was right in front of me. "Can you make it a little longer?"

"I can take her, Leo." That was Sawyer, materializing out of nowhere like a ghost—I'd been half convinced he'd left, no good-bye or explanation, like that night in the hospital all over again. "I can drive Reena home."

My father looked at Sawyer for a long minute, then back at me. Finally he sighed. "Straight home," he said, and I knew he must feel even worse than he looked. "I mean it."

"Straight home," Sawyer promised. "Absolutely."

I nodded, stood up, waved good-bye to my father. Sawyer pushed open the front door of the restaurant with one broad shoulder and swore softly as a blast of wind sliced inside. "Freezing," he said—although it definitely wasn't cold for any place besides Florida—and he took my hand so casually that I wondered if he even knew he'd done it. I swallowed and tried to ignore the petty contact, the shock waves it sent through my bones.

"Don't you have a jacket?" he asked. He wrinkled his pretty nose as we hurried around the side of the restaurant to the parking lot.

"It was in the kitchen." The sky looked heavy, full of thick, purple clouds.

"Fat lot of good it's going to do you in there," he said, opening the passenger door. "There's a sweatshirt in the backseat."

Kid had manners, at least, I thought. Lydia had made sure of that. "I'm okay," I lied.

He slid behind the wheel, groped around in the backseat,

and produced a gray hoodie. He looked annoyed. "Reena, can you forget your principles or whatever for one second and just take it? It'll be a few minutes before the car warms up."

He looked awfully good in the dark, and I found myself nodding. "Okay."

"Good." Sawyer stepped on the gas. "That wasn't so hard, right?"

I didn't answer. "It's going to cost them a lot of money," I said instead.

"That's what insurance is for."

"I guess." I pushed a CD into the stereo. John Coltrane: *A Love Supreme*. I leaned my head against the window as the music started up.

"So," he said. "About before."

I exhaled. "Sawyer, can we please, please, please just forget about before? I was a bitch for no reason. Sometimes I just act that way." That was a lie. I'd had a reason—in fact, I'd had two—but I'd rather have Sawyer think I had a random mean streak than that I'd been jealous of the attention he'd been paying to other girls. Jealousy made you vulnerable. Meanness just made you an ice queen. "Let's just not talk about it, okay? I'm sorry I was nasty to you."

"Don't be sorry. I'm not sorry."

"Of course you're not."

"Why do you keep saying shit like that to me?"

"I don't know. See? Bitch for no reason." I closed my eyes and moved as close to the window as the seat belt would allow. I didn't know what was wrong with me, exactly, but if I kept looking at him I was afraid I'd lose it completely, in front of this boy I had wanted and wanted and wanted for so long that wanting him was built into me, part of my chemical makeup, part of my bones, so that now, even when I had him, I couldn't stop waiting for the other shoe to drop.

"Okay." He was quiet then, let the music play on and on until I had lost track of how long it had been. The engine growled, steady and loud.

"Oh, Christ!" he said next, half laughing but stepping hard on the brakes.

"What?" My eyes flew open as Sawyer's Jeep skidded for half a second in the middle of the deserted road. "What's wrong?"

He nodded at the windshield. "Look."

I squinted. "Is that a . . . ?"

"I think it's a peacock."

It was. A full-grown peacock stood stock-still in the center of Campos Road, tail feathers spread. It was enormous. It blinked once. I peered at it through the glass as Sawyer pulled over. "Do we have peacocks here?"

"I don't think so." He unbuckled his seat belt.

"What are you doing?"

"I just want to see if it has tags or something."

"Like if it's someone's pet? Sawyer, that thing probably has rabies."

"Do birds get rabies?"

"I don't know."

"You're supposed to know smart-person stuff, Reena." He grinned once. "Relax over there." Sawyer got out of the Jeep. "Maybe it's from the reserve or something."

The bird allowed Sawyer to get within several feet, watching him with cautious eyes. Of course he would be a peacock whisperer on top of everything else. Sawyer crouched down. "Hey, buddy," he said.

The peacock didn't reply. They stood there staring each other down for what must have been a full minute, and eventually I couldn't take it anymore. I opened the door.

The motion startled the bird and it let out a loud squawking noise before sweeping its plumes back, a swish like a paper fan snapping shut. It galloped away toward the opposite side of the road with a lot more speed than I would have expected. I blinked. "Did that seriously just happen?"

"You scared him away," Sawyer said mildly, coming over to stand by the passenger side of the car.

"Well, I tend to have that effect on people."

"Nah." He reached down and picked up my hands, pulling me out of the Jeep and onto the grassy shoulder. I could feel the calluses on his palms. "Don't go feeling sorry for yourself."

"Oh, I don't."

"No?" His hands moved up my arms, so lightly, then back down until he was holding mine again. He pulled them up and locked them behind his neck.

"I don't even *like* birds," I said, and Sawyer laughed. I blushed a little, glanced down at the negative space between us. "I like you, though."

"Well," he said, and kissed me. "That's good."

I could still hear Coltrane. I couldn't decide if I was hot or cold. Sawyer's face against mine was soft, like an apology. He was standing closer now, impossibly close, and when I leaned back against the Jeep I could feel the metal through his sweatshirt. "You my girlfriend?" he muttered into my ear, so quiet. I laughed, loud and singing, to say yes.

31

After

Shelby's sitting at a table in back when I get to the restaurant two days after my breakup with Aaron, wiping down the thick folders we use for menus and adding the inserts with tonight's specials. "Don't talk to me," is all she says.

My stomach twists meanly. I hate the idea of fighting with her, of having screwed up the one great friendship in my life: I've been down this road before, and it's lined with total suckage. "Shelby—"

"No," she says, barely glancing up. Her red hair, curled today, falls into her face like a veil. "I need you not to talk to me for a little while. I'm pissed at you. And I don't usually get pissed at you, Reena, I don't have a whole lot of experience doing it, so what I need right now is to just sit here and wipe the crap off these stupid menus and have you let me be until I figure out what I'm going to do about it."

"That's not fair," I protest. I sit down across from her against my better judgment, hoping at least to plead my case. "You said you weren't going to get involved in whatever happened between me and Aaron—"

Shelby looks at me now, rolls her eyes like I'm being stupid on purpose. "I said I wouldn't get involved in whatever happened between you and Aaron as long as you weren't shitty about it, which—*whoops*."

I have the strangest, sharpest flash of Allie just then, that night in front of her swing set a hundred years ago. *You want to win this fight?* Here I am all these years later, still fighting with my best friend about Sawyer. It makes me hate myself a little. It makes me hate Shelby a little, too. "Fine," I say, cavalier as I can manage. "I'm a shitty girlfriend, and a shitty friend."

"Okay, *listen*." Shelby sighs noisily and sets the menus down on the table, an expression on her face like she didn't want to do this but I had to go ahead and push her, so here goes. "I know you've had a rough couple years, Reena. And it sucks in an Alanis Morissette, isn't-it-ironic kind of way that you were like, the least risk-taking person in the history of the world and all this shit still happened to you, but I feel like you did a pretty good job making a life for yourself in spite of that and now that Sawyer's back you're just acting like it's junior year all over again." She ticks off a list on her fingers, like potential side effects of some new, unapproved medication. "You fight, you make up, he's your favorite person, you hate his guts, and maybe it's out of character for you or maybe he's the only person you can really be yourself around, I don't know. That's fine, that's your business—as long as other people don't get dragged down while you're figuring it out."

"I was trying not to drag Aaron down!" I argue, bristling. "That's why I broke up with him in the first place."

Shelby makes a face. "Oh, Reena, don't even kid. You broke up with Aaron because of Sawyer, directly or indirectly. And that's not—" She stops short, shakes her head. "I don't want you to think I'm mad at you for dumping my brother."

"Then why are you mad at me?" I explode. I glance around, self-conscious—there are a couple of businessmen drinking late lunches at the bar, an elderly couple or two eating early dinners. I lower my voice. "Seriously. Why are you mad at me?"

"I'm mad at you—" Shelby sighs again. "I'm mad at you because Sawyer got back here and you like, forgot that you're kickass. It's like now that he's around again all the hard work you did doesn't even matter. And it's not anything against Sawyer, I don't want you to think that, either, especially when everybody in your family thinks he's the Antichrist—"

"Thanks," I interrupt, and Shelby pushes out a noisy breath.

"I just feel," she says crisply, "like you're forgetting yourself over a dude."

Now I'm the one who's pissed. "What am I forgetting, exactly?" I demand. "That I live at home with my father who can't even look at me most days because he legit thinks I'm the whore of Babylon? That I'm a waitress, and I'm probably always going to be a waitress? Or that I'm eighteen years old with a baby to take care of and no conceivable way of getting out of this stupid place?" God, where does she get off, honestly, Shelby with her college scholarship and brainy girlfriend and limitless doctor future, who gets to pack up at the end of the summer and fly thousands of miles from here? What on God's green earth could she possibly know about how *kickass* my life here supposedly is? I shove my chair back noisily, grab my purse off the tabletop. I'm so sick of everyone's opinions I could scream. "Thanks, Shelby," I tell her, nasty as humanly possible. "I'll be sure to keep that in mind."

Sawyer doesn't give up, of course. I've spent my life reading his face like tea leaves, and there was something about the way he looked at me before I went tearing out of his parents' kitchen the other night that let me know that, as far as he's concerned, we aren't done. By the middle of the week, it's only a question of when.

He holds out until Thursday. I'm stretched on the porch swing with my laptop when his Jeep pulls up, and even in the orange half-light I notice again what bad shape it's in these days: It was never a particularly nice car to begin with, and now it's dented like a coffee can, rust speckling the doors. From the sound of it, the muffler is shot.

The hair on my arms perks up even though it's still eighty degrees, and I close the laptop harder than I mean to, not wanting Sawyer to get a look at the screen: While all my magazine subscriptions have lapsed and I've taken my email address off the contact list of every travel website clear across the internet, I've still got a weakness for the blogs. I can waste whole nights clicking through: staring at the bright, hypersaturated images captured by women passing through San Diego or spending a year in Jakarta, reading stories about the food they've been eating and the people they've met along the way. It's torturing myself. I don't know why I go out of my way to do it.

So far, I haven't been able to make myself quit.

"Hey," Sawyer calls softly, making his way up the front walk. He's wearing dark, holey jeans and a T-shirt, and he's left his shoes in the car. His feet are pale against the concrete. There's a giant plastic cup in his hand.

"Okay, I've gotta ask," I tell him, squinting a little across the lawn. "What's with all the Slurpees?"

Sawyer shrugs, tips the cup in my direction. "Cheaper than booze."

I bite the inside of my cheek, wondering about the full story there, but in the end I just leave it alone. "Your teeth are gonna rot right out of your head," I warn him; then: "What were you going to do if I wasn't sitting out here?"

"Who said I was here to see you?" He smiles as he climbs the steps, then sits down sideways on the top one so he's facing me, leaning against my house. It's quiet inside, the windows dark. My father had a stress test this afternoon and went to bed early. Soledad followed not long after that. "I was going to knock on the door."

I raise my eyebrows. "It's late."

"Ah. Woulda thrown rocks at your window then, maybe." He nods at the laptop. "Were you writing?"

"Nope." I shake my head neatly, taking some weird perverse pleasure in saying it. "I told you I don't write anymore."

"I remember you saying that, yeah." Sawyer looks at me carefully. "It's a bummer, though. I thought maybe you were just giving me a hard time."

"Because obviously everything I do is about you?"

Sawyer rolls his eyes. "Is that what I said?" he asks, no particular irritation behind it at all. It sounds like he knows he's got to wait me out and is willing. "Seriously. Did you hear me say that just now?"

"Screw you," I fire back, imitating his tone. His patience riles me up, makes me want to fight him. "What do you want me to do?"

"I want you not to hate me."

"I don't hate you."

"You don't *like* me."

I raise my head and look at him, sitting on the floor like a penitent. I sigh and I tell him the truth. "Sawyer, me liking you has never, ever been the issue."

He smiles—I wish he didn't have such a pretty smile—and changes tactics. "Come sit by me," he says this time.

"Why?"

"'Cause I'm asking you to." He bends over and grabs a handful of shiny white pebbles from the path leading up to the porch, begins to throw them onto the lawn one by one. They skip across the slick green grass as I shake my head.

"Sawyer," I tell him. "No."

"Why not?"

I don't really have a good answer for that one—not one I can tell him, at least—so I get off the swing and perch on the top step. He slides down so he's sitting below me, his chin about level with my knee. "That one is new," I say. There's a deep blue star on his bicep that wasn't there before; it stands out against his skin like a brand.

"Got it in Tucson."

I feel my eyebrows go up, that expression Shelby calls the Big Furrow, when she and I are speaking. "What were you doing in Tucson?"

Sawyer looks up at me, smiles a little. "I worked on a farm."

"Seriously?"

"Soybeans," he tells me, nodding once. "And in a pottery place."

I laugh, I can't help it. "You are out of control."

"What's out of control about that?" he asks, all innocence. "I ran the kiln."

"I see." Of course he did. Probably Sawyer could have any job, do anything, drive a forklift or a race car or turn water into wine. "Where else did you go?"

"Oh, man." Sawyer considers. "Well. New Orleans, right when I left here. LA."

Los Angeles is dirty and full of neon. You can't drink water from the tap in Los Angeles. I know this: not because I've ever been there, but because like so many other things I read it in a book.

"Kansas, for a while."

"Kansas."

"Uh-huh. I'd never been. It's flat there."

"So they tell me."

"Missouri. Flat there, too."

I close my eyes and wonder how I am doing this, how we're talking just like we used to. On the breeze I smell the ocean, close and endless; my pulse ticks like a bomb inside my throat. I hum at him a little, unwilling to commit either way.

"New Mexico," he says, like a litany. After a moment his hand brushes my heel. "Austin."

I try not to notice—I believe in accidents—but then his palm slides up the back of my leg, across the muscles that have settled there since he's been gone. "Hey there," I tell him, and I have to clear my throat to do it.

"Reena," he says, and the sound of him saying my name is a murmur down my backbone that spreads like a flattened palm. He presses his index finger to the crease behind my knee. "I'm not doing anything."

"You really are, though." God, it would be so easy. How is it possible that it would still be so easy? I take a big breath and slide over on the step, away from him.

Sawyer lets go right away, reaches down for more pebbles to throw and, finding none, sets about pulling blades of grass from the cracks in the walkway. "Can I ask you something?" he says after a moment, not looking at me. His hands are very tan. "If I'd asked you to come with me, you think you would have?"

"What, when you left here?" I look at him curiously. "I was already pregnant."

Sawyer laughs a little. "No kidding, princess. That's not what I'm asking. I'm asking if you would have come."

For a minute I don't say anything and the silence is phosphorescent; it feels like the whole world is asleep. A small green lizard scampers by. I think of the maps folded up in my bedroom, the travel guides and atlases I'm never going to use. I think of my girl, who I love more than any breathing creature in this universe, and tilt my head back at the moon in a silent howl.

"No," I tell him finally. "Probably not."

Sawyer nods like I've given him something, confirmed what he suspected from the start. "Yeah," he says. "That's what I thought."

In the morning I wake up and find a pomegranate on my doorstep: red and perfect, round as the world itself.

32

Before

Cade and Stefanie got married the weekend after the restaurant caught fire, standing up in front of God and everyone else and promising their lifelong love and devotion to each other, for richer or poorer, till death did they part. The reception was supposed to have been at Antonia's but, since his kitchen was good and charred, Finch set up shop in ours instead. Soledad and I spent all of Saturday scouring the house, setting up tables in the backyard and filling giant vases with limes for centerpieces. Cade mostly paced.

Now, with only a few minutes to cake time, I was standing on tiptoes in my closet, rooting around on the top shelf for the shoebox containing the yearbook pictures my aunt Carin had to see *right this minute, Reena, bring 'em down.* I'd just pulled out the proofs when Sawyer wrapped his arms around my waist from behind, rested his clean-shaven chin on my shoulder. "Hi," he said.

"Hi." I grinned at my cardigans. I didn't turn around.

"Hi," he repeated, got me farther inside the closet, spun me around to look him in the face. He made for my mouth with no preamble, my back pressing into jackets and jeans: I smelled body spray and tissue paper, and laughed.

"Come to make out with me in a closet?" I asked, taking another step back. "That's very classy, LeGrande."

Sawyer shrugged, grinned a little. "We can make out downstairs, if you'd like."

I snorted. "Tempting, but I'll take a pass."

"I knew it," he said, faux-sulking. "I'm your dirty little secret."

"Oh, you so are."

He smiled. "I missed you."

"I'm really popular at this party."

"So I see." He looked out the door of the closet, glanced at the walls. "Did you paint?"

I smirked, looking around. "Like two years ago I did."

"Oh, man." Sawyer laughed. "I don't even remember the last time I was allowed up here."

"I do," I blurted immediately, then cringed. "That's embarrassing."

"Nah." Sawyer sat down on the floor of the closet and took my hand, pulling gently until I came down beside him. His index finger traced the skinny strap of my dress. "Tell me."

"No." I pushed aside a stack of *Budget Travel* magazines from last year, the pages gone smudgy and curled with repeated handling. There was one issue in particular with an article about street markets in London that I could repeat almost word-for-word—just like I could remember every detail about the last time Sawyer had been in my room. "It's dumb."

"Holdout," Sawyer teased, leaning back against the wall. It was dark down here: Jeans and dresses blocked out the light from the bedroom and it felt like we were pretending, like we were hiding in a fort. Balled up at the back of the closet was an old sweatshirt of Allie's, red with a big white cross on it from the one summer she'd spent lifeguarding. I reached for it like an instinct, pulling at one of the strings on the hood. "Come on."

"I don't know," I said, huffing a little as I thought about it—the night he came for dinner with his parents, the summer after freshman year. "It was a long time ago. Allie was here with me."

"Oh!" he said, remembering. "We played cards?"

I nodded. *Rummy*, I could have added. *Allie borrowed my tank top and you told her she looked old for her age and I wished her away for the first time in our entire friendship while we sat here, thinking maybe you'd notice me after she was gone.*

Sawyer must have seen my face change, because he

grabbed me around the waist in a hurry, tugged me even closer until my head was in his lap. I could feel the muscles in his legs beneath his gray wool pants. There was hardly any give there at all. "Don't get weird."

"I'm not getting weird," I protested, though I felt like I might be about to. I couldn't get over the notion that Allie was the third person in this relationship, that wanting Sawyer and feeling guilty and missing her so much it ground my bones to dust was all bundled up together, the strings on a hoodie pulled as tight as they'd go. I looked at Sawyer to see if he felt it too—if he felt *her*, crammed into my messy closet right along with us—but he was looking at me mildly. *Talking about it doesn't change anything*, I reminded myself. "Tell me something good," I said instead.

Sawyer raised his eyebrows. "Anything in particular?"

"No, I don't know. Anything. Tell me your favorite movie of all time."

"*The Godfather*."

"Really?" I made a face. "Predictable."

"Oh, and what's yours?"

I shrugged, muttered. "*Some Kind of Wonderful*."

"Because *that's* a bold choice."

"Shut up," I said, and he bent down to kiss me again—longer, this time, hands wandering. "Be invisible?" he asked, into my shoulder. "Or be able to fly?"

"Invisible, definitely," I said. "Be deaf or blind?"

"Blind."

"Because of the music thing?"

"Uh-huh. When are you going to let me read your essay?"

I grinned; it was a joke between us now, Sawyer saying he wanted to read the words I'd sent off to Northwestern and me feeling too shy to let him. "Someday," I promised. "We'll see."

We made out for a little while longer, ten hidden minutes with my jeans and my sneakers, the Northwestern T-shirt my father had ordered off the internet despite my protests that I wasn't even in yet. Sawyer ran his fingers through my hair. His free hand drifted down and I tensed for just one second, but in the end he just squeezed my knee, glanced up at the contents of my closet, and nodded. "You've got a lot of space in here," he said, barest hint of a grin. "I wish my closet was this big."

"To accommodate all your ironic concert T-shirts?"

"Think you're smart, huh?" he asked, fingertips seeking my sides. I scrambled up before he could tickle me, grabbed his arm to pull him out of the closet. "Come on, Slick," I said, smiling. "I need to go back downstairs."

"Mmm," he said, not moving. "No, you don't."

"I really do. My father is going to come looking for me." I grinned. "With his shotgun."

"Your father doesn't own a shotgun."

"Sure he does. He uses it on guys who try to make out with me in closets."

"Duly noted." Sawyer grinned back, and moved on. "Biggest pet peeve?"

I sighed, crouched down again so we were at eye level. "People who mispronounce the word *nuclear*."

He laughed. "English nerd."

"Favorite book?"

"*The Sound and the Fury*."

"You're lying."

"I'm not completely illiterate, you know."

"No, of course not." I blushed. "I just thought you were going to say, like—"

"*Catcher in the Rye*?"

"Well," I said, embarrassed. "Yes, actually."

Sawyer leaned toward me. "I'm not that predictable. First kiss?"

"Elliot Baxter, at the eighth-grade dance. What did you really pick up from your drummer that day?"

Sawyer frowned. "Okay," he said suddenly, up off the carpet, attempting to climb over me and out the closet door. "You're right. Time to go back downstairs."

"Yeah, that's what I thought." I dropped Allie's sweat-shirt and let him pull me out with him, slightly dizzy. We stood up in the light of my bedroom, sudden and bright. "Painkillers, right?"

"I—" Sawyer raised his eyebrows, surprised, and I knew I wasn't wrong. "What makes you think that?" he asked.

I shrugged. "I have eyeballs," I told him. Also, I had Google. "I'm not dumb."

"I never thought you were." He didn't apologize, or try to deny it. Instead he wrapped both arms around my shoulders and squeezed, friendly and familiar. "I don't do it a lot," he promised. "Every once in a while."

How often is *that*? I wanted to ask him. I thought of Lauren Werner and long nights at the Prime Meridian, of the intervention shows Shelby liked to watch. From what I'd seen in movies and on TV, Sawyer didn't *seem* like an addict—someone who sweated all the time and stole his parents' DVD player. Still, here were such huge swaths of his life I didn't know anything about—whole paragraphs blacked out of wartime letters, movies modified to fit this screen. Who *are* you? I wanted to demand, but instead I only nodded, tucking this piece of information, and everything it might mean, into the back of my head for further consideration and trying to ignore the sinking sensation in my stomach. I needed him not to be too good to be true.

"Oh Jesus," I said then, catching a glimpse of my hair in the mirror above the dresser, photos and jewelry box and deodorant scattered across the surface. Forty-five minutes' worth of Soledad's careful handiwork was completely and totally undone. "See what you did?"

He watched as I repaired the worst of the damage, kissed me on the forehead, and smiled. "You're pretty cute."

I stuck my tongue out at him. "All right, you drug-addled hair-wrecker. Let's go."

"Right behind you, you language-obsessed intellectual elitist."

I waited five more minutes after Sawyer went downstairs, snuck down as unobtrusively as I could manage. He wasn't a secret, I told myself, dirty or otherwise, but this was Cade's day, and I was happy. The last thing I needed was another grave, disappointed look from my father, the nagging feeling of something not right behind my ribs.

I grabbed a slice of wedding cake, made my way through the yard. Carin grabbed my arm as I passed by. "Reena," she said curiously, an expression on her face like I'd changed inexplicably in the thirty minutes since she'd last seen my face. "What happened to the photos?"

33

After

Fighting with Shelby makes me totally miserable. I keep going to text her—for all kinds of different reasons, stupid regular stuff, to let her know that *Center Stage* is on cable or to complain about the new Taylor Swift song lodging itself deep inside my brain—before realizing we aren't speaking and flinging my phone back onto the couch. I sulk. I remember this feeling from the year before Allie died, the weird emptiness of not having a best friend to tell things to. How it's lonelier than any breakup could ever be.

We work the same busy dinner shift at Antonia's one night, two big eight-tops and a party back in the banquet room. I catch her by the wrist by the bar during what's as close to a lull as we're going to get, my fingers curling around the half dozen bracelets she's wearing. "Shelby," I start, then completely fail to follow it up in any kind of meaningful way.

Shelby raises her eyebrows, an armful of napkins and a look on her face like whatever I have to say, it better be good. "What?" she asks shortly.

I hesitate. I want to ask her how her week's going; I want to get the latest Hipster Cara updates. I want to tell her I'm sorry, that I feel like one of those horrible girls who can't make friendships work with other girls, that I miss her a crap ton and I didn't mean to screw with her brother and I'll do anything she wants to make it up to her. I want to fix this in the worst, stupidest way, but I don't know how to do it, and in the end I just shake my head. "Forget it," I say, chickening out at the last possible second. "Never mind."

"Okay." Shelby rolls her eyes at me like she both expected this and finds it colossally lame. "Have it your way, Reena," she says finally, and after a second I let go of her arm.

The week creeps along. I'm restless and edgy; Hannah and I cruise the highway for hours every night. "You're wasting gas," Cade points out, but I just shrug, handing my credit card over to the pale, skinny attendant like a crack addict looking for a fix. The road rumbles under my feet: *keep going, keep going, keep going.*

I drive.

Five o'clock on Sunday and Soledad is cooking; the

kitchen smells delicious, a big pot of yellow rice simmering on the stove and the counter strewn with ingredients I know she pulled from memory. Soledad never makes anything from a book. "Are you going to be around for dinner?" she asks as I pull a bottle of water from the fridge. "The LeGrandes are coming over."

I tense. "Why?"

"What do you mean, why?" she asks, looking at me oddly. "To eat."

"No, I know." It was an idiotic question. Roger and Lydia still come to dinner from time to time, though usually Hannah and I do our best to scoot out the back door before they get here—it's always seemed cleaner to do it that way, and it's not as if anyone's ever encouraged us to stay. I have no earthly clue what they talk about.

"Are you not seeing Aaron this weekend?" Soledad asks me now, her expression all practiced-casual as she pulls a covered dish out of the oven, and I do my best to match it in return. He's left a couple of messages on my cell phone since I broke up with him. So far, I haven't called him back.

"Um, nope," I say, fussing a little with the magnetic letters on the fridge. REENA, I spell, red and green and yellow. HOME. "We're taking kind of a breather. Can I help?"

"Here, keep stirring this. It's sticking." She moves so I can have the stove to myself, a whiff of lilacs and vanilla as she passes by. "What do you mean, 'a breather'?"

"Hmm?" I ask, stalling, banging the wooden spoon

around in the pot with more force than is strictly called for. "I don't know. Just, like, some time apart."

"Really? That's too bad." Soledad throws some cherry tomatoes into her wooden salad bowl, then sticks one in her mouth and one into mine for good measure. "I like Aaron," she says, swallowing. "I think he's good for you."

"No shit," I say, then, "Shit. Sorry. Just, you know, you and everybody else."

"Ah." She doesn't say anything after that. The silence hangs suspended, a drop of blood in a bowl of milk. I wait, though, patient, and finally Soledad sighs. "Reena, about Sawyer."

Right away I don't like where we're heading. "Sol, please, I don't want to—"

"I know there is a certain kind of . . . *romance* in him being here. Like a movie. But I just need you to remember what the last few years have been like, all right?" Soledad has moved on to onions now. Her thin, graceful hands chop and dice. "For everyone. For your father."

"For my *father*?" I blink at her.

Soledad works steadily, the efficient sound of steel on wood. "It's been hard on everyone, is what I'm saying. And we all might have done things differently, and—" Her face softens and she is looking at me with compassion, which is why I am so surprised when she says, "Please just *think* this time, sweetheart."

I just stand there for a moment, dumb like an ox. Then

my eyes widen. "Are you fucking kidding me?" I ask quietly, and I am sure she's going to scold me for my dirty mouth, but instead she just puts the knife down on the counter and shakes her dark, beautiful head.

"No, Serena," she answers calmly. "I'm fucking not."

I've gotta go.

I don't know where—Shelby's, maybe, if she'll even talk to me, or the highway, or in my car right off a cliff—but out of this house is the first step. I pluck Hannah from her playpen and am rooting around in the couch cushions for my keys when the doorbell rings, and when Roger and Lydia come inside, Sawyer is right behind them.

Wearing a *tie*.

I stare for a minute, like the baby does when she's trying to make sense of something she's never seen before. I laugh one short, hysterical laugh.

"What happened?" he asks, before hello.

"Nothing." I lie as a reflex. "Hi."

Sawyer isn't satisfied. He nods at the keys in my hand. "Where are you going?"

Roger and Lydia are looking at me expectantly; Soledad is coming through the kitchen door. "Nowhere," I say, and it's final, like the sound of something slamming. I put the keys back down and follow them inside.

34

Before

I was walking to school one sunny April morning, totally lost in my own brain, trying to untangle a particularly stubborn knot in my headphones and planning the article I was going to pitch Noelle that afternoon, about teen travel tours for summer. When a horn honked behind me, I jumped like crazy, iPod skittering to the sidewalk. I whirled around, spooked, and there was Sawyer's Jeep parked at the curb.

"Did it break?" he called from the driver's seat. He'd pulled over a half block from my house, right along my usual route. He was wearing sunglasses, but even from over here I could see that he was laughing. Sawyer had a really excellent laugh.

I scooped the iPod up off the ground and examined it

for permanent damage, but other than a couple of scratches it seemed okay. "No harm done," I called back, shaking my head as I made my way over to the driver's side door. "Did I just walk right past you?" I asked, embarrassed.

"Uh-huh." Sawyer reached a hand out and kissed me through the open window, warm morning sun gleaming off the chrome on the Jeep. He was wearing a faded blue T-shirt that looked like it had been washed a million times, as if it might pull apart like cotton candy if you tugged on it even a little. "You," he pronounced, fingers laced through mine and squeezing, "are tightly wound."

"I am not!" I protested, holding up the headphones and shifting my weight a bit to accommodate my backpack. I had to bend at a weird angle to lean inside the Jeep. "I was concentrating."

"Clearly." Sawyer laughed again, his face tipped close enough to mine that our noses brushed together when he moved. I could feel sweat starting to prickle pleasantly on the back of my neck. "So here's the thing," he said, this quiet confidential voice like he was going to tell me something really exciting but I had to promise to keep it just between the two of us. "I woke up thinking about waffles."

I snorted. "Is that a code word?" I asked, teasing.

Sawyer raised his eyebrows. "Do you want it to be?"

I shrugged and got a little closer, nudging the sunglasses down the bridge of his nose with one finger. Inside the car it smelled like him. "Maybe," I admitted.

"Maybe." Sawyer tilted his chin in my direction, brushing a row of kisses along my bottom lip. He smiled and I could feel it in my teeth. "Get in and find out."

God, I wanted to. My stomach swooped sideways with the force of how much, but: "I can't," I told him, shaking my head. I exhaled a little, like breaking a spell. "I have homeroom in, like, fifteen minutes."

"So?" Sawyer asked. His mouth followed mine as I pulled away, still grinning. "Skip it."

I laughed, straightening up all the way and wiping my suddenly clammy hands on the back of my jeans. I was still holding my iPod. "I can't just skip it," I said—lamely, sure, but I really couldn't. I had a quiz on the first half of *Anna Karenina* and an appointment with Ms. Bowen to talk about internships for the summer, plus the newspaper meeting and a lab report to turn in. I needed to get to school—and soon, actually, if I didn't want to be totally late. "I can't."

Sawyer, apparently, was in no hurry at all. "Sure you can," he promised easily. "Here, I'll show you. Just get in the car, and then I'll hit the gas, and then boom: waffles."

I wrinkled my nose, bright sun and the headphones tangled up in my fingers, worse than they had been to start with. "Just like that, huh?" I asked.

"Just like that," he agreed.

I didn't doubt that for him it was exactly that simple: When Sawyer wanted to do something, he did it. End of story. He didn't stop to think about everything that could possibly go wrong. I wondered what it was like to be that kind of person—the kind that wasn't always worried about what might happen, about what people might think or every disaster that could potentially befall him a dozen steps down the road. He just . . . acted.

I thought again of my internship meeting and the newspaper article I'd been so psyched to pitch barely five minutes ago, but I could feel my resolve weakening the longer I stood there and looked at Sawyer's face. Even after dating a full month, it was thrilling to have him show up like this, knowing that he'd been thinking about me enough to come and seek me out. That he thought I could be the kind of person who just acted, too.

"You're a bad influence," I said finally, feeling a guilty, delighted smile spread across my face as the idea of spending a full, *secret* day off with Sawyer started to firm up in my mind. I glanced over my shoulder, then down at my feet, so he wouldn't see how excited I was. "I mean it."

Sawyer nodded ruefully. "I know," he said. For a minute it looked like maybe he felt legitimately bad about that, like he thought he was dragging me down in some way. Then he grinned like the Fourth of freaking July. "Get in."

It turned out waffles did actually mean waffles. We went to a trashy Denny's on Federal Highway and ordered big plates of them covered in whipped cream and blueberries, a giant side of bacon between us. Sawyer's warm knee pressed into mine under the table. We sat there half the morning surrounded by a bunch of senior citizens, a couple of moms with noisy kids in a sticky-looking booth by the window. Cheesy Michael Bolton music piped in through the speakers. Being here at such a weird time felt like vacation, like we were a lot further from home than just fifteen minutes: It was as if this was some great trick we were pulling off together, him and me against the world. I knew that was stupid—it was cutting school, not bank robbery or international intelligence gathering—but still, it wasn't exactly an unattractive fantasy.

"So, how many people in here do you think are spies?" Sawyer asked, taking a long gulp of orange juice and grinning like he'd read my mind. "It's the perfect cover, right?" He dragged a piece of bacon through a puddle of syrup. "Nobody would ever suspect."

"Except you," I pointed out, laughing. I was hugely full but I wanted to keep eating anyway, to hang out in this crappy diner for the foreseeable future. To drink so much coffee I began to vibrate.

"Well, and you, now." He nodded at an old lady at a table not far from ours, flowered housedress and bright orange Crocs. "Take her, for instance. You think she's just sitting there minding her own business eating her Grand Slam, but the whole time she's a special operative for the CIA." Sawyer raised his eyebrows ominously. "I'm just saying, she could be into some real crazy James Bond shit."

"Oh, yeah?" I leaned in close across the table. "What's her alias?"

"Moons Over My Hammy," Sawyer replied without missing a beat. He nudged my leg with his under the table, hooking one ankle around mine. "Duh."

Once Sawyer paid the bill we headed back to his place without really talking about it, like we both sort of knew that's where we'd end up. Purple-green weeds sprang up from between the cracks in the walk. Inside it was quiet and empty-seeming, all his various roommates out or asleep, that vaguely abandoned feeling houses get in the middle of a weekday. The air smelled a little close. There was a half-finished bag of Doritos on the grimy-looking futon and beer bottles scattered on the coffee table, plus one that had toppled over without anybody bothering to wipe its contents up off the floor. Sawyer grinned guiltily. "I, uh. Didn't clean this time," he admitted.

"It's fine," I said quickly, although in truth it bummed me out a little to think about him living here day in and day out. I thought of Roger and Lydia's airy, immaculate Craftsman, full of refurbished antiques and plush area rugs that squished pleasantly under the soles of your feet. I wondered if Sawyer had a long-term plan.

I didn't have a whole lot of time to mull it over, though, because in the next second he was wrapping his arms around me from behind, kissing all along the place where the back of my neck met my shoulder. I shivered inside my gray tank top. "You still like me?" he asked quietly, mouth tipped down low right next to my ear as he walked me in the direction of the staircase. "Even though I live with a bunch of slobs?"

And—yeah. I really, *really* did.

Afterward we napped for a while, Sawyer's body warm and solid under the covers and both of us in and out of sleep. He traced the freckles on my shoulders with one gentle thumb. I wanted to wrap him up inside the comforter and keep him for days and days, for the two of us to just hang out here forever; I was terrible at napping, normally, but with Sawyer everything felt easy and relaxed.

We were making out again, sleepy, Sawyer shifting his weight back on top of me and the slow slick of his mouth along my jaw, when his bedroom door banged open: "Yo, you home?" Iceman asked loudly, then: "*Whoops*. Sorry, kids."

I froze, hugely, hideously embarrassed, and let out a startled gasp. I'd put my tank top back on a little earlier to get some water, so it wasn't like he could see anything, exactly, but still. Sawyer's shirt was off; my hair was probably a disaster. We were definitely in the middle of something pretty specific. I felt my face flush hot and red.

Sawyer, though, seemed basically unbothered. "Hey, dickhead," he replied, rolling over and peering at Iceman like they'd run into each other in the kitchen or on the street. "Who used all the toilet paper, huh?"

Iceman snorted. "Oh, yeah, sorry, that was totally me. Here, I can make it up to you." He dug into his pocket for a minute and produced a baggie like the one I'd found in Sawyer's shoe the night I stayed over, maybe half a dozen pills inside. Tossed it on the bed. "S'what I came up here to give you in the first place." He waved to me then, like maybe it was just occurring to him how enormously awkward it was for him to be standing there looking at us like a couple of zoo animals. "Hi, Reena," he said.

"Nice," I said to Sawyer once Iceman was finally gone, rolling my eyes and throwing back the covers. I felt vulnerable and kind of gross, like whatever snow globe I'd spent the day inside had been unceremoniously shattered. For the first time since I'd gotten in Sawyer's car this morning, it occurred to me that maybe I should have gone to school after all.

"What?" Sawyer frowned up at me, still lying on his back with one arm tucked up behind his head. "Don't be upset. He didn't know you were in here. It was an honest mistake."

"He stayed and chatted for like twenty minutes!"

"He did not." Sawyer smiled up at me, winning. Held a hand out for me to take. "Okay, he kind of did. I'm sorry, you're right. I should have told him to get lost right away."

I huffed out a noisy breath, but I took his hand anyway. Sawyer tugged until I was sitting down on the bed again, tucked against the angle of his body. I picked up the baggie that was nestled in the sheets. "How long will it take you to go through these?" I asked, counting them out with my index finger through the plastic. I was strangely curious about them—they looked so innocuous, like aspirin or Altoids or something—but at the same time just being in the same room with them made me nervous. I'd never seen Sawyer use. "Hm?" I prodded. "How long?"

Sawyer shrugged into the pillows like he didn't want to answer. He was still holding on to my hand. "Long enough," he said after a minute. I didn't ask any more questions after that.

We came downstairs for food a little while later and found Iceman and Lou sacked out on the futon, *Judge Judy* blaring on the TV and the smell of weed thick in the air. "Sorry again!" Iceman called gracelessly. I cringed. "You want in on this?" he asked Sawyer, holding up the bowl. Then, to be polite I guess: "Reena?"

"Oh." I shook my head before I even really thought about it, as instinctive as not taking candy from strangers. "Nah, I'm okay," I said.

"You sure?"

I was. Sawyer wasn't, though, so I settled myself in a beanbag chair in the corner while he smoked, watching a lady in a lime-green tube top argue for child support on Channel 5. "Don't pee on Judge Judy's leg and tell her it's raining," Lou said. Sawyer laughed.

I picked at my cuticles, bored and antsy. All of a sudden I was acutely aware of everything I'd blown off. I wasn't somebody who skipped quizzes or didn't show up for meetings, not ever. By the time Judge Judy awarded tube top lady her back payments, I could feel a full-on anxiety attack nipping at my heels.

I checked my watch—it was only two thirty. If I left right this minute, I could make my newspaper meeting, at least. Maybe catch Ms. Bowen before she left for the day and explain to her that I'd been sick but felt better now. I looked around for my backpack, trying to remember if I'd brought it upstairs when we came in, and my fidgeting caught Sawyer's attention. "S'wrong?" he asked, already mellowing out. I wondered if hanging out with me all day was something he needed to mellow out from.

"I should go," I murmured, trying to climb out of the beanbag as gracefully as possible. "It's getting late."

"What?" Sawyer frowned at me from where he was sprawled on the dingy carpet, ankles crossed and back against the arm of the futon. "Why, 'cause of the weed?"

Right away I blushed, glancing at Iceman and Lou. I didn't want them to think I was some uptight killjoy—even if I kind of felt like one, like somebody who couldn't enjoy something as ostensibly harmless as cutting one day of school. "No," I said quickly, "it's not that, I just—"

"It kind of seems like it's that," Sawyer interrupted.

"Okay, well," I said, finally laying eyes on my backpack—it was right near the bottom of the staircase, where I'd dropped it before Sawyer and I stumbled up to his bedroom earlier. I got up and hefted it over my shoulder. "It's not. I just skipped a lot of stuff today, is all. I'll see you at work, okay?" I headed for the front door, backpack clutched close like the protective shell of a turtle. It felt like this day had turned around really fast.

Sawyer caught up with me on the tiny front stoop of the bungalow—a good thing, probably, since I'd realized as I crossed the threshold that I had no idea how I was getting home. "Reena," he said, scrubbing a hand over his face. "Come on, don't leave mad."

"I'm not mad," I said, and I wasn't, really. I didn't know exactly what I was. I couldn't figure out how you could go from feeling so close to a person one minute to not being sure if you even knew them the next. "I honestly do need to go. I had a lot of fun today, seriously."

Sawyer wrapped me up in a hug instead of answering, the blue T-shirt warm and soft against my cheek. I felt myself calm down some as soon as he touched me. Let myself sink into it. "Okay," he said finally, mouth at my temple and not sounding entirely convinced. "I did, too."

35

After

It's ballsy, Sawyer coming here for dinner. To be honest, I'm almost impressed. For a second I thought my father might actually slug him, but if Sawyer notices, he doesn't let on—smiling affably, telling stories, everybody's favorite prodigal son. I wonder what was going through Lydia's mind when she invited him, if it's so important to trick him into believing we're all one big happy family. If she's trying to convince him not to take off again.

We sit at the table, get the baby settled in, fill our glasses and our plates. My father recites a quick, simple prayer. I'm only half listening to the conversation around me—Lydia's low opinion of the new Woody Allen movie they saw recently, Soledad's laugh like the tinkle of wind chimes. It sounds like I'm hearing it from the bottom of a well.

"Do you feel all right, Serena?" Lydia asks as she hands me the basket of rolls; her short nails are painted a deep, glamorous crimson. For a second I imagine throwing the entire thing at her head. "You're very quiet."

"I'm fine," I murmur, glancing down at my lap. My own nails are ragged, cuticles bitten down so far they're nearly bloody.

We clink. We eat our dinners. I sit back in my chair. I feel as trapped as the very first days of my pregnancy, like I could literally burst into flame where I sit and all anybody would say is *Boy, some weather we're having*. Like possibly I don't even exist.

Hannah's not hungry, either: She's unhappy with her rice, making a mess as she spreads it across the tray of her high chair, waving her arms in the air and chattering noisily. After a moment, she begins to whine. "Uh-uh," she argues, completely unwilling to be distracted by anything I have to offer, pushing irritably at my hand when I try to tempt her with a buttered roll. "*No*, Ma."

"She's tired," I explain when the whining turns to a shriek, high-pitched and grating. I remember that day at the Galleria and think *Oh, baby, please, not now*. "She didn't nap today."

"I'll take her," Lydia says, like it's the most natural thing in the world, like she's been comforting my baby for the last year and a half and not ignoring us completely like some minor and vaguely embarrassing faux pas, the way you ignore a huge green chunk of spinach wedged in the teeth of your dinner companion. She reaches for Hannah even as I put my napkin on the table, those perfect hands under her pudgy baby arms.

"I've got it," I say, standing too quickly. I can feel the blood rushing to my face.

Lydia ignores me, undoing the high chair's safety clasp. "Serena, honey, it's fine—"

"Don't."

That stops her. It stops everybody, as a matter of fact: The whole table is suddenly silent, save my tempestuous daughter's wail.

"All right, then," Lydia says softly. She holds her hands up and sits down.

"I'm sorry." I'm embarrassed, but more than that I'm angry. I feel it pushing up from somewhere deep inside of me, red and powerful. I try to explain. "I just—you see how this looks to me, don't you? You suddenly taking an interest after all this time?"

Lydia cocks one carefully maintained eyebrow. "I don't think I understand."

"Reena," my father begins. "Let it alone."

"No, Leo," Lydia says, cool as the other side of the pillow in the middle of the night. "If Serena has something to say, by all means let her say it."

"You haven't wanted anything to do with Hannah, or with me, in *years*," I tell her shrilly. I think of broken dams, walls caving in. "You don't talk to me. Nobody talks to me. *About* me, maybe, but maybe not, even. I wouldn't know, because this is the first Sunday since Hannah was born that I've been invited to dinner." I glance at Sawyer, my gaze darting like a cornered animal. "So, you know, thanks for getting me back into the club."

"Reena—" he starts, but I ignore him, looking at our parents instead. Hannah's still crying. This is crazy—this is probably an enormous mistake—but the truth is I'm just getting started. Already I feel more powerful than I have in years.

"I'm not an idiot," I say, lifting the baby out of her high chair and bouncing her a bit on my hip. It's useless, though; there's no way to calm her when I'm this riled myself. "I screwed up, but I'm not generally stupid. Don't think I don't know how you feel about me. You've all made it pretty clear how you feel."

"Wait, what?" Sawyer breaks in again. He looks at his mother. "What did you guys *do*?"

"I certainly did not—"

"Well, Hannah belongs to both of us." I look around the table accusingly, Roger to my father to Lydia and back again. "Me and Sawyer. We had sex. We're not married. I'm sorry. And I know it's incredibly offensive to all of you, and that's fine, but I can't sit here and put on a show and . . .

repent anymore. I've been repenting for years." I pause for a second, shrugging angrily. "Nobody even threw me a baby shower!"

"Serena," says my father. His face has gone dark as his tomatoes, his eyebrows drawn together in a thick line. "Calm down."

"I *can't*," I shoot back, but even as the words come out I can hear my voice start to break. God, I don't want to cry—crying now is going to make me look crazy, is going to undermine everything I'm trying to say—but I can't help it. I'm so hugely tired of carrying all of this inside me, all my guilt and anger and loneliness. I can't do it anymore. It's too much. "I'm sorry that I disappointed you, Daddy, and I'm sorry that I brought shame on this family and that you hate me and you think I'm a slut and a whore and every other filthy thing." I'm sobbing now, big and ugly, Hannah clutched tight in my arms. "And maybe I deserve it and maybe I don't but the point is I can't do anything *about* it now. I really wish you would just forgive me already. How can you be my father and not forgive me?" Hannah is thrashing, grabbing at my hair, and I can't do a single thing to soothe her. "I mean it! Why did you only love me when I was good?"

I look at Soledad then, her lovely face blurry and distorted through my tears. "And *please just think this time*?" I shake my head, desperate. "Really? Like I don't know how hard it's been? Like it hasn't been hard for me?"

"Can someone please tell me what the hell is going on?" Sawyer demands. He's losing it himself, standing up now, a hint of the temper I remember from when we were together. His eyes are dark and angry.

"Ask *them*," I tell him, hitching up my screaming baby, leaving my dinner uneaten and heading for the door. "I'm done."

"Reena!" Sawyer is following me. "Reena, wait." He catches the driver's side door just as I'm about to slam it, and I grimace.

"I almost took your fingers off."

"Nah." He smiles what would be a really fantastic smile if it reached the top half of his face. "Got quick reflexes."

"So I recall."

He opens the door wider, maneuvers himself in between so I can't try and close it again. "Let me come with you, okay?"

I shake my head, snuffling; there's definitely snot on my face. I am not a pretty girl these days. "This is a long ride."

"That's okay."

"I do the highway."

"I don't mind."

My insides feel like they've been scraped with a fork, hollowed out like a spaghetti squash. I don't know how this got so out of control. I shrug and wipe my face, jerk my head toward the passenger side. "So," I tell him. "Get in."

We're ten minutes onto 95 before either of us says anything, and when he does his voice is quiet, the ocean at low tide. "Nobody threw you a baby shower?" he asks.

"No." I shake my head. "But that was a stupid thing to say. A stupid example. It just popped into my head."

"It's not stupid. It blows."

"Yeah, well. I am very, very disappointing to my family." I concentrate on the road and try to sound collected, matter-of-fact, resigned. I'm humiliated to have lost it the way I did; I don't act that way, not ever. I feel like I need to button up as quickly as I can. "And to yours, actually."

He shakes his head. He looks disgusted. "I don't know why I'm shocked. Of course they pulled all that Catholic bullshit with you. Madonnas and whores and whatever the hell else they can think of to make you feel two inches tall. They're hypocrites, all of them."

"No, they're not."

"Can you please get mad?"

"Obviously I'm mad, Sawyer!"

"I know." Sawyer shakes his head, scrubs at his hair with restless hands. "I'm sorry. It's just—the more I think about it, the more pissed off I get."

"That's why I don't think about it."

"You're full of crap."

I shrug. "Only a little."

"Why did you put up with it?"

"Well, we can't all run away," I say, then realize that

there's a fine line between flip and bitchy, and I probably just crossed it. "Sorry," I tell him, sighing. Sometimes it feels like my entire relationship with Sawyer has been one long apology. "I didn't mean that how it sounded."

"Sure you did," he says affably.

"Yeah, I kind of did." I'm wrung out like a washcloth. I almost laugh. "Anyway, I had nowhere to go."

"I wish you'd told me. When I first got here, I mean. I wish you'd said."

I glance over my shoulder and change lanes. "That's your family, Sawyer."

"Yeah, well." He reaches behind him to retrieve Hannah's cloth bunny, which she's dropped on the floor. Hannah grins. "You're my family, too."

We drive for over an hour, not really talking. Sawyer hums under his breath. It feels weirdly peaceful to be in the car with him, steadying, like he and Hannah and I are in our own little climate-controlled bubble, totally unbothered by the world rolling by outside. I know eventually we'll have to go back and face the music—I know that it can't possibly last—but Hannah's asleep, and Sawyer's breathing beside me, and for a while it's nice to pretend.

I'm pulling back into the driveway when Cade's wife, Stefanie, comes running out onto the front walk, her plump face worried and drawn. I blink in surprise: Stefanie wasn't at dinner. A second after that I'm hit with a cold blast of fear. I get the door open as quick as I can, my thoughts tumbling over each other and the memory of my phone ringing the night Allie died right at the center, like the eye of a devastating storm.

"What happened?" I demand loud enough to wake the baby, fumbling to unbuckle my seat belt and climb out. "Stef."

Stefanie holds her hands up, shakes her frizzy blond head. "Reena," she says, before I can even get out of the car. "It's your dad."

36

Before

Ms. Bowen wasn't thrilled with me for skipping our meeting. "That was really unlike you, Reena," she chided, a way colder tone than she'd ever used with me before. She was wearing her glasses today, a smart-looking tortoiseshell pair. "Not to mention disrespectful to me."

"I know." I felt myself wilt a bit under her gaze. "I'm sorry." On top of that, my AP Lit teacher was a hard-ass, and when I couldn't produce a doctor's note he docked me two full letter grades on the Tolstoy quiz.

I stared at the bright red *C* at the top of my make-up quiz, feeling sick. This definitely wouldn't happen again, I promised myself, trying to avoid a full-on freak-out in the middle of the hallway. I couldn't keep letting Sawyer distract me from what I was actually supposed to be doing if I was serious about graduating early.

My resolve didn't last long, though: A week or so later and I was a third of the way through a busy-ish dinner service at the restaurant, heading back to the kitchen for another basket of bread for the carb-happy tourists at a two-top in the back, when Sawyer yanked me by the wrist into the office.

"Wha—" I started, eyes going wide, but he was busy shoving the door shut behind us and then pressing me up against it, a kiss like a leash of deer rushing fleetly through my chest. He tasted like chewing gum, and under that like beer. "So how's your night going, honey?" I murmured against the sharp, sleek line of his jaw.

Sawyer grinned once, hard and bright, two warm hands against the base of my ribs where my button-down had come untucked (or, more accurately, where he'd untucked it). "My night's great," he said, and kissed me again.

I closed my eyes and sank into it a little, my fists opening and closing against the starchy fabric of his work shirt. Sawyer was a good kisser. He had one hand behind my neck now, fingertips in my hair and tugging my head back just the slightest bit so he could get to the pale, sensitive skin underneath my collar; he was working one knee ever so slowly between mine when the door to the office opened hard behind me.

I stumbled forward into Sawyer, then turned around.

There was my father, eyes dark and angry, jaw clenched hard. For a second, all he did was stare.

"Um," I said, hand flying to my mouth before I could quell the impulse, wiping with the back of my hand. Behind me, Sawyer cleared his throat. "We were just—"

"Don't." Two bright pops of color stood out against the skin on either side of his face. He opened his mouth and then shut it again, like it was taking every ounce of human restraint not to let both of us have it at the top of his lungs in front of the Holy Father and the seventy-five guests in the dining room. "Get back on the bar before I fire you," he managed finally, looking at Sawyer. "Now."

Sawyer nodded obediently, smoothed down the front of his shirt, and stepped around me toward the door. I moved to follow, my face even redder than my father's, but he got a hand around my elbow, tight enough to hurt. "You," he said quietly. "You stay."

"Leo—" Sawyer started.

"Sawyer, I swear to God that if you don't get out of my sight in another second, you're going to see a side of me you've never seen before, and I promise you you're not going to like it."

Sawyer went.

My father shut the door hard behind him and turned to deal with me. "Are you kidding me?" he demanded. He only held my gaze for a fraction of a second, like it was hard for him to maintain the eye contact. He went to the desk and dug a bottle of aspirin out of the top drawer, swallowed two without the benefit of water. "I mean it. I honestly don't know how to handle you lately. I really don't."

"Daddy," I said, trying to keep calm, the way I'd been taught to deal with an irate customer. "We were only just—"

"You were only just *what*, Serena?" he retorted, literally throwing up his hands. The phone rang on the desk, a noisy jangle, but he acted like he didn't even hear. His eyes darted to my untucked shirt. "Fooling around in my *office* and who knows what else? I'm not going to stand for it. I'm not."

I fiddled a bit with the computer wires hanging off the edge of the desk. To be fair, the office was a colossally bone-headed location for us to have chosen—it was hard for me to keep a sweaty grip on logic where Sawyer was concerned. "I'm sorry," I said, as sincerely as I could manage. I wanted so badly to calm him down. "That was dumb."

"It was," he agreed, rubbing at his tawny forehead, "but I don't want to hear that you're sorry. I'm tired of hearing that. I've treated you like an adult, Reena. I've trusted you even when it was difficult for me. I know you've had a hard time this year, and I haven't forbidden you to see Sawyer so far, but I will if it's the only way to get through to you." It was getting dark; outside the window I could see the light changing, purples and blues. "I'm worried about you, Reena. Do you understand me? More than worried. I'm terrified."

"Of what?" I demanded shrilly. "What *exactly* are you so worried about?"

My father stared at me like I was a child, like I honestly had no idea how the world worked. "Listen to me," he said slowly, looking me in the eye for the first time since he'd walked into the office. "I'm your father. And I'm worried you're going to make a mistake that I'm not going to be able to fix."

I felt my spine straighten. I was tired of my father's religion, of his judgment and his guilt and the oppressive smell of incense; I wasn't a very good rule breaker, but I was tired of being so well-behaved. At times like this I couldn't wait to leave for Northwestern, to be out from under his watchful, tyrannical eye—although that, of course, would mean leaving Sawyer, too.

"You are so beautiful," my father told me, almost pleading. "And you are so bright. I cannot for the life of me understand why you'd want to risk throwing all that away for—"

"I'm not throwing anything away!" My voice rose dangerously. "I'm sixteen. I have a boyfriend. It's normal. Not for me up to now, maybe, but for other people that's *normal*. Can you please just relax and let me have some kind of a *life*?"

My father laughed at that, low and quiet and disbelieving. "*Reena*," he told me softly, "that's exactly what I'm trying to do."

I opened my mouth to reply but he was finished with me by that point, heading for the desk to get whatever it was he'd come for in the first place. "Go back to your tables," he said, almost absent. "And for God's sake, tuck in your shirt."

I don't know when it first occurred to me that my father wasn't the only one who wasn't crazy about the idea of Sawyer and me. Lydia was looking at us sideways, for sure. "Your mom thinks I'm an idiot," I told him after one particularly awkward encounter in the parking lot of Antonia's, Lydia offering me a ride home in a way that felt an awful lot like a demand and me fumbling my way toward admitting I was actually headed to her son's. Sawyer laughed like he thought I was kidding. I wasn't entirely sure.

"She's a bully, that's all," Shelby said when I told her about it during the free period we shared—how tongue-tied I felt around Lydia, how'd I'd watched her bring a burly line cook near tears with a cool, sharp reprimand about the quality of our hollandaise and then found myself completely unable to string a sentence together when she asked me a totally simple question about the new spring schedule. How she'd shot me a bored, irritated look and walked away. "You just have to stand up to her. It's like when you punch the meanest kid on the playground."

I snorted so loudly the study hall proctor shot me an irritated glare, her enormous glasses slipping down her oily nose. I glanced down at the article about the jazz band's spring concert I was supposed to be writing, then back at Shelby. "You want me to punch Lydia LeGrande?"

"Oh my God, yes. With every fiber of my being, I want that." Shelby laughed and reached forward across her desk, tugged my braid reassuringly. "Just watch, Reena. She'll never know what hit her."

I was sitting cross-legged in bed with my laptop and a spiral notebook alternating between my jazz-band article and a cover letter for an internship at *South Florida Living* that Ms. Bowen—who'd forgiven me, sort of—seemed sure I'd be able to get, when something small and hard cracked against the window frame behind my head. I jumped, sending my notebook sliding onto the hardwood, and got up on my knees, turning around and peering out the window just as a shiny white pebble smacked the side of the house next to my nose.

I pushed my hair back from my face and felt my stomach turn over—Sawyer was standing in my driveway in a T-shirt with baseball sleeves, one hand tangled in his shaggy hair. I sighed. Of course I would be in love with the kind of boy who threw rocks at windows.

I pulled the window open to a blast of hot, damp Florida air. The sky was dark, heavy purple-black clouds rolling in from the direction of the water, and the palm trees were already starting to bend a bit with the muggy wind. It smelled like rain. "What are you doing?" I hissed. I glanced behind me toward the open bedroom door, looking for any sign of life from my father and Soledad's side of the hallway. After the scene in the restaurant office, the last thing I needed was for him to catch Sawyer at our house in the middle of the night.

"Hey," he called back. "Can you come down from there?"

"What?" I said dumbly, even though I'd heard him fine. "Sure. Yes. Hang on." I pulled a sweater on over my tank top and padded barefoot down the stairs. The kitchen was dark save the night-light under the microwave and quiet except for the low hum of the dishwasher on dry. He was standing on the back steps by the time I opened the door.

"Hi," I said cautiously, still nervous we were going to get discovered. He kissed me for a long time without coming inside, like he was waiting for an invitation. He smelled warm like the earth, not entirely clean, and when he finally stepped into the kitchen, he tracked a little mud with him. "Sorry," was what he said first, looking down. "Hi."

"Hi. That's okay." I peered past him into the driveway, but his Jeep wasn't there. "Did you drive here?"

"Nope. Walked."

"From your house?"

Sawyer shook his head. "Was at a party."

"Why?"

"Why was I at a party?"

"Why did you walk?"

"Wanted to see you."

I squinted. "Are you drunk?"

"Only a little. "

"Are you *just* drunk?"

Sawyer made a face. "Can I sleep here?"

Jesus God. "Um," I told him, hesitating. That was basically the stupidest plan in the universe. There was no way Sawyer could spend the night in my bed. I couldn't even imagine how pissed off my father would be if he caught us—he definitely *would* tell me I couldn't see Sawyer after that, and where would I be then? It was enormously dumb even to think about, a suicide mission, but: "Sure," I heard myself saying. "Yeah. Of course. What's going on?"

"Nothing. I missed you. I'm dumb. You were probably sleeping."

"Doing homework, actually." I pushed his hair off his forehead. He needed it cut.

"Oh." Sawyer's face fell, just for one fraction of a second, just around the eyes. "If you're busy, I can go."

His voice killed me, so low and rumbly, cat purr and truck on gravel. I would have listened to him read the phone book, was the truth. "Don't worry about it. Come upstairs. I can finish tomorrow morning." I cringed a little as I said it, thinking of Ms. Bowen and my C in English, the promises I'd made to myself that I wasn't going to do this exact thing. It was spring, with graduation on the horizon. I couldn't afford to screw up. Still, I slipped my hand into Sawyer's anyhow, pulling him closer. "Seriously, it's fine."

He hesitated, not moving much. "I don't want to mess things up for you," he said.

"You're not messing anything up for anybody."

"Yeah, tell that to my dad."

"What did your dad say to you?" I asked, stopping to look at him quizzically. We were standing in the middle of the kitchen now, mugs for the morning's coffee set meticulously out on the counter. Soledad never went to bed until everything was in its proper place. "When did you even see your dad?"

"I stopped by the house to pick some stuff up. I should shower."

"Sawyer. What did he say?"

His teeth grazed the top part of my jaw, back near my ear. "You should come with me."

"I'm already clean," I replied, swallowing audibly.

"So what?"

"So, if my father woke up, he'd cut your nuts off."

Sawyer tilted his head to the side like, *fair point*. "No shower, then."

I giggled and tugged on his cold, smooth hand, pulling him out of the kitchen and through the dark hallway. The old stairs creaked and groaned. "Shh," I hissed, heart pounding, fingertips curling around his shoulder to keep him where he was. God, we were totally going to get caught.

I listened for a minute and heard nothing. "You gotta be so quiet, Sawyer, no joke."

"It's not me, it's your house," he whispered back. His hand snuck up the back of my T-shirt. Even drunk he was quick and stealthy, graceful like a hunted thing. I thought of Sherwood Forest. I thought of Robin Hood.

My bedroom was half-lit by the reading lamp on the night table, and I stayed close to the door and glanced around, trying again to figure out what he saw when he came in here. I looked at the crammed bookshelves, the photos on the wall—Cade and me at the beach when we were little, Shelby on the bleachers at school. There was a shot of my mom from when she was pregnant with me, big like a beach ball, head thrown back laughing; next to that was a big black-and-white of the Seine.

"Hey," Sawyer said, exhaling, sitting down on the edge of the mattress. "Your bed is warm."

"I was on it." I locked the bedroom door to be safe, then crossed the room and knelt down in front of him. There were necklaces and bracelets wrapped around his throat and wrists, hemp and leather like a gypsy. "Are you sure you're okay?"

"Yeah. I'm sorry. I should have just let you sleep."

"I told you, I wasn't sleeping. Lay back," I instructed, and climbed in next to him. I listened to him breathe for a while, until he seemed to steady out a bit. I kept one ear cocked toward the hallway. He definitely wasn't only drunk.

I scooted myself closer until I was right up against him, one of my legs slung over his, and tucked my chin down into the crook of his shoulder. The thin skin of his neck felt warm against my cheek. I wondered where he'd been and who he'd been with, if he had more fun when I wasn't around. It felt like he could be a completely different person when he wanted, like he could morph before my very eyes.

He's not what we thought he was, I remembered Allie saying, backyard light gleaming off her yellow hair on the very last night of our friendship. I wished I could talk to her now. *Was he like this with you?* I imagined asking her—the two of us perched on the swings we were way too old for, her mom making flaxseed muffins in the house.

"Do you think about Allie?" I asked suddenly. I blurted it, quick and quiet, before I could think enough to lose my nerve.

Just for one second, I watched Sawyer disappear, somewhere in his head where I couldn't find him. Then he blinked and came back. "What?"

"You heard me."

"Maybe I didn't."

"Yes you did."

Sawyer shrugged into the pillows on my bed. "I don't know, Reena. I don't want to talk about that."

"Why not?" I asked, propping myself up on one elbow to look at him: muscles in his shoulders, hard knots of bone in his wrists. His skin was slightly shiny, a little pale.

He shook his head, stubborn. "Come on."

"Me come on?" I frowned. "*You* come on. I'm just asking—"

"Reena." He sounded annoyed, like I was bothering him somehow, like maybe he was regretting he'd turned up. "Look, I can leave if you want me to. But I don't wanna talk about that."

"Fine." I flopped back down onto my back and gazed up at the ceiling. I felt achy and uncomfortable, out of sorts.

"You're not going to like me anymore," he said quietly. "If we talk about it."

I sat up in bed. "What does *that* mean?"

Sawyer shrugged again, listless. "It means exactly what I said."

"I could never not like you," I protested, although suddenly there was a part of me that wasn't entirely sure that was the truth. "We're going to have to talk about it eventually, don't you think?"

"Why?" he asked then, flat and simple. I didn't have an answer for that. I thought of Allie's sharp chin and clown feet—of long hours spent in the DVD section of the library debating what to watch that night and the way she could make me laugh from clear across the room with the most minute twitch of her face.

Because I miss her, I almost told him. *Because I miss her like it breaks my stupid heart.*

In the end, though, I just let it alone. I don't know why,

exactly—maybe I was afraid of what he'd tell me, that once it was out there he'd never be able to take it back. Like whatever we had was so fragile—breakable as eggshell, valuable as precious stone—that I had to protect it no matter what it cost.

"What's one thing you think is really interesting?" I asked instead, curling my arms around my knees and looking down at him. "Not something obvious. Don't say your guitar."

Sawyer visibly relaxed then, his whole body uncoiling. He tucked one arm behind his head and just like that we were friends again. "Can I say chicks?" he asked, smiling a little.

"Don't say chicks."

"Can I say one chick in particular?"

"I said don't say chicks!"

"Okay." He rolled over to look at me. "Well, if I can't say my guitar, and I can't say chicks, I guess I'd have to say the weather."

"I'm sorry. What?"

He shrugged. "The weather."

"All kinds of weather?"

"Well, yeah. But that's not what I'm talking about, exactly. I'm talking about, like, how it works. Energy and fronts and stuff. I know a lot about the weather, actually. I used to want to be a meteorologist when I was a little kid."

"You did not."

"I did."

"You are full of surprises."

"So they say."

I reached over him and turned off the reading lamp. "Tell me about clouds."

37

After

The last time I was in a hospital was when Hannah was born. She took twenty-one hours to come, my baby girl, and I spent the great majority of them crushing ice chips between my molars and cursing both God and man. I stared at the bland yellow walls of the maternity ward. I cried a little.

The time before that was the night Allie died.

"Why didn't you have your cell phone?" Cade demands, before anything else. He looks unkempt, pacing like a lion across the waiting room. "I tried to call you a thousand times."

"Stef met us at the house," I say, shaking my head, trying to clear it. I hand Hannah off to Sawyer, his arms already outstretched. "What's going on? How is he?"

"He's having surgery. He had a heart attack."

"I *know*," I snap. "Stef said. What else?"

"They brought him upstairs a few minutes ago. It's a triple bypass."

"Is that dangerous?"

"No more dangerous than a heart attack," my brother retorts, his face twisting meanly.

"You don't have to be a shit about it."

"You should have had your phone."

"I left in a hurry." A fresh wave of fear and dread rolls though me, remembering my dramatic exit. I can't believe I talked to him that way, knowing that his heart is the way it is. "I was horrible to him at dinner. With Roger and Lydia. We got in a fight." I can hardly get the words out. It feels like some cruel and unusual déjà vu for this to be happening and I try not to follow that train of thought to its inevitable conclusion, how Allie and I never got to make up before she—

"Jesus, Reena." Cade shakes his head. "They're here. They went to get coffee." He glances over his shoulder at Soledad, who is as still as a dime-store Mary in a hard-backed plastic chair. Her shirt is limp and wrinkled. She looks a little like she's died. I sit down next to her, dig through her purse for the rosary beads I know she keeps at the bottom. She runs them through her fist without looking up at me.

I glance around. Sawyer is standing near the door talking quietly to the baby, explaining the contents of a nasty-looking watercolor painting hanging on the wall there. ". . . the ocean," I can hear him saying. "No swimming today."

The wall is sponged shades of taupe and beige, linoleum speckled gray like a low-budget Pollock. The soda machine rumbles and glows. A young man with a towel wrapped around his hand sits next to a bored-looking woman in a halter top who's playing on her cell phone: Besides us, they're the only ones here. Slow day for emergencies, maybe.

I cross my legs, uncross them. It's cold in here, uncomfortable, like the North Pole or a convenience store at two A.M. I think of the day Sawyer got here. I think of the night of Allie's crash. Behind the desk, a receptionist is reading *Glamour*. I swallow.

Cade told me once that the night our mother died, our father sat in the pitch-dark of our old, cracking house and played piano until the dawn came up orange and dripping behind him. Scales, Cade told me. Scales and Mozart and Billy Joel and anything else he could think of, melodies made up out of the thin air that no one, including my father himself, could remember once morning finally broke.

I have no way to account for the historical accuracy of this particular legend. Lord knows my brother loves a good story, and he's never lacked the imagination to craft one, but since the night I first heard it—whispered through the rain forest heat of our backyard years after it supposedly happened—I've believed on blind faith. There's a picture of it in my head: my father, features glass-sharp with grief, back hunched and fingers flying over the black and white piano keys. A picture so clear that, for a long time, I was convinced that maybe I remembered, too.

Now when I think about it for any length of time, I realize it's probably just a composite, some sloppy amalgam from all the other nights when I did wake up to find him at the glossy Steinway that sits in state near the window at our house. There were dozens upon dozens of those when I was a little girl: nights when I'd climb out of bed, woken by whatever heinous nightmare I'd been having, and creep barefoot and half-awake down the hall to sit at the bottom of the stairs and listen to my father play his music. With the right song, you understand, my father could atone for whatever sins had been committed against his baby daughter by the world at large. With the right song, I always thought with sleepy confidence as I leaned my dark head against the banister and closed my eyes, my father could set me free.

"Reena."

I look up and realize that this isn't the first time Sawyer has called my name—that he and Cade and Stef, who had followed in her car, are all looking at me, waiting. My ankle is jiggling wildly. I stop it. "What?" I ask, defensive.

"I'm going to take Hannah to get changed."

I almost laugh. "Do you even know how to change a diaper?" I ask, and it comes out a lot nastier than I mean.

Sawyer smiles, half a second and gone. "I'll figure it out."

We wait. What they don't tell you about hospitals, what they don't show you on TV shows about well-scrubbed doctors and the patients whose lives they save is how long everything takes. Roger and Lydia return with two cardboard trays full of iced coffees. I take one and say thanks. Stef gets food from the cafeteria. Sawyer walks Hannah around. I can hear Soledad muttering in Spanish: *"Dios te salve, Maria . . ."*

When the receptionist finishes with the *Glamour* and drops it on the counter, I walk over and pick it up, skim it to find out what girls with more money, less belly fat, and healthy fathers are wearing this season. I can hear the clock ticking, steady.

It's hours before anyone comes to talk to us, close to midnight by the time a scruffy, tired-looking doctor in rimless glasses makes his way into the waiting room to let us know that, in fact, he has nothing to report. There have been some complications, he says vaguely; there's nothing he can tell us other than that. They'll be with my father until the morning, machines beeping and cold hands inside his chest cavity. We should all go home.

"I'll stay," Cade says immediately, shaking his head like a mule. "You should take off," he tells Stef. "Reena, you should go, too."

I prickle. "If you're staying, I'm staying."

He raises an eyebrow at me. "What about Hannah?" He's a bossy bastard sometimes, my brother, but he's practical as all get-out.

I glance at Sawyer. Am I desperate enough to let him take her from me? I'm trying to think quickly now, but Soledad gets up out of her chair: As if someone has plugged in her power cord, she's back in action, taking charge. "Don't be stubborn, Reena," she tells me. "Take the baby home."

"I'll take her," Sawyer volunteers.

"Don't talk about me like I'm not here," I snap. "I'm right here."

He shrugs, all innocence. "I know you are."

"Go," says Soledad. "I love you. Put the baby to bed." Before I can react either way, she's got her arms around me, squeezing tight. "Reena," she continues softly, and it occurs to me that one day was never meant to hold so much. "Say a prayer."

Back at home I slam the car door in the driveway, the sound of it strangely startling. Wind chimes tinkle on the porch. In the trees, crickets and cicadas are rubbing their lazy legs together. "What a racket," Sawyer whispers to Hannah as he retrieves her from her car seat. We've been quiet on the ride back, one of only a handful of times I've ever been in a car with Sawyer without the stereo on. The sudden noise, natural or not, is startling.

He walks me to my door, hesitates as I dig my keys from the depths of Hannah's diaper bag. She's fully awake now, chattering nonsense syllables at the top of her voice. I get the door unlocked and Sawyer hands her off to me. So many fathers and daughters tonight.

"So," he says, standing on my porch with his hands in his pockets. I am half in my house and half out of it. "How you doing?"

I shrug, encumbered by my girl and the bag but mostly by the sudden and complete fatigue swallowing my whole body, like my skin is full of sand. "Okay. Tired."

Sawyer's not satisfied. He doesn't move. "What else?"

"I don't know." Something I can't name. "Out of my mind, maybe." Everything is so heavy and I feel suddenly, ridiculously, like I am going to burst out laughing in his face in one more second, and then:

"Do you need me to stay?" he asks, at the same time I say,

"Do you want to just stay?"

Where the hell did that come from? I do not want to go into this house by myself, is where it came from, but I'm not quite sure I want to go into it with Sawyer, either. "I'm probably okay," I say, but Sawyer interrupts.

"I'd sleep on the couch."

"No, yeah, totally," I say, fumbling all over myself. "Of course."

I'm not sure if that was agreement, but Sawyer takes it that way. "Okay," he says slowly. "So . . . I'll stay."

I blink. "Okay." I hold the screen door so he can get inside and let it slam behind me, dump the diaper bag at the bottom of the stairs with an unceremonious thud. The first thing I do is turn off the AC: I absolutely, one hundred percent cannot bear one more breath of recycled air.

I take Hannah with me, balancing her on my hip and flinging open window after window one-handed, letting the outside in. I have gotten very good, this past year and a half, at doing things one-handed.

"Hey," he says, coming up behind me in the dining room. "Need help?"

"Couldn't breathe." Maybe that's the truth, actually, now that I think about it. Maybe I haven't had a decent amount of air in my lungs since before dinner. Could be I'm brain-damaged, oxygen-deprived.

"Let's get this lady to bed," Sawyer suggests. I nod, willing to follow for now, and get Hannah changed and into the crib without much comment. "Down for the count," Sawyer says, rubbing a fast hand over his bristly head, when she's been breathing deeply for a few moments.

"Nicely done." I sink down into the rocker, exhausted.

"Go put your pajamas on," Sawyer says, noticing how tired I am. I probably look like garbage, though I can't exactly bring myself to care. "Are you hungry?"

I shake my head. "I ate, like, three packs of M&Ms while we were waiting," I tell him, accepting the hand he offers to help me to my feet.

"I know," Sawyer says. He closes the door to the nursery behind him as we step into the hallway, leaving it open a crack so that a sliver of light falls onto the gray carpet inside. "I watched you. You're an impressive woman. You want real dinner, though?"

"Yes. Maybe. I don't know."

"Well, since you feel so strongly about it." He grins. "I'll run downstairs and see what's in the fridge. You go take your clothes off."

"Shut up." I pad down the hallway to my room and change, hastily rebraid my hair. By the time I make it down the stairs, Sawyer has warmed leftovers from tonight's dinner—Stef must have cleaned up while she was waiting for us, and there are several neat Tupperware containers stacked on the counter. Sawyer's tuned Soledad's little radio to the university station, and Billie Holiday croons about her bad, bad man.

"Wanna get tanked?" he asks, poking his head out from behind the fridge door. He is holding out a bottle of white wine.

I raise my eyebrows. "I thought you don't drink anymore."

"I don't. But that doesn't mean you can't."

"No thanks." I hop up onto the counter as he replaces it. "Did you go to a program?"

"Hmm?"

"To quit drinking."

"Oh. No. I just kind of stopped."

"Wow."

"I wasn't an alcoholic. I was just stupid." He shrugs elegantly. "The Oxy, though, that I needed a little help with. What?" he asks, of my presumably gobsmacked expression. He nods as he eats a forkful of rice out of one of the containers. "I went for, like, a month in Tucson."

I blink. "Before or after the farm?"

"Before." He glances at me, amused. "Is it so hard to believe?"

"That you went to rehab? Kind of."

Sawyer shrugs. "Don't spread it around, okay? Don't want people to think I've lost my edge." He smiles, looks out the window at the shadowy yard. "But it was good. I had quite the habit when I left here, kiddo."

No kidding. I think of the not-aspirin in Sawyer's shoe the first night we were together, of Animal and Lauren Werner and the low-slung stucco house. I think of how it felt to lose him, slow and painful and confusing, and how it felt to wonder if I'd ever really had him at all. "Yeah," I say slowly. "I remember."

We're quiet for a minute, the both of us. Finally I clear my throat. "Do your parents know?" I ask him, my voice sounding loud in the empty kitchen. "That you went?"

"Nope." He shakes his head. He took his ridiculous tie

off at some point, dress shirt unbuttoned at the collar and sleeves rolled halfway up to his elbows. "Nobody does. I mean," he amends. "You do, now."

I think about that for a minute. "I wish you'd said something."

"Really?" He looks interested.

"Yeah," I reply, smiling a little. "I might have hated you a little less."

Sawyer grins back. "Probably not."

"Well, no, probably not." I pick a bit at the food on my plate. "But it couldn't have been easy."

"I mean, it didn't tickle." Sawyer shrugs. "They had a twenty-four-hour Slurpee machine, though."

Aha. I wrinkle my nose. "There's that lightbulb," I say, feeling sort of embarrassed and not entirely sure why. There's still so much about him I don't know. "Cheaper than booze."

"Cheaper than a lot of things," he tells me, and we sink into silence after that. Still, I'm glad he's here. I've relaxed: My heartbeat has timed itself to the rhythm of the music coming from the radio, syrupy slow, and *that* realization is all it takes to send me into a fresh panic. I sent my father to the hospital today. I humiliated my family. I'm a mess, miserably and in public, in so many senses of the word.

"Hey," Sawyer says. "Cut it out."

I blink. "Cut what out?"

"You didn't give your dad a heart attack."

"What?" For one crazy moment I think he's actually read my mind, but Sawyer just shrugs.

"That's what you were doing, right?" he asks. "Kicking the shit out of yourself for speaking up for once in your life?"

I consider denial, decide it's worthless. "Among other things."

"Well, cut it out. Look," he says. "You know I love your father like he is my father. I know he freaking hates me now, and that's fine, but he was never anything but good to me when I was a kid, and I don't hold it against him. But I know how he works. And I know how it must have been for you. Everything you said to him tonight?" Sawyer shakes his head. "He more than had it coming."

"Maybe."

"No maybe," he says. He steps forward, right into my personal space. My breath hitches a little. "I'm telling you the truth."

There's a lean—oh *God*, there is definitely a lean here, so close I can see the amber flecks in his green eyes—but in the end I jump down off the counter, evading. This day has gone on for years, and I don't need one more dangerous thing.

"I think I'm going to try bed," I tell him, putting a safe amount of space between us, the clean expanse of kitchen tile. "Want me to get you set up on the couch?"

Sawyer raises one dark eyebrow. "I think I can manage."

"Okay then." We load our plates into the dishwasher. I give the counters a perfunctory wipe. The moon washes in through the window, silver-pale.

38

Before

It wasn't long after the night he snuck into my house that Sawyer started taking me to parties on the outskirts of Hollywood—crowded affairs in rented bungalows far from the shoreline, thirty-racks of Bud Light in the fridge. "We'll just stop by for a minute," he always said before we got there, but in the end a minute usually took an hour or more. He held my hand at first, introduced me to a friend of Animal's or a girl who'd graduated from my high school a year or two ago, before he drifted away, promising me he'd be right back, always, that he just had to talk to this guy really quick, take care of this one thing.

"Unless you want to . . . ," he always began, then trailed off, leaving me to fill in the blanks on my own: unless I wanted to relax, finally, to let go of my mad grab for control and be, finally, finally, like everyone else. To pull off my armor. To make him happy. *Unless you want to.*

I didn't want to, was the problem, and so I sat on the counter in any number of kitchens, drinking warm beer out of a red plastic cup and watching the minutes go by on the digital clock on the microwave, hoping no one said anything to me as they moved through the room, and wishing I was home watching reruns with Soledad. My stepmother believed in dinner parties and barbecues at dusk, events that required invitations and drinks with stirs and a glass jug full of daises on the counter. "Reena, sweetheart," she would have said, if she had known how I was spending my nights, "this is not what we do."

I didn't like to think about Soledad when I was in those kitchens. I didn't like to think about much of anything, is the truth, and so I played games to keep myself occupied: Count the Drunk People, or Things I Wish I Was Doing Right Now. Once, I brought a book and hid in the pantry to read it.

Sawyer always wandered back eventually, blissed-out and mellow, quite literally feeling no pain. He was always glad to see me, though my moods were a little more unpredictable: Sometimes I was so grateful he'd turned up that I'd be super friendly, winding myself around him before we even made it home. Other times I was tired and annoyed. Tonight Sawyer was sleepy-eyed and flushed when he ambled in from the living room, and me? I was ready to kill him.

I'd been perched next to the kitchen sink, kicking at the cabinets and listening to the party sounds as bodies drifted in and out of the room. I'd by mistake put my hand in something sticky on the counter and was rubbing my palm on my jeans when Lauren crashed through the door like a tidal wave. She was wearing a drapey blue shirt and a pair of cowboy boots I'd seen in a magazine, and she was grinning widely.

"Hey, Serena!" she said too loudly. It sounded like a slap. I flinched as she got closer, peered into my cup. "You still working on that same beer?"

I tried for a smile, probably missed. "Still working."

"Good girl, good girl. Can I ask you a question?" She hopped up beside me on the counter, bumped her shoulder at mine like we were old friends. "Is it true that your family is, like, crazy religious? Is that why you don't really party?"

"I don't know that I'd call them crazy religious—" I began, wondering if Sawyer had, but Lauren plowed ahead.

"That's cool, if they are. I didn't mean to pry. I just always feel like Catholicism is one of those religions that makes girls either really frigid or really fun, you know?" Lauren laughed. "Anyway, I just left your boyfriend in the other room. He is *fuuucked* up." She tapped her nose and sniffed daintily. "Good luck getting him home tonight."

Oh God. I closed my eyes for a moment. It wasn't like I didn't know what Sawyer was doing with the pills he'd started to carry with him more and more frequently—*OxyContin produces a high similar to heroin when crushed and snorted*, thanks for the tip, Wikipedia—but hearing it from Lauren, like it was a private joke between her and Sawyer . . .

I wanted to find him, to take us both out of here, step on the gas and figure out what to do after that. I remembered, suddenly, the nights I'd spent at Antonia's when I was twelve and thirteen, sitting in a booth by the door, drinking coffee and reading while my father and Roger and Finch closed up. I wanted my father now, was the truth. The clock on the microwave said it wasn't quite midnight, and I was thinking everyone would still be at the restaurant: Lauren was a straitjacket and I was trying to formulate an escape the likes of which would have impressed Houdini himself, but the truth is I was too slow and stupid, and Harry drowned to death in the end.

"You know," Lauren was telling me, still chatting, an alcoholic lilt in her voice, "Sawyer and I used to come to parties here all the time, when we were together."

No.

He'd told me no. He'd told me that he and Lauren had never been together—but somehow I'd known, hadn't I? Otherwise why would I have asked?

I blinked. "That right?"

She was a little drunk, but not so far gone that the hard metallic glint was gone from her eyes. "Sorry. Is this, like, weird for you?"

"What?" I shook my head stupidly. "No. No, go ahead."

"It was nothing. I mean, we were just kids. It was in high school. We were both pretty wasted all the time, and, like, sixteen. We were a mess. It was comical."

Yeah, pretty damn comical. You should take that act on the road, really—brilliant stuff. I gripped the counter. I felt sick to my stomach. I had to get out of there.

Lauren's phone rang and she fished it out of her back pocket, nearly dropping it twice. "Ooh, I gotta get this," she said cheerfully, looking at the caller ID. She headed for the door, weaving a little; Sawyer wandered in as she went out.

"Can we leave now?" I asked him, before hello.

Sawyer wrinkled his eyebrows and came to stand between my knees. "Sure," he said affably, and then jerked his head toward the screen door. "There goes your friend."

"Right. You know, we actually had a really nice heart-to-heart while you were otherwise engaged." I hopped down from the counter, picked up my purse. "I told her about where I applied to college, and she told me how she sells herself for drug money."

"Ouch," he replied, following me out into the yard, around the house toward the driveway. "Those are serious allegations from such a pristine individual. She's not a crack whore, Reena."

"I know. She's the Virgin Mary." It was the middle of April and wet everywhere; the grass was slick and stuck to my feet as I crossed the lawn. "Sleep in her bed, if you like her so much. Oh, *wait*."

"Hey, hey." Sawyer frowned, an edge creeping into his voice. "What's wrong with you?"

"I like how the implication there is that the fault, dear Brutus, lies not in our stars, but in me. Give me the car keys."

"Is that Shakespeare?"

"'Give me the car keys'? No, I pretty much came up with that one on my own." I felt quick and sharp like the gleaming edge of a scalpel. I felt like I had taken something, too.

"Smart girl."

"Give 'em."

"What? No." Sawyer opened the passenger side door and motioned for me to get in. "I'm fine."

"Are you kidding? Give me your car keys or I'm calling a cab."

"Seriously?" He rolled his eyes at me, but he handed them over. "Fine. Here. You know, Reena," he said as I buckled. "It wouldn't kill you to relax every once in a while."

"And a good way for me to do that is to let you crash and kill me? Shut up, Sawyer."

"What is your problem tonight?"

"They gave the dog beer." I eased out of the driveway

and onto the road, jabbing halfheartedly at the radio preset buttons: I was so irritated at both of us in that moment that I wanted to drown us out. "Did you see that? They were giving that dog beer in his water dish. They thought it was really funny."

"They didn't hurt the dog." Sawyer snorted a little, like I was trying to be clever. "Out of everything that was going on at that party, you're taking issue with the dog?"

"No, actually, I'm taking issue with Lauren von Ho-Bag giving me a detailed history of her sexual exploits while I sit in the kitchen of a house where I've never been before and you bliss yourself out. But the dog, I have to say the dog is what really pushed me over the edge. At least everyone else was obliterated of their own accord. The poor dog was just along for the ride."

"Is that a metaphor?"

"Do you want it to be?"

Sawyer leaned his elbow on the windowsill, rubbed at his forehead like I was an unruly child. "Can we just not do this now, please?"

"Why?" I snapped. "Am I killing your buzz?"

"Is this *about* my buzz?"

"No, it's about you telling me you never had sex with that girl when clearly you did!"

"Oh God." He was quiet for a moment, leaned his dark head back against the seat. "With Lauren? Did she tell you that?"

"Among other things."

I had sort of expected him to deny it, but Sawyer only shrugged. "It was way before you. Before Allie, even. It wasn't important."

"I asked you point-blank, and you lied."

"You said it was going to upset you if I had had sex with her! You basically asked me to lie to you."

"I absolutely did not," I snapped, swinging a wide right turn onto Commercial. "I was being honest. I was expecting the same thing from you."

"Reena, sweetheart, you don't want me to be honest with you."

"What is *that* supposed to mean?"

"It means . . ." He trailed off. "It means that you somehow got this idea in your head of who I am that doesn't necessarily correspond to reality. And when I don't act the way you think Sawyer LeGrande should act, you get mad. Like I haven't learned my lines or something."

"First of all, that's not true." Was it? "Second of all, I never asked you to act any way except to be up-front with me. Honestly, I think you're the one who has a script of how Sawyer LeGrande should act. Like you have to be too cool for school one hundred percent of the time. You don't. You just have to be a human."

He shrugged. "I was just . . . I thought I was telling you what you wanted to hear."

I thought of Allie for the hundred thousandth time. *If*

you can't handle flip cup with Lauren Werner . . . It was becoming a nasty little mantra in my brain. I felt so violated sitting in his Jeep with him, swallowing back the lump I felt forming in my throat. I wanted to curl up in a corner and never let anyone touch me again. "Do you still *like* her?"

"Reena." Sawyer huffed a quiet laugh, disbelieving. "Is that why you hate her so much? Because you think I like her?"

"No, that's why I hate *you* so much. I hate her so much for many other reasons."

"Don't say you hate me." That got him, a little; his eyes narrowed like I'd landed a blow. "That's mean."

"So is lying." I turned into the driveway of the house he was living in and slammed the brakes. "Go to bed, Sawyer. I'll bring your car back here tomorrow."

"If that's what you want to do." He got out of the Jeep and for a moment I thought he was going to huff into the house without saying good-bye, but he made his way over to the open driver's side window. "Kiss me."

Up close, he wasn't looking so good: pale and almost waxy-looking, eyes bright as they'd been the other night in my room. He smelled like the inside of a bar. I pecked him on the lips, quick and antiseptic. Sawyer made a face.

"Are you serious?" he asked, shaking his head a little. "You're not going to kiss me?"

"I did kiss you."

"That wasn't a kiss."

"Sawyer . . ." I was struggling. "If you'd just eaten a whole bag of Doritos, I wouldn't kiss you then, either."

"What does *that* mean?"

"Nothing. I don't know."

"You know, Reena, I just think that maybe if you tried—," he began, and just like that I was one hundred percent closed for business.

"Don't you dare," I managed, arms crossed in front of my chest like I was freezing, even though it was eighty degrees. "Do not."

"Hey," he said, hands up, taking a step back. "Hey. It's me. Relax."

"Well, don't try to peer pressure me!"

He laughed. "I'm not trying to do anything to you. I just think everybody should try everything once."

I rolled my eyes. "That's so boring, Sawyer."

"How is that boring?"

"Why do you need me to validate you?"

"I don't!"

"So do what you want to do!"

"So don't act like I'm a piece of shit when I do it!"

"I'm not."

"You are!"

"This is ridiculous." I gripped the top of the steering wheel, rested my forehead on my knuckles. "Maybe I shouldn't go with you anymore."

"Maybe not."

"Okay then." I shrugged, threw my hands up. Blue light spilled over his face. I felt like this had gotten away from me somehow when I wasn't paying attention. "Just . . . okay."

Sawyer reached into the Jeep, running a hand through my hair and down my cheek. I turned my head and pressed my lips against his palm. "I'll see you tomorrow," he said slowly, but even then it felt like good-bye.

39

After

I'm not sleeping when the phone rings in the middle of the night—just lying in bed and worrying about my father, thoughts like a freight train hurtling stopless through my brain. I launch myself across the mattress to pick it up. "What?" I say immediately, voice panicky and shrill, demanding. "What? What? Tell me."

"Reena," Soledad says softly, and I think I've never been more afraid in all my days on God's green earth. "Reena. It's all right."

It's all right.

He's okay, she tells me calmly. He came through the surgery, critical but breathing. For now there's nothing to do but let him rest. "I love you," she says before she hangs up, my hand pale-knuckled and sweaty around the receiver, chin on my knee in the dark. "And whatever else happens, sweetheart—your dad loves you, too."

I hang up. I cry for a while. I sit silent in the center of the mattress, like it's an island in the middle of the sea.

Finally I get out of bed.

I open my door and gasp: There's Sawyer sitting on the floor in the hallway, head back against the molding and elbows on his knees. He's taken off the button-down he wore to dinner—it seems like days ago that he walked into my house with Roger and Lydia, all stupid and brave—and the cross on his upper arm peeks out from the sleeve of his undershirt. "Hey," he says, suddenly alert. "How's your dad?"

"Okay, I think. Soledad says okay." I squat down so that we're at eye level, voice quiet so we don't wake the baby. "Whatcha doing?"

Sawyer shrugs a little, half-embarrassed. "Keeping watch."

"For intruders?"

"Basically for you." He makes a face. "I'm sorry. That was a really lame thing to say. I don't mean to freak you out."

"You're not freaking me out."

"I'm freaking me out a little."

I shrug. "My dad's okay," I tell him. "For now, at least."

Sawyer smiles. "Soledad on the phone?"

I nod. I'm not surprised to find him out here, is the truth

of it—like somehow this is inevitable, the natural course of things. Maybe he's a homing pigeon. Maybe I'm his home.

"Do you ever think that this is really not the right place for us?" he asks.

I squint a bit, not entirely sure what he means. "Every day," I tell him. "But like I said before, where am I going to go?"

"Not you," he says, urgent, like there's something I'm not understanding. "Us."

"Us?"

"What if we got out of here?" he asks. "When your dad is better, I mean. Just . . . what if we took the baby and went?"

I swallow my heart back down into my chest. "Where?" I ask.

Sawyer looks right at me and smiles, huge and simple as a map of the world. "Everywhere," he says.

Everywhere.

"Sawyer." Right away I think of all the reasons why it's impossible, of the places I've never been and all the things I haven't done yet. I think of a road stretching all the way across the country and I think of all the nights I've spent alone, and when I see he's still waiting on an answer, I give him the only one that makes sense. "Why don't you just come and sleep where you belong?"

A vertical line appears between his eyebrows; his eyes turn a deep emerald color, birthstones in the dark. "Are you sure?" he asks after a minute, and his voice is lower than I have ever heard it. "Don't say it if you're not sure."

"Uh-huh." I'm surprised at the steadiness of my own voice. His fingers clench and unclench; I take one of his fists and force it open, place my own hand inside. "I'm sure."

I pull him to his feet and into the bedroom. Outside through the open window I can hear the rain starting to fall. The heat never breaks here, not really. My spine thuds softly into the sheets.

Sawyer hums a little sound into my temple: Beneath his soft, bristly hair the curve of his skull feels both familiar and strange. I get my arms around his neck to keep from flying apart at my joints and we're holding on to each other like it's the last day, when all of a sudden, all at once, Sawyer goes completely still.

"Say you love me," he orders quietly. He's not moving at all.

"Hmm?" I say into his shoulder. I look up. He's balancing his weight on his forearms and I can see the freckles across his face as he hovers over me. "What?"

"Say you love me," he repeats, and in the dark flash of his green eyes I can see this is very important to him, some kind of promise he's made to himself. He doesn't want me to make him do this without saying the words. "Reena." He is almost pleading. "Say you love me."

Don't do this to me, I want to tell him. *You can't. I can't.* When he left I held that *I love you* tight in my sweaty palm, tucked into my shirt like a talisman. *I love you.* The one thing he gave me that I didn't give him ten times over. The one thing I kept for myself.

"Sawyer," I say, thumb skating across his eyebrow, trying to stall. "Come on."

He looks right at me. "Say it."

If I say it, and I lose him again, it might kill me. If I don't say it, I might lose him right now. My heart is knocking away inside my chest. "I can't," I whisper finally, and I feel like the worst kind of coward. "I'm sorry."

He closes his eyes for a second and I tense like I'm waiting for a blow, fully expecting him to roll away from me, to pull on his jeans and get the hell out of here once and for all. But then:

"Okay," Sawyer says, on a long, quiet exhale. I can feel his ribs expand and contract against my chest. "It's okay."

"We can stop if you want," I offer stupidly. "I get if you want to stop."

Sawyer smiles down at me, quick and vanishing. "I don't want to stop."

So. We keep going.

It's strange and heartbreakingly familiar to do this with him after so much else has happened: All at once I'm remembering a hundred different things I forced myself to forget about, the telltale hitches in his breathing and the scar at the center of his chest. The back of his knee is warm when I tuck my foot there. He looks at me the whole entire time.

When it's over we lie on our sides facing each other for what might be days, gray light and the sound of the wind in the palm trees outside the window. I feel the weight of his gaze like something physical, a sheen of sweat coating my skin. Finally I can't hold it in anymore; just breathing is like a hurricane. "Seattle," I say.

He raises one eyebrow. "Seattle?"

"I think everywhere should start in Seattle."

"Seattle it is," he tells me like a certainty, and after that we fall asleep.

40

Before

Sawyer going to parties without me was almost worse than going with him. Sometimes he showed up in my driveway afterward, flicking the headlights on his Jeep, waiting in the dark until I came downstairs to let him in. I shushed him as we climbed the stairs, always terrified that tonight would be the night my father caught us. I tried not to think of where he'd just been and what he'd been doing as we lay in my bed talking about all kinds of things: music, our families, the various scientific facts Sawyer had gleaned from an early childhood spent, I learned, buried in books about the weather. "Tell me about thunderstorms," I'd whisper sleepily. Tornadoes. Droughts.

Maybe the problems started then, when I ran out of

meteorological phenomena to ask him about, or maybe they started a long time earlier, even before the night he showed up at my house way later than usual, sweaty and skittish, spacey and pale. "You okay?" I asked, once I'd locked us inside my bedroom, the two of us hidden from the sleeping world.

Sawyer nodded vaguely. "Mm-hmm."

"You sure?"

"I said yes, sweetheart."

He was always a patchy, haunted sleeper, but tonight he tossed more than usual, tangling the blankets, breathing hard. I ran my palm up and down his backbone, trying to quiet him down, but it was like he was waiting for something to attack. Like he wanted to get up and prowl.

"How many?" I asked finally, the third time he drifted off only to wake violently a moment later. He was making me nervous. Clearly Sawyer's extracurriculars skewed toward the illegal, but I'd never seen him like this. I tried to remember what I'd read about how easy it was to overdose on pills. "Sawyer. Hey. How many?"

"What?" He sounded annoyed. "Nothing. I'm fine."

"Sawyer—"

"*Reena.*" His voice was sharp. "Let it go, will you?"

Then why did you even come here? I wanted to demand. Instead I gave up, rolling over to face the wall. "Sure," I said sullenly. I had a calc test in the morning; I was more tired than I wanted to admit. "Well, try not to die, will you?"

That got his attention. "Hey," he said, moving closer, pressing the length of his body flush against my back, burying his face in my hair. "Hey. I'm okay, all right? I'm sorry. I'm not going to die. I was stupid tonight. I won't do it again."

I didn't reply. I didn't understand what I had with Sawyer: I couldn't figure out how he could make me so happy and so miserable all at once. But I let him hold me anyway, our pulses tapping out a syncopated rhythm, our breathing finally evening out. My eyes had been closed for a few minutes when he said it: "I love you," he muttered, so quiet, like a prayer whispered into my neck.

"Hmm?" I was nearly asleep myself, edges blurring; I was one hundred percent sure I'd misheard.

"I love you." He said it again, clearer this time, right into my ear, breath tickling. I felt like a hydrogen bomb. I tried to be very still, but I knew he could feel my entire body tensing, a runner ready to begin a race—

Get set—

Go.

I opened my mouth, shut it again.

Oh God.

I did love him, is the awfulness of it. I'd loved Sawyer since the seventh grade, when Allie and I began keeping a list of the places we spotted him. I loved his quick, blistered musician hands and the honest soul he kept hidden safe under all his bravado, and I loved how I was still, every day, learning him. I loved his silly, secret goofy side and the way he had of making me feel like I was a tall tree, just from the way he looked at my face. I loved Sawyer LeGrande so much that sometimes I couldn't sit still for the fullness of it, but when I opened up my mouth to tell him so, nothing came out.

I could do anything for him, I realized suddenly. I could give him anything. But not that. If I said that to him, I knew I could never get it back.

"Go to sleep now," I whispered, and he didn't say it again.

41

After

I wake up sometime after dawn, stirred by the metallic grind of the garbage truck as it clamors down Grove Street. I listen for a moment to the clang of the metal cans next door, and when I open my eyes, I'm surprised to find Sawyer still sleeping next to me: For all the nights we've spent together, this might well be the first time he hasn't slipped out before sunrise.

I take the chance to look at him, face down with one arm slung over his head, freckles dotting his back like constellations. Just for a minute I give in to the urge to touch him, run my fingers over the patterns there, but Sawyer doesn't stir. He sleeps differently than he used to. He thrashes less, breathes more deeply. It used to be that he shuddered in his sleep, trembled and muttered like the devil was in his dreams.

It's not until I get out of bed that he wakes up, opening his eyes halfway. "Where you going?" he wants to know, stretching a little.

I smile. "Gotta get up."

"Nah." He shakes his head sleepily and holds the blanket open, an invitation for me to climb back in. "Five more minutes."

"Well." I consider. "Okay." I slide beneath the quilt, rolling over onto my stomach and slipping a hand under the pillow. "Hi."

"Hi. What do you have today?" he asks, one hand on my back, thumb tracing lazy circles there.

"Um." I run through the to-do list in my head. "The hospital. And then school, if Stef can take the baby for me."

"I can take the baby for you."

"Okay." That makes me smile. "And then work at four."

"I'm on at seven." He grins. "We haven't worked together in a long time."

"When we were in high school I used to check your schedule right after I checked mine, so I would know if it mattered what I looked like or not," I confess. I feel a little giddy. "Not that you ever noticed."

"Oh, I noticed."

I snort. "You did not."

"What you looked like was never lost on me," he says, lacing one arm around my shoulder, pulling me down until my head is resting on his chest. "Nothing about you, my dear, has ever been lost on me."

42

Before

By May, the Platonic Ideal had begun doing shows under one of the pavilions by the beach—Iceman's uncle worked for parks and rec and had gotten them the gig, Tuesday and Thursday nights just after sundown. I went whenever I wasn't working, either luring Shelby along with promises of onion rings and milkshakes, or otherwise flying solo, snagging Soledad's car for the night and making the drive to the water with all the windows rolled down, humming softly out of tune. Truth was, I liked being by myself, free to sit way in the back on the low wall that separated the sand from the sidewalk behind it and stare without interruption, to listen while my boyfriend sang his songs.

Tonight I perched in my usual spot, chewing thoughtfully

on my bottom lip as the band launched into a rocky version of "Come Rain or Come Shine" that I knew Sawyer had arranged. I glanced around at the crowd, recognizing several faces from other beach shows or the parties I'd been to before I stopped going: The Wiggles were there, and I tried my best not to stare at them in their shorts and bikini tops. Sawyer was trying his best not to stare at them, too. He caught my eye and grinned, fingers moving swiftly over the neck of the bass.

He was so good, and it made me so happy to watch him. His whole body relaxed when he played his music, knots pulled from shoelaces, like he was finally free. He was wearing navy blue cutoffs and a beat-up pair of Chuck Taylors, and I had never been gladder to be his girlfriend. *I'm gonna love you like nobody's loved you . . .*

"So were we freaking awesome?" he asked later, sidling up to me after they were finished, the crowd breaking up and drifting away in clusters of threes and fours. I always tried to let him have his space at these things, always waited until he sought me out. I lifted my damp, heavy hair off the back of my neck.

"As usual."

"Dude, we're gonna head over to the Meridian for a bit," Animal called. He was standing with one of the bikini-clad girls, whom I had silently dubbed Giggles Wiggle. "You guys wanna come?"

I held my breath, but Sawyer shook his head. "Nah," he

shouted back over the rhythmic drone of the ocean. "I'll catch up with you guys later."

We got a couple of Sprites at the sandwich shop across the street, then wandered back toward the water, plopped down where the sand had begun to cool. "We don't go to the beach enough," I observed, looking out at the dark horizon. The tide was coming in, licking at my toes. "I like the beach."

"Real Floridians don't go to the beach," he replied. "It's too hot."

"What about them?" I asked, tilting my head to the right. In the distance, a group of kids a little older than us were grouped on a blanket. It was after ten, and besides them, the sand was nearly empty. "They're here."

"They're probably from Michigan."

I finished my Sprite and reached my hand out for his, which Sawyer delivered with a sigh. "Don't chew my straw."

"I don't chew straws."

"Yes you do." He planted a kiss on the back of my neck.

The skin all over my body prickled pleasantly, but I leaned forward, away from his mouth. "I'm sweaty."

"Salty," he corrected. "You taste good. Like pretzels."

"You really know how to sweet-talk a girl."

"A regular Casanova," he affirmed.

"Heathcliff," I said. "On the moors and everything."

"Don Juan."

"Juan Valdez." I giggled.

"Uh-huh. Ever had sex on the beach?"

"Real Floridians don't have sex on the beach," I informed him. "Too hot."

He poked his tongue into his cheek. "Smart-ass."

"You could try your luck with one of those girls from Michigan, though."

"Right." He grimaced when I handed his cup back to him. "Look at this," he said, holding up the straw and smirking. "You're like a woodchuck." He flopped backward, head in the sand. For a long minute, neither of us talked. "So what am I going to do when you leave, Reena?"

I blinked. I was not expecting that from him. I wasn't expecting to ever talk about it, much less for him to be the one to bring it up. *I am not long for this world*, I'd told him that day outside the restaurant, although lately graduation felt like it would be here any minute now. I checked the mailbox every day for an envelope from Northwestern. "Girls from Michigan, clearly."

"I'm serious."

Well.

"I don't know," I said carefully, choosing my words with all the caution of seventeen years spent listening for clues. "It's not like I'd ever expect you to be, like . . . It's not like I'm asking you for anything."

Sawyer's face flickered, unreadable. He wasn't looking at me. "Ouch."

"No, no, I didn't mean it that way," I said, backpedaling.

"I mean, I know you could be, like . . . faithful, I mean. If you wanted to. I just . . . wouldn't think you'd want to, is the thing. Besides," I ventured finally, when he still refused to answer, "this is all completely theoretical. *If* I get in. The magical *if*."

He shrugged, looked out at the ocean. The waves were coming quicker now: Soon we were going to need to move. "You'll get in."

He was right. I got in.

Sawyer had picked me up at school, and I grabbed the mail from the box when we got to my front door, slow and rambling. He had his fingers hooked into the belt loops on the back of my jeans as I pulled out the bills, a *TV Guide*.

And.

A big envelope. From Northwestern.

"Oh," I said, more like a sigh. I sat down on the steps, a handful of catalogs and envelopes fanning out onto the porch. "Oh my God."

"Big is good, right?" he asked, sitting down beside me, although he had to know it was—after all, he'd applied and been accepted to college the year before. But he was still wearing his sunglasses, and I couldn't see his face. "Big means they want you?"

"Big means they want me."

"Of course they want you. They'd be idiots not to."

Congratulations, the letter said.

The storm door creaked open; Soledad stood at the screen wearing a pale pink tank top, all tan skin and freckled arms. "How was your test?" she wanted to know, then: "Hey, Sawyer."

"Good," I said, turning around and looking up at her. I held out the letter. "I got into Northwestern."

Soledad's face bloomed open, a wide, delighted grin. "Reena!" she cried, hurrying outside and throwing her arms around my shoulders. "Oh, Reena, sweetheart, that's wonderful!"

God in his golden heaven, I wanted to go. I wanted that writing program, I wanted to study abroad—to own a pair of corduroy pants and read fat Russian novels in coffee shops and tromp down the street in yellow snow boots all frozen winter long. I wanted to be someone totally different. I wanted to see places I'd never been. I'd wanted all those things for as long as I could remember, but I'd wanted Sawyer for even longer than that, and now that I had him and the choice sat before me, it didn't feel as easy as it once had. I thought of Ms. Bowen, of all the hard work we'd put in so I could graduate early. *A lot of kids don't want to miss their senior year.*

Sawyer hung out at my house late that night. The two of us sat on the floor of my bedroom until almost eleven, door wide open per Soledad's instructions, playing an epic game of rummy: He was the only one who'd ever managed to learn Allie's convoluted set of rules. I ran downstairs to get us more ice cream out of the freezer, tossing a giddy "Don't cheat!" over my shoulder, and came back five minutes later with a pint of Super Fudge Chunk in my hand to find him not where I'd left him on the carpet, but standing at my desk with his ankles crossed casually, reading my college application essay.

"Um," I said, staring at him and trying not to feel as irrationally caught out as I did, as exposed and weirdly spied on. After all, I'd always told him I'd let him read it eventually. "Where'd you get that?"

"Was on top of the pile," Sawyer said, nodding at the truly explosive mess on the desktop: textbooks and test papers, an email from *South Florida Living* asking me to come in and talk to them about that internship. He didn't look guilty at all. He was smiling. "This is really good, Reena."

"Yeah?" I asked, some of the shrillness seeping out of me. I knew it was pretty good, objectively—after all, it had gotten me into Northwestern—but it was different to hear Sawyer say it. I set the ice cream down on the dresser. "You think so?"

Sawyer nodded and sat down on my bed; instinctively, I glanced out into the hallway, but my father and Soledad were both still downstairs. "How come you never let me read it before now?" he asked.

"Dunno," I said, sitting down beside him. Brushing two of his fingers with two of mine on top of the quilt. "Felt shy, I guess."

Sawyer smiled. "You don't have to be so shy all the time," he said. "It's just me." Then, a beat later: "You're really gonna go to all these places, huh?"

I looked up at him, surprised. There was something about the way he said it that made me think he was just wrapping his brain around it for the first time, the fact that I was really going to leave at the end of the summer. "That's the plan," I said quietly.

He nodded again, sinking back into the pillows. He slept over so much my sheets had started to smell like him. "Maybe I need to get out of here, too," he said after a moment.

I raised my eyebrows, reaching for the ice cream. Vague as it was, it was the first time I'd heard him talk about anything resembling a plan. "I mean," I said, leaning off the bed to grab our spoons out of the empty bowls on the carpet, "I hear Chicago's a good music town."

"Oh, yeah?" I looked over and Sawyer was grinning, broad and open. I felt something like hope expanding like a yellow balloon deep inside my chest. "Well," he said, clinking his spoon with mine like maybe we were deciding on something together. "Maybe I'll need to check it out."

43

After

It takes us half an hour to get downstairs, Hannah dressed and fed and into the playpen in the dining room, right next to the kitchen door. "I'm going to make you breakfast," Sawyer decides, heading for the fridge.

I shake my head. "I'm not really hungry."

He makes a face. "You didn't eat last night, because you were upset, which is fine. But today is a new day. Thus, eggs." He grins at me, and I sit down, content to be taken care of for a few minutes. Content to let him do it.

The doorbell chimes. "It's probably Shelby," I tell him, standing up. Her mom is a nurse at the hospital, and there are a slew of messages on my cell. The phone in the kitchen begins to ring. "Can you get that?" I ask Sawyer over my shoulder.

I hurry into the living room and swing the door open without checking the peephole, realizing my idiocy one second too late. It's not Shelby coming to see me, this sunny summer morning: It's Aaron. There is one second in which I think, *shit*.

"Hey!" I say brightly, taking a step back to let him a foot or so into the house, but no more. He's freshly scrubbed and wearing a T-shirt with the marina's logo on it, ships sailing off to sea.

"Hey," he says. "I heard about your dad."

"He's okay, we think," I tell him. "I'm going to go by the hospital in a bit."

"Want some company?" he asks. "We could grab breakfast real quick."

I'm trying to decide how to answer that when Sawyer's voice reverberates through the living room, all noisy and cheerful. "Is that Shelby? Invite her in! I'll make her some eggs."

Damnit.

Aaron's face changes, hardens. "I'm sorry," he says. "I didn't realize you had company. It's only your car in the driveway."

"No, it's just—" It's just what? It's not just anything. It's sex with Sawyer LeGrande.

"Shelby Fitzsimmons, star of stage and screen," Sawyer calls, making his way through the dining room. He sees Aaron and freezes for just one second before he recovers, a nearly undetectable smile quirking at the corners of his mouth. Already I want to slug him. "Oh. Not Shelby."

"Not exactly," Aaron says slowly, and God, *God*, I feel like garbage.

"Well, hey, man, good to see you," Sawyer says, recovering. If you didn't know better you'd think he was totally decent. "I'm, uh, making eggs, if you're interested."

"Thanks, but I have to get going," Aaron says, edging his way to the door. "I have to get to work. I just came by to make sure Serena's dad was okay."

"I just got off the phone with Soledad, and she says he's doing great."

"That was Sol?" I ask, forgetting for one moment the massacre going on in front of my very eyes.

"Well, then, I guess that's that." Aaron looks from me to Sawyer and back again. "I guess . . . I guess I'll, ah, see you around, Reena."

"Aaron—" What am I going to say? I've been terrible to him, this good person, this soul who brought me flowers and made me smile on my ugliest of days. There's no excuse in the world.

It doesn't matter, really; Aaron's already out the door. "Give your dad my best," he calls over his shoulder, retreating like possibly my house is on fire and I'm just too stupid to notice and save myself.

"Shit," I say, when his car is gone from the driveway. "Shit!"

"What?"

I turn on him savagely. "Shut up."

"Oh, come on." Sawyer has held it in as long as he can; he's smiling now. "It's not that bad."

"No, actually, it's *exactly* that bad. You don't understand. You definitely do not understand." I think of how angry Shelby is at me already. I think I've just annihilated our friendship for good. "I have just completely screwed myself."

"Well." He side-eyes me a bit, mischevious. "I wouldn't say *that*, exactly."

"I said shut up!"

Sawyer rolls his eyes. "Can I ask you a question? Do you even like him? Or is he just, like, practical? Because I've gotta tell you, Reena, he's like the human equivalent of a bowl of shredded wheat."

"Go to hell, Sawyer. You don't know him. He's a really nice guy."

"So is Mister Rogers, but that's no reason to jump into bed with him."

"First of all, who I do or do not jump into bed with is none of your business. Second of all, speaking of things you don't know anything about, he was a really good boyfriend." I turn and stomp toward the kitchen. "And third of all, Mister Rogers is dead!"

That stops him for a moment. "Mister Rogers is dead?"

"For years!"

He follows me through the dining room, stopping to tousle Hannah's hair. "Can you quit running away every time I try to have a conversation with you?"

"You're one to talk about running away," I shoot back, turning off the stove and replacing the eggs in the fridge.

Sawyer makes a face, like maybe that particular refrain is wearing a bit threadbare for him. "Well, I'm here now," is all he says.

"Right." I bounce around the kitchen like a pinball, tossing various and sundry items into the backpack on the chair: phone, keys, crackers for Hannah, a couple of juice boxes, a stuffed stegosaurus. "Until you get the itch or the urge or whatever it is that makes you do the lame-ass things you do and you take off again and I'm back where I started, except that now I have completely alienated the one guy in my entire life who actually treated me well."

Sawyer doesn't like that. His soft mouth thins. "I treated you well."

"Mm-hmm. I especially appreciated the part where you peaced out without even having the decency to make up a lie about going out for cigarettes."

"How long are you going to hold that against me?"

"Until I'm not pissed about it anymore!"

"So, forever?"

"You were gone for two years! You've been back for two weeks!"

"You know, what I love about all this is how conveniently

you forget that you were on your way out, too, when I left. You told me every day."

"I was going to college!"

"You were getting out of here a full year before you had to, and never coming back. You were going to go do something great and amazing and a hundred times better than the restaurant and this town, and a hundred times better than me."

"Sawyer, don't be such a baby. I never said that."

"You said it in a hundred different ways. You were leaving anyway. I just thought I'd get the jump."

"Jesus God." I roll my eyes, try to think for a moment, and when I do there is only one logical conclusion for me to draw. I feel mean as a rabid dog. "This was stupid of us."

He looks at me suspiciously. "What was?"

"This." I spread my arms out. "Last night, this morning, all of it. It was a bad idea. I was upset. I shouldn't have let you—"

"*Let* me?" he explodes. "You came looking for me! I was ready to sleep on the damn couch!"

"Whatever. It doesn't matter. What matters is that I'm a maniac, and you make me that way. You've been back for thirty seconds, and I'm acting like an idiot all over again."

"Well, *that's* not far off."

God, I am so frustrated with him. I am frustrated with my whole life. "Screw you."

"Nice." He's angry, too. "You know what? Let's just forget about it."

"You know what? Let's."

"Fine," he says, and he could be giving me the weather report but his eyes are cold like marbles. "It never happened."

44

Before

"What are you wearing?" Sawyer wanted to know.

I glanced at myself in the mirror as I cradled the phone between my ear and shoulder. It was the Friday after I'd gotten my letter from Northwestern; he was supposed to be picking me up in twenty minutes for what, he promised, was going to be a Very Big Date. "Why?"

"Because I want to make sure we're not wearing the same thing."

"Shut up." It was the middle of May, uncomfortably hot. "Everything I put on makes me sweat. So maybe nothing."

"I see." He was smiling, I could hear it. "Now there's an idea. Be ready in ten, yeah? We're celebrating. My girlfriend got into college this week."

We drove to South Beach that night, windows of the Jeep rolled all the way down; the air conditioner had finally given out a few weeks before, and I smelled ocean and summer. Charley Patton twanged out into the heat: *Took my baby to meet the mornin' train . . .* Sawyer kept one hand on my leg as we made our way down 95, breaking contact occasionally to rub at a twitching muscle in his jaw.

"I like your wrists," he commented suddenly, glancing over at where my hands were resting in my lap. He traced the underside of my forearm with the tip of his finger.

I looked at him skeptically. "My wrists?"

"Yeah," he said, half smiling as he switched lanes. "Relax. I don't have, like, a weird wrist thing. I just like yours. They're small. Like bird bones."

"Bird bones," I repeated.

"Yeah." He paused. "See? Now you ruined the moment."

"You were making a moment?"

"I was trying!"

I laughed. "Sorry. Do it again."

"No!" he said. "The moment is over." But he was laughing, too.

South Beach was shiny like a carnival, all Art Deco buildings and neon storefronts, but the Breezeway, where we wound up, made the Prime Meridian look like the bar at the Ritz. We had to walk down a dark, garbage-strewn alley to get to the door, and I wondered how Sawyer knew where he was going. *You drove all this way to bring me* here *when all of*

South Beach is lit up like Christmas? I wanted to ask him, but I wasn't in the mood for a fight.

Sawyer held my hand as he expertly wove through the crowd, pulling me along like deadweight. It seemed to me that he liked crowds, big noisy crushes of people. It seemed to me that he was good at them.

He let go when we got to the bar, peering through the smoke like he was looking for somebody. "Wait here," he said in my ear. His breath tickled, set my dangly earring swinging.

"Why?" I squinted, suddenly suspicious. I had to raise my voice to be heard over the music, something thumping and loud I didn't recognize. "Where are you going?"

"Just wait a sec. We'll go grab dinner right after this, I promise."

I sighed and headed for the bathroom. I'd downed a soda on the ride. When I was finished, I killed time by reading the graffiti on the wall next to the empty Tampax dispenser, making up stories in my head to go with the scribbled initials, the doodled hearts, the swears. I was getting very good at killing time. My shoes were sticking to the floor, and I was picking my way toward the exit when I heard one yell, a woman's, rise above all the others.

"What's going on?" I asked a slightly inebriated guy as I rounded the corner from the small hallway that housed the restrooms. It had gotten more crowded since I'd been gone, and I couldn't see the action.

"Two idiots got into it," he told me, after looking me up and down in a way that made me shudder. Then, as if perhaps that wasn't clear enough: "Fight."

I looked around for Sawyer, saying a quick prayer that I knew was useless even as it ran through my brain. Standing on my tiptoes, trying to see over the crowd, I realized that one of the two idiots getting into it was absolutely my boyfriend. Suddenly, our little trip to the Breezeway made a lot more sense.

"You've got to be kidding me," I said, realization dawning bright and harsh. I could see the bouncer and the bartender moving in to break it up, and I stood frozen for endless seconds, debating whether to move toward them or flee. I whimpered as a fist connected with Sawyer's cheek, and felt the acid rising up in my throat as he reared back and slammed his knuckles into the other guy's mouth. He was a good fighter, I realized dully, then turned around and pushed through the crowd toward the door.

I was on my heel and into the alley even before the guy Sawyer had talked to at the door pulled him out of the bar. "Dude, I'm not wasted," he was saying, but the bouncer didn't seem to care. "He started it, I swear."

"He belong to you?" the man asked me.

I almost said no. Sawyer looked at us sullenly. "Yeah, I guess," I replied. "Thank you. Sorry." The bouncer nodded and shrugged and turned to go back inside, and I pulled Sawyer's car keys from his back pocket as we walked toward the street. I was tired of driving home. "Get in the car," I said.

"Reena, that was supposed to be so quick, but that guy—"

"Don't talk," I interrupted.

"We were going to go somewhere else—"

"I said don't talk to me!" I started the car. "Is that why you brought me all the way down here?" I demanded. He didn't reply—because I'd told him not to, I suppose—so I barged ahead. I was close to tears, I was so angry. "Seriously? And you tried to make it look like a date. Because I got into *college*? Jesus. I don't believe you. I seriously do not believe you."

"It was supposed to be a date," he muttered. "I was going to take you someplace else. It would only have taken a second if that guy hadn't been such a douchebag."

"Right. It's his fault. It's your *drug dealer's* fault." I flinched just looking at his ruined knuckles. There was blood seeping from them. "This is ridiculous." I glanced out the window, put my blinker on. "Do you know that this is ridiculous? This isn't real life. This isn't how I operate."

"What are you doing?" he asked, instead of answering me.

"I'm stopping at Walgreens."

"Why?"

"Because I'm going to get stuff for your hand! Jesus!"

"I'm fine."

"There are teeth marks! You want to get rabies?"

He barked a laugh. "Nobody's getting rabies."

"You want to get AIDS?" I almost gagged on the words. I turned off the Jeep in the Walgreens parking lot and, after debating for a minute, pocketed the keys.

"Nice," he said. "Where exactly do you think I'm going to go? You think I'd leave you here?"

"Who knows what the hell you'd do?" I slammed the door and headed into the store, where I spent all the cash I had on me on peroxide, gauze, a tube of Neosporin, and another soda. I wished for my father, for Shelby, for Soledad, for Lauren even. I didn't want to go back out to the car. I could feel him receding, going so far that I couldn't catch him, and I didn't know how to stop it.

The cashier surveyed my purchases and looked at me half-sympathetically and said, "Hope your night gets better."

"Thanks." I had to look into the fluorescent light to keep from crying.

"Goddamnit, Sawyer," I hissed, switching on the overhead light in the Jeep. He looked worse than I'd thought. He was going to have a shiner. I thrust the soda at him, and he applied it to his rapidly swelling eye. I hoped he had a headache. "You know, why would I even want to go to college when I can stay here and play Florence Nightingale to you?"

"Beats the hell out of me. Shit," he said, when the peroxide hit his knuckles, breath hissing from him like a balloon. "That hurts."

"Good."

"Look, don't even bother," he said, pulling his hand away. "I'll take care of it myself. Let's just go."

"Fine. Have it your way." I threw the Jeep into reverse. I hated this car, and this town, and the entire state of Florida. I thought of speeding north toward Alligator Alley, of driving us right off the road into the swamp. "I can't believe you're going to act like this."

"Well, you won't have to endure it for much longer," he pointed out, slouching in his seat like a baggy pair of jeans. He crossed his arms.

"Honestly? You're mad at me about Northwestern?"

"I'm not mad at you about anything."

"Liar." I sighed. "It's not like you didn't know I was going. I said to you right from the beginning that I was getting out of here."

"No shit."

"No shit," I echoed, and we were quiet for a while after that, the radio drowned out by the hot blare of the wind. Sweat trickled grossly down the back of my neck. Finally I just said it. "I want to talk about Allie now."

That got his attention. "What?"

"You heard me."

"You want to talk about this now?"

"When would be a better time?" I asked. "We've been doing this for six months and we basically haven't talked about it at all."

He sighed. The soda bottle was still pressed against his face, and I wondered briefly if his hand might be broken. "What about her?"

"What made you like her?"

"Reena, why do you want to do this?"

"Just answer me."

"I don't know!" he said, sighing noisily, head back against the seat. Eventually he started to talk. "She was really . . . open, I guess. And mellow. Like nothing ever worried her." I wondered if he was framing this description specifically to hurt my feelings, to highlight the differences between my best friend and me—his old girlfriend and his new one—or if we were just such polar opposites that he couldn't help but sound that way. "She was just . . . fun."

Fun. Right. I took a deep breath, peered at a road sign, took a wide right turn. "Would any of this ever even have happened if she hadn't . . ." I trailed off.

"She *died*, Reena." He wasn't looking at me, was staring out the window instead, watching the lights blink by. "You might as well just say it, if we're going to talk about this. If she hadn't died."

"If she hadn't died." I swallowed. "Would you ever have wanted to be with me if Allie hadn't died?"

"What the hell is up with you, huh?" he asked. "Can we not do this?"

"Just answer me!"

There was a long silence. He seemed to be weighing his

options. "I don't know," he said. "I don't know! And there's shit you don't know about me, and there's sure as hell shit you don't know about that night—"

"Well, then *tell* me!"

"I *can't*!"

I didn't argue. What was I expecting, really? Surely it was dangerous for me to be driving like this. Surely it would have been smarter to pull over, to sort it all out. But I was tired now, and I wanted to go home. I stopped short at a light I hadn't realized was red.

"Careful," he said quietly.

"Shut up," I replied.

We rode without speaking the rest of the way, the croon of the radio the only sound inside the Jeep. *You know you done done me wrong . . .*

The sky was a full, heavy purple when I pulled into Sawyer's driveway. Probably it was going to rain. The yellow house loomed like something haunted. I screwed up my courage. "You need help, Sawyer."

"Oh, please." He made a noise, something dismissive, in the back of his throat. "Don't start that with me."

"Well, you do!"

"Stop it."

"You're not in school, you have half a job that you're constantly on the edge of losing, you're wasted *all the time*—"

"I am not!" he interrupted.

"Honestly, Sawyer, the only thing you have going for you right now is me, and you're doing everything you possibly can to mess that up, too!"

"Right," he muttered. "It's all me messing this up."

"I can't help it that I'm going away!"

"It's not *about* you going away!" he shouted.

"Then what *is* it about?"

He didn't answer. "Well?"

Still nothing.

"Do you like this?" I demanded. "This stupid badass act that you pull all the time? Is it working out for you?"

"You keep asking me that. Do you like always being the good girl? Does that do something for you?"

"It's not being the good girl, Sawyer! It's being myself!"

"Well, maybe that's what I'm doing, too. Just being myself."

"That's not you!"

"Maybe it is."

"Then I don't know you."

"Maybe you don't." He sighed, opened the door of the Jeep, and slid out.

"Do you anticipate quitting all this bullshit anytime soon?" I called out the window.

He smirked. "What bullshit is that?"

"You know what bullshit!" I wanted to hit him. I wanted to be as mean as I possibly could. "I'll tell you, Sawyer, the novelty of you is really starting to wear off."

Sawyer recoiled, then got very still. "The *novelty* of me?" he asked quietly. And that was the moment I realized I'd gone too far.

"Look, I'm sorry," I told him. "I didn't mean— I just—"

"Forget it."

"Sawyer—"

"I've gotta get out of here," he said, almost to himself. He was on his feet, across the yard, almost before I knew what was going on. His hands were like white spiders in his hair. "I'll see you around, Reena."

This time, he didn't kiss me good-bye.

45

After

I drop Hannah off with Stefanie and drive too fast to the hospital, a change of clothes and a bagel for Sol on the passenger seat beside me. She looks like hell, but my father looks all right, considering: He's groggy and sallow, an IV taped to the back of his hand. I have fifty things to tell him but none of us says anything and I sit at the edge of the bed while we watch the *Today* show, an incredibly boring segment about finding the best summer produce. It makes me want blueberries. I fidget. I think of how disappointed he'd be if he knew I'd just spent the last twelve hours repeating every stupid mistake I ever made with Sawyer, or if those are just the kind of bad calls he expects from me after all this time. I feel so foolish on top of everything else, letting myself think I could make it work after everything that's happened.

"You scared me," I tell him finally. I want to say *I'm sorry* but I don't know where to start. "Don't do it again."

"Yes, ma'am." He nods and leans back against the pillows, the skin beneath his eyes pale and gray. His cheeks are speckled with a day's worth of beard. "Soledad already read me the riot act."

"I'll come by later with Hannah," I promise on my way out. I kiss him on the forehead and don't cry until I get to the parking lot. I feel like a bad bruise.

Sawyer shows up at ten to seven to take over for Joe, who slips me a butterscotch Dum Dum for Hannah before he heads home to his wife. Sawyer grew up behind that bar, just like the rest of us, and right away he makes himself at home amid the SoCo and grenadine, setting up as if he's never been gone.

I try as hard as I can not to watch him, not to notice as he flashes an expert grin at a middle-aged woman in heavy makeup or chats baseball with a couple of suits in town for a conference. Still, we're not particularly busy, and the restaurant isn't offering a whole lot by way of distraction. I hide in the kitchen for a while, fill Finch in on what's happening with my dad.

By eight the place fills up enough that I can get into a strange, familiar kind of rhythm: split checks and olive oil, extra knives and plates. I ring my drink orders in from the computer in the back hallway and I don't look at Sawyer at all.

Eventually he notices me not noticing, though, catches my eye as I head toward the kitchen with a just-balanced armload of dirty plates. I don't know what I'm expecting, exactly, but it's not the bland newscaster smile he shoots my way. "Something you needed, Reena?" he asks.

There is, actually; I just haven't plugged it into the system yet. "Two Amstels," I tell him, no preamble. It's the first thing I've said to him all night.

Sawyer raises his eyebrows, teasing me. "What's the magic word?" he asks.

I scowl. "Sawyer, shut up and get me the beers."

"*Testy*," he says, sticking his tongue out. He turns around to grab the glasses, muscles moving inside his shirt in a way I do my best not to notice. I roll my eyes to cover, trying to sound as annoyed as humanly possible.

"You know," I tell him shrewishly, "if I were you, I'd be careful what I did with that tongue."

"That so?" His gaze flicks up and down my body, overt. "Where would be a safe place for it?"

"Seriously?" My stomach twists so hard it almost hurts, like car parts scraping against one another. I'm still holding four dirty plates. "Shut up," is all I come up with.

Sawyer smiles. "Why do you always tell me to shut up?" he asks pleasantly.

"Why do you always deserve it?" I fire back, and go to dump the dishes in the bin. I come back a minute later and find him leaning forward over the bar, both beers waiting.

"Why'd you pick Hannah?" he asks, as if he's picking up the thread of an earlier conversation, like we've been talking like old friends all the live-long afternoon.

"Huh?" I snatch the bottles off the bar. "Pick Hannah for what?"

Now it's Sawyer's turn to roll his eyes. "You know what I'm asking. What's it mean?"

"Grace of God."

He nods his approval, thoughtful. "Nicely chosen."

"I had a book."

"Efficient," he says, then: "What about yours?"

"Serena?" I shrug and deliver the beers, then come back against my better judgment. "Just what it sounds like. I was misnamed."

"Nah," Sawyer says, shaking his head. He's still leaning over the bar, dark head tipped close like he thinks I'm going to tell him some kind of secret. "Ever look me up?"

"Nope," I say; then, because that looked like it hurt his feelings—and honestly, what is *that* about?—I frown. "Okay, can you stop?"

Sawyer frowns back. "Stop what?" he asks, as if he honestly doesn't know.

"Whatever you're doing," I say. I feel so stupidly close to the edge here, like anything could set me off. For some reason idle chatter seems worse than the nastiest of fights. "Asking about names. Being my buddy."

"I'm being civil."

"Well," I tell him, "*don't.*"

Sawyer snorts. "That's very mature."

"Do you even have feelings?"

He stares at me. "Do I have *what*?"

"Feelings," I repeat, as if maybe I just wasn't speaking loudly enough. "Do you have any? Or was there some kind of genetic fluke?"

For a moment Sawyer just gapes, shaking his head slightly. "Okay," he says finally, flipping up the wooden partition and stalking around the front of the bar. He grabs my arm, not gently. "That's it."

"What are you doing?" I hiss as he pulls me down the back hallway, past the office and the kitchen. He flips the lock on the patio door and pushes it open. "Let go of me," I tell him. "It's raining."

"No shit. It's Florida." He turns to face me once we're outside, half covered by the awning over the door. The air is hot and muggy; my right shoulder is getting wet. "You know, this is classic," he says, like he honestly can't believe we're still having this conversation after all this time. "This is *great*."

"What is?" I ask, playing dumb. I don't want to do this. Not now.

"*You*, out of *everyone*, asking me if I have feelings." He scrubs at his eyes with the heels of his hands. "You know, I always thought it was messed up when people said you were an ice queen, like maybe they just didn't know you well enough, but honestly, at this point—"

"You're not so sure?" I round on him. "Well, can't say I didn't warn you." I shove past him, aiming for the door—I'm *done* here, done with him—but he catches my arm again.

"*Reena*," Sawyer says sharply. "Can you stop?"

I shake my head. "Look, I'm sorry," I tell him, trying to get away as cleanly as I can, as if that's even a thing that's possible with Sawyer. "Last night, all of it, I'm just—"

"Don't apologize," he orders. "Look, I don't— I just don't want this to be another way for us to leave each other, okay?"

Oh, come on. "Each *other*?" I look at him skeptically. "I've been *right* here."

"I know," Sawyer agrees. "And now you don't trust me as far as you can throw me, I know that, too. You've been pretty clear." He bends down close to my ear. "But I think you're glad it happened that way."

I snort derisively. "Oh, yeah, it was awesome."

"I'm serious," he says, and I can tell by his voice that he really is. "I think secretly you love it because it gives you an excuse to be closed off to everyone and not give anybody the chance to mess with you." Sawyer gets closer, both of us still under the patio awning, this place we've known all our lives. "But the truth is, you wouldn't let me mess with you to begin with. You never let me that far in. And now you get to hold me at arm's length and tell yourself I deserve it, and maybe I do, but that's tough because it's not good enough this time." He's got me backed against the exterior wall of the restaurant, right up in my space like he wants to make one hundred percent sure I know he's not going away. "You hear me, Reena? I want more than that."

I shake my head again, wishing I didn't have to hear him. "Shelby's never going to forgive me," is what comes out.

"God*damnit*, Reena," he says, voice rising; oh, I'm making him mad. "Can you please let me in for *one second*?"

"Seriously?" I demand. I feel myself get a little bigger, my shoulders broadening out. "Let *you* in? The whole entire time we were together I tried to get you to talk to me."

That gets his attention. "About what?" he asks, sounding genuinely curious.

"About everything!" I tell him. "About your family, about your friends, about Allie—"

"I gave Allie the keys to her car."

"What?" It's so sudden I think I've misheard him, and when I look at his face I can tell he's surprised himself. For a second we only just stare at each other, recalibrating, but then he takes a breath and goes on.

"The night she died." It looks as if it's physically painful for him to say it, as if the words taste like gravel or bone. "I had her keys. And I let her have them."

I don't— It feels like he's speaking Mandarin. "But we

were together the night she died," I say, still not understanding. "At the ice cream place."

"Before that." Sawyer exhales, rakes his hands through his hair. All of a sudden the tenor of this conversation has changed completely, like it's about so much more than just him and me. "Before I came to the restaurant. We were at a party with some people. Lauren and all of them. We didn't drive together, but she gave me her keys because she didn't want to carry a purse. She had that big stupid purse, you know?" Sawyer shrugs and heads across the patio even though it's still raining, leaves the safe harbor of the awning for the glider at the edge of the yard. After a minute I follow.

"We were there for like an hour," he tells me, swinging just a little, picking reflexively at the seam of his work pants. "Maybe an hour and a half. And we started to argue."

"Okay," I say softly. I perch beside him on the glider, same as the night just after Allie's funeral. It makes it easier, somehow, not to have to stare him in the eye. I can hear the restaurant sounds just like I could the last time we did this, the same underwater sensation. "I'm with you so far."

Sawyer nods. "She said she was leaving," he continues after a minute. My heart is thudding hard behind my ribs. "She yelled at me to give her the keys, and she wasn't—she wasn't sloppy, you know? It wasn't like she was falling down. But she'd had a couple beers and there was that look in her eye, and—" He breaks off all of a sudden, shrugging helplessly. He looks about ten years old. "I never, ever should have let her go. But I did. I threw her the keys and I told her to get the hell lost, if that's how she felt about stuff, and I—"

"—and you came to the restaurant and found me."

Sawyer nods like all the breath has gone out of him. The rain is slipping down the back of my neck. "So," he says eventually, eyes on the other side of the courtyard; *Get the hell lost*, he told her, and she did. "Now you know."

Now I know.

For a long time neither of us says anything, rain spritzing down on the pavement. I think of Sawyer carrying that secret across the country. I think of Allie dying before she ever got to live. I cry for a while, sitting there on the glider, remembering the purple ribbon I didn't wear in the weeks after the accident, like no pretty length of grosgrain would stretch around whatever it was I'd lost. Sawyer's arm is warm and damp against mine. "What was the fight about?" I ask him finally.

"You." Just like that, no hesitation at all: Sawyer lifts his head to look at me, his expression wry and heartbroken and honest. "We were fighting about you."

"Me?" My stomach lands somewhere around my shoes. I can't believe this was true the entire time we were together. I can't believe he hasn't told me this until now. *"Why?"*

"She said you were in love with me."

There's a sound, this quiet gasping whimper, and it takes

me a minute to realize it's coming from my mouth. "What?" I manage. "She said—*what*?"

Sawyer shrugs. "You heard me," he says quietly, a simple matter-of-factness in his manner that leaves no doubt in my mind he's telling the truth. "She said you were in love with me even though you'd never admit it, and you had been for a long time, and she thought—" He shakes his head. "She thought I loved you back."

"What?" I say again, just the one word on repeat like a CD that's gotten stuck. My first reaction is this totally irrational embarrassment on behalf of my fifteen-year-old self, although—what with our kid being big enough to walk and talk—it's probably a little late to feel humiliated at the idea of Sawyer knowing I had a crush on him back then. Still, knowing that Allie sold me out like that, used my most private feelings for some kind of messed-up emotional currency in a drunk fight with her boyfriend—that stings. For the hundred thousandth time I wish she hadn't crashed her car and disappeared forever, if only so I could tell her what a bitch move that was.

Then again: I betrayed her, too. I think of the very first time Sawyer ever kissed me, on the hood of the Jeep outside the ice cream place on the very last night of Allie's life. There's no limit to the ways that we managed to fail each other as best friends, Allie and I. It makes me feel so colossally sad.

"For what it's worth, I don't think she meant to hurt you," Sawyer says now, watching my face as if he's trying to read hieroglyphics carved there. "I think she was just . . . upset." He shrugs one more time, honest and regretful. "And anyway, it's not like she was wrong."

I stare at him. I blink. "Meaning . . . ?"

"Are you kidding?" Sawyer looks at me like I'm deranged, like we're still on two totally different sides of the river. "Why do you think I came looking for you that night, Reena? To see if it was true. *I left my drunk girlfriend with her car keys* and I came and I found you, do you understand that? Why the hell would I ever have done that if I didn't care whether or not it was true?"

"Uh-uh." I shake my head stubbornly, refusing to believe it. "You never paid one speck of attention to me before—"

"No, *you* never paid one speck of attention!" Sawyer's voice rises. "You were so worried about making sure I never knew you felt one way or the other about me so that you wouldn't have to be embarrassed or vulnerable or *whatever*—" He stops and gets up off the glider. Turns around to look me in the eye. "Well, guess what, Reena? I never knew you felt one way or the other about me." He shrugs a little, elegant shoulders just barely moving. It's the saddest thing I've ever seen him do. "So I guess you won."

We gaze at each other for a moment, the rain still hissing steadily all around us and my heart beating fast like moth wings, so small and whisper-quiet inside my chest. I know it's my move here, that Sawyer's told me the worst and most honest thing he can think of. I remember the fight I had with Allie that night at the party: *You want to win this fight, Reena?* It doesn't feel like I've won anything at all.

"It means woodcutter," I tell him finally, wiping either rain or tears off my face with the back of one cold, damp hand. I don't know why it suddenly feels like it matters.

Sawyer physically startles at the sound of my voice. He looks at me, blinking. "Huh?" he asks.

"Your name," I manage after a moment. "One who saws."

It's not what he was hoping for; the sag of his body makes that much unmistakably clear. Still, Sawyer musters a smile. "Makes sense, I guess," is all he tells me. Offers a hand to pull me to my feet.

46

Before

I dropped Sawyer at home after our miserable night in South Beach, drove back to my house, and beelined directly into the downstairs bathroom. I threw up everything I'd eaten all day.

Everything.

I sat on the tile for a long time after that, head against the wall, waiting for my stomach to settle, for my breath to stop coming so quick. I sobbed for a while, feeling pathetic. I thought my insides were actually in revolt. In the morning, Soledad brought me toast and tea and sat at the edge of the mattress reading novels in Spanish, thumb stroking absently along the arch of my foot while she listened to me try not to cry.

"What happened?" she asked once, around lunchtime. I shrugged into the pillows on the bed.

I felt better by dinner, thought of calling him, decided against it.

I sat awake in bed till the sun came up.

The morning after that, I got sick again. Then a day of nothing.

Then again the day after that.

(That was when I started to freak.)

I drove all the way to a Walgreens in Pompano Beach to buy a pregnancy test, went over to Shelby's to take it. I curled my arms around my knees on the carpet-covered lid of the toilet. Shelby sat cross-legged on the floor.

"Just look at it for me, okay?" I told her, watching the second hand creep along the face of my watch—slowly, slowly. I couldn't get over the notion that this absolutely could not be happening to me. I almost wasn't even nervous, that's how sure I was that it wasn't real. We'd been careful, hadn't we? I'd made sure we were careful. "Just . . . look."

"I'm looking," she said, peering at the stick and frowning. She was wearing denim cutoffs and a T-shirt with the Mario Bros. on it. "But it's not—it's not doing anything yet."

"How is it not doing anything?" I demanded, leaning forward to grab it out of her hand. "It's got to be—"

Shelby pulled it back, looked more closely; she glanced again at the picture on the back of the box. "*Reena*," she said then, and she looked so *sorry*. I closed my eyes so I wouldn't have to see.

47

After

There are complications following my father's surgery, bleeding that requires a second operation. We spend a week's worth of days and nights in that waiting room, Cade and Soledad and I, taking shifts, going home for showers, making dinners out of Diet Coke and Fritos from the vending machines. Shelby's mom leaves casseroles on our doorstep. Lydia brings changes of clothes. Hannah comes down with a summer cold that keeps us up nights and turns me, for all intents and purposes, into an extra from a movie about the zombie apocalypse; Sawyer turns up at the hospital to take her off my hands for twenty-four hours, hands me a Tupperware container full of risotto I can tell he's made himself.

"I owed you dinner," he tells me, hitching the baby up on his hip.

"You owe me more than dinner," I tell him, but there's no real heat behind it. I grab his free hand, squeeze a little in spite of myself. "Thanks."

Sawyer smiles. "You're welcome."

We don't talk much, my family. Cade paces. I read magazines. Soledad prays. She's stopped eating almost entirely; I think of Jesus in the desert, fighting his demons for forty days.

"About the thing," she says suddenly, one night when I come to relieve her. She's watching Leno with heavy-lidded eyes. "I shouldn't have said that to you. I shouldn't have told you to think. I know you think."

"It's fine." I shrug. "It doesn't matter."

"It does, though."

"Yeah," I say eventually. "I guess it does." I hold up a bag of takeout and think of how Cade and I used to beat the crap out of each other as kids and then move on a minute later as soon as something more important came up, like nothing had even happened. Maybe that's just how families work. "I brought you food. Drive-thru was the only place open."

"Thanks, sweetheart." She sighs. "Sawyer has the baby?"

"Mm-hmm."

"He doesn't do a bad job with her," she says. "I have to hand him that."

I think of Seattle, of rainy woods and coffee on cloudy mornings. I think of the desert and hot, arid air. I think of the middle of this country, the endless rolling green of it, and I want so badly, badly, badly to get out of this place.

"Yeah," I tell her. "You really do."

On the way home the next morning, I stop by Target and pick up a road atlas of the continental United States.

Just to see.

Hannah and I are splitting a PBJ in the kitchen when the bell rings—not once, but five or six times in a row, incessant. I pad barefoot through the living room with the baby on my hip and fling it open: There's Shelby on the other side of the door, wearing a Ms. Pac-Man T-shirt and a scowl, holding a big glass tray of marbled brownies. "I made these," she says curtly, thrusting them at me. "Eat them or don't."

I reach my free hand out like a reflex, barely catching the tray before it crashes to the tiles. With everything that's been going on around here, our paths haven't crossed in a couple of weeks. "Thanks," I tell her, a little shocked; then, trying for a smile: "Did you poison them?"

Shelby's eyes narrow. "I should have," she huffs. She squares her shoulders, muscles past me into the house. "I told you I wasn't going to be shitty as long as you weren't shitty," she announces, flouncing onto the couch. "Well, you *were* shitty. But I'm gonna be cool."

I blink, not totally understanding, resting the tray of brownies on top of the TV. "Really?"

"Yes, really." She still looks annoyed, but she holds her arms out for the baby, waits for me to hand her over and cuddles her in the crook of her freckly arm. Hannah babbles her giddy pleasure—she loves Shelby, always has. Shelby traces her thumb over Hannah's downy ear. "I feel like maybe you haven't had a whole lot of breaks. So I'm giving you one."

Right away I feel a lump rise up in my throat. My hands flutter sort of helplessly at my sides. "You always give me breaks," I manage, voice cracking a little bit—and I don't deserve her, I don't, somebody as fierce as Shelby to help me fight my wars. "You're my best friend."

Shelby cocks her head to the side, wrinkles up the edges of her mouth like maybe she's worried I'm going to get her started, too. "Oh, stop it," she orders gruffly, but then: "You're my best friend, too."

Well, that does it. I'm crying for real when I sit down on the sofa, everything so painfully close to the surface all the time. "I'm sorry," I tell her, almost too far gone to get the words out. "I didn't mean to mess with your brother. I didn't mean to screw everything up."

Shelby slides an arm around my shoulders so she's holding me and Hannah both. "I know," she tells me, her ginger temple bumping softly against mine. "I'm sorry, too. I should have come over here right away, when your dad got sick. That was really shitty of me."

"I thought you were going to hate me forever," I tell her, and realize that it's true: I thought for sure our friendship had gone the way of mine and Allie's, that I'd lost her for good and would never be able to find a way back. I'm so hugely relieved that she's here.

Shelby smiles. "I could never hate you, dummy," she tells me. "I love you too much for that." She sighs a little, squeezes. Waits for me to quiet down. "Shh, Reena. You're okay." She says it again a minute later, just quiet: "You're okay," she promises softly, and there's something in her voice to make me believe.

48

Before

I sat on the floor of Shelby's bathroom for a long time, forehead on the edge of the tub, not talking. The porcelain felt cold and clean against my skin. Shelby leaned her back on the door, cross-legged and patient, dragging the edge of the cardboard box beneath her nail. I could hear her mother moving around in the kitchen, making dinner and singing along to the radio, the sound of life spinning on.

I was pregnant.

Me.

"Jesus Christ, Shelby," I finally whispered, bracing my hands on the tub and looking up. My head, as I lifted it, felt heavy enough to snap off my neck entirely. I wished for a swamp to swallow me. I wished for my mom. "What am I going to *do*?"

I had to tell Soledad.

I had to tell my father.

I had to tell—

Oh *God.*

I splashed some water on my face and drove south down 95, toward Sawyer and the crumbling stucco house. It was past twilight, palm trees silhouetted gray and graceful against the darkening sky. I sped. I sped a *lot*, actually, and also I was crying again, and when I made the left turn onto Powerline Road I came within centimeters of smashing into a canary-yellow pickup truck and very nearly killed myself.

I very nearly killed myself and my *kid.*

The blaring horn faded in the distance and I pulled over as soon as I could, two hands shaking on the wheel. I thought of Allie and near misses, wondered why on earth things happen the way they do. I missed her more than I ever had, if that was possible. My breath came in crazy gulping sobs.

"Congratulations," I said suddenly, talking to her like she was sitting in the passenger seat beside me, feet up on the dashboard and singing along to the radio, her head thrown back to laugh loud and hard. I'd never done that before, not in all the months she'd been gone. "You were right. I couldn't handle it. I *can't* handle it, and it just—it would have been great of you to stick the hell around and help me out."

Cars whizzed by on the avenue. Allie didn't reply.

Finally I pulled it together enough to make it the rest of the way to Sawyer's, gliding silently up to the curb across the street. I shut off the engine and got out, flip-flops sinking into the dry, brittle grass. The remains of two broken beer bottles were scattered on the pavement, green and sharp.

I had a long stare at the low, sprawling house: It looked worse than I'd remembered, dirty aluminum awnings over the windows and a weird rusty stain creeping up the exterior near the door. A random orange traffic cone sat overturned on the lawn. I'd thought it was some exotic clubhouse, romantically shabby. Now it just looked bleak.

The windows were dark but Sawyer's Jeep was in the driveway, and I was talking myself into crossing and ringing the bell when the front door opened and there he was: slouching and feline, angry and sad. I hardly even recognized his face. He'd lost a startling amount of weight, I realized. I hadn't noticed that before. His shoulders jutted oddly beneath his T-shirt, fiberglass or shale.

Actually, I thought as I stood there: They looked sort of oddly like wings.

He didn't see me. He wasn't looking. He was holding a backpack, some ridiculous old camping number I happened to know was his father's, because my father had one, too. They'd bought them together when they were teenagers, back when they used to do things like camp.

Sawyer crossed the lawn, threw the pack in the backseat

of his Jeep and slid into the driver's seat. I stood there and watched him, struck dumb. I didn't know where he was going. I didn't know how long he'd be gone. I waited as the engine turned over, loud and cranky—Reena in the background, watching as usual. The taillights glowed like two red coals.

Wait, I almost shouted, but didn't, and that would be my burden to bear. Instead, I stood on the curb and I watched him disappear, lights fading in the distance like waking up from a dream.

I stood there for a long time, feet rooted to the sidewalk, and in my head the stillness began to make a sick kind of sense. I wasn't going *anywhere*, I realized numbly—not college, not Chicago, not off into the sunset to see the great wide world. This was it. Sawyer was gone—*gone* gone, I knew already, the way you know you're hungry or that it's about to rain—and I was going to have to stay in Broward. I was going to have to do this—whatever *this* was—on my own.

I was crying again, silent and stupid, right there on the curb like the worst kind of fool. All that careful planning, all those maps and magazines, those nights I'd dreamed myself to sleep. The places I was going to explore, the stories I was going to write when I got there—and for what? I looked down at the damp, cracked pavement, felt the boundaries of my life constricting around me. The air was heavy and oppressive, pushing against the surface of my skin.

At long last, I pulled it together, wiped my eyes and scrubbed my palms against my jeans. I took a deep breath and headed for the only destination that made sense at this particular juncture:

I got back in the car and drove toward home.

49

After

My father gets released in the middle of August, twenty pounds lighter and considerably worse for wear. He spends most days in the living room or at physical therapy, groggy or annoyed, but he is alive, and that is good enough for now. We settle into a new routine, all of us Monteros, full of medicines and lists. I start cooking dinner. Silence descends like a shroud. A few times a week, Sawyer's Jeep rumbles to the curb and he takes Hannah to the park or the zoo for a couple of hours.

"How are you?" he always asks, when I bring her outside.

"Fine," I always tell him, and watch him disappear down the road.

During the day I am a dutiful daughter. I weed the

garden. I salt the soup. At night I read my atlas like a Bible, imagining my escape.

It goes on like this for a while, a steady drone and the hum of the central air, until one afternoon when I come downstairs after putting Hannah down for a nap and find my dad sitting on the couch, flipping the channels. "Do you need anything?" I ask automatically. "You hungry?"

"I'm all right," he says. Then, clicking the TV off: "Come here for a minute, daughter of mine."

I feel the nerves stir in my stomach—a warm prickly rush of guilt and anxiety, though I know there was a time when I felt safer with my father than with anyone else on earth. "What's up?" I ask, trying not to sound afraid. My hands move in front of me like butterflies. My toes curl down against the rug.

"Sit down," he tells me, and I do, perching on the edge of the sofa beside him, feet still planted on the carpet like at any second I might jump up and bolt.

"I want to talk to you about that night at dinner," he says.

"I'm sorry," I say immediately, trying to avoid the inevitable lecture: If he's going to lay into me again, I'd rather just take the blame right off the bat and be done with it, preempt the whole affair. My textbooks are piled on the desk in my bedroom. I've got finals starting next week. "I shouldn't have lost my temper like that."

"It's not that," he says, which is surprising. He shakes his head, sighs a little. "I owe you an apology."

"It's just been a really difficult—" I stop. "You do?"

"I do." There's something stilted about his speech, like he's been practicing. I wait. "You were right, Reena," he begins after a moment, "about what you said at the table. I didn't protect you after—" He breaks off, tries again. "Once the baby came. I was angry. You know that. I said rotten things to you, and I'm ashamed of myself for that. I'm sorry." He swallows. "This isn't the life I imagined for you."

I shrug, hands still twisting in my lap. I tuck them between my knees to still them. "It's not the life I imagined for me, either."

"I know. But as your dad, I think it felt—it felt like a personal failure to me, to see you lose Northwestern. A baby at sixteen—it's not the way I raised you. I'm sorry if that's difficult for you to hear, but it's true."

My cheeks feel hot. "I *know*."

"But that's not an excuse." My father sighs again; he looks so old lately, his face gone slightly slack. "I did a terrible job once you told me you were pregnant. I did a miserable, piss-poor job. You probably needed your parents more than you'd ever needed your parents in your entire life, and what did I do? I walked away."

I start to deny it, an absurd reflex. It's bizarre to hear him talk this way. Finally I nod. "Yeah," I tell him, which is about all I can manage. "It's been hard."

"But look at you," he says. "You've handled yourself

with a lot of grace. You're responsible. You took up your cross. You do a good job with Hannah. You might think I don't notice that, but I do."

I feel my eyes start to well up, that familiar clog in my throat. I feel like I've been on the verge of crying for the last two years. "Thanks."

"I know a lot of people have left you in your life," he tells me, and that's when the tears start for real. He gets a little closer, puts a heavy hand on my back. "Your mother, and Allie. Sawyer. And me, too." His arm slides down around my shoulder, pulls me close; he smells like laundry detergent and limes. "But what I want to tell you, sweetheart, is that that's not going to happen again, all right? I'm not going anywhere. No matter what happens, what you do or where you go—you're not going to lose me again."

Well, that rips it. All of a sudden it's like he's given me permission to let go of everything I've been holding on to so tightly—the guilt and fear I've walked around with since the night of his heart attack, the huge anger that's burrowed in behind my ribs. I rest my head on his shoulder and let myself a cry a little, leave a wet splotch on his shirt the way I haven't since I was a little girl. My father pets through my hair. I know this won't fix everything between us—I know we have many, many miles to walk—but it feels, at the very least, like a start.

"There's something else," he tells me, once I've pulled it together a little bit, hiccups instead of sobs. His hand is still on my back, familiar after all this time. "It's about Sawyer."

"Honestly?" I groan. "There's nothing going on between me and Sawyer."

"It's not that." My father shakes his head. "Although whatever decision you make about him is just that—it's your decision." He clears his throat again, straightens up. "There's something I never told you about Sawyer, about the time right before he left."

I feel my eyebrows shoot up; I can only imagine. "What?"

My father reaches for the glass of water on the table, takes a long sip before he goes on. "He came here, to the house. Looking for you."

"Wait," I say, blinking. "Before he left for good?"

He nods. "This was when things between us weren't so friendly, and I didn't invite him in, but his car was full of all kinds of nonsense, like he was going on a trip." He sets the water glass back down on the table. "I didn't know then that he was leaving, but I also never told you he came by."

I sit there for a minute, recalibrating. I feel like I've been hit with a wrecking ball. I think of Sawyer outside my house the other night, of him asking: *If I'd asked you to come with me, would you have?* I wipe my sweaty palms on my jeans. Maybe that's not even what Sawyer wanted that day—maybe I'm understanding it wrong—but if there was a bunch of stuff in his car it means that the day I watched him pack up and leave the crummy stucco house forever, he came to say good-bye before he went.

"Well." My father sits forward a bit, exhales like he's sort of exhausted himself. "I just wanted to tell you, Reena, that I'm sorry that I've been so hard on you. I've sat in judgment, and that was a mistake. If there's something—I'd like to try to make it up to you."

I struggle for a moment, trying to fit all the pieces together—to come up with some cure-all, a plan for living our lives in a new way. I'm about to tell him to forget it, that both of us just need time—when all of a sudden it occurs to me, as clear and as terrifying as the Book of Revelation. "I need your blessing for something," I tell him.

He hesitates for a moment: He thinks it's Sawyer-related, I'm sure, but to his great credit, he comes through. "Name it."

I raise my head, wipe my eyes, and stare at my father dead-on. "I'm going to take a trip."

50

Before

Back at home after leaving Sawyer's I shut the bedroom door and packed up all my guidebooks, threw my maps into the recycling. I ripped down my posters of Paris and Prague. I took the winter coat I'd gotten for Chicago—"I know it's jumping the gun a little," Soledad had said when she showed me the catalog, "but it's good to be prepared"—and shoved it into my closet, deep in the back, past where Sawyer and I had fooled around the afternoon of Cade and Stef's wedding. I imagined I could smell him, soapy and faint.

I had to take two breaks to throw up.

When I was finally done I sat in the middle of my bedroom floor for a while, looked around at my empty bookshelves and my naked walls. I leaned back and stared at the ceiling, two hands on my stomach. I cried for a while. I thought.

Eventually I wandered downstairs where Soledad was sweating onions, humming along to Dolly Parton under her breath. "Meat sauce," she told me, instead of hello, then: "I didn't know you were home." She laid one cool hand on my cheek like she was checking for a fever, for something she sensed but couldn't prove. "You feeling any better?"

I shrugged and then hugged her, impulsively and hard. She smelled clean and familiar, vanilla and home. "I'm okay," I managed, breathing her in to try and keep it together. "I'm fine."

"Well," she said, kissing my temple. She sounded surprised, and it occurred to me that maybe I hadn't let her hold me in a while. "Set the table, then."

I stuck close to the house for a while after that, reading next to Soledad and shadowing my father in his garden, plucking tiny crimson strawberries from their vines. I wanted, a little bizarrely, to spend time with both of them while I still had the chance: I knew I was going to lose them anyway, sure as if I was moving clear across the world. I knew they were never going to look at me the same way again—and honestly wasn't sure if I'd even want them to. Still, part of me missed them already, and I wanted to soak them up while I could.

So I pruned the tomatoes and helped Sol with dinner, got used to the way my life would be. I sat in the yard underneath the orange trees and tried to tell myself it could be enough, that I could be happy this way, that I wasn't terrified and lonely, that the walls weren't pressing in on all sides.

I thought he might call. I watched the phone like a sentry.

He didn't.

Saturday night and my father was flipping through old movies on cable, tonic and lime on the table beside him. He looked at me a little curiously as I came in. "Hi, sweetheart," he said and wrapped his heavy arm around my shoulders. He looked so glad to see me it almost broke my heart. "You're not going out?"

"Nope," I said, did my best to keep my voice even. "I'm staying right here."

It took everybody but me more than a full week to realize Sawyer was gone.

I guess I couldn't totally blame them. His attendance at work and family dinners was spotty, to put it mildly; he came and went from the dingy stucco house as he pleased. So when he didn't turn up for his shifts for a couple of days, and then a couple of days after that—well. "Goddamnit, Sawyer," I heard Roger mutter one night, manning the taps in the middle of the dinner rush. "Pain in my ass."

If I suspected that Sawyer wasn't coming back anytime soon—and it was more than a suspicion, honestly; it was something I knew in my bones—I certainly wasn't telling. I wasn't saying much of anything, really. I went to school and I worked at the restaurant and I kept my mind studiously, fastidiously blank; every time I tried to wrap my brain around what was happening or make some kind of a plan, my thoughts just kind of . . . slid away. It felt like I was shuffling through my days wrapped in a thick swaddle of blankets, everything muffled and coming from some far-off place.

I didn't know how to deal with what was coming.

So I didn't.

That worked, for a while. I flew under the radar as best I could. I knew somewhere in the darkest corner of my mind that I was going to have to speak up sometime, about Sawyer and about the rest of it, but as the days ticked by there was some small insane part of me that began to think maybe I'd made the whole thing up. Maybe I'd imagined taking the test in Shelby's bathroom. Maybe I'd never been with Sawyer at all.

One afternoon at the end of May I came through the front door a bit later than usual, having spent a good fifteen minutes staring at the contents of my locker with absolutely no clue what books I might need to take with me, then managing to make two different wrong turns as I drove home from school. I was scaring myself a little. I was having trouble motivating myself enough to care.

I was going to head straight upstairs to my bedroom—I'd been spending an awful lot of time staring at the wall—but my father and Soledad were sitting on the couch side by side like a couple of tin soldiers, waiting. "Hi, Reena," they said, when I came in.

I blinked. "Um," I said, dropping my bag on the floor where I stood. I felt vaguely sick. "Hi."

My first thought was that they knew about the baby somehow, that they'd intuited just by virtue of knowing me, and the wave of relief I felt in that moment was tidal and huge. Then I realized that wasn't it at all.

"We need to talk about Sawyer," Soledad told me. "Roger and Lydia need to know where he is."

"Sawyer?" I repeated. I had a sharp, ridiculous urge to laugh. "I have no idea."

"Reena," my father snapped, "this is no time to play—"

"Leo," Soledad interrupted; then, to me: "Have you heard from him? Did you kids have a fight?"

I shook my head once and sat down hard in the armchair, this feeling like a physical collapse. Suddenly I was so, so tired. "He took off," I said, shrugging just a little. "I don't know where. But I don't think he's coming back."

That took them both by surprise; I don't know what they'd been expecting me to tell them, but it wasn't that. "When?" Soledad asked softly.

"Ten days ago?" I guessed. The days had started to seep together into a dark, endless river, whole weeks like an underwater blur. I couldn't keep this secret a whole lot longer. "Two weeks?"

My father had been listening quietly, dark gaze fixed in my direction. “Reena, sweetheart,” he said, clearly baffled. “Why didn’t you tell us?”

I took a deep breath, raised my chin to face the music. “There are a lot of things I haven’t told you,” I began.

To say my father didn’t take my pregnancy well would be like calling a category five hurricane a little bit of inconvenient drizzle. He yelled—Jesus Christ, he *yelled* at me, all kinds of hateful accusations I would like never to think about again. I cried. Soledad cried. And my father cried, too.

Then the quiet came in.

Soledad crept into my bedroom some nights, rubbed my back and whispered prayers in my ears. Shelby held my hand and told me jokes. They did what they could to soothe me, to make me feel less alone; still, I spent those long foggy months sure of nothing so much as the feeling of standing on the edge of a canyon and screaming, waiting for an echo that refused to come.

51

After

And so it happens. They find a replacement for me at the restaurant; Cade gets me new tires for my van. I come home from my last day of finals—a multiple choice from Professor Orrin that, true to form, still had a URL printed across the bottom—and find Soledad and my father drinking tea in the kitchen. "Hannah napping?" I ask, dropping my schoolbag on the counter. We need to run errands for some last-minute supplies—sunscreen and notebooks, novels on tape. We're scheduled to hit the road at the end of the week.

Soledad shakes her head, glances in my direction over her big ceramic mug. "She's in the garden," she tells me, once she's swallowed. "With Sawyer."

That is not what I'm expecting. I turn to my father, gaping a bit. He gazes back with an expression that isn't quite a smile. "Things change," he allows, eyebrows arcing with the barest hint of amusement. His color is much better, these days. "You of all people should know that."

I smile back, I can't help it, a disbelieving grin that pulls at the edges of my mouth. "I guess so," I tell him, and head outside into the heat. Sawyer and Hannah are sitting in a lawn chair reading *The Runaway Bunny*, Hannah's face flushed and sleepy and leaning back into Sawyer like she's known him all her life. I think of the first day he held her, how starkly terrified he looked, and marvel for a moment at how fast he learned to swim. I sit on the patio to listen, pulling my feet up onto a lounge chair and waiting for the bunny to come home.

Normally by the time a book is finished, Hannah's up and crowing for the next one, or otherwise she's bored and wants to play; today, though, she stays where she is, like she's waiting for something. Sawyer smoothes her dark hair back off her face. "Heard you're going," he says to me after a moment, eyes still on the baby—the delicate slope of her jawline, the birthmark on the side of her mouth. She looks a little bit like both of us, is the truth.

I nod and glance away myself, focus on the heavy, ripening tomato plants. It should feel more satisfying than it does that this time he's the one who'll be left behind. "Seems that way," I reply.

“Thought it through?”

“Of course,” I tell him, a bit of heat behind it. I feel my shoulders straighten, think of the itinerary I’ve planned so carefully my entire life. “I’ve got money saved. I’m smart, and we’ll be safe.” I shrug. “Anything happens I don’t know how to handle, my family is a phone call away. I want Hannah to grow up seeing places, you know? I want her to always know what’s out there.”

“Easy, tiger.” Sawyer smiles, unconcerned. Hannah’s falling asleep before my very eyes. “That’s not what I meant. Of course I know you wouldn’t be going if you didn’t think it was a good idea for the baby.”

I blink, look at him for a minute. “So then . . . ?”

“So then.” Sawyer shrugs a little himself. Still, he’s not looking at me. “I don’t know. I think I could have been a good dad.”

I close my eyes for a moment and lean back against the chaise. If you’d told me six weeks ago that this conversation even existed in the realm of human possibility, I would have laughed until my sides were sore and splitting. “I know,” is all I can think to say.

“I would never, ever ask you not to go, Reena,” he says softly. “Go. Do what you need to do. I already screwed up your plans once in this lifetime. I’m not going to do it again.” The baby’s asleep now, peaceful against his chest; Sawyer shifts her warm weight in a gesture I recognize as one I perform a hundred times a day, a series of small, necessary readjustments. "But I guess I'm just telling you I'll be here when and if you decide to come back."

For a second I only just stare at him. He's got to be kidding. He's got to be *nuts*. "What are you going to do, *wait* for me?" I ask, laughing a little. "In Broward?"

Sawyer doesn't smile. "That's the plan," is all he says.

"And do *what*?"

He considers it for a moment, that exaggerated thinking face he puts on to disguise the fact that he's already thought. "Who knows?" he asks finally, and I know I won't get another straight answer out of him this afternoon as surely as I know he's already made up his mind. "Work on my tan."

"You're insane," I tell him. Sawyer cocks his head like, *possibly*, and I roll my eyes at him, annoyed and stupidly fond of him at the same time. A warm, wet breeze shuffles the leaves of the coconut palms. "My father just told me," I say eventually. "That you came by before you left. I never knew that until now."

Sawyer raises his eyebrows, nods a bit. "Yeah, well," he says, tipping his chin in my direction. "Probably for the best, right? You said yourself you wouldn't have come."

"I said hypothetically."

"You wouldn't have," Sawyer tells me, then smiles. Around his neck is the silver half-moon pendant he gave to Allie years and years ago, tarnished and familiar. I wonder when and how he got it back. It's strange to see it again after all this time, pieces of our old lives slipping seamlessly into our new ones. "And you'd have been right."

I don't know what to say to that so I don't say anything, picking a bit at the seam of the cushion and tilting my face up into the sun. Sawyer leans back and closes his eyes. Hannah just dozes, sweet and oblivious, secret dreams fluttering inside her baby head.

52

Before

I graduated, at least.

I sleepwalked through the ceremony, sat in my big black robe in the air-conditioned auditorium listening to the valedictorian quote Dr. Seuss and trying not to barf. Shelby sat three rows in front of me, kept glancing over her shoulder and giving me the thumbs-up. My biggest accomplishment for the day was managing to cross the stage and pick up my useless diploma without bursting into tears.

Ms. Bowen came up to me afterward, threw her arms around me in congratulations and asked to meet my family. "You made a winner here, with Reena," she told them happily; if she was at all baffled by the fact that their collective disposition on this most auspicious of days was somewhere in the neighborhood of the Addams Family at Disneyland, she didn't let on. "I can't wait to hear all about how she does at Northwestern."

There was a moment of silence then—probably only a second or two, although to me it felt like it lasted sometime between nine months and an entire lifetime. Soledad *hmmed* noncommitally. My father cleared his throat. I could feel them both watching me, baffled, but in the end I just smiled my widest and most artificial, told her she wasn't the only one.

I tried to keep working my normal shifts at the restaurant, but in the end I called in so often that finally they went ahead and replaced me with someone new, a dishwater blonde with a pale, zitty complexion. She was nice enough and a decent worker, Shelby reported, but Lydia picked on her to no end. "Mama LeGrande is on the warpath," Shelby warned me, having dropped by with a movie and a magazine and a generous side of gossip that, thankfully, wasn't about me. "I'm thinking now is probably an awesome time to tell her that I'm gay."

I grinned. "Lydia wouldn't care that you're gay," I told her as I flipped through the glossy tabloid. The TV jabbered cheerfully in the background. "You could tell my parents if you wanted, though. Maybe take some of the heat off yours truly."

Shelby didn't smile. "You don't have to do this, you know," she said suddenly. She was painting her toenails dark blue, window opened to the sticky heat outside because the fumes made me sick to my stomach. Her ripped-up jeans were rolled halfway up her calves. “Reena.”

I sighed a bit, rolling over on the bed so I was staring up at the ceiling. There were faint tape marks up there, left over from a poster of the Brooklyn Bridge Allie had helped me hang when we were in middle school. I’d pulled it down along with all the rest. “Yeah, I do.”

“No, I mean. Not to like, hit you over the head with a Planned Parenthood brochure or anything, but”—Shelby looked at me pointedly—“you really don’t.”

I laughed in spite of myself, a dark, hollow sound. “You think I haven’t thought about that?” I asked her, propping myself up on one elbow. “You think it just, like, hasn’t occurred to me? Of course I’ve thought about it, Shelby.”

Shelby put the cap back on the nail polish, feet resting on the windowsill. “So?” she asked.

“So, nothing.” I shrugged into the pillows, resigned. “My father would hate me, for starters.”

“I hear that,” Shelby said slowly, “but not wanting your dad to be mad at you is not a good enough reason to have a baby when you’re sixteen.”

“Thank you, Captain Obvious.” I made a face. “I didn’t say he’d be mad at me. I said he’d *hate* me. I mean, he already hates me, but it’s the kind of hate I can maybe see mellowing out after a while. If I had an abortion, I might as well just pack my bags and forget I ever had a family.” I picked at a loose thread on the quilt, watching it unravel. "Anyway, that's not even really it."

"Okay," Shelby told me. She pressed a thumb against her big toe to make sure the polish was dry, then came over and flopped belly-down onto the bed beside me. Her hazel eyes were sharp and curious. "Then what is it really?"

I shrugged a little, trying to think how to explain it—how to tell her that in some weird way I'd already made a break between my old life and my new one. How to tell her that I just sort of felt it in my bones. In spite of myself I'd already started thinking of the person growing inside me as a *person*, a half-formed heart beating steady underneath my own. Late one night I'd found a chart on Google that talked about the size of the baby in relationship to different kinds of fruit: *Your baby is a grape, your baby is a mango*. It was me and this mango-size baby now, is what it felt like. We were all that we had in the world.

"I don't know," I said finally, turning to face her. I curled my knees up alongside my chest. "I get that this is going to change my entire life, Shelby. It's just, like . . ." I trailed off and shrugged again, determined and afraid. "My life is already changed."

Shelby looked at me like only a real friend can, like what I'd said made one sliver of sense. Then she sighed. "Well, all right then, baby," she said softly. "Let's rock and roll."

53

After

Shelby brings over a bottle of wine and a pint of ice cream on Friday, clomps up the stairs like a Clydesdale to help me pack. "Are you sure you don't want me to come with you?" she asks again, refolding a pair of jeans and tucking them into the duffel bag on my bed. I am packing light. Hannah sits nearby, playing with her lamb and duck. "We'll be like Thelma and Louise, only without the murder and fiery death."

I laugh. "I would love for you to come with me," I tell her, "but I need you to go back to school so you can make lots of money and support me in my decrepit old age."

"And keep you in the lifestyle to which you have become accustomed?"

"Exactly."

"Well, I have my orders, then." She sighs. "How I'm going to survive the rest of the summer without you, however, remains to be seen."

"Oh, stop," I say. "We'll be meeting up in Boston before you know it. And until then you'll be busy with Cara the hipster poli-comm major."

Shelby makes a face like, *Fair enough*. "True," she admits, smiling a secret sort of smile. "I do intend to be busy."

I'm missing Shelby's girlfriend's visit by two days: We're leaving tomorrow, Hannah and I, on a jaunt across the country in my crappy old car. It feels like pretend, but I'm dead serious this time: After all, you can't be a travel writer if you've never been anywhere, and I'm done sitting here waiting for my real life to find me. I have a giant atlas, a dozen blank notebooks, and no real plan except to take my girl and go. I am terrified and thrilled.

Shelby flops onto the bed, lifting Hannah onto her chest and grinning. "Hey, girlie," she says. She turns to me. "So everything is okay now? With your dad and Sol?"

"I wouldn't say that, exactly." I dig a couple of tank tops out of my dresser, toss them on the bed. "But better. I feel better about it. Good enough to go."

"Well, thank God for that." She makes a face. "About time. That's what makes me crazy about you Catholics. You torture each other over stuff that was finished and done with during the Holy Roman Empire. Force everybody to repent and repent and repent, world without end, amen. Makes me nuts."

I blink at her. "What did you just say?"

"I said it makes me nuts."

I just stand there for a minute.

What have I been doing, if not exactly that?

Above all, love each other deeply, because love covers over a multitude of sins. That's Peter. Peter, I always liked.

"Hey!" Shelby squints. "What?"

"Nothing." I jump on the bed with my two best girls and give them both a good long snuggle. "Nothing at all."

It's just first light when I reach Sawyer's house, dawn coming up gray and dripping behind me. I stopped at the gas station to fuel up and grab last-minute provisions; Hannah's asleep in the car seat, put out by the early hour. The radio bumbles, a low, soothing sound.

I dig a couple of pebbles out of the planters in the LeGrandes' front yard, then cut across the cluster of coconut palms on the lawn and toss them, one by one, at his window. Barely seven A.M. but it's already humid, the slick of damp Florida air across my skin.

Nothing happens. I hold my breath: This is a stupid gesture, way lamer than it is poetic, but it made a weird kind of sense on the way over here. I'm just about to give up when Sawyer raises the screen and looks. "That for me?" he asks. Even from a full flight down, he's got a hell of a smile.

I smile back, big and reflexive, and heft the enormous Slurpee in my free hand in a ninety-nine-cent salute. "Looks that way."

Sawyer nods a little, sleepy and impressed. "It's early," is all he says.

"I know. I didn't want to waste any time." I hesitate, and then I say it: "I just stopped by to find out if you felt like taking a trip."

Even from all the way down here I can see his dark eyebrows arc. "Where you going?" he asks, leaning a little further out the window, like he's trying to get a good look at my face.

I shrug, raise my hands a little helplessly. "Not sure," I admit, still grinning. It feels hugely powerful to say. "But I brought a lot of notebooks."

"Oh, yeah?" he asks, faux-casual. "Gonna do some writing?"

"Thinking about it," I tell him, equally glib. It feels like we're circling something here, like maybe we both know where this is headed. Like maybe we sort of always have. "Gonna start in Seattle."

Sawyer nods his approval. "Seattle is nice," he says mildly. His tan fingers curve around the window frame. "When are you leaving?"

"Right now."

Sawyer doesn't say anything for a moment, then: "Wow." He's looking at me like he's known me forever. He's looking at me like I surprise him every day. He straightens up in the window, tall and familiar; the cup is damp and heavy in my hand. "I mean. Can you wait five minutes for me to put clothes on?"

I laugh out loud and sudden, like there's something fizzing and effervescent inside my veins. I didn't realize until right this second that I was holding my breath, but letting it out is hugely relieving, years and years' worth of tension draining away. "I think so," I say, still giggling—*giggling*, seriously, like I haven't done in forever. Like Allie and I used to when we were little kids playing outside. "That sounds fine."

"Good," Sawyer says, and starts to tug the window down. "Stay put. I'll be right there."

"Okay," I tell him, then: "Hey, Sawyer?"

He stops, peers back out at me. "Yeah? What's up?"

I stand there. I gather my courage. I take a breath so deep it feels like it comes from the ground underneath my feet, and then I jump: "I love you, you know that?"

"I—" Sawyer breaks off, grinning hard and bright and happy. He looks like a little kid himself. "I do know that, actually," he says after a moment. "But—*Jesus*, Reena." He laughs a bit, disbelieving. "It's nice to hear."

It's nice to *say*, I want to tell him, then realize I've got a whole country to say it. I've got a whole continent. I've got the whole world. The sun is rising, orange, a glowing circle in the sky.

"Come on," I call, tilting my chin up. "I'm driving this time."

Acknowledgments

The list of people responsible for turning *How to Love* into a reality is so long as to leave me completely dumbstruck. A simple *thank you* feels absurd and inadequate, but my gratitude is deep: to Josh Bank, Sara Shandler, and Joelle Hobeika at Alloy, for plucking me out of the pile and quite literally making my dreams come true—I couldn't ask for a sharper, smarter, more hilarious team. To Alessandra Balzer and everyone at Balzer + Bray for their bottomless energy and wisdom. To the lovely ladies of the Fourteenery, for the moral support and the hundreds of goofy, insightful emails. To Shana Walden, Adrienne Cote, Erin Guthrie, and Rachel Hutchinson: They know why. To Chris, Frank, and Jackie Cotugno, for putting up with my particular brand of perpetually distracted mania for almost thirty years now, and Tom Colleran, who is and always has been my truest of norths. I count my blessings daily. I love you all so very much.

Read on for a sneak peek at

Katie Cotugno's next novel, 99 DAYS

DAY 1

Julia Donnelly eggs my house the first night I'm back in Star Lake, and that's how I know everyone still remembers everything.

"Quite the welcome wagon," my mom says, coming outside to stand on the lawn beside me and survey the runny yellow damage to her lopsided lilac Victorian. There are yolks smeared down all the windows. There are eggshells in the shrubs. Just past ten in the morning, and it's already starting to smell rotten, sulfurous and baking in the early summer sun. "They must have gone to Costco to get all those eggs."

"Can you not?" My heart is pounding. I'd forgotten this, or tried to, what it was like before I ran away from here a year ago: Julia's reign of holy terror, designed with ruthless precision to bring me to justice for all my various capital crimes. The bottoms of my feet are clammy inside my lace-up boots. I glance over my shoulder at the sleepy street beyond the long, windy driveway, half-expecting to see her cruising by in her family's ancient Bronco, admiring her handiwork. "Where's the hose?"

"Oh, leave it." My mom, of course, is completely unbothered, the toss of her curly blonde head designed to let me know I'm overreacting. Nothing is a big deal when it comes to my mother: The President of the United States could egg her house, her house itself could *burn down*, and it would turn into not a big deal. *It's a good story,* she used to say whenever I'd come to her with some little-kid unfairness to report, no recess or getting picked last for basketball. *Remember this for later, Molly. It'll make a good story someday.* It never occurred to me to ask which one of us would be doing the telling. "I'll call Alex to come clean it up this afternoon."

"Are you kidding?" I say shrilly. My face feels red and blotchy, and all I want to do is make myself as small as humanly possible—the size of a dust mote, the size of a speck—but there's no way I'm letting my mom's handyman spray a half-cooked omelet off the front of the house just because everyone in this town thinks I'm a slut and wants to remind me. "I said where's the *hose*, Mom?"

"Watch the tone, please, Molly." My mom shakes her head resolutely. Somewhere under the egg and the garden I can smell her, the lavender-sandalwood perfume she's worn since I was a baby. She hasn't changed at all since I left here: the silver rings on every one of her fingers, her tissue-thin black cardigan and her ripped jeans. When I was little I thought my mom was the most beautiful woman in the world. Whenever she'd go on tour, reading from her fat novels in bookstores in New York City and Chicago and L.A., I used to lie on my stomach in the Donnellys' living room and look at the author photos on the backs of all her books. "Don't you blame me; I'm not the one who did this to you."

I turn on her then, standing on the grass in this place I never wanted to come back to, not in a hundred million years. "Who would you like me to *blame*, then?" I demand. For a second I let myself remember it, the cold, sick feeling of seeing the article in *People* for the first time in April of junior year, along with the grossest, juiciest scenes from the novel and a glossy picture of my mom leaning against her desk: *Diana Barlow's latest novel,* Driftwood, *was based on her daughter's complicated relationship with two local boys.* The knowing in my ribs and stomach and spine that now everyone else would know, too. "Who?"

For a second my mom looks completely exhausted, older than I ever think of her as being—glamorous or not, she was almost forty when she adopted me, is close to sixty now. Then she blinks, and it's gone. "Molly—"

"Look, don't." I hold up a hand to stop her, wanting so, so badly not to talk about it. To be anywhere other than here. Ninety-nine days between now and the first day of freshman orientation in Boston, I remind myself, trying to take a deep breath and not give in to the overwhelming urge to bolt for the nearest bus station as fast as my two legs can carry me—not as fast, admittedly, as they might have a year ago. Ninety-nine days, and I can leave for college and be done.

My mom stands in the yard and looks at me: She's barefoot like always, dark nails and a tattoo of a rose on her ankle like a cross between Carole King and the first lady of a motorcycle gang. *It'll make a great story someday*. She *said* that, she *told* me what was going to happen, so really there's no earthly reason to still be so baffled after all this time that I told her the worst, most secret, most important thing in my life—and she wrote a best-selling book about it.

"The hose is in the shed," she finally says.

"Thank you." I swallow down the phlegmy thickness in my throat and head for the backyard, squirming against the sour, panicky sweat I can feel gathered at the base of my backbone. I wait until I'm hidden in the blue-gray shade of the house before I let myself cry.

DAY 2

I spend the next day holed up in my bedroom with the blinds closed, eating Red Vines and watching weird Netflix documentaries on my laptop, hiding out like a wounded fugitive in the last third of a Clint Eastwood movie. Vita, my mom's ornery old tabby, wanders in and out as she likes. Everything up here is the same as I left it: blue-and-white striped wallpaper, the cheerful yellow rug, the fluffy gray duvet on the bed. The *Golly, Molly* artwork a designer friend of my mom's did when I was a baby hanging above the desk, right next to a bulletin board holding my track meet schedule from junior year and a photo of me at the Donnellys' farmhouse with Julia and Patrick and Gabe, my mouth wide open mid-laugh. Even my hairbrush is still sitting on the dresser, the one I forgot to take with me in my mad dash out of Star Lake after the *People* article, like it was just waiting for me to come crawling all the way back here with a head full of knots.

It's the photo I keep catching myself looking at, though, like there's some kind of karmic magnet attached to the back of it drawing my attention from clear across the room. Finally, I haul myself out of bed and pull it down to examine more closely: It's from their family party the summer after freshman year, back when Patrick and I were dating. The four of us are sitting sprawled on the ratty old couch in the barn behind the farmhouse, me and all three Donnellys, Julia in the middle of saying something snarky and Patrick with his arm hooked tight around my waist. Gabe's looking right at me, although I never actually noticed that until after everything happened. Just holding the stupid picture feels like pressing on a bruise.

Patrick's not even home this summer, I know from creeping him on Facebook. He's doing some volunteer program in Colorado, clearing brush and learning to fight forest fires just like he always dreamed of doing when we were little and running around in the woods behind his parents' house. There's no chance of even bumping into him around town.

Probably there's no good reason to feel disappointed about that.

I slap the photo facedown on the desktop and climb back under the covers, pushing Vita onto the carpet—this room has been hers and the dog's in my absence, the sticky layer of pet hair has made that much abundantly clear. When

I was a kid, living up here made me feel like a princess, tucked in the third-floor turret of my mom's old haunted house. Now, barely a week after high school graduation, it makes me feel like one again—trapped in a magical tower, with no place in the whole world to go.

I dig the last Red Vine out of the cellophane package just as Vita hops right back up onto the pillow beside me. "Get out, Vita," I order, pushing her gently off again and rolling my eyes at the haughty flick of her feline tail as she stalks out the door, fully expecting her to turn up again almost immediately.

DAY 3

Vita doesn't.

DAY 4

Imogen doesn't, either. When I was staring down my summer-long sentence in Star Lake, the idea of seeing her again was the only thing that made it feel at all bearable, but so far my *hey, I'm back* and *let's hang out* texts have gone resolutely unanswered. Could be she hates me, too. Imogen and I have been friends since first grade, and she stuck by me pretty hard at the end of junior year, sitting beside me in the cafeteria at school even as everyone else at our lunch table mysteriously disappeared and the whispers turned into something way, way worse. Still, the truth is I didn't exactly give her a heads-up before I left Star Lake to do my senior year at Bristol—an all-girls boarding school plunked like a missile silo in the middle of the desert outside Tempe, Arizona.

Absconded under the cover of darkness, more like.

By the next day it's been a full ninety-six hours of

minimal human contact, though, so when my mom knocks hard on the bedroom door to let me know her cleaning lady is coming, I pull some clean shorts out of the pile of detritus already accumulated on my floor. My T-shirts and underwear are still in my giant duffel. I'll have to unpack at some point, probably, although the truth is I'd almost rather live out of a suitcase for three months. My old sneakers are tucked underneath the desk chair I notice while I'm crouched down there, the laces still tied from the last time I wore them—the day the article came out I remember suddenly, like I thought I could somehow outrun a national publication. I had sprinted as hard and as fast as I could manage.

I'd thrown up on the dusty side of the road.

Woof. I do my best to shake off the memory, grabbing the photo of me and the Donnellys—still facedown on the desk where I left it the other night—and shoving it into the back of the drawer in my nightstand. Then I lace my boots up and take my neglected old Passat into Star Lake proper.

It's cool enough to open the windows, and even through the pine trees lining the sides of Route 4 I can smell the slightly mildewy scent of the lake as I head for the short stretch of civilization that makes up downtown: Main Street is small and rumpled, all diners and dingy grocery stores, a roller rink that hasn't been open since roughly 1982. That's about the last time this place was a destination, as far as I've ever been able to tell—the lakefront plus the endless green stretch of the Catskill Mountains was a big vacation spot in the sixties and seventies, but ever since I can remember Star Lake has had the air of something that used to be but isn't anymore, like you fell into your grandparents' honeymoon by mistake.

I speed up as I bypass the Donnellys' pizza shop, slouching low in my seat like a gangbanger until I pull up in front of French Roast, the coffee shop where Imogen's worked since we were freshmen. I open the door to the smell of freshly ground beans and the sound of some moody girl singer on the radio. The shop is mostly empty, a late-morning lull. Imogen's standing behind the counter, midnight dark hair hanging in her eyes, and when she looks up at the jangle of the bells a look of guilty, awkward panic flashes across her pretty face in the moment before she can quell it.

"Oh my God," she says once she's recovered, coming around the counter and hugging me fast and antiseptic, then holding me back at arm's length like a great-aunt having a look at how much I've grown. Literally, in my case—I've put on fifteen pounds easy since I left for Arizona—and even though she'd never say anything about it, I can feel her taking it in. "You're here!"

"I am," I agree, my voice sounding weird and false. She's wearing a gauzy sundress under her French Roast apron, a splotch of deep blue on the side of her hand like she was up late sketching one of the pen-and-ink portraits she's been doing since we were little kids. Every year on her birthday I buy her a fresh set of markers, the fancy kind from the art supply store. When I was in Tempe I went online and had them shipped. "Did you get my texts?"

Imogen does something between a nod and a headshake, noncommittal. "Yeah, my phone's been really weird lately?" she says, voice coming up at the end like she's unsure. She shrugs then, always oddly graceful even though she's been five eleven since we were in middle school. Somehow she never got teased. "It eats things; I need a new one. Come on, let me get you coffee." She heads back around the counter, past the rack of mugs they give people who plan to hang out on one of the sagging couches, and hands me a paper to-go cup. I'm not sure if it's a message or not. She waves me off when I try to pay.

"Thanks," I tell her, smiling a little bit helplessly. I'm not used to making small talk with her. "So, hey, RISD, huh?" I try—I saw on Instagram that that's where she's headed in the fall, a selfie of her smiling hugely in a Rhode Island School of Design sweatshirt. As the words come out of my mouth I realize how totally bizarre it is that *that's* how I found out. We told each other everything—well, *almost* everything—once upon a time. "We'll be neighbors in the fall, Providence and Boston."

"Oh, yeah," Imogen says, sounding distracted. "I think it's like an hour, though, right?"

"Yeah, but an hour's not that long," I reply uncertainly. It feels like there's a river between us, and I don't know how to build a bridge. "Look, Imogen—" I start, then break off awkwardly. I want to apologize for falling off the face of the earth the way I did—want to tell her about my mom and about Julia, that I'm here for ninety-five more days and I'm terrified, and I need all the allies I can get. I want to tell Imogen everything, but before I can get another word out I'm interrupted by the telltale chime of a text message dinging out from inside the pocket of her apron.

So much for a phone that eats things. Imogen blushes a deep sunburned red.

I take a deep breath. "Okay," I say, pushing my wild, wavy brown hair behind my ears just as the front door opens and a whole gaggle of women in yoga gear come crowding into the shop, jabbering eagerly for their half-caf nonfat whatevers.

"I'll see you around, okay?" I ask, shrugging a little. Imogen nods and waves good-bye.

I head back out to where my car's parked at the curb, pointedly ignoring the huge LOCAL AUTHOR! display in the window of Star Lake's one tiny bookstore across the street—a million paperback copies of *Driftwood* available for the low, low price of $6.99 plus my dignity. I'm devoting so much attention to ignoring it, in fact, that I don't notice the note tucked under my wipers until the very last second, Julia's pink-marker scrawl across the back of a Chinese take-out menu:

dirty slut

The panic is cold and wet and skittering in the second before it's replaced by the hot rush of shame; my stomach lurches. I reach out and snatch the menu off the windshield, the paper going limp and clammy inside my damp, embarrassed fist.

Sure enough, there it is, idling at the stoplight at the end of the block: the Donnellys' late-nineties Bronco, big and olive and dented where Patrick backed it into a mailbox in the fall of our sophomore year. It's the same one all three of them learned to drive on, the one we all used to pile into so that Gabe could ferry us to school when we were freshman. Julia's raven hair glints in the sun as the light turns green and she speeds away.

I force myself to take three deep breaths before I ball up the menu and toss it onto the passenger seat of my car, then two more before I pull out into traffic. I grip the wheel tightly so my hands will stop shaking. Julia was my friend first, before I ever met either one of her brothers. Maybe it makes sense that she's the one who hates me most. I remember running into her here not long after the article came out, how she turned and saw me standing there with my latte, the unadulterated loathing painted all over her face.

"Why the fuck do I see you everywhere, Molly?" she demanded, and she sounded so incredibly frustrated—like she really wanted to know so we could solve this, so it wouldn't keep happening over and over again. "For the love of God, why won't you just go away?"

I went home and called Bristol that same afternoon.

There's nowhere for me to go now, though, not really: All I want is to floor it home and bury myself under the covers with a documentary about the deep ocean or something, but I make myself stop at the gas station to fill my empty tank and pick up more Red Vines, just like I'd planned to.

I can't spend my whole summer like this.

Can I?

I'm just fitting my credit card into the pump when a big hand lands square on my shoulder. "Get the fuck out of here!" a deep voice says. I whirl around, heart thrumming and ready for a fight, before I realize it's an exclamation and not an order.

Before I realize it's coming from *Gabe.*

"You're *home*?" he asks incredulously, his tan face breaking into a wide, easy grin. He's wearing frayed khaki shorts and aviators and a T-shirt from Notre Dame, and he looks happier to see me than anyone has since I got here.

I can't help it: I burst into tears.

Gabe doesn't blink. "Hey, hey," he says easily, getting his arms around me and squeezing. He smells like farmer's market bar soap and clothes dried on the line. "Molly Barlow, why you crying?"

"I'm not," I protest, even as I blatantly get snot all over the front of his T-shirt. I pull back and wipe my eyes, shaking my head. "Oh my God, I'm not, I'm sorry. That's embarrassing. Hi."

Gabe keeps smiling, even if he does look a little surprised. "Hey," he says, reaching out and swiping at my cheek with the heel of his hand. "So, you know, welcome back, how have you been, I see you're enjoying your return to the warm bosom of Star Lake."

"Uh-huh." I sniffle once and pull it together, mostly—God, I didn't realize I was so hard up for a friendly face, it's ridiculous. Or, okay, I *did*, but I didn't think I'd lose it quite so hard at the sight of one. "It's been awesome." I reach into the open window of the Passat and hand him the crumpled-up take-out menu. "For example, here is my homecoming card from your sister."

Gabe smoothes it out and looks at it, then nods. "Weird," he says, calm as the surface of the lake in the middle of the night. "She put the same one on my car this morning."

My eyes widen. "Really?"

"No," Gabe says, grinning when I make a face. Then his eyes go dark. "Seriously, though, are you okay? That's, like, pretty fucked up and horrifying of her, actually."

I sigh and roll my eyes—at myself or at the situation, at the gut-wrenching absurdity of the mess I made. "It's—whatever," I tell him, trying to sound cool or above it or something. "I'm fine. It is what it is."

"It feels unfair, though, right?" Gabe says. "I mean, if you're a dirty slut, then I'm a dirty slut."

I laugh. I can't help it, even though it feels colossally weird to hear him say it out loud. We never talked about it once after it happened, not even when the book—and the article—came out and the world came crashing down around my ears. Could be enough time has passed that it doesn't feel like a big deal to him anymore, although apparently he's the only one. God knows it still feels like a big deal to me. "You definitely are," I agree, then watch as he balls up the menu and tosses it over his shoulder, missing the trash can next to the pump by a distance of roughly seven feet. "That's littering," I tell him, smirking a little.

"Add it to the list," Gabe says, apparently unconcerned about this or any other lapses in good citizenship. He was student council president when he was a senior. Patrick and Julia and I hung all his campaign posters at school. "Look, people are assholes. My sister is an asshole. And my brother—" He breaks off, shrugging. His shaggy brown hair curls down over his ears, a lighter honey-molasses color than his brother's and sister's. Patrick's hair is almost black. "Well, my brother is my brother, but anyway he's not here. What are *you* doing, are you working, what?"

"I—nothing yet," I confess, feeling suddenly embarrassed at how reclusive I've been, humiliated that there's virtually nobody here who wants to see me. Gabe's had a million friends as long as I've known him. "Hiding, mostly."

Gabe nods at that. But then: "Think you'll be hiding tomorrow, too?"

I remember once, when I was ten or eleven, that I stepped on a piece of glass down by the lake, and Gabe carried me all the way home piggyback. I remember that we lied to Patrick for an entire year. My whole face has that clogged, bloated post-cry feeling, like there's something made of cotton shoved up into my brain. "I don't know," I say eventually, cautious, intrigued in spite of myself—maybe it's just the constant ache of loneliness but running into Gabe makes me feel like something's about to happen, a bend in a dusty road. "Probably. Why?"

Gabe grins down at me like a master of ceremonies, like someone who suspects I need a little anticipation in my life and wants to deliver. "Pick you up at eight" is all he says.